THE WOMAN

A LINDA DARBY MYSTERY

DAVID BISHOP

This book is a work of fiction. Names, characters, places and incidents have been produced by the author's imagination or have been used fictitiously. Any resemblance to any actual persons, living or dead, or to any actual events or precise locales is entirely coincidental or within the public domain. Sea Crest, Oregon, lives only in the mind of this author, inspired by the quaint Oregon coastal towns of Depoe Bay, Yahats, Newport, and Canon Beach. If you wish to further capture the flavor of Sea Crest, visit these beach towns in Oregon and you should feel that connection.

The Woman

Please visit David Bishop, his books and characters at www. davidbishopbooks.com
You may contact David Bishop at David@davidbishopbooks.com

The publisher does not have any control over and does not assume any responsibility for author or third-party websites or their content.

Cover designed by Telemachus Press, LLC

Cover art copyright © iStockPhoto # 12415881 Woman Walking on Beach

David Bishop
#1 BESTSELLING MYSTERY AUTHOR

Version 2019.02.09

The Woman captured my attention in the first two pages. It is a great book. I have read books by Flynn, Margolin, Connelly, Thor, Baldacci, Morrell and many others. I just finished David Bishop's books, *The Woman*, and *The Blackmail Club* and have enjoyed these books as well as any I have read.

∾

You might be a little tired of James Patterson and if you are seeking a new storyteller, you just found him! Wonderfully drawn characters, descriptive locations and very convoluted situations ... all in a very good mystery.

∾

My Third David Bishop Read and I'll be back for more. This guy can really, really tell a story.

∾

Just finished my second David Bishop read. If you like a who-dun-it that doesn't satisfy your curiosity until the bitter end, *The Woman* is for you!

∾

The minute I started this book by David Bishop, I was hooked. It was very interesting and entertaining all way through. I could, at times, only imagine the desperation she felt running for her life. I believe it was well-written and thoroughly entertaining. I am looking forward to reading his other novels.

∾

The first book I read written by David Bishop and I finished it in 2 days. Good story line that keeps you wanting to turn the page.

∽

Being relatively new to Kindle books, I have to say that this book was probably the best that I have read so far. I was thinking that it would be a romance novel and it turned out to be a thriller. I would highly recommend this book and I will definitely read more books by David Bishop.

∽

This is my first David Bishop reading and I am already a fan. *The Woman* was an enjoyable read with good pace and interesting characters.

∽

I was looking for a book that could be loaned. Along the way I found a favorite new author. Love his writing. Will be reading him from now on.

∽

Linda Darby seems like many of us—maybe a little prettier and more toned from jogging on the beach, but a divorcee who lives quietly and whose idea of a good time is movie night at her friend's—a friend with a dark, mysterious and dangerous job.

Toby Neal, author Blood Orchid, the Lei Crime Series.

∽

This is the first novel I read from David Bishop but will not be the last. I enjoyed it because it was believable. How many mysteries do you read that you ask yourself, "What a stupid thing for the victim to do?" Like go after the trained killer alone or purposely place themselves in a situation where there is little chance to escape. No, the story line here is strong enough to provide suspense without relying on the ridiculous. The characters are well drawn out and the author ties everything up nicely and sensibly at the end. Kudos to David Bishop!

∼

This book had everything that I love: suspense, action, and deception. The lead characters backgrounds were fleshed out pretty well. I can't wait to read Mr. Bishops other books!

∼

David Bishop's mystery *The Woman* is much more than a clever detective story could be. Bishop has written a story that tells another story: he writes of today's world, its political corruption, personal greed, and efficient killings. Terry Crawford Palardy, author

∼

With Linda Darby, author David Bishop has given us a character to cheer for, worry about, and applaud along the way. The story is a fast-paced high tension ride with the perfect amount of details to keep it flowing in living color before your eyes, right up to the dynamite final scene. Sure to be a big hit with action/crime novel fans everywhere!

∼

I enjoyed David Bishop's writing style, easy without any extra unnecessary description. The dialogue sounded accurate to what the characters portrayed in the book. I will be reading more of David Bishop.

~

Mr. Bishop has written a remarkable book that has something for everyone but doesn't feel like it is too much. You are drawn into the story and almost feel as if you are a part of it which compels the reader to continue reading.

~

Overall, a very well crafted, satisfying and entertaining read. I tend to be somewhat conservative in my ratings, but I have now re-read this again and it's going to stay to be re-read. Those books [like this one] are the only ones I give my 5-star ratings to.

~

We go along living our safe and sometimes boring lives, much as Linda Darby does in her little quiet sea side town. Fortunately, most of us won't be thrust into running for our lives from unknown evil forces; wondering who to trust and not to trust. Bishop, entrusts his mystery, 'The Woman', to a great character, Linda Darby; smart, strong and braver than even she knows.

~

This one is about THE Woman, a remarkable character involved in a very original plot. The secondary characters are equally well portrayed and, to me, they are also memorable. I would call this a psychological thriller. The Woman has many twists and surprises, and the end is totally unpredictable. It rings true. And, once again, the dialogue plays a big part in this novel's appeal. The last sentence is proof of this.

～

This is an absolute gem of a book. It has everything that a suspense thriller story needs; shadowy political/intelligence operatives, fake identities, lots of money and a bit of sex. The author shows throughout that he really does know what he is doing.

～

"*The Woman*" grabbed me and had me hooked within the first few pages. This is the first David Bishop book I've read and I was on the edge of my seat the entire book. I kept trying to figure out what was happening to Linda Darby and what the big picture was, but I was kept pleasantly guessing. It was a fun thrill ride full of mystery and suspense!

～

The only negative aspect of David's books are that I find myself reading them way too fast and then wanting more. So David, if you are reading this, please make more books. I know I'll be buying them if you do.

～

David Bishop has mastered the art and does it without having to take you on a journey to the center of the earth with a thousand slow moving pages. It moves along quickly, surprising you at every turn, and never releases its grip on your imagination. I am a fan. Gerald Lane Summers, author of *Mobley's Law*

Novels by David Bishop

Mysteries currently available – By Series:

Matt Kile Mystery Series (in order of release)

Who Murdered Garson Talmadge, a Matt Kile Mystery
The Original Alibi, a Matt Kile Mystery
Money & Murder, a Matt Kile Mystery Short Story
Find My Little Sister, a Matt Kile Mystery
The Maltese Pigeon, a Matt Kile Mystery
Judge Snider's Folly, a Matt Kile Mystery
The Year We Had Murder, a Matt Kile Mystery

Maddie Richards Mystery Series (in order of release)

The Beholder, a Maddie Richards Mystery
Death of a Bankster, a Maddie Richards Mystery

Linda Darby Mystery Series (in order of release)
All Linda Darby stories, co-star Ryan Testler

The Woman, a Linda Darby Story
Hometown Secrets, a Linda Darby Story
The First Lady's Second Man, a Linda Darby Story
Heart Strike, a Linda Darby Story

The Ryan Testler Character Appears in: (order of release)

The Woman, a Linda Darby Story
Death of a Bankster, a Maddie Richards Mystery
Hometown Secrets, a Linda Darby Story
The First Lady's Second Man, a Linda Darby Story

Heart Strike, a Linda Darby Story

Jack McCall Mystery Series (in order of release)

The Third Coincidence, a Jack McCall Mystery
The Blackmail Club, a Jack McCall Mystery

Short Stories

Money & Murder, a Matt Kile Mystery Short Story
Love & Other Four-letter Words: a Maybe Murder, a novelette by
fictional author Matt Kile, as written by David Bishop
Scandalous Behavior, a novelette by fictional author Matt Kile, as
written by David Bishop
The Twists & Turns of Matrimony and Murder, by David Bishop

To be notified when each of the above titles are available:
Send your email address to, david@davidbishopbooks.com

For more information on books and characters visit: www.
davidbishopbooks.com

Each forthcoming novel will have a new list of titles and dates.

DEDICATION

This novel is dedicated to the many fine novelists whose writings have influenced my own in ways too numerous and too beneficial to list. Thank you all. The book is also dedicated to my first granddaughter, Brandi Bishop, whose love is among the things I most cherish, as well as Jody Madden whose love, happiness, and enthusiasm for life is the wind beneath my wings. And all the others who know I love them. Also those wonderful and special people who are faithfully willing to read and critique my manuscripts before publishing: Martha Paley Francescato, John Logan, Kim Mellen, Gerald Summers, and Jody Madden.

PREFACE

The woman marked for death was prettier than most, but otherwise, in many ways, an ordinary woman living an ordinary life in a quiet let-the-world-go-by beach town on the coast of Oregon. For Linda Darby, Sea Crest was a retreat, an escape, a place to hide. She had grown up knowing only that she did not want to become her mother: housedresses, housecleaning, and a butt too wide. That mindset had led to her present state, an ex-husband and enough one-night stands to have stopped counting.

Linda jogged on the beach most mornings. There was nothing better for maintaining trim legs and a tight butt. She dined alone most evenings before returning to her computer to enter any day trades she wanted executed upon the next opening of the financial markets. She had positioned the desk in her oceanfront condo so she could watch the comings and goings of her neighbors, whose lives seemed more exciting than her own. She was good enough at day trading to have bought her condo with cash, and several jumbo CDs that provided a steady living income.

Day trading was flexible work and Linda appreciated the insulation from the questions of coworkers: Do you have children? What happened to your marriage? She just wanted to be left alone.

Then Linda Darby went out the door to go for a walk, and nothing for her would ever again be the same.

CHAPTER 1

*T*he mild beach town night air cooled Tag's arms. Despite being well muscled, his arms felt chilly. He considered asking his partner to hold their position while he drove back to the motel to get his windbreaker. He could be back in fifteen minutes. But he knew he couldn't chance it. The call could come at any moment, letting them know Linda Darby had settled in for the night. They were ready. The drop cloth and dental instruments were in the back of the rented van. Tag's partner would have her talking nonstop in no time. No one resisted the dentist for long.

Linda Darby did not believe in the supernatural, yet tonight felt different somehow, as if gods long forgotten were whispering just beyond human hearing. She worked her tongue against the roof of her mouth. It felt dry and tasted metallic.

Her fortieth birthday was fast approaching. Perhaps her premonition had been born of that and nothing more. The days came and went, the seasons repeated, and all of it merged into history. Another year spent without any real change. The only constant, the horizon at sea always looked close enough to reach out and trace with her fingers. But her life remained just as she had made it, a mire. Every day aged her, gradually but definitely. Her body had never screamed, *you're getting old,* at least not in any meaningful way, but her mind knew. Men still noticed her. Thank God. She hoped they always would, but one day they wouldn't, at least not in the same way. Time remains the true enemy of us all.

Her sense of foreboding had started just before dusk, but Linda had forced herself through her routines. She entered her stock trades for the morning. Then called Cynthia Leclair to confirm they were on for lunch tomorrow. Her friend had sounded distant and preoccupied on the phone. Perhaps Cynthia also sensed whatever was crawling along the edge of Linda's consciousness.

Her neighbors were home, but she was too restless to spend another evening watching others. She decided to go for a walk. The pleasant evening, along with the easy breeze carrying the sounds of the tossing surf might just blow away her sense that something unseen was on tilt. She had not jogged on the beach this morning, so all this second sense could be nothing more than her body craving some activity. If so, the four-mile-roundtrip walk into town might be just what she needed to trim the crust off her mood.

She would stop in at Millie's Sea Grog. Millie's was mostly about drinking, but the place had the town's best clam chowder, not to mention a nightly crowd of area hunks wallowing in the town's bawdiest bar talk. Millie's also meant getting hit on, but, by now, the message on the boys' boner network said: Oh, sure, Linda Darby puts out, puts out rejections. She had heard the rumors: Linda is a lesbian. Linda has a secret lover. Linda is an old-fashioned girl with a steady guy overseas. Whatever. She could deal with those guys, and she'd enjoy the laughs.

After drawing her hair back into a ponytail and strapping on her fanny pack, she paused at the mirror. She didn't like the plumpish look that came with the pack, and neither would the fellas in Millie's. She unhooked the pack and dropped it on the chair in her bedroom. When she glanced at the ocean through the back slider, she saw low clouds on the far horizon moving horizontally, a mist more than a fog. She'd seen this pattern many times. There were no white caps out beyond the breakers which meant mild wind off the ocean. Her prognosis, she would be home before the dampness reached the shore. She grabbed her purse and headed out the door.

"Linda Darby's on the move," the voice said into Tag's earphone. "She walked up Ocean Road and angled onto Main Street, on the inland side. It looks like she's heading into town. I'll let you know if she changes direction. If you don't hear from me, you know where to take her."

Linda brushed back the strands of hair the breeze had swept across her forehead and eyes, and angled onto Main Street. In the next block, a local couple came toward Linda, rollerblading their way home as they did each night after closing their glass blowing shop in town. They coasted across Main and began laboring up the only street cut into the hilly inland side. They lived on that side street, their property cut out of the tangled wild berries that crowded in wherever man had left the local land to its own devices. About one mile up, that side road deteriorated into a gravel trail fit more for deer and four wheelers than passenger cars. After another two miles that road crested over Pot Ridge, the local spine that separated the coastal dwellers from the enterprising growers who had emigrated from California's thriving marijuana fields.

The lady rollerblader wore a lightweight sweatshirt about the color of a blouse Linda had tried on last week. The top had a cowl neckline. She had liked the fabric, just not the price. Over the years she had tried on a lot of clothes that she liked at the moment, but had forgotten about within a week. This top she had remembered,

3

that proved something. And it had fit her just right. What the hell, you only live once. She'd stop in the House of You. Besides, she thought, the new top might just be the ticket to shake off her funk —therapy. She smiled, thinking that maybe her doctor would give her a prescription for the top. The young doc liked to look at her, and he had a tight body that made going to see him more pleasant than any doctor she'd used in the past. But she dated no local men, no exceptions, not even for doctors.

Downtown Sea Crest was like a morgue after dark, shrouded by a billion living stars. Linda had never understood why this one clothing store stayed open until nine. She stepped off the curb into the intersection that began her favorite stretch of downtown. The air here tasted of donuts from the nearby shop, and there had been no scientific studies claiming you could get love handles just smelling them. On Sundays, she often walked down to get one glazed and one cream-filled bismark. Nothing beat donuts, hot coffee, and the Sunday newspaper on her deck overlooking the ocean.

The House of You was just past the hardware store on the other side of the alley. She quickened her pace toward the store, its light reaching out across the sidewalk.

Then, just as the pungent odors from the alley pushed the heavenly donuts from her nostrils, Linda stopped smelling everything.

CHAPTER 2

A strong hand clamped over Linda's mouth and nose, a wide hand, a man's hand, a suffocating hand. His strength coiled around her shoulders pinning her right arm. He wore a short-sleeve shirt, his arm carpeted with tattoos of snakes coiled around a busty topless woman. His other hand gripping her left elbow, allowed him to steer her deeper into the alley.

Oh, God.

She staggered, twisting her head in a desperate attempt to free either her mouth or nose. She fell back against his head and shoulders. He was clean shaven. His height nearly matched hers, five-eight, but he was powerful. She needed to remember all she could so she could tell the police. But for now her attention was riveted not on staying alive, nothing that long term, but on her desperate hunger for one more taste of air.

This is only a robbery. Only a robbery, she kept telling herself as each erratic step pulled her deeper into the darkness between the rows of two-story brick buildings.

Linda's attacker abruptly jerked her arm, navigating her around a filthy puddle in the trough gutter that centered the alley, the action momentarily easing his grip.

She sucked a mouthful of air through his smelly, tobacco-stained fingers.

5

He smokes. All right, that's something else I know about him.

Just as quickly, his hand tightened again and the two of them went back to stumbling as if their clothes were sewn together. An idea had come with that quick breath. Her right arm was pinned against her side, but she controlled her hand. She opened it, letting her purse drop to the pavement.

There's my purse. Take it. Leave me alone.

The tattooed man ignored the purse.

Desperately she searched for another idea. Something. Anything. Nothing more came.

Take my purse. Let me go. Please. Please.

Linda could no longer see the brightness from Main Street. The meager light finding its way back this far had been frayed by the century of grime coating the twists and turns of the buildings lining the alley.

Her holder suddenly jerked her to a stop. The foul-smelling trough water penetrated the canvas uppers of her walking shoes. His breath slithered down the back of her t-shirt. "I'm going to let you breathe. If you scream, I'll hurt you."

Tag knew the assignment was not a straight hit. First they needed to talk with Linda Darby to learn what she knew. If the woman resisted, the dentist would start with his gum pick and battery-operated drill. No one resisted for long, but someone would hear the screams. Tag had worked under the field leader for this mission before. The man was competent, one of the best, but Tag did not agree with his decision to use the alley for this interrogation. The woman would have been home in an hour or so. They should have waited.

Linda breathed, heaving breaths, again, and again. The damp, salt-rich air raced through her body. She considered screaming. But she had been warned. Instead, her voice scratched out from her dry throat. "What do you want?"

His hand moved from her arm to the top of her shoulder, his fingertips burrowing into her collarbone like a carving fork piercing a roast turkey. She buckled some, hoping to alleviate the pain, but he increased the pressure.

A second man stepped out from the shadows, his belly waging war against the lower buttons of his dress shirt. His tie loose at his neck, the collar unfastened. His head in constant motion, a turret mounted on lumpy shoulders. Her holder was clearly the brawn, could this one be the brains? Not that brutalizing a woman took great brainpower.

The near electrical punch of her adrenal gland stunned Linda. Her legs buckled. Her head felt light. She didn't recognize this as a panic attack. But labels didn't matter. Escape mattered.

I'm a jogger. If I can get free, I'll have a chance.

The second man started to move toward her. No. He had only bent his knee, putting the flat of his foot up behind himself, against the wall of the building on his side.

Suddenly, the man holding her from the back jerked upward onto his toes, exhaling a loud painful grunt. From the corner of her eye Linda saw the outline of a third man fully in the shadows.

My god, he kicked the man in the balls.

Her holder released her, his hands instinctively cupping his groin as if he were holding a fledgling fallen from a bird's nest.

Kick him again. She screamed inside her head. *No, hold him and let me kick 'im. I'll drive his dick up behind his eyes.*

In a flash, her helper slammed a brick down onto the man's spine. Then he kneed her assailant in the face, and his head slammed back against the brick wall. His tattooed arms flopped like a gate with a broken hinge. He went down. Flat. His face in the gutter trough where Linda's had stood only a moment earlier.

7

Linda staggered back until her shoulders thumped that same brick wall.

As the shock of surprise wore off, the taller one on the other side of the alley brought his foot down from the wall. He reached inside his jacket. In that same moment, the third man hurled the brick he still held, striking the taller man in the shoulder. His hand inside his coat paused. In that split second, the third man drove his fist into the other man's gluttony, followed by two quick blows to his face. The taller man collapsed, a circus tent dropping to the dust of a deserted fairground.

Her helper wore a full-head stocking mask. In the shadows, she hadn't noticed. He stepped toward her. He grasped her arm and pulled her close, then touched the bottom of her chin.

Her head came up, fear occupied her face.

His warm whisper touched her ear. "You're okay." The scent of his light cologne found her nose. "Go home," he said. "Do not call the police. They cannot be trusted."

He got her walking toward the street, out of the alley. On the way she scooped up her purse, the strap seeming to reach up for the hand it knew. Ten yards from the sidewalk, he let go of her arm, turned and, betrayed only by the fading sound of his footfalls, retreated into the swallow of the darkness.

Linda spoke into that darkness. "But—"

"No buts," his voice returned from seemingly nowhere, "go straight home."

When Linda reached the sidewalk, she began walking briskly, nearly jogging, her gaze often backward. The police station was on Main Street at the corner of Oak. Three blocks. She could make three blocks. She had to make three blocks.

At the station she grasped the door handle, pulling it part way open, and then stopped. She stood there. Then let go.

He did save me. He must have had a reason for telling me not to go to the police.

After walking to the next corner, feeling unsafe in the town where she had always felt safe, she got into a taxi, giving the driver her home address.

The hack spoke without turning his head. "Are you all right, Miss?"

The voice was louder, less of a whisper, but it sounded much like the man who saved her in the alley. She decided to find out. "If not for you," she said, "I would likely have died tonight."

"If you had, in that last moment, what is the one thing you would have missed having in your life?"

"The right relationship with a man, maybe even a family of my own."

"But you have been married."

"How do you know that?"

"Not important."

After a minute or two of silence, she spoke again. "I thought my husband was the right man.... My hormones keep telling me he was.... Then, eventually, I just knew ... "

"Then what?"

"I blamed the man. All my girlfriends told me I was right to leave him. I was sure at the time."

Sudden squeals and pops from the taxi's tires fighting for footing startled Linda as the cab drove off the blacktop onto the graveled roadside. "You're home," the hack said without turning his head.

"Who are you?" Linda asked.

"I teach high school social studies. I'm on vacation."

"You expect me to believe that?"

"I also teach P.E."

"I'm not going to get an honest answer, am I?"

"You were smart not to go into the police station. The authorities cannot be trusted."

"But I have to do something?"

"Yes, you do. Go inside. Take a warm shower and go to bed. You will sleep. Don't worry. I got your back."

*L*inda awoke to the patter of windblown rain striking the window, and the crescendo of the breaking surf a hundred yards from her deck. God, she loved these raw natural sounds. They allowed her to live alone without feeling isolated. She lingered, her head nested in her pillow. After a while, the rain stopped and she could hear the calls of the gulls taking flight, soaring and swooping down to skim the surface of the sea.

As always, she had left the Venetian blinds open on a slant, the morning sun and the waves acting as a gentle alarm. She parted the blinds and peered outside. Everything had that fresh look, the sky brightening wherever the sun reached through seams in the billowy clouds. A hummingbird furiously worked the airspace above her deck, thrusting its rapier-like beak in and out of the orange blossoms of a honeysuckle flourishing in one of her patio pots.

The shards of last night's terror began worming back into her mind. She poked the power button on her bedside radio, turned the volume up to cover the bathroom noises, turned on the light over the sink and opened the faucet to let the water heat. Her morning routine, everyone had one.

She had not as yet decided what, if anything, she would tell Cynthia about last night. She didn't want to worry her older friend, but she just had to tell someone, and there was no one else close enough for such a sharing. She also needed to find out why last night, on the phone, her normally upbeat friend Cynthia had sounded so melancholy.

The local radio station she habitually played each morning told of the theft of one of Sea Crest's two taxis. Then, the announcer said the thief had abandoned the cab on a side street.

Linda went still. She had ridden in that cab. As she reasoned the events, the taxi had been stolen, at least borrowed, by the man who helped her and then drove her home. He had certainly not been a cabbie for he had not asked for a fare.

I hadn't realized that until right now. And why did I tell him all that stuff about myself. Things I've never told anyone but Cynthia. Why did I do that?

Her body went rigid, the hair dryer poised above her head, warming only the air. The radio had gone on to report that two men had been found dead—murdered, the announcer said, two strangers. Police Chief Benjamin McIlhenny reported having found no identification on their bodies. They had been found in the alley behind Sea Crest Donuts. Both shot in the head.

Linda's windowless bathroom shrank, cramped. The sensation of a belt tightened around her chest made her fight for the next breath, just as she had in the alley. The dead men had to be the two who attacked her. There were two men. Found in the same alley. They had been killed that same night. They had to be. Who else could they be?

She recalled the touch of the repulsive man who'd held her close. He had rough hands. And sour breath. She shuddered. Then her mind saw the cruel face of the second man, his sagging stomach.

The radio station described these killings as the first local murders ever, according to the Sea Crest Gazette, the town's twice-a-week newspaper: Wednesday and Saturday mornings. The station went on to inform its listeners that no one knew exactly which year the Gazette had issued its first edition. Old man Jory, now retired, whose family had once run the ice house just outside of town, called in to say his pa had once said the Gazette began publishing in October 1881. The paper's first lead story had been the shootout between the Earps and the Clantons at the OK Corral in Tombstone, Arizona. Since then, the Gazette had reported many murders, but none in their own quiet hamlet. That had changed this morning. The tone of the announcement almost seemed proud. Like Sea Crest had finally made the big time, had qualified to be on the map.

Such nonsense.

Her next thought struck like a claw hammer.

My mysterious helper must have killed them... . Who else? I have to tell Chief McIlhenny. No. First I want to talk with Cynthia.

Linda left her condo at eleven-fifteen so she could arrive at O'Malley's Bistro in time to get their regular table by the front window. The establishment had a side wall of stainless steel equipment that kept things cold and a back wall behind the bar crowded with more stainless equipment that kept other stuff hot. Other than the ubiquitous well-known fast food mainstays, O'Malley's Bistro along with Millie's Sea Grog comprised everything about food and drink for those who called Sea Crest home.

From the table at the front window, Linda always saw Cynthia come out of her job across the street at SMITH & CO. At sixty-two, Cynthia was twenty-five years older than Linda, at least seventy-five pounds heavier, and had weak ankles. Linda always opened the door to O'Malley's from the inside and helped Cynthia to their usual table.

SMITH & CO. occupied a plain brick, standalone building with no windows and only a small sign: SMITH & CO., CONSULTING. No glass door. No sign welcoming visitors. In fact, the building, framed by alleys on its north and south sides, projected an image that said: not welcome. Cynthia had never invited Linda to stop at the office, and had always deflected inquiries about her place of employment.

As usual, Clark Ryerson came to Linda's table. He always waited on her, trading tables with other staff when necessary. Rumor was that Clark had come to town after being hired to provide security for the marijuana growers. Then one day Clark rode his Harley into town with a horrible cut on his side, blood steadily dripping from the bottom of one pant leg of his Levi's. He told Dr. Mulvihill he'd foolishly backed into a cutting machine. The story seemed suspicious, but nothing else suggested trouble in the growers' nearly autonomous region a few miles to the east. Mulvihill stitched Clark's wound, but the man had lost a great deal of blood and needed a transfusion. Clark told the doctor to forget it. His blood was Bombay Phenotype. The state's blood banks had none. The U.S. Army had trouble getting Bombay. Only one person in every quarter-million was Bombay, and their bodies rejected blood of any other type. To Clark's surprise, the doc had one other patient with that type. Linda Darby.

The doc had called Linda at home. "You share or the odds say this fella dies." She donated what the doctor needed.

After that Clark stayed in town. He got a job waiting tables for O'Malley who ordered Clark to get rid of his earring, cut his hair above his shoulders, and work clean shaven.

Everyone had expected Clark would tell O'Malley to stick his job where the sun didn't shine and put the coastal dwellers in the rearview mirror of his hog. Everyone was wrong. Other than drinking with some of the growers when they came to town, and letting them crash at his place when they were too drunk to drive back over Pot Ridge, Clark had apparently walked away from that part of his life. He had become a coastal dweller, a quiet citizen of Sea Crest. On more than one occasion, Linda had considered surrendering to Clark's persistence. He stood about six feet, had a well-muscled torso and a melt-you-inside smile, but he didn't fit Linda's first criteria, no locals. No relationships.

Linda drank an ice tea and a refill Clark brought, without seeing Cynthia as usual, struggling while stepping off the curb on her side of Main Street. There were never many pedestrians in Sea Crest, and those few were mostly regulars. But now and again she saw a stranger, including one passing right now, a camera case slung over his shoulder. Cynthia had recently told her about a new man in town who always carried a camera. Maybe he was that man. Cynthia, having already pitched Linda on behalf of all the eligible men she knew, had moved on to promoting men she had only observed. "After all, honey, it's the visceral stuff that rings your chimes."

The stranger had dressed to blend in. Dark shoes with soft soles, khaki pants and a windbreaker pinned down by the strap of his camera. His head covered by a dark baseball cap, nothing embroidered on its front. Linda enjoyed watching people and over the years, while waiting for Cynthia, had watched hundreds walk by SMITH & CO. Never before had anyone paid any real attention to that brick building. It had been built in the age when contractors didn't trowel off the mortar protruding between bricks. But this man had paused at the alleys on each side of the building. His pauses were nearly imperceptible, but clearly he had paused to study the unwindowed sides as if the building was a lingerie shop, and he had x-ray vision.

The man tugged his cap lower, and then suddenly faced in Linda's direction. Instinctively, she turned away. Then, realizing her reaction had been unnecessary, she looked back, taking note of a cleft in his chin, his small waist and broad shoulders.

When the man turned at the corner, Linda stared for a moment at the last space he had occupied, then went back to sipping her ice tea and watching two elderly men near the bar playing checkers, each nursing a draft beer.

When Cynthia was thirty minutes late, Linda asked Clark to bring her a Cobb salad with honey-mustard on the side, and a croissant. That is, after rejecting Clark's latest request to take her out to dinner. She said no politely, without explanation, and Clark respected her answer. While waiting for her salad, she checked her cell phone to be sure it was on and operating. It was and it held no messages.

The two women had been meeting at O'Malley's for lunch once a week for more than six years and never had either of them just failed to come. Linda's concern grew, but she clung to the thought that Cynthia would soon contact her with a rational explanation.

At one-thirty Linda paid the bill and left without having seen or heard from Cynthia. She walked her normal route home through the sweet smells from the donut shop. When she neared the alley into which she had been dragged, the alley in which the two dead bodies had been found, she stepped out into the street giving the mouth of the alley a wide berth. She also went cold remembering the squatty man's hard touch on her breast. She still had no idea why she had been attacked. She had assumed a rape at the time, but that seemed likely only due to the absence of any other plausible reason. Now she knew there had to be another reason, she just had no idea what it could be.

CHAPTER 4

*L*inda went out to sit on the deck of her condo, hoping to calm herself by watching the ocean.

Sea Crest had always provided Linda a safe place to watch sunrises and sunsets, and read novels next to the fireplace or on her patio overlooking the Pacific. She had exiled herself to Sea Crest following the death of her marriage. In part, she had selected Sea Crest because when she first visited, the town projected the feel of a Thomas Kinkade painting, a slice of Americana she believed existed only in the hearts of romantics. But here she had felt it, and here she had moved. In the beginning she had called the move a peaceful getaway, a place to calm herself and reset her ambitions. But with time came honesty. She had selected Sea Crest as a hideaway, not a getaway. Last week had completed seven years and still she remained, in hiding. That was the truth, in hiding.

The only times she left Sea Crest were the nights she dressed the way she had once dressed regularly. On those nights, her celibacy growing intolerable, she went bar-hopping in one or another of the not-too-distant cities. She avoided the dives populated by lost souls, choosing instead the upscale watering holes frequented by the successful men of commerce and finance. These one-night stands usually occurred near the end of each month, perhaps the result of the fecundity of her id. These forays were daring, yet safe, both for the same reasons. She did not know the men. She did not use her real name. She never agreed to see any of these men a second time. These couplings were not in search of a relationship, only in search of a servicing. That said it crudely, but, when talking to oneself, plain talk was just fine.

Her life had become much less than she had once wanted, once hoped, but she desperately clung to the belief that marooning herself in Sea Crest would be enough. More recently, with the help of Dr. Shaw, she had begun to acknowledge a few truths. Avoiding all chances for a new loving relationship could protect her from the agony of being hurt, but such a choice also assured the lingering anguish of loneliness. Only through finding a successful lifelong relationship could enduring sadness be avoided. Still, Dr. Shaw had, at least tacitly, admitted the odds of finding such a relationship were not all that good in today's world.

While she had been on the deck the hummingbird returned, a distant friend, comfortable, yet suspicious. She had hung a feeder filled with red sugar water to which the bird seemed a constant visitor. She doubted any hummingbird had a weight problem given their highly aerobic pace. A sudden dart, the envy of any helicopter made, took the hummer away as suddenly as it had appeared. She wished she could as abruptly stop wondering about Cynthia, her only real friend, and the stranger who had, to say the least, acted curiously while passing SMITH & CO.

The man remained clear in her mind. He stood about six feet, and had medium brown hair with a slight natural frosting just above his ears. Actually, he might have had more gray, even been bald. She hadn't been able to tell because of his cap. She estimated his age to be mid forties. He strode gracefully, but without gentleness, confidently, without swagger or military march. She recalled the cleft she had seen momentarily when he turned toward her. He had not looked right at her, but in her direction. Still, his gaze had made her momentarily look away. She enjoyed watching men more than watching women, but did not enjoy them being aware.

Then a thought swirled in her mind the way a floating leaf circles in an eddy. *Clark could have been the man in the alley. He has a similar build, but the voice hadn't sounded like Clark. But then, in my state of mind, I can't be sure I'd have recognized his voice.*

Linda shook off these thoughts and again called Cynthia. Again she got no answer. She was no longer concerned. She was worried. Enough so that she decided to return to town and go to SMITH & CO., a company without a listed business phone. That had always seemed strange for a consulting firm, regardless of their brand of consulting.

Linda walked to town quickly. When she arrived at SMITH & CO., she found the door locked. She knocked. No answer. According to her watch the time was four-fifty-four, but she had been there at least a minute, probably two. She walked a little further to check the time in the window of the antique shop in the next block. There, the grandfather clock in the window displayed one minute after five, her watch now saying four-fifty-nine. Apparently, Cynthia and her coworkers had left a little early, but, in truth, she didn't know their hours of business and they were not posted on the door.

Linda spent that evening doing the same things, worrying and wondering. Leaving messages on Cynthia's cell phone and praying her friend would return her calls. She even checked with the nearest hospital and urgent care center, both twenty-five miles up the coast. Cynthia had not gone into or been taken into either. Thank God for that, but it didn't change the facts. She had been attacked. Her friend had disappeared. What were the odds of those two things happening in Sea Crest on consecutive days?

Linda fell asleep with that discomforting thought and the resolve that in the morning, if Cynthia had not reappeared, she would return to SMITH & CO., and demand to see her friend.

CHAPTER 5

*T*he sun had been up for about ten minutes when Linda rolled out of bed. The sun came up later in Oregon than it did farther south. But the process was the same. The black diluted into ever lightening grays, at first dull and matte. Then the colors started as the new day quickly blossomed into the vibrancy of youth, without any of youth's silliness or petulance.

With the morning light, Linda backed out of her decision to go to Cynthia's place of employment, admonishing herself for having spent the previous night being overly dramatic. She even convinced herself she would laugh upon hearing Cynthia's explanation. Besides, she wouldn't want to embarrass her friend who had often made it clear that she should not come to SMITH & CO.

Oh, bull feathers, Linda said out loud a few moments later. A dress on a pig can't change what you have. Something was very wrong. She had to stop vacillating and take action. Cynthia was one of the most polite people in the world. For her not to call to explain and apologize was completely outside her personality.

Halfway through her first cup of coffee, Linda settled on a new explanation. Cynthia did not have a land-based home phone, only a cell phone. She could have accidentally left the cell at work and became too sick to go in. That would also explain why all the workers had left yesterday before five o'clock.

By the time Linda stepped out of the shower, she had a new reasoned calm plan. She would take the bus and go to Cynthia's home. After all if Cynthia was that sick she might need help, just as Linda needed Cynthia's help. She had decided to tell the wise older woman about her being attacked in the alley, and about the mysterious man who saved her and then warned her not to go to the police. Linda was certain Cynthia would agree that the two men found dead in the alley had been the men who had accosted her. Together they would decide whether or not Linda should confess it all to Police Chief Ben McIlhenny.

The number three bus stopped in front of Cynthia's condo building. And Linda could catch the number three at the park two blocks from her own home. There was a light rain, but no real wind. She would walk the two blocks.

Her decisiveness excited her. She felt alive. She began to dress, and then realized she had inadvertently gone to the closet in the spare bedroom in which she kept the clothes she wore when going bar hopping.

She had stopped dressing to attract the attention of men seven years ago, following her crushing divorce which had been final on her thirty-second birthday. A divorce she had gradually come to think of as her finest birthday present ever. She still wore a size eight, but she had purposefully begun wearing plain pants or dresses and skirts below the knee, and discontinued low-cut tops and enhancing undergarments. Since the change she got no more whistles. No grunts. No lusty comments. She missed the bawdy attention, but continued to resist her urges to bait the boys.

As Linda approached the bus stop, she saw the man from yesterday. His chin cleft appeared darker than when she had seen him across from O'Malley's. Perhaps he had not shaven this morning. He stood in the light rain far enough away that the other person waiting for the bus paid him no mind, but she knew he was the same man.

Today, he wore a dark turtleneck sweater, black she thought, inside a dark peacoat. The collar turned up. His hands jammed into the pockets. The image made Linda think of Captain Ahab, stoic and vigilant on the foredeck, impervious to the crashing waves and salt spray. His eyes fixed on the horizon, searching for any sign which might point the direction in his relentless pursuit of the great white whale. She had read *Moby Dick*, and many other seafaring adventure stories, old classics such as *Mutiny on the Bounty* and newer classics including *The Hunt for Red October*. Read them sitting on her deck looking out toward the ocean, imagining the stories playing out before her.

Captain Ahab's presence near her bus stop was completely illogical. Yet there he stood without provocation or intimidation. He was watching Linda. She had no doubt she was his reason for being there. Why? Why would she attract the interest of such a man?

Linda knew almost nothing about Cynthia's place of employment. With some prodding, Cynthia had once shared that she was the manager and had a staff of three, and that they analyzed things, stuff too boring to discuss. Her tone had said, "Let's not talk about my work." After that they never did.

This did nothing to lessen Linda's wild suspicions about SMITH & CO., suspicions she had repeatedly dismissed as the over active imagination of an avid reader. But the last twenty-four hours or so had not been the product of her imagination. She really had been attacked. A mysterious man had really saved her. The two men in the alley were really dead. Cynthia had really disappeared. A mysterious stranger had really watched Cynthia's place of employment, possibly the same man who had saved her. That mysterious stranger had really reappeared at her bus stop. Common sense told Linda these events could not be related, but her built-in warning system screamed the hell with common sense. *All of this is somehow connected to me.*

The two women met every Friday evening, usually at Cynthia's home to play cribbage. Linda knew that Cynthia had begun to think of her as a daughter, and she liked that feeling. The regular Friday routine included taking an overnight bag, staying the night at Cynthia's, and going home on the Saturday bus, then taking a long run on the beach. Before her divorce Linda had run suburban streets with her husband, their dream being to one day live where they could run on the beach. Now she ran on the beach alone and had come to enjoy it that way. She did no day trading on Saturdays so these runs, after getting home from Cynthia's, were always her longest.

The earlier rain had stopped and the sun, struggling through the clouds was bringing new warmth, while a light breeze helped the trees shed their held water. The number three bus pulled through a wispy coil of steam rising from the wet pavement, an airy whoosh signaling the opening of its door.

Linda chose a seat from which she could watch Ahab by shifting her eyes without turning her head. A clunky sound announced the closing of the bus door. Then the big box pulled from the curb. As the bus turned at the corner, she looked back to see Ahab still standing where he had been next to a tree about fifty yards into the park.

Perhaps it's a coincidence, his being here and all. Or, perhaps Ahab doesn't need to follow the bus. Perhaps he knows my destination.

She twisted around and squinted while looking out the window at the back of the bus, but saw nothing that indicated Ahab had followed.

Or, perhaps, I'm just daffy. Ahab may just like parks in the rain.

Linda, sitting with her hands on her lap, instinctively leaned to her right as the bus turned at the next corner. Back on the straightaway, she opened her purse and looked at the small picture of Cynthia she carried in her wallet. The woman had the rounded cheeks, close-set brown eyes, and thick mouth reminiscent of the early pioneer women who immigrated to America from any number of feeder countries. Women with neck moles and calloused hands eagerly awaiting the challenges ahead, prepared to do what became necessary in their adopted America. That was Cynthia. Tough. Dogged. Thick. Plain. Lovely.

As for Captain Ahab, well, the man could have been in the ocean side park on a wet morning dressed to film a commercial for Old Spice aftershave. She smiled at the thought, admitting that explanation was likely as plausible, or more so, as some of the spellbinding explanations she had conjured.

CHAPTER 6

*T*wo years ago, Alistair Webster had assigned oversight of the Sea Crest mission to Ryan Testler, the most seasoned man in his private five-man force, and Webster's best field coordinator. Each of the five sometimes employed others under the strict order that no one else was to know Webster's identity.

While Webster had given Testler oversight of the Sea Crest operation, he had not ordered Testler to go there until three weeks ago. At that time Webster advanced the Sea Crest operation from oversight to cleanup and disposal because Cynthia Leclair had discovered his identity and how he used the information her company, SMITH & CO., had developed for Webster. After his first two weeks in Sea Crest, Testler had called in two other operatives, a man called Tag and a master interrogator known as The Dentist. Both men were scum, enjoying their work a bit too much, but they always got the job done.

At first the cleanup and disposal had gone well, then Webster began receiving reports about another woman, a friend to whom Cynthia Leclair may have told what she had learned about Webster's activities. The local woman, Linda Darby, had gotten away from two of Testler's men.

Webster used his satellite phone to call a Sea Crest man on his payroll, a local man who had installed surveillance equipment in Leclair's consulting company.

"Tell me the latest on Linda Darby."

"The two men who took her are dead, killed in a downtown alley... No. I have no idea who took them out. Do you have any other operatives in Sea Crest?"

"I have kept your secret," Webster said, "in return for your maintaining electronic surveillance inside SMITH & CO., and keeping me informed of anything you learn concerning that company or Cynthia Leclair. Who else I may or may not have on the scene, is not your concern. You'll be informed in the usual way if your assistance is needed further."

"Listen, whoever you are, this has become more than I bargained for. Sea Crest has no history of violent deaths. The town fathers are demanding that I solve these killings. This is not some Chicago ghetto or Brownsville, New York."

"Christ, man, stop being a cunt," Webster snarled. "You've got a town full of yokels. When we've finished our work there, I'll provide closure that will satisfy your locals."

The snitch made some sniveling sound before saying, "I should have just told the truth back in Jersey. Maybe I should just tell the truth now. Be done with it."

"Oh, stop yanking your pisser," Webster said, preferring to talk to his minions as if he were a thug himself. "Truth is a wisp of smoke. People reject the truth more often than they accept it. The truth nearly always lacks the substance of preparation that accompanies a well-planned lie. Leave the thinking to me. Now go get laid and forget about all this shit. What about that local banker's wife? That woman has an ass that can make boys into men, and turn men back into boys. But I'm not telling you anything you don't already know. I've got some great pictures of the two of you."

"You know about that?"

"You should know by now that I know whatever I need to

know. And as long as you do what you're told, her husband won't get the pictures. I've paid you a lot of money in the past for doing nothing but maintaining that bug. If your town fathers knew what I know about you they'd drop you out beyond their breakwater. If I can't count on you, I don't need you. Do you understand me?"

Webster also realized that once Linda Darby had been removed and Sea Crest had settled back into its sedentary lifestyle, he would need to remove this mealworm. This conversation had convinced him there was no way he could rely on this man staying quiet about all this for the rest of his life.

"What do you want from me?"

"Just keep your eyes and ears open," Webster said. "Scan and send me copies on the secure line of all police reports. I want to know a minute after you, everything that is even remotely relevant. Everything. And, remember, we're watching you as well. I may have more for you later so get a grip on yourself and be ready. Linda Darby is the ticket to keeping your past from finding its way into your present."

"I won't do anything more without at least knowing who you are."

"You'll die before you know who I am. The relevant point is I know who you are. So shut up and take care of the assignment I've given you." Webster hung up.

Webster paid enough to get obedience without having to answer unnecessary questions. Testler knew his identity, but not any of the men working under Testler.

Webster's immediate problem, Testler would not get back to Sea Crest until the day after tomorrow. For those two days, the only eyes Webster had in Sea Crest would be his now unstable snitch. He considered immediately ordering Testler to return to Sea Crest, but decided against doing so. Webster had ordered Testler to come east so he could watch the man's eyes while he explained his failure to interrogate and eliminate one ordinary woman.

Webster also knew that Testler had nearly a year ago inserted one of his own men into Sea Crest, a sleeper with instructions to become part of the local community, to watch Cynthia Leclair and SMITH & CO., and Police Chief McIlhenny. He would confirm that Testler had put that man on alert while he would be gone, but the man was only an observer. Webster had approved that expenditure, telling Testler that he would be held responsible for the conduct of his undercover man. And that under no circumstances was Testler to disclose Webster's identity.

In the meantime, Alistair Webster had an embassy ball to attend. Several politicians and members of the Foreign Service would be attending, insiders with whom Webster needed to stay in contact. To twist the necessary political arms, Webster needed to participate as a connected man in the nation's capital. Quietly. Socially. And those same people expected Billionaire Webster, as he was called, to attend. Politicos always used the "B" word to segregate out those who could be counted on to write checks for almost anything asked of them.

He smiled at the thought of politicians thinking they were using him when it was he using those empty suits. The favors Webster bought and extorted from regulators and congressmen had made millions, even billions for Webster's clients, and for himself.

CHAPTER 7

*L*inda stepped off the bus in front of Cynthia's condo building and, finding a sun-dried bus bench next to the curb, sat down to see if Captain Ahab would show up, knowing full well that if he did, it would freak her out.

After ten minutes of not seeing anyone, she rose and opened the cranky iron gate that announced all entries into the courtyard of the Oceanview Condos.

Cynthia's condo, located halfway back on the side, lacked the quality ocean view promised by the name of the development. Cynthia had told Linda she had difficulty seeing distances so she chose a unit close enough to allow her to listen to the surf, without paying for a view she could not fully appreciate. When the weather permitted, Cynthia often walked down onto the beach to watch the waves break and spread silently across the smooth sand. She often commented about the popping of the tiny bubbles over the breathing holes from the clams, or whatever lived in the basement of the sand.

Hope and fear met in Linda's throat as she pressed Cynthia's doorbell.

No answer.

After ringing again, she noticed that yesterday's Portland, Oregon newspaper, a bit wet, lay beside the door. She rang a third time, and keeping her ear close to the door she heard the bell, a melodic tune she couldn't quite place. Cynthia always needed a few extra minutes to get to the door and this time she was likely coming from a sickbed. Linda stood back nearer the rail, cleared her throat and waited hoping Cynthia would soon open the door and clear up the mystery. When that didn't happen, Linda got out her cell phone and dialed one more time, with each ring beseeching her friend to pick up the phone and assure her that all was well. But the phone, like the door chimes, brought only empty promises.

Linda reached into her leather shoulder bag for the key to Cynthia's condo. Linda had never before let herself in, always choosing to respect her friend's privacy by knocking and waiting until Cynthia opened the door. Several years ago Cynthia had said, "Take this key, dear. I want you to have it, just in case."

Linda decided that right now defined *just in case.*

Linda hollered through the open door, "Cynthia!" Hearing no reply, she stepped inside. "Cynthia? Are you home? It's Linda."

Cynthia's living room looked normal, even smelled normal. Cynthia used plug-in air fresheners, changing fragrances each time she plugged in a new one. Cynthia always chose flower scents, but this one had an aroma not reminiscent of flowers. Perhaps the old woman had left some food out on the kitchen counter.

Cynthia's hobby, ceramic dolls, stood in silent vigil on the high shelf rimming the room. Early American furniture, arrayed on medium-length cut pile wall-to-wall carpeting, looked as it always did: neat and orderly. A flowered TV-tray with gold metal legs fronted the red rocker, a throw blanket over its back. Cynthia's bifocals, waiting flat on their temple bars, were on the table beside the rocker. Her prized Thomas Kinkade lithograph silently looked out from over the tweedy couch against the far wall. Two stone coasters, the kind that absorbed moisture, waited on the small kitchen table where they had been left last Friday when their cribbage game ended.

She found no food on the kitchen counter, only the day before yesterday's newspaper, an inside page folded over to the crossword puzzle. Beside the puzzle lay an opened box of facial tissue. Cynthia's normal morning routine would have included bringing in yesterday's paper to compare her puzzle work against the completed version shown in the next day's paper. But the paper with the puzzle solution had still been on the landing outside the front door.

The only furniture not straight out of Aunt Bea's home in Mayberry was the 55-inch TV that helped Cynthia watch her favorite shows. Like a larger-than-life buccaneer, wearing a black eye patch, the large dark-screen silently watched Linda as she moved through the condo.

Despite having been in Cynthia's home on many occasions, Linda felt like an intruder. Still, she had to get to the bottom of her friend's disappearance so, thinking that maybe Cynthia was asleep, Linda tiptoed toward the rear bedroom where Cynthia slept with a high window ajar to let in the sounds of the sea.

She found Cynthia.

Linda's heartbeat eased, she had reasoned it out correctly. Cynthia had apparently taken ill, and not had her cell phone. Her friend, lying on her side, appeared asleep. The covers pulled up over her shoulder. Relieved that all appeared to be okay, Linda looked around and saw a large crack in the dresser mirror, a broken piece having fallen onto the dresser top.

Confused by the broken mirror, she approached the bed. She had to be certain Cynthia was okay, and didn't want some company or need anything, perhaps a cup of tea.

When she touched her friend's shoulder, Cynthia rolled onto her back. And Linda instinctively pulled back her hand, holding her breath. Cynthia's face was a patchwork of dried blood. Her eyes were open. Her stare was blank.

A fly crawled out of Cynthia's open mouth.

Linda wanted to scream, but no sound came. Her eyes welled. She sat on the corner of the bed, just looking at her friend. The only portions of her face which looked normal were the drooping folds of skin below her eyes. Unable to look any longer, Linda turned away.

After what seemed to be forever, she again looked. It was clear now that her friend had suffered greatly before her death, likely even prayed for it to come. Those last minutes had to have hurt beyond description. Linda guessed Cynthia had been shot, but Cynthia's face had been brutalized to such an extent that Linda was unsure she could recognize a gunshot wound to the head. Linda's father had taught her to shoot quite well as a youngster, but after a childhood friend was accidentally killed by an unidentified hunter, Linda had never again touched a gun.

Linda gathered her hands on her lap without conscious consent. She just sat staring at a drop of crusted drool on her friend's wrinkled chin. She couldn't just walk out. She couldn't just leave Cynthia lying there. She had to call Chief McIlhenny.

What should I say? She asked herself. *Should I also tell him about my being attacked? About the stranger who saved me? That I saw a stranger pausing as he passed SMITH & CO.? That the man had reappeared near the bus stop? That all three of those men could be the same man? Was it time to tell all of it? Should I tell none of it? Or, should I just admit I may be nuts.*

The one thing certain, she could not just leave Cynthia dead in her bed. She had to report the death of her friend, the rest she would figure out when the time came. Long ago, Linda had put the police department, along with the fire department and the local hospital and ambulance service in her cell phone. She highlighted "PD" in her directory and hit the call button.

"Hi, Pamela, this is Linda Darby. I need to talk with Chief McIlhenny."

"Hi Linda, how's things? The chief just checked in by phone. He's at a domestic disturbance on the far side of town. His deputy is off today."

Linda explained the reason for her call, gave Cynthia's address, and said she would wait there until the chief arrived. After Pamela cautioned her about crime scene contamination, Linda said she would wait outside on the deck.

Actually, the wait would be good. She needed more time to decide just what she would tell Chief McIlhenny. After a few minutes, she went back inside and into Cynthia's bedroom. She tried not to look at her friend on the bed. She had come to take another look at the room. She had remembered it correctly. The mirror over Cynthia's dresser was more than just cracked. It was a maze of fractures, like a car windshield hit by a rock. Cynthia's face had been that rock.

CHAPTER 8

"*M*s. Darby?"

Chief McIlhenny's deep Montana voice slightly scorched by the nasal sounds of New Jersey came from inside Cynthia's condo.

"Out here, Chief," Linda hollered, "on the patio."

"Hello, Ms. Darby. Linda." The chief left the slider open. "I'm sorry you had to see this; I already peeked in the bedroom. What can you tell me about all this?"

Linda crossed her arms and leaned against the railing. "Not all that much. Despite the difference in our ages, as you know Cynthia and I were best friends. We met once every week at O'Malley's, for lunch. Day before yesterday, Cynthia didn't show up. She didn't call. My calls to her cell over the past day and a half have gotten no answer. Eventually, I became worried enough to come on over."

"How did you get in?"

"We have keys to each other's home. I came in when she didn't answer the doorbell."

The chief stepped closer. "I'll need to go in and look around a lot more. You up to going back in, with me? You've already been in there so ... I understand if you don't ... it's just that, well, you might recognize something that's missing or different. You game?"

33

"If it'll help." Linda ran her tongue over her dry lips before following the chief inside.

Linda walked through Cynthia's condo with Chief McIlhenny. Then he asked, "Well, did you see anything missing or out of place?"

Linda shook her head before saying, "Everything looks right except her bedroom and bath."

A moment later, McIlhenny picked up an unfinished crossword puzzle from the table. "What's a seven-letter word with an 's' in the center, that means two?"

"Ambsace," Linda said after thinking for a moment. "Does that mean something?"

"She was working the down words, with all the ones above having been crossed out. Did Cynthia work crosswords?"

"Passionately. I do, too. But not like her. She was addicted. What does that matter?"

"Just wanted to make sure it wasn't the killer who did crosswords. That also explains the magnifying glass next to the puzzle."

"That would seem unlikely, wouldn't it, Ben?"

"Hey, stranger things, you know. I'm just covering all the bases, without being all that sure what in hell all the bases are."

He led Linda back into Cynthia's room. The chief looked closely at Cynthia. Linda looked away.

"Your friend was shot twice, head and heart. Looks like her face had been smashed against the dresser mirror, over there." He pointed with his note pad. "Her teeth and gums are bloody. My guess is she'd been beaten quite a bit before the mirror came into play. Holy shit. Look." Linda did not. "A hole has been drilled in her front tooth, two of her teeth."

"Why would someone do that?" Linda asked with an expression of pain and confusion.

"They wanted something from her. Maybe they got it, maybe not. Either way, they ended up killing her."

"I've been here over an hour and I'd really like to get away from ... all this. You still need me?"

"You go on. I need to get the official stuff going anyway. Once I figure out what all that is. Sea Crest is part of what's called a joint violence task force. The way it's supposed to work is the state police provide a homicide investigator. This here's the first time I've had to call on it. Bradford city police, Bradford's the county's seat, will send down a fingerprint guy and somebody who knows more about forensics than I do. All of which means he doesn't need to know much to outsmart me on that stuff. Sorry we had to see each other under these conditions."

Linda paused at the door and looked back at Chief McIlhenny.

"I'll likely need to talk with you some more," he said. "After I get things going here, I plan to mosey down to where she worked. What can you tell me about SMITH & CO.?"

"Not a thing. Cynthia never talked about her work. I never even had a work phone for her, only her cell."

"Ever meet any of her coworkers?"

"No. When I said, Cynthia never talked about her work I meant it. Never."

"What kind of consulting do they do, anyway?"

"Search me," Linda said. "I meant it literally. Cynthia never told me anything about her work so I'm as curious as you are about that place."

CHAPTER 9

*R*yan Testler's flight had passed the high point over the Rockies, not far from Denver, on its way to Reagan National Airport in Washington, D.C., and Ryan had still not decided how he would handle his meeting with Webster. The man always demanded the truth, and until now Ryan had always delivered the truth.

Testler had placed a local observer to watch SMITH & CO., and more specifically, its owner, Cynthia Leclair, and to assist in picking up the surveillance tapes from the dead drops. A man he could count on, not like the scum who had killed Leclair and accosted Linda Darby. Testler had instructed this man to melt into the local scene, to be accepted in the community, but to stay in the shadows.

Men like Webster always had or envisioned forces opposing him. If Testler denied knowledge of who killed Tag and the Dentist, Webster would be left to choose between not believing Testler, and believing that someone opposing his agenda had intervened.

Testler had been with Webster for nearly ten years and never failed him. Truth is men like Webster who bought muscle would accomplish little without men like Testler. Given that reality,

Testler expected that for now Webster would believe him, would need to believe him.

The men in Testler's family, as far back as the revolutionary war, had always been in the military and he had followed that tradition. He was a natural athlete who had easily taken to the training and physical demands of being a special-forces soldier, and the enduring patience required of a sniper. He had tested at the expert marksman level or higher using multiple hand and shoulder fired weapons, as well as earning high status in several forms of martial arts. He had allowed his country to hone him into a killing machine. And, as far as the world knew, he had even allowed himself to be killed in the battle to drive Iraq from Kuwait. That was when he became Ryan Testler, and he had now been Ryan Testler for so long he no longer thought of himself as the name under which he had been born and raised in a small Nebraska town.

Testler had been introduced to Alistair Webster by a retired general and a senator who chaired the foreign intelligence committee. Later, Webster claimed he acted as an outside conduit for off-the-books jobs for the government's intelligence agencies. Over the years, Testler came to know the acts of violence he carried out on Webster's orders served only to assist Webster in extracting huge sums from his clients when they needed a favorable ruling or vote from some regulator or member of congress. At other times, Webster worked through compromised congressional staffers who generally held great sway over those by whom they were employed.

Testler no longer deluded himself about Webster. The man was a parasite, not a patriot. The problem for Testler was that he had become a shadow citizen and Webster had become his only source of income, an excellent source of tax-free cash. Two years ago, Testler began recording some of his meetings with Webster. Webster fancied himself an intelligence expert, but his belief came from ego not expertise. Testler's plan had been to continue doing

Webster's bidding for another three to five years, and then retire. The recordings would protect him from Webster having him permanently retired.

Testler knew some of the history of Webster and Cynthia Leclair, the rest he could surmise. Cynthia Leclair had been discharged by the CIA in a budget cut, and Webster had convinced her to gather information for him. Webster used that information along with leverage he could gain through the use of prostitutes, gamblers, and other temptations to draw his targets into compromising situations.

At first, Webster had led Leclair to believe her work was being done for the CIA, off their books. Testler guessed that Leclair was killed because she had learned the truth, or at least suspected the truth. But, in the final analysis, Testler saw Leclair as an insider. And, in his view, everyone who worked in espionage, or intelligence as it is more often called today, accepted that an unexpected death was part of their life, even though for most it never came to that.

To the contrary, Linda Darby personified the citizens for whose protection Testler had first become a Marine and, later, a defense department sniper. Killing Linda would strip away the veneer that allowed him to think of himself as more than a killer for hire. Conversely, he could save Linda Darby. At least he thought he could. However, doing so would end his lucrative income and turn him into an unemployed assassin, without an employer capable of providing him insulation. Left without that protection, Testler's best option would become work as a mercenary in Asia or Africa with greater risks for lower pay.

The pilot announced the approach to Reagan National Airport without Testler having resolved his dilemma. Should he save Linda Darby, or kill her and keep his retirement plan on schedule?

CHAPTER 10

*T*estler drove off the airport grounds holding his phone. He had just dialed the number for one of Linda Darby's neighbors. He had the phone numbers for all her neighbors, and had chosen an elderly couple after noticing the meticulous care with which they nurtured their small patio garden. They would take pride in doing things well and pay close attention to detail.

The woman of the house gladly agreed to get Linda and bring her back to the phone. He waited.

"Hello?" Linda said into her neighbor's cordless phone.

Testler had first noticed Linda's smoky sensual voice, the night she sat in the back of the taxi while he drove her home. It had somehow sounded familiar, listening without seeing her helped him make the connection. She sounded like Julie London, a torch singer from the 1950s. His father's favorite.

"Miss Darby. Linda. I drove you home after your incident in the alley behind the donut shop. Do you remember?"

"I will never forget a thing about that night." Linda glanced up as the elderly couple retreated into their bedroom and closed the door. "Who are you?"

"Not important. I have only a few minutes. I am not in Sea Crest, but I will return. There are a few things you need to know. I expect there will soon be another attempt to abduct you. You need—"

"What is this about?" Linda said, interrupting. "Tell me what this is about?"

"Someday, but right now, your life depends on your listening. Do I have your attention?"

"Yes."

Testler spoke through Linda's short, rapid breaths. "Your home phone has been bugged, that's why I called through your neighbor. Continue to use your home phone for routine innocent calls. If you stop using it all together, it will alert those who are listening. Do you understand?"

"Yes."

"Stay dressed at all times at home. Sleep fully clothed, including the shoes you run in on the beach."

"How do you know about my running on the beach?"

"Not important."

"It is important." Linda protested. "How do you know so much about me? Why do you want to? I've got to know what's going on. Is this related to the torture and murder of my friend, Cynthia Leclair?"

"No time now. Listen to me. You have a canvas bag hanging on the clothesline just below your deck where you hang your wet bathing suit and sweats. Do you know where I mean?"

"Yes."

"In the bottom of that bag, under the clothespins, I have left you five thousand dollars in cash so if you need to run you'll have money. If you run, do not use any credit cards. Not even once. Not for anything. There is also a cell phone in the bag. It is safe. If you need to reach me, press the send button. It's programmed to my cell. I will answer. If that cell rings, it will be me calling you. It is otherwise dysfunctional. It has no phone number you can find in the cell so don't bother looking. It is only to connect us, particularly if you go on the run. There is also a gun. It cannot be traced anywhere. It is loaded. Do you know how to operate a handgun?"

"Well, there's at least something you don't already know about me. Yes I can handle a gun. My dad taught me. But I don't like guns."

"You may need to rethink that. With what you're involved in, a gun might be the only thing that keeps you alive."

"And just what am I involved in?"

"I said later. For now, keep the things I left in that clothespin bag with you. You can't know just when you'll need them."

"Not the gun, I will never shoot one again."

"Get over it, woman. You'll likely be better off running and hiding than trying to shoot it out with the type of men who will be coming. But keep the gun close. If you are cornered, you have one advantage. They will want to take you alive. Let them get close without knowing you have the gun. Then use it. Always aim for their broad center, then close in and put one in their head."

"You're scaring the shit out of me."

"Good, if you're going to survive that's how you need to be, scared, but keep your wits about you. Don't trust anyone. And say nothing to Police Chief McIlhenny. I'll be in touch with you when I get back there, probably tomorrow. When you call me, always say hello first. Your first word, your very ... first ... word. I'll always say hello back. My very ... first ... word. If you are in danger say hello a second time, after I've said hello back to you. Got it?"

"Yes."

"Do you keep a diary, Ms. Darby?"

"What?"

"Simple question, do you keep a diary, a ledger, a journal, anything like that?"

"No. But what does that have to do with anything?"

"Not important. Do you have any questions about our use of

the word hello to first begin and first reply in our phone conversations?"

"I understand that, but nothing else."

"That's all for now. I'll call you tomorrow night to let you know I'm back or when I will be. Until then you are on your own. Stay alert and ready. Do you have any questions about what I have told you?"

"Plenty, but apparently you won't answer them."

"I will later."

"From what you've said I may not have a later."

"Then the answers won't matter."

After hearing the dial tone, Linda held the phone in front of face, looking at it as if it were a severed umbilicus cord.

After thanking her neighbors, she went home, hooked the chain lock on the front door and got into bed fully clothed, even her running shoes. After a few minutes, she got back up, went out the front door and walked around to the back of her condo. The ground sloped down enough so she could stand under her deck. From a distance, even in the ambient light, she could see the canvas bag on the clothesline looked extra plump. Inside she found everything Ahab said would be there. She took out the money and the cell phone, putting them in her pockets. Then she took out the gun. The first time she had held a gun since she was twelve. She held its coldness, stared at its hardness. No. She would not take the gun into her home. Instead, she took her black sweatshirt off the clothesline and wrapped the gun in its hoodie. Then she buried it in the sand beside the sea grass on the far side of a berm, a short distance behind and to the right of her condo. Away from the trail the locals used to go down to the beach.

Back inside, after relocking her front door and checking the window locks, she sat on her bed. Too nervous to sleep, even to lie down, she went to the kitchen sink and filled her tea pot. While at the sink, she looked out the window. The night seemed unusually dark. Most nights the moon, glancing off the surface of the ocean, provided ambient light that gave the sand a sheen as it snaked around the scattered berms crowned with sea grass. But tonight the choppy surface of the ocean denied the reflection, reducing the moon to a ragged spot on the distant water, the sand to a lifeless matte gray.

CHAPTER 11

"*M*s. Darby. Linda. It's Chief McIlhenny. I hope this isn't too late to stop by?"

"It's only a little after nine." Linda stood back and held her door open. "Come on in."

Ben was a solidly built man around six-foot-three, with good facial features, except for his habit of cropping off his sideburns level with the tops of his ears. When he had on his service cap it looked as if he had no sideburns.

"How you doing, Linda? Have you had any dinner?"

"Haven't felt much like eating. I'm making some tea, though, chamomile. It's steeping. Wanna join me? I got a full pot on."

"That'd be nice."

"Can we sit outside, Chief? It's a little cool, but I like the night."

"Outside is good. Call me Ben, Linda. We've known each other too long."

Linda had met Ben McIlhenny two years ago when he first took the job of police chief. He had asked her out, more than once. Twice she had come close to accepting his dinner invitation, but so far she had held fast to her self-imposed rule: no relationships beyond one-night stands and never with men who knew her for real.

44

"I'm sorry," she replied. "I didn't mean to be overly formal ... I just don't know how one should talk about ... a murder."

She walked toward the back of the house. He pushed the sliding screen door over, the glass slider was already open. They stood looking at the ocean for a minute or two. Then Linda swiped at a tear. Ben came to her and put his hand on her shoulder. She collapsed against him. Her head pressed into his chest, and she let her tears flow.

Ben said nothing, just held her in a comforting way. After a few minutes, she stepped back and went inside. When she came out, she handed Ben a cup of tea.

"While you were inside," he said, "I noticed the way the moon dies in the rough sea. Still, at night, the ocean ... well, it's just beautiful, the stars. We don't need to talk right away, drink your tea."

Linda sipped. The warmth relaxed her some. She had great difficulty accepting that a man this sensitive, this gentle, could not be trusted. Neither of them said another word until their cups were empty. Then the chief broke the mood.

"I've been police chief for a few years and outside of an occasional bar fight over a ballgame or a woman, Sea Crest doesn't have much that takes any big-time law enforcement. No drugs. Well, hardly none, sometimes a little marijuana from the growers over the ridge. A home burglary now and again, and there's a guy who books a few bets, penny-ante stuff. The guy even has a full time job to support his family. Now... this." He waved his hand before letting it fall to his side. "I guess I better get on with it. So, you and Cynthia Leclair were really close?"

"Close enough that I told her about my terrible teens: wearing red tennis shoes, chewing gum with my mouth open, wearing tops just because they showed my bra straps, having my lip and nose pierced for rings. Like the girls I see downtown now, anything to show a little rebellion, get some attention. It all seems so childish now." She looked toward the ocean. "Yeah. We were that close."

"Well, you've grown into a woman who doesn't need those kinds of things to get noticed. But I'm not so sure you want to be noticed."

"Thank you and you're right. I prefer staying to myself, living quietly. Was this more than a social call?"

"I guess I should get down to business. Have you thought of anything more about Cynthia's house? SMITH & CO.? Anything Cynthia said or did lately that seemed outside her normal behavior."

"No, but then I'm not yet thinking all that clearly, maybe in a day or two."

"Well, let me bring you up to date. An investigator from the state police and the boys from the Bradford police department spent most of the afternoon with me. Cynthia's clothes were wet. Her tub was half full and a lot of water had been sloshed onto the floor. Two of her fingers had been broken." Linda put her hand to mouth. "Do you wanna hear these details?" Linda nodded with her hand still over her mouth. "Okay," he went on. "Her dresser mirror was a real mess. You knew that. Some of the glass was embedded in her forehead. There were also cigarette burns on her breasts. Bottom line: She had been worked over pretty good. Hell, I'd a told 'em whatever they wanted, so I'm figuring that's what she did."

McIlhenny took off his service cap and held it on the tips of his fingers. "You okay?"

"Yes. Well, hell no. I'm not okay, but, yes." Linda took the last sip of tea into her mouth, held it there for a moment and swallowed. "What's next, Chief? Uh, Ben?"

"Too late tonight, employees would all be gone, but I plan to start my morning over at SMITH & CO. Find out more about Cynthia and it's about time we learn just what in damnation them folks consult about. And for who? Or is it for whom?"

Linda smiled, "Whom. For whom."

The chief slipped his cap back on. "I'll find my own way out.

46

But you might want to lock the door behind me, and the slider, too, while you're inside. Thanks for the tea. It was a nice break in the nuttiest day of the year. Goodnight."

Linda kissed him on the cheek.

A moment later, he knocked on Linda's door and came back in.

"You heard about the two men found shot in the alley two nights back?"

"Sure. Who hasn't?"

"Here's their pictures, sorry for the gore. You ever see either of them with Cynthia or anywhere else?"

"No."

"You know, Sea Crest's not exactly the murder capital of the country. Hell, we never had one before. Now we have Cynthia and these two. The only difference being the men took two in the noggin, while Cynthia got one in the head and one in the heart. I figure all of it is linked up somehow. You got any thoughts?"

"None, but what you say makes sense."

"If you had to guess at a connection, among the three of 'em, I mean knowing Cynthia so well, what you figure that connection would be?"

"I wish I could help you, Ben."

"Well, had to ask. Never know which question will bring forth something helpful. I'll stay in touch. You try to get some sleep. I'll stop back by sometime tomorrow to check on you and bring you up to speed."

I should have told Ben about those two men. At some point I'll have to tell him, also about Captain Ahab, all of it. But when Ahab comes back, I don't want Ben waiting to arrest him. The man saved my life.

a lovely woman with a daring measure of cleavage took Alistair Webster's coat while welcoming him to the Italian Embassy. The pop of champagne corks punctuated the quiet notes emanating from the piano and harp in the far corner of the grand foyer. Then a young man approached with the grace of a ballroom dancer. He bowed slightly and extended a tray crowded with flutes filled with champagne.

"A lovely evening, sir," he smiled, "would you like champagne?"

"Yes. Thank you." Webster circled his fingers around one of the crystal stems and turned from the server.

Actually, for Webster it had not been a lovely evening. The Sea Crest mission had called for SMITH & CO., to be completed and the full team extracted before any of the bodies were found. From what Webster had learned not even the work at SMITH & CO. had gone according to plan. Cynthia Leclair had not been at her office, although Testler's men had effectively improvised to find Leclair at her home. Then, another glitch, Linda Darby, a woman who had initially been seen as nothing more than a loose end, had become a thorn. Testler had sent his two men to question Darby, and then terminate her in a staged rape and murder. But some unidentified force had stepped in and saved her, killing Testler's two men.

The loss of the two men itself was not a problem. Testler had always been able to put together specialized teams. The remaining problems were Linda Darby and the identification of the forces that had saved her. Webster needed to know who had interfered. But for now, he had appearances to maintain, and one contact, in particular, he wanted to make at this pompous gathering.

Webster had been to the Italian embassy on Whitehaven Street in Washington, D.C., on several occasions. Tonight's gathering was a smallish affair commemorating the latest update of the Memorandum of Understanding between the United States and Israel regarding the prevention of weapons and war materials to terrorists. He did not understand why Italy was hosting the event.

Webster drifted outside onto the marble balcony and leaned up against the balustrade. He had long been convinced that the industrial and political world was effectively shrinking. The business activities of all countries needed to be based on free enterprise principles. All of it ultimately controlled by a few international kingpins capable of not only grasping the big picture, but of making the hard decisions needed to keep it all in balance.

Traditional democratic governments, wallowing in their need to posture to sound like they were serving the people, had outlived their effectiveness. The selection of leaders could no longer be left in the hands of the fickle rank-and-file citizenry. The overwhelming majority of American voters simply voted for whichever candidate promised the most wrapped in the no-cost lie: a boldfaced falsity told repeatedly by both parties while they spent the taxpayers' money for anything they believed would garner them votes or campaign contributions. The predictable results were broken promises, bigger deficits, and more and more convoluted laws. In his lifetime, the voters had shown themselves incapable of dismantling the platforms of lies upon which the current political process had been built.

The developed world needed to be run by the multinational corporations. Once in charge, the multinationals, not the people, would elect a council responsible for setting policies designed to see that consumers were treated fairly in the marketplace. Laws would be simplified. Justice would return to the swift status that existed in early America when the hammer building the gallows would ring as if an echo to the rap of the judge's convicting gavel. Life sentences would be abolished as such terms of incarceration only burdened society. If the crime was sufficiently evil to warrant life in prison, then the verdict should be death by public hanging. Let the public see the results of violating the law. It worked in early America, before the nambie pambies took over.

While competing brands of the same products would be tolerated, efficiency would dictate fewer competing brands, and that would mean higher profits for the companies and lower prices for the citizens. People would live in comfort and not have to endure the unsettling and contentious political cycle of lies and disappointments. In the end the people only wanted to be cared for, to be protected. That was why the people believed the preposterous lies upon which politicians commonly rode to victory.

Citizens who did not meet the requirements of education, healthy living, and obedience to the law would be incarcerated with the goal of rehabilitation or, for repeat offenders, termination. This new era of American efficiency and wealth would bring happiness to the four corners of the globe. There would be only one military which would be under the control of the multinational council.

As it currently was, and always had been, with rare exception the voters, in their mindless allegiance to the thirty-second sound bite, voted for the candidate who spent the most money campaigning. The voters appeared to pay little attention to the content of political speeches, ingesting only the syrup of their delivery. These empty messages were overwhelmingly persuasive with the fast-growing, less educated, poorer portion of the populace. The politicians had learned a significant portion of the voters were drawn to idle promises, particularly when that portion of the population paid little, if any, of the income taxes that would fund the promised largess or the rising massive national debt used to finance it. After the election, the winning candidate rarely delivered on the promises, blaming the political opposition for their having been unable to come through for the voters. Then, next election, the process repeated with those same voters likely believing the next round of lies, and so on, election after election. It all had to stop, and Webster saw himself as the man to stop it.

Still, the current abscessed political process had to be used to achieve the laws that would allow the multinationals to take more and more control over the running of the country. Thus, in the short run, it was Webster's self-appointed task to see that the right candidates got the necessary money to win elections. Webster's genius was that he used the corrupt political process to generate the very funds needed to back his chosen candidates. Funds obtained through being paid vast sums by those for whom he curried political loopholes and lax regulatory oversight. On those few occasions when his clients' dirty dealings were exposed, the government, choosing to not bring light on its own culpability, cried that they lacked sufficient regulations. When, in fact, the failings were in large part a result of failure to enforce regulations that already existed. These failures, often brought about by Webster employing his bribes and leverage over legislators and regulators, could result in a failure to measure the safety of deepwater oil drilling rigs or the requirement to test their functionality. Or, a blind eye turned toward an unscrupulous investment broker whose real business was building a Ponzi scheme.

Then Webster saw Aviv Cohen, Israel's Defense and Armed Forces Attaché. Webster casually drifted in his general direction until the military attaché saw him and moved out onto the rear patio. Webster followed. When they were both on the veranda, they each feigned surprise at seeing the other and came together along the balustrade.

"How are things, Webster?" Cohen asked.

Nearly everyone in power called him Webster, something he did nothing to discourage. In turn, he called most by their given names.

"Couldn't be better, Aviv, thank you for asking." This was a lie, of course. For the first time ever, Testler had failed him, and Webster would not sleep until Testler explained what went wrong.

Then Webster bulled into what had brought him here tonight. "What's the latest on Iran's nuclear program?"

"They continue as they always have, lying to the world as they move still closer to nuclear weaponry."

Normally such information would not be discussed with the power brokers from the financial world, but Webster had long ago bought his access.

"How soon?" Webster asked.

"A year, maybe as long as three, but not likely."

"What are the influences?"

"If they are left unconstrained, one year. The more successful your president is in bringing pressure through Russia and some countries in the Middle East, the longer some of their testing will be delayed. Your president could do much more to make it difficult for Iran to get some of the necessary materials and equipment."

"We agree, my friend," Webster said with his hand on Aviv's shoulder, "but we can't count on President Jackson being very effective. The man is surrounded by fools who advise him that Iran is not a serious threat even with nuclear capabilities."

"Reference to a nuclear threat or any other for that matter is always determined within the context of *to whom*. In the case of Iran, the sooner threat will be against my homeland. And, as Hezbollah expands its control in Lebanon, nuclear weapons from Iran will find their way there as well. In any event, left to their own devices, over time the Iranians will enhance their launch capacities to reach central Europe, and one day over the pond into your Virginia countryside."

"I trust Israel will take action before your homeland falls within that shadow."

"Ah, my friend, even with you I cannot discuss our positions on that subject. However, such actions, if necessary ... perhaps, I should say when necessary, would be much easier if your president would step up to the plate on this one."

The tap of a woman's high heels on the Italian marble flooring pulled the two men's attention. A voluptuous woman on the arm of a man in a white dinner jacket stepped out through a second door, moving in their general direction. Webster nodded. She smiled. Her escort nodded.

"They're with me. Security," Aviv said. "They won't come too close."

Webster moved to the other side of the Israeli Deputy. From that position the Israeli agents could not read his lips. Then he said, "Yes, well, I'm still working on getting you a statement of clear support from our president. A statement that will tell the world America will support Israel, should such action become necessary."

"Sadly," Aviv said, "I can't see that coming from President Jackson. And this situation may well boil over before your next election."

CHAPTER 13

*a*t precisely midnight, Webster heard the light knock for which he had been listening. Plush carpeting muffled his steps as he moved across the open seating area of his hotel suite. He looked through the peephole before opening the door. Ryan Testler came in after glancing each way down the hall. The two men nodded, but did not shake hands.

"This is your first absolute failing," Webster said, ignoring any pleasantries. "I want to know why. And I want it straight."

"First off," Testler began, "the major piece of the mission, SMITH & CO., went just as planned, a success not a failure. I shipped you their hard drives and backup disks."

"I've been told they've arrived. They're being looked at as we speak. Now tell me about Darby. That should have been the easier part of the assignment."

"I wish I knew more than I do," Ryan said, taking a seat on the arm of an overstuffed chair after Webster had first sat on the facing couch. "I had two men, men we've used before, skilled men set up to take Linda Darby at her home. Five minutes from launch, she unexpectedly left to go for a walk. I dispatched the operatives to an alleyway she would pass. I considered waiting for Darby to return home, but we couldn't chance where she was headed. She often got together with Cynthia Leclair. Darby could have been heading

54

to Leclair's home. She could even have had a key or she could have walked to SMITH & CO., expecting to meet Leclair. Had she walked into the middle of either of those scenes, she would have called the police. Had that happened we would not have gotten to Darby in time to learn what, if anything, Leclair had told her. The alley would have made her death appear more random for her killer could have been anyone. With my two men positioned in the alley, I went into a restaurant/bar where I have often been seen by the locals. I wanted the staff to be able to confirm I had been there when Darby went down."

"You could've stayed close enough to observe."

"To stay near the scene would offer the possibility of someone seeing me there. That would bring me into the investigation. Make it possible for some local to say, 'The new guy in town. The one who's always taking pictures, I saw him near the alley.' Sea Crest is a small town. There was no need for that risk. I had two men handling a small task, and the target was a nonprofessional. To set my alibi, I had dinner and then drank until midnight."

"But something did go wrong," Webster said, his eyes burning into Ryan's.

"Yes," Testler admitted. "Something went wrong, that's field ops. They often aren't smooth."

"So what happened?"

"I have no information on that, sir. When the men didn't report back, I went to the alley after leaving the bar. They were both dead. I didn't linger."

"You saying they bungled the job?"

"That's obvious, sir."

Webster frowned, and then got up from the couch. "You want something from the mini bar?"

"No, thank you. I had my fill on the plane."

Webster sat back down forgetting about the mini bar. "Were these good men?"

"I've used them several times. They are rough men. One is a

great interrogator, and both would behave exactly as two hooligans. They were the right men for that job."

"The results don't say so," Webster said. "If you're right about their skills, I can't imagine any local being able to take them out."

"And certainly not the woman on her own," Testler added. "What counter forces are in play?"

"That's not your concern."

"Look. I don't really give a rip what you're up to. You pay well and I do my job, but the fact remains that your damn compartmentalization complicates things. Had I known what other force might be in the field against my mission, I could have taken that opposition into account."

"Perhaps, but, need-to-know is the best policy. And you didn't. Still don't."

"Generally, sir, I agree. However, you're not filling me in on that appears to have contributed to the failing."

"Be careful, Testler." Webster said, pointing his finger. "I don't tolerate insubordination."

"Now listen here, Webster, I have years of getting it done for you, always with proper restraint and respect. You asked for this report, ordered me back here to give it. That makes it my job to lay out what I know and the possibilities of what went wrong. I mentioned you not telling me of any possible forces only as part of that report, albeit mostly supposition."

"In that context, I accept your criticism."

"Thank you, sir. And, while I'm at it, let me add that I personally watched Linda Darby for more than a week, up close and from a distance. I tapped her phone and searched her home, including electronic surveillance. I even perused her email when she would go out for the night. I don't believe you have anything with which to be concerned. In my judgment, Linda Darby knows nothing about Cynthia Leclair's work at SMITH & CO., or that firm's activities. Therefore, I recommend you leave Darby alone, and let things in Sea Crest return to normal. Another killing isn't needed. Darby is not part of our world even tangentially. She is an innocent bystander."

"You may be right. But what if you are wrong? No. We must be sure. We must question her. Then, she must die."

"I don't think that's wise, sir."

"You aren't paid to think beyond how best to carry out your assignments."

"Your judgment has always been superior," Testler said, knowing he could not push it further without casting suspicion on his loyalty. "If you don't have another assignment, then, sir, I think I'll take a holiday for a week or so. I'll check in when I return."

"Not so fast, mister, I want you back in Sea Crest."

"I can return if you'd like. I use photography for my cover. The area has a beautiful beach, backstopped with miles of mountain country. The camera lets me take whatever pictures I need."

"You should know," Webster said, "I've sent Blue to Sea Crest. He will be there within the hour. If we're lucky, he may just wrap up the Darby matter tonight."

"Sir, you put me in charge of this mission, why send another man?"

"The time delay while you came here to report was too great. If Darby knows something, we can't leave her flopping about until you get back."

"I tell you again. Darby knows nothing."

"What we are involved in, well, it is too important to America, to the world, to be left to chance. Against that, Darby is insignificant, if only as insurance against Leclair having talked out of school. No. Darby must be questioned and eliminated. And, if she passed on anything she heard from Leclair, you have my approval to follow that trail to whomever it leads. I don't want to hear any further opposition on this. I've decided."

"Of course, we should be certain," Testler said. "One thing I'll need, have Blue give me the time and place he plans to take control of Darby. I need to be somewhere else at that time. Just like with the alley, if you want me to linger in Sea Crest to read what happens I need to be sure I don't become the stranger who came into town and whose whereabouts can't be accounted for when these events took place. Give me Blue's number. I'll call him after I leave you so we can coordinate his actions."

"No need. It is likely Blue will have finished with Darby before you can return to Sea Crest. Trust me, he's better than the two bozos you used. And, assuming he completes his assignment while you're in transit, your being somewhere else becomes ironclad. In any event, I still want you there for that extra time, listening for rumors about why Leclair and Darby were killed."

Webster stood. "Enough talk." He led Testler to the door. "Get on your way. Fly out tonight. You've got a job to finish."

After shutting his hotel room door, Webster called Blue. "I'm on a hotel phone. It's not private. Have you arrived?"

"Yes. I've located the property in which you are interested."

"Good. You know what to do. Proceed immediately."

As Testler had expected, Webster had not bought his argument that Darby should be left alone. He had also anticipated that Webster might send Blue or his other operative named Charlie. That had been why Testler had alerted Linda. Why he had left her money, a gun and a cell phone.

On the other hand, maybe it would be best if Blue finished Darby. Testler had saved Linda Darby once, and he left her the gun to give her a fighting chance against Blue. He didn't want Linda to die, but he also didn't want his name added to Webster's hit list. One thing he did know, Linda Darby was facing a major challenge. In Testler's opinion, Blue was Webster's best operative, aside from himself of course.

CHAPTER 14

en McIlhenny had always wanted to be cop. His love
for law enforcement had started as a child watching
cowboy movies with his father. His favorite was Bill Elliott
playing Red Ryder. Growing up in Montana, he never lost his love
of cowboys and traditional westerns. But he also came to
understand the job of law enforcement involved much more than
just riding into town knowing that the saloon owner would be the
head of the bad guys.

In his teen years he left Montana to move in with an uncle who
lived in New Jersey where he obtained his bachelor's degree in
criminology, joined the Newark Police Department, eventually
earning his detective's shield. He wanted police work to be his life,
and everything had gone wonderfully until one evening after an
off-duty dinner and drinks with friends. That night, two unrelated
events, occurring within less than one hour, intertwined to destroy
his plans for a big-time career.

While Ben stopped at an intersection, a kid rode up on his
bicycle, leaning forward, his pencil-thin arms crossed over the
handlebars. An NBA Nets tee-shirt creeping up his back revealed
the handle of a gun jammed behind the waistband of his crack-
revealing pants. At the next intersection, McIlhenny flashed his
badge through the window and told the boy not to move.

McIlhenny confiscated the gun, which still had bubble wrap on the barrel. The youth also had a box of bullets.

The kid had no drugs on him and had not been drinking. He swore that he and some other kids had just found a canvas bag full of handguns and bullets in an empty lot about ten blocks away. At first, he said he didn't know the other kids, but later admitted belonging to a gang that Ben had already identified from the tattoo on the boy's forearm.

A young nurse Ben had been seeing with some regularity had left a text message on his cell phone which he had read after leaving the restaurant. "I'm about to hop in the shower," her message had said, "then I'll be over. You're forty-five minutes away from a night you will never forget." He either had to let the kid go or call the nurse and explain, not tonight, honey, the job, you know. He wasn't about to let that happen.

He kept the weapon and told the kid to get lost. Tomorrow he would follow up with the boy's gang to try and recover the rest of the weapons. This plan wasn't according to the book, but he wasn't about to blow off his date with this nurse, particularly with her in the mood her message had promised. As the kid stood up on his pedals and rode away, he looked back over his shoulder, smiled, and flipped McIlhenny the finger. Had the fabulous nurse not promised a dose of home health care, McIlhenny would have gone after the kid, explained the word ingrate, and run him in for felony possession. For even a child, this would have been a serious charge.

After that, the rest of the night had gone quite differently because Ben McIlhenny had left his police radio on. Several blocks later, he heard a call reporting a domestic disturbance in an upscale neighborhood about two blocks west from his current position. He had to go. He could get there faster than any other officer. These complaints were often based on nothing more serious than a neighbor fed up with listening to swearing and breaking dishes, but other such calls involved out-of-control people who had turned violent. This meant a cop could walk into the middle of anything, anything at all.

McIlhenny pulled to the curb, the situation was as he expected. He was first on the scene. The front door of the home stood open a few inches. He didn't have his police issue. Rather than take it on his dinner engagement, where he expected he might do some heavy drinking, he had left it in his locker at the station. He loaded the handgun he had taken from the kid with the bullets he had gotten at the same place. Most likely, he wouldn't need the gun, but domestic calls sometimes went sideways. He stuffed the confiscated weapon behind his belt, quietly closed his car door, and moved toward the house while stabbing his arms into the sleeves of his blazer.

Through the bedroom window he saw a man pistol whipping a woman. The woman had collapsed down onto her knees. Her face was pulp, a bone protruded through her cheek. Still the man continued using the gun barrel to rain down blows to her head and neck. Then the man picked up a two-liter plastic Pepsi bottle and stuck the gun barrel into the neck of the bottle. McIlhenny considered breaking the window and ordering the man to stand down, but such a course might lead to a gun battle. Instead, estimating he had sufficient time, McIlhenny took off for the front of the house where he eased the door open. Inside, he hastened down the Persian carpet runner that centered the hallway. His hand tightened on the boy's gun.

By the time he reached the bedroom door, the man, having wrapped duct tape around the barrel of the handgun, was busy holding the bottle steady between his thighs while twisting the tape around the neck of the plastic bottle.

"Newark, PD," McIlhenny hollered. "Drop the gun. Kick it over here. Get your hands behind your head. Do it. Now."

The man spun toward McIlhenny, sweat flying from his hair. One hand held the roll of duct tape, the unfinished Pepsi silencer in the other. His face dotted with the woman's blood.

"Don't," McIlhenny warned. "You won't make it."

The man froze in that position, half twisted at the waist, one corner of his mouth curled. McIlhenny knew the man was weighing his options. Then he dropped the gun, kicking it away. With the plastic bottle partially taped on the end, the gun didn't kick very far.

McIlhenny ordered the man onto his knees. Next, he had the suspect—suspect hell, he had watched the blows pound the beauty out of the woman's face—scoot back to the far wall keeping his hands still behind his head. After quickly looking around, McIlhenny picked up a hunk of lingerie that had been torn from the woman's body, and used it to pick up the odd-looking customized gun.

The woman lowered her head and collapsed onto the carpet. It didn't surprise McIlhenny who could only imagine the woman had stayed in the kneeling position by habit. She went down silently. No moan. No audible exhalation. As a tent would after someone had jerked the center pole.

With the butcher compromised, McIlhenny took a closer look at the woman. The side of her beaten-in head no longer gushed blood. He placed his fingers on her carotid artery. She was dead.

A moment later, McIlhenny had the man's gun in his hand, the bottom of the Pepsi noise suppressor blown open. The scum sat slouched against the wall. Dead like the woman only he had died more mercifully. The bullet had entered just above his right eye, too quickly for him to have seen it coming. McIlhenny had pulled the trigger without recalling his conscious decision to do so. True to its purpose, the plastic bottle had swallowed the residual blowback.

Other officers could arrive at any moment so McIlhenny wiped the gun clean, pressed it into the dead man's hand, and then dropped it on his dead lap. Then McIlhenny left. From what he could see outside, once the loud arguments had stopped, the neighbors had lost their curiosity. The next officers to arrive would easily put together the facts: the woman had been beaten to death by the dead guy and that animal had subsequently been shot by a third unknown person. The homicide guys would go through the motions, figuring the bastard got what he deserved, and then file the case among the unsolved.

To McIlhenny's surprise, the U.S. Marshall's Office and the Federal Bureau of Investigation took control of the case. Over time, he learned that the woman had been in the Witness Protection Program, and that the man was a New York mob enforcer, and the woman's ex-husband. She had foolishly contacted her mother and the suspicion was that the mob had maintained a tap on her mother's phone.

Three years later, McIlhenny resigned at the request of the Newark Police Department for repeated drunkenness on the job. After going through rehabilitation, McIlhenny had moved to the west coast and secured a uniform job with the Bradford city police. Two years later, he successfully applied for the position of police chief of Sea Crest, one of the state's lowest paying senior law enforcement positions. He had been the only applicant for the job.

The FBI never solved the Newark case, but, unknown to the Newark Police, the feds had a voice-activated audio tape running in that house, that night. A year after McIlhenny became the chief of Sea Crest he received a voice print matching his voice to the voice of the unknown man who had killed the hit man in Jersey. McIlhenny didn't recall having said, "You no-good piece of shit," but his voice was on that tape saying just that. He had said it immediately before the muffled roar of a bullet tore the creases out of the end of the soda bottle.

Not long after, McIlhenny heard from a man who made it clear the time had come for Police Chief Ben McIlhenny to pay the piper. The threat included a promise: After we have finished our business in Sea Crest, you will never hear from us again.

The chief had no reason to believe that promise, but he had little choice if he hoped to sustain his rebuilt life. The next Sunday night, he followed his first order by installing electronic surveillance equipment inside SMITH & CO.

He also realized, now, that decision had started the chain of events that had led to these deaths and put Linda Darby in harm's way.

CHAPTER 15

*T*he visit from Police Chief Ben McIlhenny last night had made it impossible for Linda to remove the images of the brutality that had been inflicted on Cynthia. Last night, not wanting to rely on the gentle service of the morning sun coming through the blinds, Linda had set her alarm. If Ben didn't come by early, she would go find him. She needed to know what he had found out at SMITH & CO. The answers had to be there.

Linda put a bagel in her toaster oven and got out the cream cheese, then stopped. She had no appetite. Fortunately, on mindless remote, she had set the coffee to come on in the morning. She dropped the still warm bagel into the trash, and poured what would become the first of three cups of coffee into one of her white ceramic mugs silk screened with a pictograph of Oregon's rocky coastline.

By 9:30 she had lost her patience waiting to hear from the chief. She grabbed her purse and headed for the door. With the knob in her hand, she pulled back startled by the knock of an unseen hand. After gathering control of her emotions, she opened the door to find Ben McIlhenny standing on the other side.

"Good morning, Linda, I hope you got more sleep than I did."

"Morning, Ben. I'm surprised you had trouble sleeping. I thought you law dogs could sleep through anything. Let me get you a cup of coffee. I just turned off the pot, but it's still plenty hot." With the chief two steps behind, she headed for the kitchen, asking over her shoulder, "Have you already been to SMITH & CO.?"

"Went last night."

"I thought you were going this morning?"

"That had been the plan up until my deputy called last night after he got a missing person call from Wilbur Sharp, an old man that lives three miles out of town on Windward Road. Turns out Wilbur's son had called him, wondering if the old man had seen his son's wife. She hadn't been home since leaving for work the day before yesterday. Guess where the daughter-in-law worked?"

Linda stopped pouring, her trembling hand holding the pot over the partially filled cup. "SMITH & CO."

"SMITH & CO."

Hearing the chief repeat the name, Linda thought it odd that no one ever pronounced it as Smith and Company. Their small, nondescript door sign read, SMITH & CO., and the whole town, knowing nothing else about the enterprise, had always referred to the business just that way.

Linda sat Ben's coffee on the bar in a mug that matched her own, while he pulled out one of her bar stools and sat down.

"So?" Linda said while picking up a bowl of fruit. He shook her off. "You can't just say you went there, talk to me. What did you find at SMITH & CO.?"

Ben took the bowl of fruit she still held from her shaking hand and put it on the counter. "They were all dead. Alice, the missing daughter-in-law, and two others shot twice: heart and head, just like Cynthia."

"God help us, Ben. First Cynthia. Now ... what's going on?"

"Tell me about it. With the two in the alley, I'm dealing with six murders after none around here in what, four-hundred years or something?"

"Are they all connected?"

"Logic says they are. The bodies are up in Bradford for autopsies, but the cause of death for all of 'em is pretty straightforward. Ballistics has told us the two in the alley were killed with the same gun. Cynthia was shot with the same caliber, but a different weapon. We won't know for a while about the three in Cynthia's office. Don't repeat the part about the two shots to the head for the fellas in the alley versus one in the head and one in the heart for the others. We're holding that back to help identify the shooter."

After a minute or so of just looking dumbfounded at the chief, Linda poured herself another cup, not bothering with the splash of hazelnut flavored cream she normally added. She had never before drunk four cups in one morning. But then she'd never been in the middle of whatever she was in the middle of now.

"Chief ... Ben ... I need to tell you something."

"What is it?"

"Something I didn't tell you before, but should have, as it turns out anyway."

"Go ahead. I don't know what any of this means, but holding back surely won't help us figure out much."

"The two men in the alley."

"You know something about them?" The chief's eyes narrowed a bit. "So far the Bradford police report their fingerprints don't check with any known prints. Do you know who they are?"

"No. Not who they are. This likely won't help at all, but ... well, I should have told you before."

The chief frowned, the movement furrowed his eyebrows.

"The night they were killed, I'd say around eight or so, I walked into town. When I passed the alley, a man grabbed me. He dragged me back to a point behind the donut shop where another man waited. That's where the paper said the bodies were found. I believed they were going to rape me. But I got away. Now, I'm wondering if maybe they wanted to make me another victim. Why? I mean, I'm nobody special."

"They didn't rape you?"

"No."

"Are you sure?"

"I think I would know, Ben."

"Ladies don't always admit being raped. So tell me, were you?"

"Last time, Ben, I was not raped. Next question."

"Okay. They grabbed you, dragged you into the alley. Then what?"

"Only one grabbed me, the shorter man, the one with all the tattoos. When he got me back near where they were found, the second, a heavyset man appeared in the shadows, leaning against the wall about ten feet away, his foot up against the bricks. The one who forced me back there held both my arms. When he got me there, he relaxed his grip. I pulled my arm free, hit him in the nuts and ran. At the time, like I said, I thought I had gotten away from being raped." Linda crossed her arms tightly, each of her hands in her armpits. She shuddered. "Now, I don't know, maybe from being murdered."

"You outran them both?"

"I run on the beach nearly every day. You've seen me. They chased me until I got to the street. After a block I looked back. They had stayed in the dark. After another block I stopped running. They weren't chasing me. I walked home. That's it."

"Why didn't you come to my office? It's on your way home."

"Turns out, I should have. But at that point, well, nothing really had happened. I had gotten away. I assumed they'd just scurry back into the hole they had come out of. I didn't want an attempted rape police report. The paper picks that up. I didn't want folks fussing when they saw me. I live a quiet life, Ben. You know that."

"Okay. So what did you do?"

"I walked an irregular pattern, cutting back here and there until I got home. I never saw them again. I assumed they didn't know my identity or where I lived. That they had been drunk or something and just grabbed the first woman that passed the alley."

"Turns out, they never left the alley. Did you have a gun with you, Linda?"

"No, Chief McIlhenny, I did not. Certainly, you don't think I shot them. That I could hit them each twice in the head, even if I did?"

"I suppose not. My job's to ask."

"I understand. Is it possible those two killed Cynthia and everyone at SMITH & CO., and then were killed in turn by someone else?"

"We got ourselves a long list of possibilities. The medical examiner from Bradford's doing the autopsies, but his preliminary opinion was that Cynthia and her coworkers had all died earlier than the two men in the alley. He felt very sure about that. If so, that'd line up with what you just said. They killed the others, then, having done their job, were eliminated themselves. Why or by who is anybody's guess. You'd think, with my having worked as a detective in New Jersey that I'd know a lot about murder investigations, but I don't. My time there was spent mostly working home burglaries. The last couple years I worked vice. Now I'm a small town police chief. I'm guessing this is the work of a professional. Sure looks that way."

"At Cynthia's," Linda said, "there were aspirins and a sleeve of decongestants on her kitchen counter. I also saw a box of Kleenex on the small table near her bed and another on the table in her living room."

"You'd make a good detective," Ben said, "I saw that, too. The way I figure it, they planned to kill Cynthia along with the others at SMITH & CO. But, when they got there, Cynthia had not come in due to being sick. So after they did their thing at her company, they made a house call."

"Maybe all this is about murdering SMITH & CO., not

Cynthia. You need to find out just what kind of consulting they did."

"I agree this may have been about SMITH & CO. So far, we haven't found anything out except there was no one named Smith. According to the state corporation commissioner's office, Cynthia owned SMITH & CO. Certainly you knew that."

"No," Linda said. "Cynthia always told me the owner was an out-of-town guy named Smith. That she managed the place. Mr. Smith doesn't like visitors, she'd say, so don't ever stop at the office. Smith doesn't even like us talking about the work we do. Blah. Blah. Blah. They had computers. A little time with them should tell you all you want to know about their work. Their clients. Mail. Files. The answers should all be in that office."

"Only one problem."

"What," Linda asked.

"The computers are there, but the hard drives are gone. And the file cabinets are empty."

"They'll have back-up disks somewhere. Every business does nowadays."

"Appears those things were all kept in a fireproof safe in the office. We found the door standing open and the safe empty. There was not a piece of incoming mail or an envelope prepared to be mailed anywhere. Cascades Bank said they had no safe-deposit box. I'm supposed to pick up a copy of their bank statements later today. The post office said their carrier never took or picked up mail at the business. O'Malley, at the bistro across the street, says Fed Ex trucks came there every day. And O'Malley never saw anyone enter or leave that office except for Cynthia, the three dead employees, the bottled water delivery guy, and the Fed Ex driver. They got no mail through the post office. None. Zip. Now that's odd as hell, don't you think?"

CHAPTER 16

*L*ast night, the sky had been red. Old-time sailors say a red sky at night, meant sailors delight. This morning, the weather had provided some measure of proof. The air had been still and cool, the sky azure blue with high smeary clouds.

Later in the day, Linda left for a walk on the beach, but she would do no jogging this morning. No reading. No day trades. This walk was about trying to make some sense out of the recent events that had upended her life.

She began her walk heading up-beach. The locals considered the direction toward their small town always to be up-beach. Conversely, the direction away from town was always referred to as down-beach. The appropriateness of the terms was dictated by one's location on the beach with respect to the direction toward town.

With the afternoon maturing toward evening and the sun sliding toward the horizon, Linda ignored her stomach's overdue notices and continued walking and thinking.

A few hours later, with the sun seemingly sitting on the edge of the distant water, she turned from the surf and started up toward her condo. She had been walking since before noon. Her legs felt exhausted and she had grown quite hungry. She had found no answers. Soon she would go inside, to eat. She had homemade bean soup in the freezer for dinner. She would add some crackers to get back some of the salt lost while walking.

Fifty yards from her condo, she stopped in one of her favorite spots, snuggled down her beach hat, and sat behind one of the sand berms to watch the sea. Over the ages, violent storms had pushed the sand inland. The shaping winds contoured the berms with the seabirds pitching in to help spread the seeds. That mixture was then left to Mother Nature's mild spring temperatures and hot summer hands.

On the coast, the sun drops from the edge of the horizon to behind it in a matter of minutes. About that time, being resigned to the fact that she would find no more answers sitting and thinking than she had found walking and thinking, she turned her position sufficiently to watch her condo through the wind-combed veil of sea grass. After a while, she startled when her two living room lamps, fixed with timers, came on. The lamps were positioned so that anyone moving inside would cast shadows. Ten minutes later, having seen no indoor shadows and not wanting to longer endure the demands from her stomach, she rose and trudged up the slight, steady incline to her condo.

She ate the bean soup and crackers in silence. She did not turn on the television or put on music, just watched as the deepening night pulled its dark blanket over the coast and began energizing the lamps in heaven. Then she went to bed.

Some hours later, she woke suddenly. Perhaps her subconscious had been reviewing her investments. It would not be the first time she had awakened with a decision regarding a buy or sell she had been pondering, but not this time.

She had awakened because something didn't seem right, nothing she could put her finger on, just something she couldn't ignore. Living alone, she had learned the personality of her home as one might come to know the personality of a spouse or roommate. And all was not right. Her bedroom seemed too dark.

Then she felt a whisper of movement, nothing more than a breath, but not her own. She glanced peripherally, opening her eyes just far enough. The Venetian blinds beside her bed were closed. That accounted for the darkness. The problem, she always kept the blinds slanted open so the sun could gently wake her each morning.

Someone had been in her house.

Someone had darkened her room.

She remained motionless, feigning sleep, searching for a rational explanation. Yesterday morning, Ben McIlhenny had stopped by. But she had stayed with him the whole time. They hadn't come into the bedroom although she had long known he desired to do so. At times she had found the thought appealing. Ben was a powerfully built man and that power would likely fuel his lust. But no, whoever had closed her blinds had come in earlier today. While she was on the beach, there was no other explanation. But why hadn't he or they stayed to capture her when she came back inside?

A small odor came to her. Faint. Unmistakable. The smell of a human. Not body odor or flatulence. Musk? Yes, Musk, a man's fragrance she found too bold. She could not think of a man in Sea Crest who wore musk. Yet, here it was. In her home. In her bedroom. Discernible even as it mixed with the salt air coming through her open glass-sliding door.

Ahab had told her someone would come.

She could see him now.

One man.

At least she could see only one man. He sat in the overstuffed chair near the door to the living room. She had placed the chair there for putting on her shoes, but instead she always sat on the side of the bed. The chair was comfortable, but her butt sank into the cushion below her knees, making it hard to lean forward to tie her shoes and a little klutzy to get out of.

His slouch suggests he might be asleep or at least drowsy. Why hasn't he taken me? The neighbors' small lamp next to their TV is still on. Even with her blinds drawn closed, she could see the light from their undraped window. They go to bed after the eleven o'clock news. Could he know that? So, it's still earlier than midnight. He figures I'm asleep and he's waiting until the deadness of total darkness.

She had gone to bed fully clothed, just as Ahab had warned her to do. But she had not kept the gun with her, something she had also been warned to do.

If he moves first, gets out of that chair, I'm a goner.

She eased back the covers as one does when getting up to go to the bathroom during the night. She paused, sitting on the edge of her bed, and with her back to the man, ran her hands through her hair. She stood. Reached up and ran her hands under her breasts, rubbing an area that sometimes got itchy while sleeping. Through it all, she denied herself even the slightest look toward the man. He had not moved. If he had, she would know it. No one could rise from that chair easily even at her height, and her glance had noticed he was still taller.

She took one unsteady step toward the bathroom, then a second. Each of her strides appearing to be those of a sleepwalker's stagger. She was now no more than five steps from the man. Two steps from the mostly open sliding glass door. If awake, he would soon recognize she was dressed in street clothes.

She moved first.

She ran those two steps like a sprinter leaving the blocks, turning sideways slightly to burst through the screened slider which flew off its track, bent and flopped outward onto the deck. She stumbled briefly, regained her balance and ran directly toward the long side of the deck. There, she planted her hands on the top of the railing, just to the right of the hummingbird feeder, and vaulted over, dropping one floor onto the sand below, an area busy with her footprints and those of her neighbors. From there she withdrew into the darkness below her deck, shards of moonlight squeezing through the spaces between the deck boards above her head appeared to slice the sand beneath her feet.

She pressed her back against the masonry wall and listened.

CHAPTER 17

*T*he glass slider slammed against the wall after the man violently pushed it full open. His foot slid when he stepped onto the fallen screen door. He quickly regained his balance by grabbing the wider plank at the top of the deck rail.

Linda took advantage of the cover provided by that noise to open the wooden, unlocked door to the storage area under her condo where she had planned to hide. But she was repulsed at the thought of being confined. Instead, she left the door standing open to give him the opportunity to assume she had gone in and enter himself. If that happened, she might be able to slam it shut and latch it with him inside. That door would not hold him inside for long, but perhaps enough for her to have time to determine if he had a helper out front. If he did, that second man might come to let him out. If so, she could make the front street and get far enough that they would not be able to find her.

No. The door was plywood, the latch small. He would smash through it as easily as she had burst through the screen door.

She looked up. The man remained on the deck. She remained beneath him, his bulk turning jagged the lines of moonlight passing through the deck planks. She then glanced toward her neighbors still watching News at Eleven. She prayed they had heard the commotion and had called the police, but nothing at their place looked any different. The neighbors played their television loudly. They had not heard anything. These madmen had already killed six people so they would not hesitate to kill two more.

The man just stood there. Listening. Watching. She imagined his hand above his eyes as he strained to find her running across the sand. She expected he would soon abandon that effort and drop down off her deck that had no stairs to the beach.

Linda kept her eyes upward while easing backward to the wall, then sideways, scooting her flat hand across each masonry block, down into each mortar line, then out and across the rough texture of the next block.

The sky went dark, a fleeting cover in the moon's nightly hide-and-seek game with the earth. Her next move would take her out from under the deck and across open sand before she would reach the first patch of sea grass. That position still a full twenty yards from where she had left the gun wrapped in her sweat hoodie.

Damn it. I should have listened to Ahab, kept the gun with me.

She scooted forward on her belly the way she had seen soldiers do in the movies. Then stopped and parted the grass. The man was down off the deck now. Standing. He had not panicked. He had not rushed off in one direction or another. He had again paused, anticipating his eyes would soon find his prey. Her.

Like her hunter, Linda didn't move. She wanted to. She felt eager to touch the cold of the gun. Turn it warm with her hands, feel its hardness. But to move now, would mean he would reach her before she reached the gun. She needed him to move a few yards farther, just a few yards. She again cursed herself for not having kept the gun. Had she slept with it, she could have flipped on the lamp and confronted him. But that wasn't her reality.

Move. Damn you. Move.

Then, as if her will alone had been sufficient, he moved. He didn't run, just a brisk walk toward the surf.

He wants to get beyond the sea grass, where he can look up and down the beach. He's guessing he'll see me running along the

*harder packed sand, and feels confident he can catch me. When he
doesn't see my tracks, he'll know I'm here in the knee-high grass.*

She rolled over twice before stopping to find him with her
eyes. He was standing close to the surf's edge. She glanced at the
sky to confirm the cloud cover would hold a while longer, and then
rolled twice more. Then she looked again. He remained in the
same position, hands on his hips. She glanced at the sky. Then she
focused on the nearby terrain. She had looked at these berms many
times from her deck, watched the wind move through the sea grass,
at times rhythmically, sometimes violently. Those same berms
looked different from down below. Then her eyes found the goal,
the clump where she had cached the gun. Ten yards, nine, maybe.
No distance at all if a casual pursuit. But he was a hunter and she
the prey. She raised enough to see that he had turned. He was now
facing down-beach. Like the two in the alley, this man was a
stranger, with one common bond with the two in the alley. They
had all come for her.

She still hated guns, but right now getting that gun was the
only thing in her mind.

She glanced again. He remained statue steady, staring. He was
smart and careful. Without moving himself, he could more easily
detect her movement. After another minute, the man turned
quickly twice, each turn one hundred eighty degrees. First down-
beach, then immediately back to up-beach, away from her position.

Linda moved through one more patch of sea grass. Then she
rolled down the far side of the berm nearest the gun. There, she
frantically dug the sand away. The gun was still there, right where
she had left it. She pulled the hoodie open and looked at the gun
without disdain. She clutched it tight, crawled up the berm and
parted the grass. The man had turned, his concentration again
down-beach.

Linda knew the pattern of the berms, where she would find the
highest and densest grass. She also knew where she would
encounter flat stretches of sand without grass or berms. Some of

those stretches were parted by the small streams of fresh water that endlessly wound down from the hills east of town, under the main road, across the beach and into the sea. A few of those streams fed tide pools, parts of the ecosystem that kept beach things living. Hopefully, these same forces would also help keep her living.

The next time she looked for the man, he had left the surf line and was moving back toward the berms generally toward her condo. He must have concluded, she thought, having found no tracks on the firm sand that she had not gone into the surf or run upon the denser sand.

He stopped.

Then he stared off to Linda's right, then exactly in her direction. Her heart raced. Then he looked off to her left. He was searching methodically, setting up the beach in visual grids, hoping that when he looked exactly toward her that she would panic and take flight like a flushed bird. She also knew that eventually she might have to do just that, but not yet. For now, she would continue her gradual progress up-beach with each opportunity. A few feet at a time, a yard, perhaps two, as much as she could whenever his behavior allowed her to move. She was in a game of hide-and-seek with death for the booby prize.

He was about fifty yards from her. If he broke into a short hard sprint, he could halve that distance before she could get up and get moving at top speed. Her options were quickly disappearing. If he kept coming, she would soon need to rise up and run for her life. She had the gun but lacked the confidence to get in a shootout with a man she imagined to be a trained assassin.

The wind was mild so she had to be careful about causing erratic movements in the grass. She continued to increase the space between them each time he looked away. Once with him facing toward the surf, she crab walked through an opening to reach another berm. She wanted to gain a hundred-yard lead before it became a footrace. With the hundred yards, she believed he would be unable to catch her. She had to assume he could run faster, but unless he was also a jogger, she figured he would be unable to endure a hot pace as long as she.

Suddenly, without warning, he ran hard away from her, his fluid gait unlabored, even in the sand.

Oh, Shit. He's a runner.

Linda grasped the opportunity to roll over another berm, crab across a patch of open sand, roll through the next berm, then, on all fours, she crossed one of the fresh streams. After one more berm, she stopped, turned, and looked back.

He had stopped running. He was just standing, staring. He was definitely trying to flush her, to panic her into rising up. His strategy was good, but so far his direction had been bad. She looked one more time and, in the full moonlight, saw him change direction to run hard toward her.

Each of his strides ate into her safety zone, now down to seventy-five yards, not the hundred she had hoped. For a moment, she held her position, hoping he would veer off or at least stop. When he didn't, she knew.

The time for sneaking had passed.

Her feet began pushing small, soft piles of sand this way and that, her legs pistons forcing her forward. As she ran, she glanced back. He saw her. She knew he would. He had changed his angle slightly. He was now running directly at her.

Her life had become escape tonight or die tonight.

CHAPTER 18

*T*he cat and mouse had ended. From here on, Linda's life would be a flat-out race. She couldn't treat it as a sprint, there was too far to go. She would need to pace herself some but make no mistake this was no jog. His stride would be longer than hers so she would need to run harder than he. Many years ago, she had run a short marathon called run-for-life. That one had been for charity. This time was literal, a run for her life.

Linda hit full speed in a few strides. Then she angled toward the surf. The firmer sand there offered less change of hitting a soft pocket and falling. Her legs already felt heavy after her long day of walking.

As she ran, her mind searched for a way to turn her intimate knowledge of this beach into an edge. Some kind of advantage that could increase her odds of making it, of seeing tomorrow's sunrise.

The gun was working loose in her waistband. She reached down and pulled it free, gripping it in her right hand. Not like she would hold it to shoot. Just clutched it, strangled it. Her hand circled the trigger housing. Her pumping fists punctured the sky with each stride. She had jogged in this direction countless times. She knew where to angle out and in to avoid the spreading waves from snatching at her feet. Like a winding mountain road, the surf line jutted in and out repeatedly.

If she were to survive, she had to beat him for about three miles. Life had become that simple. That precise. That frightening. Three miles. Live or die.

The road in front of her condo would have been a mile shorter. She had considered dashing through her house, past the man in the chair, out the front door, but then she might run into the arms of his accomplice waiting out front, if he had one. She would not have had time to get her car out of the garage. She would have had to run the paved road to town because the tangled berry fields on the inland side were impenetrable. At this time of night, there was seldom anyone on the road and her pursuer would have followed in a car. She could have gone to a neighbor, but the killings at SMITH & CO. said these men had no problem killing innocent bystanders. Hell, I'm an innocent bystander, she thought, and they want to kill me. Besides, she had wanted to go out the back of the house to get the gun she now clutched. She hated guns. Right now, she loved this gun.

She had made the right decision, use the beach she knew. That was an edge in her favor. Would it be enough?

A moment later, Old Gray, a mangy dog who seemed to live on the beach, and had long ago accepted Linda as a fellow beachcomber, came out of the grass to run beside her.

Then a shot rang out, and Old Gray darted inland, disappearing into the sea grass.

She didn't know where the bullet ended up, but it hadn't ended up in her. A warning shot? A stop or I'll-shoot-you, shot? This stretch of beach had no facing houses. No one would have heard the shot, not over the sound-swallowing sea. She guessed he had fired in the air hoping to scare her into stopping. If he was there only to kill her, she would have died in her bed. The same had been true when the two men forced her off the street into the alley. They wanted to control her first.

Why do they want me? What for?

Right now the why didn't matter, not in the slightest. Survival, that's what mattered now. Run. Get to town without being caught. She ignored the messages from her muscles and drove herself forward. She could not afford to give up any more of her shrinking lead. She needed to lengthen that lead.

Ahead another hundred yards or so, she would come to a group of beached trees, bleached white by salt and sun. North of town, the hills sloped down to the water and raging storms sometimes tore out huge hunks of hillside. When that happened, some massive old trees belly flopped into the surf where their branches were sheared off by the same storms that had torn them free of their roots. The trunks then followed the tide until the current beached them like albino whales with defective sonar.

Linda planned to jump over those tree trunks, and then hunker down to wait until her pursuer came close enough to see the whites of his eyes. If she were lucky, she could then put a shot or two into him.

Don't try for a head shot Ahab had said. Shoot for the broad center of his body. Stop him. Make him bleed. Slow him. If you're lucky, you'll hit his heart, putting him down for the count.

As the logs came into view, the stubs of their branches in the distance appeared as pocks, the way eyes disfigure a freshly scrubbed potato. Two more strides brought the logs into clear view. Stretched across the sand, blocking her passage the way a military checkpoint impedes the progress of travelers on a desolate mountain road.

By the time Linda had drawn near enough to think in terms of the exact point in the expanse that she would attempt to hurdle, she changed her mind. Ahab had said, "Shoot only if you must." At this point, the must didn't apply, at least not yet. Still, she had to leap. If she did not, the time she spent circumventing the logs, her pursuer would spend to purchase more of her lead. He would come straight. He would leap. She had to leap. But she would not shoot. Hopefully she would never shoot. She feared his plans for her.

Still, she didn't want to shoot him. She didn't want to shoot anyone.

She pushed down as hard as she could on her right leg, and extended her left leg out in front of herself, as straight as she could make it. Her left foot cleared. *You made it, girl.* Then the toe of her right foot stubbed against the log. *Damn. I should have turned the foot to put my toe to the side.* Still, her momentum had kept her moving. Her right foot dragged across the log. By the time she had regained her balance on the other side, she had been slowed to a walk. She needed a new plan, at least a revision. She needed a breather, a way to regain some of her lost lead. She turned and ran away from the surf, toward the grassy berms. Ten yards first. Then twenty yards inland, at thirty yards she dove into the grass.

Her legs, even her chest and stomach had passed aching. If she had been jogging, she would have long ago given in to her racing heart, caught her breath and walked home. She wanted to stay in the grass, become another beach creature living in the privacy of their ecosystem. But hers was a different reality. She rose, and then ducked back down.

The quick look confirmed he had changed direction. He was now headed directly toward her.

She stayed out of sight, moved below the grass line, and worked her way back to the fallen logs. From there she crawled along their edge until she returned to the hard sand. There she stood and resumed her frantic race toward town. Her detour had failed. Her lead had not been lengthened. In fact, her rough estimate said she had sacrificed some ten yards of the space that separated them, but she had gotten a short breather. Then again, he had to slog through the soft sand and grass to get back to the packed sand. She prayed that by then she would have recovered the ten yards, maybe even more. It was maddening that the choice between life and death would be measured by a few yards of sand.

The lights of town came into view. She was getting closer.

Since the race began, her lead had been cut by more than half, but she had come more than half way.

She glanced back. His gait appeared as smooth as it had at the start. He had to be a jogger, maybe an accomplished runner. Maybe he was one of those Special Forces types who could run all day with a fifty-pound pack on his back. Certainly he had not spent the day, as she had, walking in the sand. She knew he could see her struggling. Her gait was unmistakably uneven. He had to be encouraged by her staggering. He had to believe he was gaining. He was gaining. Still, in a worst case scenario, he didn't need to catch her. Should he conclude he could not, he only needed to be close enough to shoot her in the legs. Like the two in the alley, this man wanted more than to simply kill her. They all wanted to question her, but why? She had nothing to tell. She knew nothing. Maybe Cynthia had nothing to tell either. Maybe he'll drill holes in my teeth like he did, someone did, to Cynthia's mouth.

My God, I can't let him catch me.

A rocky crag jutted out near the water's edge about a half mile ahead. At low tide, there was about twenty feet of open sand. The high tide reached the rocks. She had no idea what time she had awakened and run for it, so she had to guess at the tide, but it looked close to full high. If so, no more than a narrow strip of sand might remain between the crag and the surf.

Linda could now smell the urine and fecal matter left by the homeless who often slept in the sand on the downwind side of the rocky crag. The rocks blocked the glow from their small fires. Most nights, Linda could have run to their cardboard hooches and pleaded for help from the half dozen or so men, but not tonight. This morning, Linda had seen the rotating lights above the Sea Crest squad car reflecting off the rock face while McIlhenny's deputy ran them off for the umpteenth time. The deputy never arrested the sad sacks, but, before leaving on her walk, using her binoculars she had watched them bundle their meager belongings and leave. She had no idea where they went, but somewhere they liked less than the beach because they always returned a few days later.

Linda's gait was now much less than a run. More like the stumbling progress of a lost vampire found by the morning sun.

The rocks were only twenty yards ahead. Just beyond them, the coastline turned inland. He would not be able to see her again until he, too, had passed the massive rock. She willed herself to widen her shrinking lead, her heart pounding as if it were about to burst free of her chest.

As she neared the rock face, she learned she had reasonably guessed the tide, a small strip of sand did remain. She intentionally drifted into the shallow surf. She wanted him to see her kicking up water as he lost sight of her with the turn of the coastline. When she had gone far enough past the rocks to close off his line of sight, she swung around and ran back toward the crag. The mere thought of going back toward the man filled her with fright. But she knew he was gaining too fast for her to beat him to town and up the cardiac steps.

She had also grown tired of being chased.

At the crag, relying on arms less weary than legs, she began climbing the side of the rock face. Needing her hands free, she held the gun in her teeth. It tasted of wet metal, gun oil, and sand. She bit down so she would not drop it.

Two years ago, Linda had climbed onto this crag to watch a rising storm. She had climbed high enough to stay there until the storm had quieted and the tide lowered. It had been glorious to see, but a foolish, freezing, and frightening night as the fury of the storm had not broken until nearly noon the next day. Still, that experience let her know where to climb. Where she could find cover within the rocks, while she waited for the terror that drew closer each second.

She settled into a cavity pounded out by the crashing waves of a thousand years. The pain traveled her legs like a hamster trapped in a wheel cage.

She had used more than a minute climbing. He had to be close. Then she saw him. He was twenty yards out. His gait still smooth, his white shirt reflecting the moonlight. He was trim, with a thin waist and broad shoulders. His chest calm despite the roughly two miles he had run.

Near the crag, he slowed to a walk. His dark weapon in a leather holster beneath his arm swayed gently with each step. She had waited. He had caught up. They were only a few yards apart.

Her mouth dried.

Linda receded into a water-pooled pocket ten feet above his head. She briefly considered hiding there and letting him pass, but the moonlight would reveal her footprints returning to the rock ledge. Whatever would come now would come. The footrace was over. She took the gun into her hand, then added her other hand to try and steady the shake.

When he was directly below her position, she screamed. "Why?" That was enough. There were a thousand whys. Why are you chasing me? Why does someone want me killed? Why was Cynthia tortured? Why was Cynthia murdered? And more whys, but plain "why" was enough.

The man stopped. His hand instinctively reached for his gun.

"Stop," she demanded. "Stop or I'll shoot."

He turned toward her. His back to the open sea. His feet receding deeper in the surf as the tide pulled around him. He smiled. His smile was pleasant. His physicality impressive.

"I see you have a gun," he said. "The surprise is on me." His manner remained casual. In a different setting he might even seem charming. But this was not a different setting. This was now. This was life or death.

"I know how to shoot," she said, her voice rising like some nervous child with a shaking hand. She cleared her throat. "Maybe not as good as you, but well enough to put several in your guts before you can reach your gun."

"You think you can make me talk? You? A woman?"

"This woman can make you dead. That's your choice. Talk or die. First, take your gun out. Slowly. Use your left hand. Two fingers."

The moonlight reflected off the barrel of the handgun dangling from the tips of his fingers.

"Wrap your left hand around the trigger housing," Linda commanded. When he had done so, she ordered him to toss it back over his head. "Throw it hard. Do it. Now."

He did.

She saw and heard the splash.

He smiled; his teeth bright in the moonlight. "Why don't we go have a drink and talk this over?"

"You think you can charm your way out of this?"

He moved slightly when the ebb pulled at his feet. "I can be a charming fellow if you give me half a chance."

"You can be a dead fellow if you don't do what I say."

"You're not really going to shoot me, are you?"

"Maybe not if you answer my questions. All of them."

"I may not be able to do that. I've got loyalties."

"A man like you has no loyalties."

"Well, then, I've been well paid. And what do you think it would do to my reputation if I were to be bamboozled by a woman?"

"Make your decision," Linda said, her hand now steady. She had no options. "Talk or die. Why am I being hunted?"

"You were a close friend of Cynthia Leclair."

"Why was Cynthia killed?"

"I won't tell you."

"What made my friendship with Cynthia put me on your radar?"

"She may have told you things the man I work for doesn't want anyone to know."

"What things?"

"Things about her work. That's all I know."

"Cynthia never talked about her work. Never."

"It doesn't matter whether I believe you or not."

"Who sent you?"

"No way, lady. I can't say anything more."

"You mean you won't."

"Have it your way. I won't."

"Is that your final answer?" She felt like a fool using the question she had heard so often on that TV game show.

"Final answer." He grinned.

Him or me time had arrived. At this moment, it was that simple. No doubt. No gray. She took the slack out of the trigger. The gun jumped in her hand.

The man went down like droppings from the seagulls suddenly quieted by the roar of the gun. The white seabirds scattered to wait somewhere in the sky until the night sea again became theirs. He had guessed she wouldn't shoot. He had guessed wrong.

She stared at her hand holding the gun, warmed by the explosion of its fire, stared as if trying to identify just whose hand had done this thing. But she knew.

The Sea Crest that had brought her peace, which had allowed her to hide, was gone forever. Her life had turned. Toward what, she did not know.

Linda remained still as if frozen on her ledge. She watched as several incoming waves washed over his face. The ebbs pulling the water back into his nose without him reacting. He was dead.

She climbed down and stood silently in the surf, the retreating sand now pulling at her ankles. She had never before shot anything but paper targets. Paper targets with neat clean holes. Paper targets that didn't bleed.

The red splotch on his shirt over his heart was already pinking out in the rinsing sea water. The moonlight brightened his face. His was not an ugly face. Not grotesque as one might expect on the face of a killer, the face of a torturer. She guessed his age to be around forty, maybe forty-five. His full head of hair darkened with sea water. The ghoul inside, released, hopefully dead, like its host body.

Her stomach turned queasy. She stepped into the surf. Scooped up saltwater and splashed her face, a second handful circled her neck, cold rivulets crawling down her back and front.

Linda turned back to the man, squatted, and went through his pockets. No wallet. No car key. Not even a hotel key or airline ticket. Nothing. In the many mystery novels she had read, this guy would be called a professional. He was dead now, but not his employer, some truly evil man about whose existence she no longer kidded herself. He would send others. What had happened here had ended only the immediate danger.

In another half mile she could take the wooden stairs from the beach up the sand wall to Ocean Street. These stairs were the only way from the beach to the highway up-beach from her condo. Clark, who worked for O'Malley, lived on Ocean Street, just on the other side of the vacant lot where the stairs came up. She could hide the gun under the top step, and then go to Clark's for a short rest to gather herself.

What body in the surf, Chief McIlhenny? I didn't see a body. It was dark when I jogged the beach. It likely washed up at high tide, after I had passed.

She had moved up-beach another hundred yards or so when she felt a fist of ice starting down toward her stomach where a ball of fire waited. She knew the feeling and ran thigh-deep into the surf where her puke would not be found. After several saltwater rinses, she walked out of the eternal waves. The distant inland sky, adorned with faintly flickering stars, appeared as strings of lights suspended along the crest of Pot Ridge.

The civilized world liked to hang onto its rules separating right from wrong, the rules we learned as children with all of it contrasted as clearly as black and white. With maturity comes confusion because there is no line with all the black on one side and the white on the other. It is wrong to kill. Still, that man had come to take her life, first making her suffer pains she couldn't imagine. Instead, she had taken his life. Killing should not be dismissed as wrong in every instance.

After walking another minute or two, she stopped, then turned and walked back to the man lying dead in the surf. She straddled him, looking down at his face now as innocent as a neighborhood paperboy. She put one foot on each side of his midsection, cradled the gun with two hands, aimed, and squeezed the trigger. Her first shot had found his heart. This second, purely symbolic shot had struck where she aimed, his forehead.

Linda fully expected Chief McIlhenny would notice the similarity to Cynthia Leclair, but she hadn't considered that when she fired this second shot. Then again, she really didn't give a fuck. It had made her feel good to strike back, even though her behavior had sickened and frightened her.

"You got off lucky," she said to his silence. "I didn't have a chance to first do to you what you or someone like you did to my friend."

Before leaving, she again straddled the now harmless killer, this time with her face toward the shore. She grabbed the belted top of his trousers and strained to drag him a little farther out into the surf, but the sand had ebbed around him. She had moved him a few inches when an incoming wave smacked her on the backside, knocking her face down on top the dead stranger, her face to his groin.

She rolled off and stood up, her shoes filling with wet sand, her heart racing as if King Neptune had chosen to resurrect this man rather than accept him into the kingdom of the sea.

CHAPTER 19

*L*inda continued up-beach with her heart slamming her chest as if she were being pummeled with medicine balls. If the man she had left in the surf had an accomplice, he could have driven toward town, looking for a place Linda might climb up from the beach. That place would be the wooden staircase she now approached, the stairs near Clark's house. Yet she had no better choice. If she turned back, passed the man she killed and returned to her condo from the beach, the accomplice could be there.

Before starting the climb, she stood for several minutes, her eyes fixed on the ledge that topped the one-hundred stairs, the crest of the cliff top. Then, holding the gun behind her right thigh, she started up the back-breaker, another of the local names for this climb. She paused at each of the several landings to again study the crest and to prepare herself for the next stretch of rising stairs. She was now pulling herself each step using more arms than legs.

She slowed near the top, her eyes focused on the clearing, alert for any kind of movement. But there was no one, no movement other than Old Gray, who apparently had his own way up the hill without using the stairs. The dog, being at the top, assured her that the accomplice, if there was one to begin with, was not up there. Old Gray didn't like strangers.

At the top of the stairs, seeing no one, Linda reached through the backless step to nest the gun amongst the trash the wind had back flushed into the dirt cavity.

Clark was home. The front door was open except for a latched screen, its dry wooden frame grayed by weather. The inside was dark except for flickering lights dancing on the far wall. Many of the owners of these beach-facing houses had screened in their ocean facing decks. She guessed the one Clark rented had done so and the light was from a television around the corner on that deck.

"Clark?" she hollered through the screen. "Are you home?"

A moment later, his head peeked around the side of the archway that partitioned off the back part of the house. He immediately moved toward the door, his fist tucking his white T-shirt into the elastic waistband of his gray shorts. "Linda? Is that you?"

"Yes. May I come in?" She asked as he reached the other side of the screen. "I'm exhausted from a late jog. I remembered you lived nearby so I thought I'd stop by for a few minutes before heading home, if I didn't come at a bad time."

His finger slapped the hook out of the eye screw that held the screen shut. "Sure. Linda. Sure. Come on in."

She stepped inside. "Thanks, Clark. I appreciate this."

"Anytime... You look a mess, a good mess. Did you fall?"

"Sorta. I'm okay though."

"What happened?" He latched the warped screen to prevent it from sagging open.

"I don't need questions, just a place to sit for a while. Okay? If not, I can head on home."

"Hey, chill." He took her arm and led her toward the back from where he had come. She sat. He turned off the television.

"Leave it on, will ya? Anything. No violent stuff. Okay?"

"Sure. I'll put on a music channel. We can just sit. Talk if you wanna."

"Thank you."

After looking down for a moment, he said, "I was real sorry to hear about your friend, Cynthia. I didn't know her except for seeing her in O'Malley's with you. But she was your friend, so she was aces in my book."

"Yes. Cynthia was... aces."

"You know, the town's full of rumors about that company where she worked. Some say she owned it, others claim they brokered drugs. In O'Malley's I hear it all. That kinda talk turns real shitty in no time at all. Everybody trying to top the last crazy thing they heard somewheres else."

"She did own SMITH & CO.," Linda said. "The rest of all that's ... a bunch a bull."

"I figured as much. You wouldn't be tight with somebody selling shit."

"Can we just sit quietly?"

"Sure."

After a few minutes, Linda said, "So, you happy living here in Sea Crest?"

"Sure. Nice town. I love the ocean. O'Malley's good people, tough, but in a nice way, you know. The tips, well, they could always be better. But it's clean work, which is a huge change from my life before I came here. So, yeah, everything's cool."

Linda rubbed her upper arms. Clark got up and shut the two partially open sliding windows. "Did somebody attack you? It don't look like you're hurt, but you've been, I don't know, hassled or somethin'."

"I went jogging on the beach tonight. You know those logs at the surf line about a mile or so down-beach? Stupid me, I tried to hurdle 'em." She stood back, holding her arms out from her sides. "I tumbled in the sand, a wave washed over me. My pride hurts the most."

Clark raised his eyebrows. "Okay, Linda, if that's the way you want to play it."

"That's what happened. I really don't need your doubting attitude."

"No offense." He raised his hands as if somebody had put a gun against his back. "Whatever you say, is cool for me. I'll back you all the way."

They sat through three songs before either spoke again.

"You wanna shower? I got a clean pair of sweats you can wear, and a T-shirt. That might take the edge off your done-in look."

"I'd like that. Thanks."

"Let me show you the way. Excuse the mess. You know us bachelors, give us a toilet and a shower, a bed and a TV, micro and refrigerator, and we're set for life." She smiled. He did too.

The hot water pounded the top of her head, cascading down over her breasts. The trailing water stung her thighs, chafed from sand grinding on wet skin. She shampooed and rinsed her hair, then stood under the spray until the hot water withdrew into warm and surrendered into cold. Clark had put out a fresh pair of sweats, a clean T-shirt, and a pair of clean socks across the tops of her wet tennis shoes, along with a plastic bag for her wet things.

She dressed and went back into the bathroom to fuss with her hair. When she came out, the plastic bag was gone. She rejoined Clark, leaned down and kissed him on the cheek.

"This was a good idea. Felt great."

"I'm glad I was home."

"What did you do with my wet clothes?"

"I burned them in the fireplace. They smoked quite a bit. You can probably still smell it."

"Why did you burn them?"

"The front was stained with a red smear. You musta fell in something. I didn't think it would come out. There was none on your shoes."

He knows. How can he know?

"Look. If you wanna talk, really talk. I got some beers. Cold Coronas with lime just like at work. You drink them sometimes. Listen, if tonight's earned me the right to a guess, I'd say somebody's pressed you about something, forced you to act. You know."

Linda said nothing for a moment, and then stood. "I'm leaving now. Thank you very much. This was just what I needed. I'll get your clothes back to you in a day or two."

"I can run you home on my hog. Let the air blow dry your hair."

"Another time. I'd like to walk."

"No hurry on getting those sweats back, I got a ton. They fit you okay. Well, a bit big, but I'll bet they think they're on vacation being on you instead of me."

She hugged him. "You're a good man, Charlie Brown. Thank you."

She stepped outside and closed the screen. Then she turned back at the sound of his voice.

"By the way," he said. "We had cheeseburgers and watermelon for dinner. Shared a six-pack of Coronas, put on some music and watched the ocean." She started to protest. He held up a hand. "Just in case somebody asks where you were tonight. You walked down here a little after five and left about now. Don't say you were jogging on the beach tonight because too many people might have seen you on the beach all day."

"Why is this necessary?" she asked.

"I don't know that it is. It's just there, if you need it. Like I said, I got your back. And let me say this, please. I've never heard of you taking up with anybody, but if some dude's giving you a hard time, you tell me and I'll see that he stops." He pushed open the screen and looked straight at her. "Even if it's Chief McIlhenny. I've noticed the way he watches you."

"The chief is always a gentleman." She touched her still damp hair, then his cheek, turned and walked down Main Street leaving him holding the edge of his screen door. She heard the snap-click when Clark reengaged the latch hook.

She wanted to go back and ask Clark to drive her home, to go in with her and make sure no one was waiting for her. But, flimsy as her story had seemed to him, she wasn't about to tell him what had really happened on the beach. She also saw no reason to bring him into the danger that had crowded out everything else in her life.

A minute later, she stopped at the top of the beach stairs to retrieve her gun from under the top step. There was a gun there, fully loaded, but not the one she had left.

CHAPTER 20

*W*ebster didn't know the time but it was earlier than four in the morning because that was when the master timer turned off the lights under the eaves of the cabana about fifty yards from the main house. And the cabana lights were still reflecting off the pool.

Webster could feel the lushness of the grounds surrounding his estate, even detect the mild aroma of the horse stables on the far side of the helipad. From where he stood the stately trees at the back of the property silhouetted against the moon. A chorus of crickets reminded him that God had made creatures of all kinds, but selected only a few to protect and preserve the balance and order of life. He would not fail that duty.

One day he would put a stop to the drunken spending by politicians in their endless pursuit of the votes they needed to keep themselves in power. Like addicts everywhere, selling their very souls for the next fix. For politicians, the next fix was campaign money for the next election. For now, it served Webster's interests to be one of their main suppliers.

He loved walking and thinking in the quiet of the night. In the distance, the sky lightened with what he believed to be the glow of the nation's capital. The White House. The Capitol Building. The

U.S. Supreme Court. The three centers of power. The rest of D.C. was about posturing and pomposity, along with serving the big three. All that would be his once he had sufficiently tightened his noose around the big three.

No one in the modern world could conquer America from the outside, but complacency, arrogance, and voter apathy had made the country highly vulnerable from within. His plan: claim power silently, one member of congress at a time, then, eventually, the presidency. The banks in which he held considerable influence would play their part. They could be counted on to go along with any structure that took the government's growing yoke from their necks. The leaders of the major banks, along with the technology giants and the makers of armaments would be at the apex of his multinational world government.

The same excessive debt and out-of-control spending that ruins families and companies would eventually ruin the entire country. The need to give everything necessary to garner votes required a government powerful enough to first take all that the people had. A benevolent dictator was needed to prevent that, one insulated from the vicissitudes of politics.

Now this nobody, this Linda Darby, had become a tumor growing on the side of his plan.

As for Ben McIlhenny, who had handled the installation and monitoring of the surveillance equipment in Cynthia Leclair's company, he would be of no help with the Darby matter. In fact, McIlhenny would soon become another loose end that required tying off.

Webster had dispatched Blue, his best operative, aside from Ryan Testler, to Sea Crest on the same day he had ordered Testler to come east to report in person. Blue had called in earlier to report having located Linda Darby's residence, but that she had not been at home. Not wanting to be seen hanging around, Blue had driven to the bigger town north of Sea Crest to get something to eat before going back to see if she had returned. Webster had gone out to walk his estate grounds to keep himself awake while waiting to hear from Blue. He had to know what Cynthia Leclair had told Linda Darby, and in turn if Darby had leaked that information to others. West coast time was three hours earlier, but Blue should have reported in by now.

More than three thousand miles to the west, as Linda Darby walked home from Clark's house she decided she would no longer be a sitting duck. They—whoever in the hell they were—had come for her in the alley and a mysterious stranger had saved her. Soon thereafter they came for her again and she had been ready, well somewhat ready, warned at least, thanks to the same mysterious stranger. She couldn't indefinitely count on luck and the shadowy man she thought of as Captain Ahab. She had to take more control and change things for herself. To continue to follow her routines, to live as she had, would only help them through her behaving as a reliable sitting duck.

Could Ahab have left the new gun? He had said he was out of town. But who else?

By the time Linda got to the intersection where Main Street split off to form Ocean Street she had decided she would leave in the morning. She didn't know where she would go, but then, if she didn't know, whoever wanted to torture and kill her wouldn't know either. In the end what mattered was going. The simple act of being on the move would provide some sense of safety. It just had to.

One thing was certain. Sea Crest was no longer the quiet, sleepy ocean hamlet she had embraced. The town had become the murder capital of America, at least on a per-capita basis, and, insane as it seemed, somehow these murders all revolved around her. After walking another block, she changed that thought to somehow these murders all seemed to revolve around Cynthia Leclair, and an innocent friendship with Cynthia had sucked her into its vortex.

She unlocked her front door and stepped inside, the new gun held with two hands as she had seen done in the movies. After being sure no one was inside, she drew the drapes and turned on all the lights. She felt exhausted, but knew she couldn't sleep.

She got out her travel suitcase, the smaller one she took to Cynthia's on Friday evenings, and experienced a melancholy moment realizing she would never again do that. The travel size would be enough to hold her toiletries and a couple of outfits, anything else she could buy on the move. Her bills were mostly utilities, and her bank credit card which she used to pay for most everything else. She got those statements online so she could pay them no matter her location. She had paid the homeowners' association dues through the end of the year. The cash in her purse, augmented by the five-thousand dollars Ahab had left in the clothespin bag, totaled just more than fifty-two hundred. Not enough to run very far, but enough to get started. She could have her investment brokerage house sell some shares. They had an office in Portland and in most principal cities. It wasn't much of a plan, not yet anyway. She would customize it as she went.

In addition to not knowing where she was going, she had no idea how long she would be gone. She would monitor the happenings in Sea Crest, and maybe not return until things quieted down. The FBI was another possibility, although there had been no crime, as she understood it, that would qualify bringing in the FBI. Chief McIlhenny seemed more appropriate, but then Ahab had warned her against him. Those decisions would come in due course. For now, she just had to stop waiting patiently in her home by the sea for the next visit by the grim reaper.

She put her travel case on the cedar chest at the foot of her bed and opened it to see a large manila envelope, the kind with a red string wrapped around a little disk. On its face were two words in hand printed block letters: LINDA DARBY. Just below her name a ring of three keys had been taped to the envelope. Inside the big envelope she found a smaller envelope with the caption: TO BE OPENED ONLY BY LINDA DARBY, AND ONLY IN THE EVENT OF THE DEATH OF CYNTHIA LECLAIR.

CHAPTER 21

*P*olice Chief Ben McIlhenny couldn't sleep. The killings troubled him for he knew somehow his bugging of Cynthia Leclair's company had contributed to her death, as well as the deaths of the others employed there. He was also coming to realize that somehow Linda's friendship with Cynthia had drawn Linda into it. He had thought the surveillance he had arranged had been connected to some kind of industrial espionage or perhaps off-the-books government work, not something that would result in killings and chaos.

The morning after the first call McIlhenny received from the person who had demanded that he carry out the unlawful surveillance, he had found in the backseat of his official car the most sophisticated audio-visual surveillance equipment he had ever seen. His government theory was further supported because that caller had possession of the tape that had been playing inside the home of a person relocated under the Federal Witness Protection program. As it turns out, the house had been equipped with an audio system that allowed the former federal witness to record any suspicious phone calls or people at her door or on her property that made her suspicious. That recorder had been engaged the night Newark police detective McIlhenny killed the mob hit man after that man had brutally killed the woman being hidden by the Feds.

Over the past two years Chief McIlhenny had, at various times, received phone calls identifying a new dead drop where he was to cache the spent audio-visual discs from Smith & Co., to be picked up by a person unknown to him.

Since his days in the military, Ryan Testler had been unable to sleep in an airplane. Despite the obvious dangers of military missions, the scuttlebutt back then said that Ryan Testler would sleep on his way to hell, a place no worse than some of the deeds he had carried out for Webster.

He had started with Alistair Webster after Webster had resigned from a deputy director's chair in the Central Intelligence Agency. Webster believed America had enemies that needed to be eliminated. At first, Ryan had believed that Webster's retirement was orchestrated so he could handle black ops outside the watchful eye of the congressional committees with oversight of the agency. The first two years, the targets assigned to Testler had all been foreign, after that the assignments increasingly became domestic. And it became increasingly obvious that his missions had nothing to do with the goals and objectives of the government's intelligence network.

A year ago, Testler began to mentally review each of his assignments. Foreign military and political targets had quickly been replaced by missions centering on compiling information about selected Americans. The kind of information Webster could use to threaten bureaucrats into doing Webster's bidding. And, on occasion, Testler had been ordered to eliminate individuals. A few of Testler's missions had included cleaning up, one way or another, soured love triangles from which Webster clients had been unable to comfortably withdraw. For all this Testler had been well paid. He had no gripe on that account.

Over time, Testler had been forced more and more often to listen to Webster rant about the government's drunken-sailor spending. The hollow election-time promises of more and more government largess. These promises were accompanied by another falsity, all this would not cost Americans anything, or that the needed funds could all be obtained by increasing taxes only on America's wealthy. Americans liked to say there was no free lunch, yet their gullibility at the polls said they would still believe in free lunches when promised within smooth campaign speeches. Webster had said on two separate occasions, in Testler's presence, that the elected government needed to be replaced by industrialists and financiers who would, free of the whoring decisions of politicians, make the cost-benefit-balanced decisions necessary to deliver, not just promise, a comfortable, safe and controlled life for all citizens.

Testler had not yet decided when and how he would openly oppose Webster, but he had grown certain that one day he would. He could simply kill Webster as he had killed others on Webster's behalf. The issue was never the difficulty of killing a rich soft man, although killing any powerful protected person was not all that easy, particularly one who had become paranoid. The real issue was how the death of Webster would drastically alter Testler's life. According to military records, Testler had died in Desert Storm, at least he had under his real name. Since then, he had lived in the shadows using false driver's licenses and passports, all of which checked out in government data bases, all courtesy of Webster's connections. In addition, Webster always provided Testler with witnesses who could, if needed, confirm Testler was elsewhere at the time he was carrying out Webster's assignments.

As for money, Webster had generously rewarded him and Testler had secreted funds in the U.S. and Europe, enough to allow him an adequate lifestyle. However, if he stayed with the current plan for another two or three years, he could have the lavish retirement that fuels the dreams of most Americans.

He had to decide. He would be back in Sea Crest by noon tomorrow. If he wanted to retire in luxury, he needed to stop fooling around and interrogate and eliminate Linda Darby.

CHAPTER 22

*T*he letter began,
    Dear Linda:

First I must tell you what you already know. After my daughter was killed in Iraq, I replaced her in my heart with you, loving you as a mother loves a daughter.

I know you have a thousand little questions like how did I get this package into your travel case. You gave me a key to your home and I know that you jog each morning. Other questions of similar magnitude don't matter. And there is no time. A short while ago my company discovered things we were never expected to know. I should have shut down the operation and disappeared. Instead I decided to hang on, hoping to bluff it out for a few more weeks. That would have provided the time I needed to blow the lid off this entire mess. Your reading this now confirms I did not get those few additional weeks.

I am dead, likely a violent death, probably during questioning. You are either under threat or not. My guess is you are, your friendship with me has put you there. Had I only imagined such an outcome, I would have long ago ended our relationship, even though my time with you was the only loving, warm part of my life. If you are not under threat, you must decide what to do, if anything, with the information that will be made available to you. From this point forward, what I have written assumes you are under threat and have opened your travel case to pack and run.

Inside the big envelope are a state driver's license and a passport in the name of Nora Jean Larick. Also, a birth certificate that is real. Nora Jean and her parents are all dead. She had no brothers or sisters. You will see your picture upon these documents. Yes, you look different, thanks to face-altering software. You were always good at changing hair styles and good with cosmetics so I doubt you will have trouble capturing this look. As Larick, you should carry a large colorful purse. It will draw people's eyes away from your face. The information shown on the enclosed documents is real, the rest you will need to make up. Choose bits of background information which are as difficult as possible to be confirmed. Spend time on this background detail until it becomes you. Oh, the signatures are obviously forged as Nora Jean Larick died at age two.

The signature is an expert's rendering. I had accumulated many things you had written, thus the expert was able to approximate how you would sign Nora Jean Larick. The first time, simply sign your new name without even looking at the forged signatures on the documents. Then compare, make changes as needed and practice until it is second nature. You will be surprised how alike your signing will be to the signatures on the documents.

I have not provided credit cards. Do not use your own. I realize you will not walk away from the amounts you have in stocks. Fly to the national headquarters of those brokerage firms, taking all the statements and documents you will need for identification and have them release all that money to you. Tell them you plan to take their check to their bank and cash it. Given the amounts you have in those accounts, be sure to get the name of a brokerage executive since the bank will likely want to call that executive for confirmation. Then go immediately to the brokerage house's bank, the exact branch on which the broker's checks are drawn, and cash them. Cash only. No check. Then put the cash in banks you choose using deposit boxes, not checking or savings accounts. For now, maybe forever, you must consider Linda Darby to be dead. Those who will hunt you will know that is not true, so you must act as if it is if you do not wish to be found.

This envelope also contains twenty-five-thousand dollars. I have provided considerably more cash as you will see when you go to the bank in Portland, Oregon. The bank where you stopped in to have something notarized when you and I last went there for a weekend of shopping. The safe-deposit box is in your new name along with a phony name I used for myself, the name of my favorite movie actress from the 1930s, you know that name. In that box you will find several additional sets of identification and further explanation about what has brought this evil upon you.

I pray you forgive me for getting you in the middle of this thing. I guess I should have seen it coming. I am so very sorry.

The keys: One is to the safe-deposit box in Portland. One of the other two is for a padlock on number seventeen in the you-store-and-lock garages on the corner a couple of blocks from your condo. Inside the garage you will find a used car, the last key is the ignition key. The car registration is in the glove box as well as an insurance card. Both are shown in your new name, Nora Jean Larick. Use them. You are no longer Linda Darby, at least not for the foreseeable future.

Leave now. Every minute you remain in Sea Crest you are in grave danger. Do not return for my funeral. They will watch for you there.

I love you,
    Mother Cynthia.

〜

The light from the morning sun, not yet cresting the mountains to the east, crept through the trees when Nora Jean Larick left Linda Darby's condo, locked the door, picked up her travel case and started walking toward storage garage seventeen.

CHAPTER 23

"Chief, we've got a dead body in the surf, down near Cypress Rock."

"Where?" Chief McIlhenny said into his phone.

"You know, the big rocky area where the homeless hang out, just north of town. You know."

"Who is it?"

"No clue," said Clyde Martinez, Chief Ben McIlhenny's newest deputy. "I've never seen this guy around town."

McIlhenny had found his new deputy's name an odd ethnic blend. Then he learned Clyde was half Hispanic on his father's side, with his given name coming from his mother's grandfather who raised her. "The guy's been shot," Clyde stated, as if the cause of death were an afterthought.

"What is this, a frigging epidemic?" blurted Chief McIlhenny. "Are you sure?"

"No doubt, Chief. Old Dickie, you know him, the unofficial head of the Sea Crest homeless group, called it in. The guy's got a cell. Can you imagine? I never heard tell of a homeless guy with a cell phone. Dickie tells me it's some new federal program that provides the poor with free, limited use cell phones. Can you believe it? What is this country coming to?"

"Clyde, did you call me to discuss homeless people, cell

phones, government policy or the dead guy? So far you've told me more about all that than about the corpse."

"Not much to tell, Chief. The guy's dead. He's carrying no ID. Not real bloated so my guess is he hasn't been in the surf long. The crabs and birds haven't chewed him much, but then, hey, what do I know. You coming down, Chief?"

"Quick as I can. Keep people away. Make sure the morning tide doesn't pull him out to sea. Now that he's come visiting, let's do what we can to make him feel welcome."

"That's sick, Chief."

"I'm on my way."

On the highway above Cypress Rock, Nora Jean Larick drove by in the car Cynthia had left in rental garage seventeen on her way to the county road which eventually became a state highway. The state highway would connect up to I-5, north to Portland, Oregon, where she hoped to learn more about the insanity that had taken over her life.

Six minutes later, Chief Ben McIlhenny pulled his car off Ocean Street onto the sand and gravel road that angled out onto the beach a few miles north of Cypress Rock.

An hour later, the chief drove back up that makeshift road without having learned much beyond what Deputy Clyde had told him on the phone. The man was fit, about six-foot, around one-hundred-seventy-five pounds, a wild guess said he had been in the water less than a day. As Clyde had said, the man had no ID. Even the labels had been cut out of his clothing. McIlhenny had noted one more thing. The man had been shot two times. One in the head and one in the heart, just like Cynthia Leclair.

Besides the police and the medical examiner, only the shooter and Linda Darby knew that Cynthia Leclair had been shot once each in the head and the heart. What troubled McIlhenny most was his involvement. Had his installation of surveillance equipment inside SMITH & CO. also led to the murder of this man? He wanted to think no, but he feared yes.

He pulled to the side of the road and picked up the empty, disgustingly brown foam cup that had for too long been substituting for the broken plastic screw cup to his thermos. If he wanted coffee now, and he did, he would have to use that cup. He poured from his thermos until the coffee covered the old stains. After promising himself he would get a new thermos or at least a new white foam cup, he took a sip and licked his lips. The hot coffee would sterilize the gunk. At least he hoped that was the way this kind of thing worked. But, bottom line, the taste was right and that's all that mattered right now.

After he got back to his office and finished the paperwork on the crime scene, he'd go see Linda Darby. She jogged mornings, but was usually back by noon. He figured she must be good at day trading as it appeared her only means of support. Then again, she could have had an inheritance or perhaps a divorce settlement, maybe both. Police work was habitually nosey in that it led to analyzing everyone, breaking them down as to resources and peculiarities, even sexual proclivities. It was that last one, when it came to Linda that he couldn't quite figure. She had a fabulous body. All the men in town knew that, not that she showed it. Fact was she dressed a bit dowdy. No cleavage, yet there was no doubt she had an ample supply. She just didn't share it. She never wore short skirts or even cheeky shorts during the summer. Still, she had this unmistakable air about the way she looked and walked.

The chief would tell Linda about the Fed Ex packages SMITH & CO. mailed having been sent to a Mr. John B. Smith at a residential address in Baltimore. The occupant of the house, a retired elderly man, confirmed that Mr. Smith rented an upstairs room. He explained that Smith was a traveling salesman who only came to Baltimore a couple of times a month and hated hotels. The owner knew about the packages, being retired he was home and had signed for and taken in all of the packages. He estimated the number to be a couple dozen at least over the last two years or so. He simply held the packages until Smith's next arrival. The home had burned to the ground the day Linda had found Cynthia Leclair's body. The Fed Ex driver never again saw Mr. Smith.

Chief McIlhenny planned to get a bit more direct with Linda. He had always sensed she was holding something back, and with this latest body the time had come to pressure her to come clean.

Clark sat having coffee on his back patio before leaving for his lunch shift at O'Malley's. He had not slept well. He was worried about Linda Darby. The woman's blood had saved his life. She had given it to help a complete stranger, a man she knew only as a motorcycle rider who worked for the marijuana growers. Now she was in trouble. She didn't say so. She didn't have to. He knew. He had seen enough violence to know the red blotch on the front of Linda's jersey the night she came to his door had been blood. After his lunch shift, during the break before the dinner crowd, he would take another run at getting her to talk. While he had been a biker and before that in the Navy Seals, he had seen or been involved in a lot of mayhem, Linda Darby was involved in something for which she was ill prepared. Some of his past activities gave him pride. Others did not. But he had learned things. He could help Linda, if she would ask before it was too late.

Around two in the afternoon, Chief McIlhenny got out to Linda's place. She didn't answer her front door. He followed the wooden walkway that wrapped from her front porch around to her rear patio. She wasn't on the deck, but the screen door was, bent. He had once walked through his own when he thought it had been pulled back. He smiled at the thought she had likely done the same thing. He looked over the rail down to the beach but he couldn't see her running or walking in the surf. He went back and looked more closely at the back slider. A carefully cut wooden dowel lay in the trough inside the rear sliding glass door to prevent it from being opened from the outside. On his way back to the front of the house he stopped where the side walkway bumped out to provide space for her barbeque. His peek through the glass insert of the locked kitchen door told him nothing. He would come back later.

Interstate five stretched like a steel-gray ribbon winding through the easy hills of central Oregon. Linda had never particularly thought it before when driving the nation's roadways, but each car traveling with her or passing from the opposite direction carried people with their own distinct lives, their own troubles and joys. She hoped none of them were traveling, as was she, in a desperate attempt to escape an invisible threat. At least she had no family to also be trapped into her terror. Not even an extended family. She had chosen to live in seclusion, to not let others into her life. And now, with Cynthia's death, her wish had become completely true. She was truly alone except for a cell-phone in the bottom of her purse, an umbilical cord linking her to a violent stranger. She lowered her window and took out the cell phone. Looked at it in her hand, turned it over and considered tossing it into the brush bordering the interstate. Then she stuffed it back into her purse.

A few hours later, the southern outskirts of Salem, Oregon, came into view. She would be in Portland in less than three more hours. There she would rent a room and get something to eat. Then she planned to sleep, something she hadn't done at all last night after her exhausting encounter on the beach. In the morning she would need to make herself look like Nora Jean Larick before visiting Key Bank where, hopefully, she would find more answers, maybe even a way out of this consuming nightmare.

Clark had never been invited to Linda's home, but he had followed her home once. It was not exactly gentlemanly of him, but it was one more piece of knowing her. Today, he planned to press her into telling him what the hell was going on. She had not fooled him when she came to his home last night. She had not fallen while jogging and been covered by a wave. Her mind had been fried. Her hands were covered with small scratches. The scratches were not from a log. His guess being she had climbed the lava rock which had eons ago reached the cool hands of the Pacific Ocean. This lava flow appeared in only a few spots along the Sea Crest beach. There had been green stains from sea grass on her knees and red blood-like splotches on her front. From his deck, he had watched her, through his binoculars, cautiously walk up the beach stairs, then after moving to a side window he saw her hide a gun under the top step. While she had been in the shower, he had replaced the gun with a new one, untraceable. When she left his place he waited a few minutes then followed her home, at a safe distance. After everything had looked okay at her place he went home, disassembled the gun she had left under the stairs and scatter tossed the pieces into the surf. That is, he did except for the barrel. Tomorrow morning he was going out as a crewman on a friend's early half-day fishing charter. He would drop the barrel necessary for ballistics tests into the deepwater coastal channel.

Clark got no answer when he knocked on Linda's front door. He walked back to his hog, then just as he freed the kickstand from the soft gravel in front of Linda's condo, Chief McIlhenny pulled his police car up behind him.

Clark reset his kickstand and walked back. "Hey, Chief, what's doing?"

McIlhenny got out of his car and leaned his arms across the top of the still open door. "Hello, Clark. You come by to see Linda?"

"Yeah. Social call. She isn't home. Can you tell me why you stopped by?"

"Can't see that I should. Police business."

"Fair enough. Some of my lunch customers in O'Malley's were talking about a dead body. Made it sound like a new one, not the two found in the alley. They characterized it as another murder. That true, Chief?"

"It'll be on the news in an hour, so it's no national secret. A guy washed up on the beach a mile or so from your place."

"That must've been down by the big lava rock."

"Yep."

"Drowning?" Clark asked.

"Murder. Two shots."

"Head and heart like Cynthia Leclair?"

"Now how would you know that?" the chief asked.

"People talk without much noticing a waiter, your dispatcher and deputy for example."

"You're a pretty observant guy, Clark. I've noticed the way you watch things, people. Even in O'Malley's. Why haven't you ever applied to be a deputy?"

"Thought about it once, really did. Don't know if I could handle being on the side of the law."

"You don't fool me with that tough, ex-biker business. I checked you out, back when you decided to stay in town. You had a solid military career in the Navy Seals, and that's not so easy to come by. You had no trouble with the military police or with the civilian cops. There's a big hole for the years after the military, up until you roosted in our town. That your time with the biker gang?" Clark nodded. "I watched you calm a near fight inside the bistro. Millie told me about you handling an out-of-control drunk down the street in her place. Settled it right down, she said, and Millie has endured more than her share of drunken scenes. You got yourself a knack for handling difficult situations. The city provides great benefits. You likely don't get any at O'Malley's. Pay's likely better as well. You'd need to shorten your hair."

"I already did that for O'Malley."

"More for me."

"I'm flattered Chief. I'll think on it. Better than that, would you let me know next time you have an opening?"

"Be glad to. In the meantime, if you hear anything or have any thoughts about this craziness that has infected our town, my door is open. And, yes, I came by to see Linda about the killing on the beach. She sits on her deck a lot, thought she might have seen something. Routine stop, I'm paying a visit to all the beach houses."

"Thanks, Chief."

"See ya, Clark." Chief McIlhenny got back inside his car. As he pulled around Clark's motorcycle, he lowered his passenger side window. "If you hear from Linda, let's all sit down and powwow. Okay?"

"That the same deal if she contacts you instead of me?"

"From what I can tell, you listen to a lot of rumors, but you don't spread any. So, yeah, if I hear from her, I'll ask her to agree to your sitting in."

Clark offered his hand through the car window and said, "Chief. You didn't answer my question. Was this guy you just found in the surf shot the same as Cynthia Leclair?"

"Exactly, head and heart, but keep it under your hat, although it appears most of the town may know by now."

"Small town, Chief." They both nodded.

CHAPTER 24

A few minutes after noon, downtown Portland, Oregon, came into view, the sun overhead a jagged bright spot on the Willamette River. Linda had decided she would stay in the northwest area of the city known locally as Nob Hill. But first she bypassed the exit for downtown. She wanted to shop in Nordstrom's Department store at Lloyd's Center, a major shopping mall, east of town.

In the making of Nora Jean Larick, Cynthia had morphed a different hairstyle and lipstick colors onto Linda Darby's face using a picture of Linda wearing a black cardigan sweater over a white blouse. Linda easily matched that outfit in Nordstrom's, and left the store wearing it. She had also bought a large colorful purse as Cynthia had suggested in her letter. The kind of purse she had never before carried. Still, after looking at herself holding it in the mirror she liked it. She would wear this outfit in the morning when she went to the bank.

Linda needed no reminder that hers was a dangerous endeavor, yet the prospect of dressing up and acting out being someone else filled her with excitement. She hadn't done that since the high school plays she acted in which were among her fondest memories. She had lost her virginity in the backseat of a Chevy to a senior who had the male lead in her first play. That double experience had filled her with thoughts of an acting career and, after all, everyone knew a young starlet could not be a virgin. Now, these many years later, she wasn't just acting, she was trying to stay alive.

Linda's room in the Silver Cloud Hotel in the Nob Hill section was a pleasantly appointed room with a 42-inch plasma television, wifi, and well-insulated walls. The hotel had an exercise room where she could jog on a treadmill. It wasn't the beach, but it would have to do. She would use the treadmill late at night when there were no other guests in the exercise area.

An hour later, she left the hotel dressed as Nora Jean, including hoop earrings like the pair Cynthia had cropped onto her picture as Nora Jean. Hoop earrings were among the items which drew people's eyes away from a woman's face. Despite the help offered by this distraction, Linda felt incapable of carrying off her charade.

In the next block, she stopped to sit on a bus bench. She closed her eyes, breathed slowly, and fought back against her insecurity. She had no real choice. Tomorrow she would have to go to the bank. Cynthia had left more information there so she had to make it work. She got up and continued walking, continued projecting herself as Nora Jean, continued letting people, strangers, see her as Nora Jean. With each passing she gained some confidence, damn little, but it helped.

After a few blocks, Linda settled on a more brazen walk than she used for herself. Each foot placed more in front of the one behind. This enhanced the sway of her hips, which in turn accentuated the movement in her butt. The walk the swells in the early 1900s called the cakewalk. She paused at every shiny window to look at her reflection, seeing herself again and again as Nora Jean.

As a young single woman, Linda had briefly lived in downtown Portland. Perhaps some of her friends from those days were still around, but she doubted it. They had been mostly kooky artists, writers, and college grads looking for the mythical high-paying, low-working jobs capable of funding their party lives. Those days were before the black fingernail polishes and multicolored hairdos she saw adorning so many of today's loitering street people. She had lived long enough to now realize what all older generations came to know: each generation of young people thinks they invent antisocial behaviors, with the truth being they only alter the manner in which each generation manifests its rebellion.

She hadn't been in Portland for more than a few hours at a time in many years, but the city hadn't changed all that much. The downtown area near the Willamette River had been glamorized, but then Portland had always been a cool big city.

At this hour, traffic was light and the pedestrian count low. She kept a casual pace, like the others ahead of her and coming the other direction. Distant music came to her as she turned at the next corner. The base notes most discernible. Then it was gone. Perhaps the door on a club had closed. Or the street musicians had collected enough in tips to pay for tonight's room. Mostly, however, she saw the quiet faces of office workers and store clerks. Their gaits reined in after faster-paced days.

In the distance, she could see the high-rise Koin Center with its illuminated blue dome. The building's array of lit windows contrasting the night sky as might diamonds loose on a jeweler's black cloth.

In the next block, Linda noticed a strong looking, attractive man crossing at the approaching intersection, coming to her side of the street. His eyes traveled her length, and then away before coming back for an encore ogle. As he stepped up onto the sidewalk on her side, about twenty yards in front of her, he glanced across the intersection to her left. Then he moved toward her. She darted into a bookstore on her right and watched as he passed without looking at her. A minute later, she stepped back out of the store and glanced to her left. The man had turned around and was now walking the same direction. She quickened her pace and in the next block she entered the Nob Hill Bar & Grill on Twenty-third and sat in a vacant booth along the window, putting her large colorful purse against the wall, the strap flopping over to touch the glass.

A moment later that same man entered, looked right and left, then walked up to her table.

"My apology, I didn't mean to startle you out on the street. It is simply that, well, I was out alone to find a place to dine. May I join you?"

"No," Linda said, "perhaps another time."

"Well, then, if you will give me your number, I'll call and invite you in a more proper manner." He reached into his pocket and withdrew a small portfolio, prepared to write down her number.

"Do you live alone?" Linda asked.

"Why yes," he said, his body appearing to percolate a fresh rush of interest.

"My name is ... Nora. Nora Larick. Give me your card, and leave it to me to call you some other time."

His face sagged, but he extended his hand, holding his card. "I'm Nathan. Until then," he said, refreshing his smile. "Goodnight, Nora."

He turned and left, leaving Linda to wonder if he was simply a man on the make or another henchman who would be waiting outside. Linda put his card in her purse. He was a contact in Portland. Put another way, he was the only person in the entire world who knew Nora Jean Larick.

After a few minutes, a tall middle-aged waitress, with fingers long enough to suggest she suffered from Marfan's syndrome came to her table. "If you'd like to know, that fellow's a local. He comes in here maybe once a week, usually alone. I think he lives nearby. Seems like a decent sort." Linda thanked her and ordered a cheeseburger and fries, and to offset the accompanying rush of calories she added a diet coke. She smiled at the thought of how silly it was to think a diet soda would somehow miraculously counterbalance a session of pigging out.

While eating, she looked out onto the sidewalk, making eye contact with passersby. She needed to confront her sense of panic that each person who looked her way would yell faker or imposter. Before tomorrow's trip to the bank, she wanted to develop a higher level of comfort with herself as Nora Larick.

CHAPTER 25

*U*nder the spur of the alarm clock, Linda nearly leapt from her bed. Then the phone rang, "Ms. Larick, your 6:30 wake-up ma'am. Please enjoy your day in our beautiful city."

Ms. Larick. She said to herself. *Get used to it, girl. This just might be you forever.*

She found comfort in the simple thought of having a forever, under any name.

The sun crested the building across the street and rushed through her window. She had purposely left the blackout drapes open so that, along with the alarm and the wake-up call, she would rise early enough to get to the bank when it opened. She prayed the contents of that box would explain the insanity that had destroyed her quiet life.

Cynthia, please tell me what this is all about and how the hell I can end it.

She started some coffee using the small pot, the pouch of grounds and the filter placed in the room for guests. Then turned on the television and found the news channel. On her drive to Portland she had kept the radio on the news the whole way, half expecting and fully fearing a public announcement: "Linda Darby is wanted for questioning with regard to a murder on the beach just north of her home in Sea Crest, Oregon." But no such announcement had come. She had killed in self-defense. Still, she felt like a fugitive. She had shot a man to death and, apparently, no one wanted to ask her about it. Then again, no one knew she had been the shooter, no one except whoever had taken the gun she left under the step near Clark's house. The missing gun carried her fingerprints and the prospect for a matching ballistics examination.

She had read that in the 50s the overwhelming majority of murders in America had been solved, but in modern time, despite the massive gains in the collection of crime scene evidence, less than half were now solved. She prayed that she would be in that new majority. The killers who had never been called to account for the deaths caused at their hand.

She knew that Clark had not been satisfied with the story she had given him about what happened to her that night on the beach. But, she felt she could trust Clark. Truth being, that night she had little other choice than to trust Clark. Besides he owed her his own life. She also hoped that Chief McIlhenny would never think of her as a suspect. Still, there was the suspicion that would be generated by her disappearance from Sea Crest. On that score, it would help if she returned to Sea Crest, but doing so would put her where those trying to kill her were looking to find her. She could call Chief McIlhenny. Tell him she was scared. That she took off and would be back after all the craziness had stopped. That with all he had on his mind, she didn't want him worrying about her as well. But then, Ahab had told her not to trust the local police, which meant don't trust Chief Ben McIlhenny.

She would let the decisions about that wait until she knew more, until she had perused the contents of the safe-deposit box.

Linda had always considered Cynthia Leclair to be sweet and thoughtful, a too-good-to-be-true surrogate mother. Now she knew there was much more to Cynthia than she had ever imagined. Cynthia had told her that she managed SMITH & CO. for Mr. Smith, an absentee owner. She now realized that had been Cynthia's way of creating an outside authority with a policy against visitors, while it had been Cynthia who had not wanted visitors. The records, Chief McIlhenny had said, showed Cynthia owned the company. Cynthia had said they did boring research. Well, no one kills everyone in a business that does boring research, and steals their computers, including their back up disks. A company doing boring research uses regular mail service, which SMITH & CO. never used. What research could be so horrible that Cynthia wouldn't talk about it? What research could be so terrible that others would torture and murder people to learn the fruit they picked?

The bank would not open for twenty minutes and right now each minute passed like an hour. She was ready. She had fussed with her hair long enough to make it look at least similar to the style Cynthia had used in the ID picture. And she had practiced signing as Nora Jean Larick for an hour the night before. Cynthia had been right. Her Nora Jean Larick signature was very close to the way Cynthia's expert had put down after studying Linda's own handwriting. She wanted to get on with it. Get it over with. Still, she didn't want to be at the bank where she could be watched while waiting for the doors to be unlocked.

She spent most of the twenty minutes pacing the room, listening to the news between trips to the mirror to check and recheck her hair. Her makeup. Her Larick smile. She needed to project the errand-running manner of a calm person, not the panic of a woman running from murder.

No. Not murder. Damn it, girl, get this straight. Self defense, the right of every citizen.

She stared at the clock on the night stand between the two double beds. She could feel her tension mounting with each round of the second hand. Still, she didn't feel just right about her appearance. With a now practiced hand, Linda tucked her hair behind one ear to fully reveal her hoop earring. The picture Cynthia had used to create Nora Larick had been at a time when Linda had put on a few extra pounds, which had mostly shown in her face. Her face was a bit thinner now. She reasoned that Nora Larick could have lost a few pounds since the picture was taken so, so what. That thought made her feel a little better about the likeness.

The automatic closer drew her room door shut as she walked down the hall toward the elevator. The bank was not that far. She would moderate her pace sufficiently to allow her to reach the bank a few minutes after it opened.

Okay, girl. The curtain's going up.

CHAPTER 26

a thin woman with round eyes looked down the bank counter. Her tongue darted through a deep red swath of lipstick. "I'll be with you in a moment."

Too nervous to speak, Linda raised her arm and dangled her box key so the woman could see it. The woman replied through an index finger held in the air.

She's stalling, while the police close in.

Linda placed her hands flat on the counter to steady her nerves and looked around. There were two other tellers, each with that tanning bed look—they probably went together after work. Peripherally, Linda noticed a woman stand from behind a desk fronted by a small brass name plate with the title Bank Manager. She wore a respectably short skirt and a slightly tight sweater, her heels a bit high, but not platforms. She walked toward Linda, and stopped at a closer desk. She had no ring on the third finger of her left hand. Did she purposefully hire female employees to help establish her as the diva?

Calm down. Your thoughts are all over the place.

The teller's voice startled her out of her bizarre thoughts, her tongue again in play. "You want to access your box?"

Linda nodded. When the woman turned to obtain the signature

card, Linda took a deep breath and willed her hand to be steady while she signed her new name: *Nora Larick*.

"Your box is co-owned with whom?" asked the teller.

"Glenda Farrell," Linda said, recalling the 1930s actress favored by Cynthia.

The teller nodded, then buzzed open the chest high gate.

Linda followed the woman's slight figure through a vault-like door into the innards of the bank. The fear that inhabited her spine whispered run. Run from the bank. Drive back to Sea Crest. Sit on your deck. Walk the beach. Live your life and wait for the inevitable. But she did not. She had to know what was in that box. She had to know why Cynthia Leclair had died. So, she braced herself and followed the teller's bony backside deeper into the bowels of the bank.

The boxes were kept in the bank vault, which gave her path the feel of entering prison. Her heart clamored like an inmate riffing a tin cup across the bars of a cell. She swallowed hard and willed herself calm.

"I'll need some time alone with the box."

"Of course, Miss Larick, we have viewing rooms for your use." The enthusiastic teller smiled and looked at her own narrow finger pointing toward three adjoined rooms that rose to shoulder height. "They're very private, yet open at the top for air movement. Can I get you anything? A cup of coffee perhaps?"

"No, thank you," Linda said, while thinking that banks should serve martinis.

The teller took the key from Linda and slipped it into the lock next to where she had already inserted the bank's key. The box was a large one near the floor. After turning both keys, she pulled out Cynthia's inner box, rose and carried it into the nearest private booth where she placed it on the counter, smiled, closed the door, and left.

At last, Linda was alone with Cynthia's secrets of the private dealings of her mysterious SMITH & CO. Linda's heart raced when she read the notation on the face of the top envelope inside the box.

OPEN ONLY IN THE EVENT OF THE VIOLENT DEATH OF CYNTHIA LECLAIR.

Linda held the envelope as if it might dissolve, its contents absorbed by the very air. At that moment, she again felt the urge to run, drop everything and leave all this shit behind. Permanently become Nora Jean Larick and drive until she found some small town somewhere with a John Wayne type sheriff who would keep her safe.

But she couldn't. Whoever had found her in Sea Crest would eventually find her no matter where she went. And her traditional view of justice still hoped that whoever had tortured and killed her friend would be identified and hunted down. She looked back over her shoulder to be sure the short door was closed and latched. Then she looked to each side to be sure that no cameras had been positioned to record the contents of the box. After a deep breath, she nervously lifted the envelope with the ominous message.

Before reading anything, she inventoried the full contents of the box. There were two larger envelopes folded over and held that way by thick rubber bands. On the outsides of each, Cynthia had written in pencil: one-hundred-thousand dollars. There was also a tube filled with diamonds and a list of jewelers in major U.S. cities where Linda could sell them, no questions asked. A third large envelope held five more sets of identities carrying different names. Each ID had Linda's picture, but with unfamiliar hairdos and different styles of clothing. One of five wore no earrings, another no glasses.

With the general inventory taken, as well as additional glances at the closed door and the upper ledge of the partial walls around the booth, Linda sat down and opened the letter-size envelope. Inside were two handwritten pages, unmistakably by Cynthia's hand.

She held the pages in front of her face, and again looked over each shoulder as if she were sitting in the middle of a bus station. Finally she leaned back, took a deep breath, crossed her legs and began reading.

"Dear Nora Jean:

Well, how are you enjoying being someone else? I often fantasized disappearing, becoming someone else, starting all over again. Fresh! Well, I never did so that doesn't matter any longer.

"I am dead or you would not be here. And I have died violently or you would not have opened this envelope. And, I expect you are running for your life. This man does not like loose ends and, unfortunately, he will see you as just that, a loose end. I expect if you do not already know, his men are under orders to capture you so they can learn what I might have told you, and then kill you. Do not doubt they have this intent. There is no reasoning with these men.

"The morning I expected them to come for me, I called in sick. Actually, I was sick, a cold I think, or maybe just a case of nerves. Then I came to your home and left the letter while you were out jogging on the beach. By the way, I apologize for standing you up at O'Malley's for lunch and not answering your calls. I knew I could not have fooled you. The night before, when you called to confirm our luncheon, I could tell even then you sensed something was wrong.

"I considered going to the FBI, but chickened out because I would have ended up in jail. I should have for two good reasons: 1) to protect you, and 2) to hopefully bring this man's evil to an end. Instead, I clung to the hope that somehow I had it figured wrong and they might let me be. That decision was stupid and selfish. After a lifetime in espionage and intelligence work, I accept the fate that sometimes goes with the territory. But you don't deserve what is happening to you and I am sorrier than I can say.

"After leaving your place, I drove here to Portland to put these things in this bank box. This box should be safe, the actress's name I used for myself I have not used for anything else, and my partiality for that actress is not real. I told you her name several times the week this became a possibility. The wisest course may be for you to keep some of the money and diamonds with you and split the rest up in other boxes in other cities under your other identities.

"The man looking for you is powerful and very well connected. He has access to all government records and the computers used by banks, credit bureaus, and credit card companies. Leave no trail. The likelihood is he will not learn of this deposit box, but I cannot say that with certainty. His bribes are so huge that his reach is unimaginable. Therefore, I strongly urge you to dump these contents into your purse and leave now. This minute. Read the rest of this letter later. The other bank boxes you open will be in your other identities without my involvement. That will add another layer of safety for you."

Linda desperately wanted to read the rest now, but she did as Cynthia had warned her to do. She put the contents in her large shoulder bag and walked out of the bank.

CHAPTER 27

hief McIlhenny answered his personal cell phone.

"Get somewhere we can talk. Now!"

McIlhenny did so before saying, "What do you want?"

"What can you tell me about Linda Darby?"

"She has lived here in Sea Crest for some years. A quiet lady. Day trades for a living. She was a close friend of Cynthia Leclair. Why did you have to murder everyone at SMITH & CO., and steal their computers? I had them under surveillance. I was giving you everything. You knew what was going on there."

"Why, Chief, what makes you think I had anything to do with that awful tragedy?"

"Spare me your bullshit. You paid me to install electronic surveillance in their office soon after I became chief of police. You've had me send you the results every week or so. Now they are all dead. It had to be you."

"I have no idea what you're talking about, Chief. And, may I add, you don't want to think anything else. I shouldn't need to remind you that if I'm involved, you're involved. If they were killed for what they discovered, you were an accessory. Am I making myself clear, Police Chief Ben McIlhenny?"

"Yes." Ben sighed, and then repeated in a lower tone, "yes."

"Now, tell me more about Linda Darby."

"What do you want to know?"

"Is she still in your town? Has anything happened to her or at her home?"

"Yes and not to my knowledge are your answers. Now, let me be clear. Linda Darby is off limits. If anything happens to Miss Darby, I'll take the wraps off and blow your entire deal wide open."

"Do I hear a little lovesick swooning?"

"Listen asshole. Nothing is to happen to Miss Darby. Your threats to keep me in line won't work any longer. Too much has happened. You hear me, nothing!"

Then the line went dead. McIlhenny had punctuated his message by hanging up.

Ryan Testler returned to Sea Crest, checked back into the motel just outside town, threw his bag in his room, and went to Millie's Sea Grog for a late lunch. He wanted to be seen back in town. And he wanted to hear the latest rumbling about town. Millie's and O'Malley's were the town's rumor centers. There were seven customers in Millie's plus the staff, four at one table, and three at another. All seven were men and all men he had seen in Millie's before, locals. Beef dips and nachos and a pitcher of beer were on each table. There were no women, although he could hear enough to know women were the subject under discussion at both tables.

After a crab Louie with Thousand Island dressing, he drove down and parked close to the public beach access near Linda Darby's home. From there he studied her condo through his Swarovski binoculars. Linda did not appear to be home. If she had jogged this morning, by now she would be back. She was not sitting on her deck, and she was not at her computer. Before leaving, he used the zoom lens on his camera to snap several pictures for later study, including a zoomer of her clothespin bag so he could determine if the money and gun were still there. Then he walked back to his car intending to call the cell phone he had left for her.

~

More than two thousand miles away, Alistair Webster walked out of his mansion after finishing a three-course meal. The cook had eaten in the kitchen. His two bodyguards, Victor and Mark had eaten with him.

Webster's estate dated back to revolutionary days, but little of the original structure remained. The remnants of a few outbuildings were in disrepair, but he had the old slave quarters razed to remove any stigma that might connect him with things politically incorrect. As far back as he knew, the property had always been known as The Continental. Over the years, it had been owned by four congressmen and one associate justice of the U.S. Supreme Court. There was a time when Webster had considered becoming a congressman but chose not to join such men. He desired to control them, to influence and dictate a fair amount of law and regulation without having to be accountable to the fickleness of the voters. Elections were a waste of time when money and blackmail, not the vote, ruled the application of power.

The Continental was the nerve center of his nefarious dealings. His most secure place where he kept all the files he had on those in power who were subject to his influence. J. Edgar Hoover, the once mighty head of the Federal Bureau of Investigation had compiled and used similar files to protect his fiefdom. Hoover had been Webster's inspiration, but Webster believed he had taken the idea to greater heights and to serve a loftier purpose.

Webster meandered toward the pasture with a cube of sugar in his hand. The nights he dined without guests, his ritual included a walk of the grounds and the bringing of a sugar cube to Oval, his riding horse. The stallion had an oval-shaped mark on its face, but

DAVID BISHOP

only Webster knew the name had been for the Oval office, not the stallion's marking. On these evenings, Oval would walk inside the corral fence along Webster's path and at his master's pace. When his walk was finished, Webster would let Oval eat the cube from the palm of his hand.

Thirty yards behind Webster and Oval, walked Victor, one of Webster's two resident bodyguards, Victor's brother having gone up to man the security gate at the entrance to The Continental. Webster insisted that his bodyguard maintain that spacing in case he received a phone call. He always wanted the calls private and his staff knew to keep a safe distance. Inside the house, they had been instructed to immediately leave the room and shut the door.

"Come here, boy. You've been following along, waiting politely. Here it is."

The horse came close, neighed and extended his head over the split rail fence.

Webster's scream pierced the night. Victor came running. "Mr. Webster, What happened?"

"That damned horse bit me." Webster held out his hand. "Look."

"That's a nasty little nip, sir. Maybe you cupped your hand a bit too much and Oval caught the skin. It doesn't need stitches. It should heal nicely."

"I never cup my hand," Webster said incredulously. "I've been feeding Oval cubed sugar for years."

"I'm sorry, sir. I only meant it was inadvertent, an accident."

"I'll show you an accident. Give me your weapon."

"What?"

"Give me your weapon. Now."

Victor drew his Smith & Wesson, flipped it around in his hand and extended it. Handle out. "Sir, don't overreact. Please. You love that horse."

"That's why I'm going to put him down."

"Sir?"

"I won't allow him to be fed after he bit the hand that feeds him. I should let him starve to death, but I won't."

Alistair Webster took the handgun, turned toward Oval and without hesitation shot him in the head.

"I want his remains off the estate before sun up."

"Yes, sir," Victor said, his head lowered.

CHAPTER 28

*L*inda left the bank and after walking a block entered a convenience market where she bought a diet soda and two candy bars.

Two blocks later, she suddenly turned into a bar, walked through it and out their back door, across the rear alley and into the back of a card store, and then left by the front door onto the main street. At the end of that block she walked into her hotel, went up to her room, engaged the deadbolt on her door and drew the blackout curtains. On some level, all this seemed a bit melodramatic, still, following the steps to lose a tail she had learned from books and movies provided her some measure of comfort.

She nested back into the layers of decorative bed pillows, twisted the cap off the diet soda and tore open one of the candy bars. This was not a lunch designed to enhance her waistline, but then, right now, she'd settle for living long enough to get fat.

She reopened Cynthia's letter and continued reading:

"You deserve to know what type of research we did and who is hunting you and why.

"For years my company did surveillance work for the CIA, electronically culling countless cell phone and email communications between people in certain regions of the Middle East, and people within the United States. Our computers had been programmed to alert us of any messages that contained key words. An example: for years, *Big Cold*, was the code Al Qaeda used to refer to Russia. Our job was to cull out correspondence that needed human reading and analysis. Other than the potential of those communications, the work was rather tedious.

"A few years ago, after my contract with the CIA terminated, a private individual, Alistair Webster, contacted me to do some clandestine work for him, largely the same, only with regard to communications totally within the U.S. This work was illegal. He implied he was doing this for the government, outside congressional oversight. These things are done, so I assumed this was legal illegal work—if there is such a thing. Anyway, I recently was able to confirm my growing suspicion.

"The work for Webster was illegal surveillance of select Americans: some business executives, but mostly members of Congress, some of their staff, and also regulatory agency personnel. The identity of the targets eventually made me suspicious, but, by then, good old American greed had me hooked. I received substantial amounts of money, for which I sold my integrity. I saw it as the pension I would soon need. My eyes were failing and I was alone. We certainly can rationalize when we want to. My three employees did not fully understand the nature of what they were doing or, if they came to suspect something was afoul, they, too, were paid extremely well so they chose not to rock my boat. The employees only gathered the data. I was the analyst. It is likely they, too, have been killed to protect my client from the blowback of anything they might have learned. I suspect that is essentially why you are being sought, a possible blowback from anything I might have shared with you.

"We dug up dirt on Americans holding influential positions, stuff that could be used for blackmail. Little by little, using the training and equipment I had, I was able to conclude my work was not off-the-books for the government. Still, I had to know that Webster wasn't fronting for some unfriendly foreign government or non-state terrorist.

"Six days ago, one of my employees said she had seen a stranger in our town. She thought the man had been watching us. That night, I searched the office and found surveillance equipment. I called Chief McIlhenny. He came over and convinced me to leave it in place so he could watch to see who came for it and to whom it was passed. That evening, a man followed me home. I spent the next day using my online skills to follow the phone calls and emails of Alistair Webster. Staying late that night I went back over everything we had on the communications he had us tracking. I then cross referenced searches for those individuals. He had to be using the data to blackmail regulators and members of Congress to support legislative or regulatory actions he wanted taken or not taken, supported or opposed. That evening, you called to confirm our meeting for lunch the next day. I didn't want to lead them to you, but it would now appear they had already known about our relationship. The next morning, while you were out jogging, I left the first letter in your travel bag.

"I'm sorry I never told you. I wanted to keep you close to me. My selfish decision put you right in the middle. The fact that these men will kill is obvious. They have. This money will help you run. Hide. Rent units offered directly from owners, not leasing companies. Do not open any accounts. Do not purchase anything online. Buy only in stores and only for cash.

"Do not seek revenge or justice for me. It's of no consequence. For men like Webster, appropriate justice does not come in the courts. Don't try it. Use your new identities and the monies I have left to find another Sea Crest, perhaps in another country. If you feel it is too unsafe for you to go after your investment accounts, let them be for now. Research how and when assets escheat to the state to learn the frequency you will need to make periodic contacts to the brokerages to avoid that from happening. Never mail anything from anywhere close to where you hole up. If three years pass without any threats, you might consider going to the brokerages to get your funds. After another five years without a threat, go back to your own identity. The money and diamonds I have left will easily support you for those years.

"I have also left my condo to you. It is free and clear. My will is with my attorney, Maxwell Crane. His office is in the building at the corner of Main and Seventeenth. I recently made arrangements with him that if he did not hear from you within two weeks of my death he should rent out the condo and wait until he does hear from you. He understands that he may not hear from you for several years. He was confused but accepted the instruction.

"You have the advantage that Webster will not use the authorities to find you, at least not officially. The fact that you have no living family will help you. Do not contact anyone. It isn't worth the risk.

"I don't mean to sound insensitive, but you need to recapture the bold confidence you lost after your divorce.

"Disappear.

"I'm so sorry.

"I love you,

"Mother Cynthia."

Linda sat clutching the letter, no longer reading the words, just staring while tears washed her cheeks. There had been so much to Cynthia Leclair that she had never known. Her friend had been part of a world Linda thought existed only in novels: Spies. Traitors. Killers. Then there were those they victimized, the foolish, gullible and greedy who sell their souls for money. The two men in the alley had been part of that world, as was the man she killed on the beach. This was also true of her mystery man, Ahab, her hero.

What happened to the line that separated good and evil? Maybe that line existed only in the fairy tales that parents tell their children with the hope the next generation will rise up and reject evil in all its forms. What happened to the world Linda thought she knew? The world she thought she lived in. This is wrong. That is right. It had all become a blur.

A moment later, her deep thoughts were shattered by the ring of a telephone.

CHAPTER 29

*L*inda looked at the hotel phone, but the rings were more distant and muffled. Her ears followed the noise trail to her purse. Ahab. She had forgotten the cell phone he had given her was still in the bottom of her big, colorful Nora Larick purse.

She swung her feet off the bed and grabbed the bag. Then she stopped dead still. Did she want to answer it? Maybe she should run from him as well. After all, he was part of the world that had sucked in Cynthia, a world Linda wanted no part of. In her letter, Cynthia had said, "No contact with anyone. Just disappear." During her uncertainty, the phone went silent, action taken through inaction. She briefly considered throwing the phone away, but decided she would keep it in case her thinking changed.

Linda's gaze went to the window, the outside light muzzled by the open-weave drapes. She had opened the blackout drapes after the sun had passed over the top of the hotel. She burrowed into the warmth of the pillows, exhausted, and eventually her eyes closed and she fell into a fitful sleep.

〜

At some point during the night, Linda suddenly opened her eyes.

She still faced the window, but the night had darkened the room. Perhaps she had been startled by a bird that had flown through the muffled outside commercial light, a seagull maybe. There were seagulls in downtown Portland, although mostly nearer the Willamette River. She watched for a while but saw no birds.

Straining her senses, she detected a presence. More like feeling a presence, not like in Sea Crest. Then she had smelled the musk fragrance he had worn. This time there was no aroma, just awareness. Maybe her mind had replayed the incident about the man who had been in her bedroom in Sea Crest, the man she had shot dead and left lying in the surf. She closed her eyes and tried to put this awareness out of her mind. But it would not leave.

She did not recall having taken off her clothes. She must have done so sometime during the night, too asleep to remember, because she now wore only her panties. If her instincts were correct and she was not alone, the room had no sliding screen door she could break through and vault onto the sand. Her only way out would be past whoever was in the room watching her, right now.

After trying with only modest success to calm her breathing, she groaned and turned over the way she imagined she might while sleeping. After lying in that position for a minute or two, she eased her eyes open far enough to see through her lashes.

The occasional chair had been moved close to the bed.

A man sat in that chair.

Close enough to reach her.

Suddenly, he raised one hand. His palm turned toward her. He curled his fingers a few times in a child's wave. Linda fully opened her eyes.

"Ahab! What are you doing here?"

"Who the hell is Ahab?"

"It's a name I've given you. Oh, it doesn't matter. What are you doing here? How did you find me?"

"It's what I do. I'm impressed that you were able to sense my presence for I gave you no way to detect me. You have good instincts. Trust them."

"What do you want?"

"To protect you, of course."

"How did you find me?"

"Not important. What is important, it's likely no one else will as long as you do what Cynthia Leclair told you to do in her letters."

"How do you know about Cynthia's letter?"

"You left it over there on the table. I read it."

"You read it?"

"I think I just said that." He shifted in his chair and crossed his legs. "I'm thirsty," he said. "Do you mind if I raid your minibar? Can I get you something?"

"No, nothing for me. Help yourself."

He flicked on the light in the bathroom, its spreading brightness tunneled across to the small refrigerator.

"How dare you read her letter?" Linda sat up and leaned against the headboard, before quickly pulling the sheet up over her exposed breasts. "That letter was private."

"Oh, spare me the indignant outrage. This isn't some kid's game. The more I know, the more I can do to protect you. There is one thing I would have had you do differently. You should have immediately gone to your brokerage houses and cashed out your investments. Before the people looking for you could get their sweeps fully set up. Then again, Cynthia had no way to know which data filters were already in place. Still, I agree, your funds are safe enough for now."

"You said letters," Linda said, "but there is only one letter."

"Ah. You've got a good ear for details. You could be great in my business. The plural is correct however. There were two, counting the one in your travel bag back at your condo."

"How did you know—"

"I followed Cynthia the morning she put it there. When she

went back home, I went in your place. You were still out jogging. It's how I knew you were here in Portland."

"Okay. But, well, how did you find me in this hotel?"

"It's what I do. I'm not Allstate, but you're in good hands."

"I don't want to be in your hands. Get out of here. Get out of my life. Cynthia's letters don't tell you which cities or banks I'll choose, and when I'll go to each so there is no great harm to your having read her letters."

"If you want it that way. By the way, the money and diamonds, tempting as they are, you'll find are still there on the table. If I wanted to harm you, you'd be dead. The payment I've been promised for dealing with you, plus that two-hundred-thousand in cash, not to mention the diamonds, would equal the price on the head of a president of a small African country. But sending me away is a mistake."

"Oh. And what mistake is that?"

"You need me." He leaned down and took off his shoes, then his socks, stretching them out neatly across the tops of his shoes. "Besides, how can our romance blossom if you run out on me?"

"What romance? Get out of my room. Leave me alone."

"It hasn't exactly been a pleasure watching your backside. Well, that's not exactly true, watching your backside is definitely a pleasure. But, then, as you wish. I drove half the night to get here and I'm tired. I'll leave in the morning." Then he took off his pants and his shirt, laying it on top of the slacks he had just draped over the end of the dresser, the leg pleats straight. Lastly, he took a handgun from somewhere behind him and placed it on top of his shirt.

"Just what do you think you're doing?"

"I need some sleep. Move over."

"Go to hell. You're not sleeping in this bed."

"Yes I am. I'm exhausted. And we've got a full day tomorrow."

Right then his gun and shirt slid off the dresser and thudded

146

against the floor like the carcass of a small dead animal. Linda's eyes fixed on the dark weapon then widened and went round. "Then you're sleeping alone." She got up, bent down to pick up her clothes from the floor, slipped her top on and moved to the chair where Ahab had been sitting. He shrugged and got into the bed.

The seat of the chair was warm. She sat looking at his open eyes, barely discernible in the ambient light coming through the open weave drapes. After a while she spoke. "Whatever made you decide to ... this'll sound hokey, become a bad man?"

"In my line of work you learn there are lots of shades of bad. Not since the crucifixion, has anyone been purely good. So, there are lots of shades of that, too."

Then, like a thought tossed aside, he closed his eyes.

~

"Hello, Nathan?"

"Yes. Who is this?"

"It's Nora Larick. We met in the Nob Hill Grill."

"Who?"

"You've forgotten me that quickly?"

"Oh. Nora. Yes. Yes. I remember. Forgive me. It's the middle of the night. But no, how could I forget you? ... Nora, it's five-thirty in the morning?" It was a statement of fact, he had said like a question.

"Listen, Nathan. I understand this is a bit odd. A lot odd, I admit. It's just that, well, I had gotten up and checked out of my hotel to get on the road early. Then, a few miles out of town, I got a call telling me I needed to stay in Portland for a meeting this afternoon. And, well, to tell the truth, I could use a few more hours sleep. So, I got to wondering, you said you lived alone and worked days, so, well, how'd you like some company? I could cook you breakfast. Get you off to work. Then sleep a few hours and be out of your way before you get home. I come back to Portland a couple times a year and, well, next time we'd know each other... Dumb idea, huh?" she said into the lingering silence. "I'm sorry I woke you."

A few minutes later she hung up the hotel lobby phone and walked outside holding the directions to Nathan's place.

Late that afternoon, Linda had left Nathan's home, an older house nearby in a neighborhood filled with homes that could qualify for favored financing as historical structures. Nathan had been a nice man, lonely, hard working, and he was the only person in the entire world who knew Nora Larick. Her contact of Nathan had been more daring, more brazen than her passive behavior in the upscale taverns of the towns near Sea Crest. She felt both shocked and proud she had pulled it off. Despite this difference, the memory of him felt the same as the memories of the men from the bars, empty and meaningless.

Today might become the day she would die and, if she did, after last night she would not die horny.

She smiled and pressed the accelerator.

CHAPTER 30

*L*inda drove south from Canon Beach through the darkness along the coast toward Sea Crest seeing very little traffic in either direction. Around three-thirty in the morning, no longer able to stay awake at the wheel, she stopped at a beachside rest area to take a short nap in the car. The moon glowing off the Pacific whitecaps appeared as bright pinpricks in the night sea. When she closed her eyes, the sounds of the surf let her think she was back at home, safe in her own bed.

Two hours later, the first subtle glow of the morning moving across her stretch of the road announced the new day. Later today she would play cat and mouse with Police Chief Ben McIlhenny.

After driving fifty miles, she used a drive-through to get a large coffee and a fast food breakfast. Then she was back on the road.

In daylight all roads look safer, less secretive, even the roads with which one is familiar. The tree shadows cast on the road ahead moved in a cadence with the wind. She was nearing home. It felt good, even though she would not actually go home, not this trip anyway, if ever.

She entered Lincoln City, Oregon, a few minutes after nine and stopped to use a pay phone to call Ben McIlhenny. "Hello Ben. It's Linda Darby."

"Linda. Where are you? Are you okay?"

"I'm fine. I just had to get away for a few days. Clear my head. We need to talk. There are things I haven't told you."

"I can come by your place."

"No. Not my place. This is a nice day, how 'bout the turnout just north of town. We can sit on the benches near the cliff overlooking the ocean."

"When?"

"I can be there in an hour."

"I've got a meeting with the violent crime task force that starts in fifteen minutes. Give me two hours. Will that work?"

"I'll make it work."

"Linda. I'd like to bring Clark Ryerson with me."

"Why?"

"Two reasons. He cares about you. And he's my new deputy, just started yesterday."

"That was fast."

"Small town means less red tape. You know."

"What happened to ... what's his name? Your other deputy."

"Clyde? He quit. Said he signed on to be a cop in a quiet little beach town. I guess all these murders melted his backbone."

"Don't fault him, Ben. He's probably the only sane one out of all of us."

"Clark's got great instincts. I s'pose as my deputy I could just bring him along, but I'd like you to be okay with it."

"Sure. No problem. I trust Clark, but no one else. Whoever else is on this task force of yours, I don't know those guys. I don't want to feel ganged up on. Just the three of us, okay?"

"Sure. Clark and I will see you at eleven-thirty."

The drive from Lincoln City to Sea Crest would take less than an hour, so Linda took time to eat something more substantial than fast food. It also gave her time to use a gas station restroom to brush her teeth, freshen up a bit, and change a few appearance things to recapture the real Linda Darby look.

She had one more problem. Ben McIlhenny knew her car, and

if he saw her driving the car Cynthia left for her it would lead to questions she'd rather avoid. Since he was a cop, he might just run the plates letting him link her to the name Nora Jean Larick. She didn't plan on telling Ben about Cynthia's letter, the bank box, the cash or diamonds, or the fake identities. After meeting with Ben and Clark she would be back on the road. Back on the run so she needed that stuff to remain a secret. Besides, she had not completely shaken off Ahab's warning about Ben McIlhenny. Truth was she didn't know exactly what to make of Ahab. He had saved her life in the alley. Then again by warning her and leaving the gun she had used to kill the man who chased her on the beach. Then, last night, he could have killed her in her hotel room and taken the cash and diamonds. Still, none of that changed one thing, he was an assassin who apparently had a contract on her.

She considered swapping over to her own car, but couldn't be sure someone was not watching her condo. Then she'd have to switch back to the Nora Larick car. She decided that simpler was better. She would park in the small neighborhood on the east side of the highway and walk to the cliff-side turnout.

The high sun striking the windshield prevented Linda from seeing the occupants when Chief McIlhenny's four-wheel jeep wagon pulled into the turnout. And right then she realized that her choice of where to meet had pinned her against the sea cliff. If Ben had come to arrest her, she would have no way of escape.

Calm down. Ben has no reason to arrest me. I'm a victim, not a criminal. I killed. I didn't murder.

The driver's door opened. Ben stepped out stretching his tall frame, and tugging and pushing on the wide leather belt on which he carried his gun and other official paraphernalia. A moment later, Clark got out of the passenger seat, similarly fussing with the leather ensemble wrapped around his waist. No one got out of the back. They had come alone.

"Hello, Linda," Ben said, as he got close.

Clark winked, and then took off his cap. "Are you okay?"

She nodded. Clark's transition from a motorcycle gang member to a waiter, to a cop, was measurable through the changing lengths of his hair. Standing there, clean shaven, the sun on his face, he looked good in his uniform.

"Please sit down," Ben said.

Linda managed a nervous smile. Then sat, placing her hands on top of the wooden picnic table. She had read in a book that when people were nervous, they rarely knew what to do with their hands. It was true. She moved them to her lap.

"Well, Linda," Ben began, "this is your meeting. You take the lead. We'll listen. Tell it your way. Try to keep it chronological, if you can. Okay?"

"I'll try," Linda said.

They all instinctively turned toward a loud wave, large enough that it climbed over the seagull-whitened rock polyhedron about a hundred yards out from where they sat.

Linda knew it was time to do what she had returned to Sea Crest to do. Come clean. Well, part way clean anyway.

Ben and Clark sat facing Linda. Ben rested his hands and forearms on the table. Clark sat on the end of the bench, his legs crossed, his arms relaxed on his lap.

"It all started the night before the two men were found dead in the alley," she began. "Like I told you before, Ben, I had decided to walk to town. Do a little shopping, and then go to Millie's for some chowder and cheese bread."

Fifteen minutes later, she had told the two men everything including the mystery man who had saved her and drove her home, most likely in the taxi that had been briefly stolen that same night.

"You had told me about being accosted in the alley and getting away," Ben said, "but not about the man who had saved you. Why not?"

"He warned me not to come to you, said you could not be trusted."

"Why? Why did he say that?"

She noticed that Ben's voice had risen, and, at one point, cracked.

"I have no idea. Besides I didn't want to get him in trouble. He saved me. I thought from being raped. Now it appears more likely from being tortured and murdered like Cynthia."

"Did he kill those two men?"

"When I left the alley, they were both alive, just unconscious, so any claim that he killed them is only supposition. I didn't even know the two men were dead until the next morning when I heard about it on the radio. All I knew—know—is that he saved me and the two men were found dead."

"Come on, Linda, who else could have killed 'em?"

"Yes, it seems logical to assume he killed them. But I don't, we don't, know that."

"But he never told you about why he felt you shouldn't come to me?"

"He didn't," Linda replied. "Let me ask you, why would he doubt your trustworthiness?"

"I think he just didn't want you telling me about him. It was to his advantage for the authorities not to know there had even been another man in the alley."

"That makes sense," Linda said. But she hadn't liked Ben's body language. His eyes were normally right on her, but while saying this, he had looked away. Ahab had been right. She knew it now. Not why. Not how. But, Ben McIlhenny was involved.

"Then what happened?" Clark asked.

"Ben knows the rest. I went to Cynthia's and found her.... . Called him and waited until he arrived."

"But why did you run?" Ben asked.

"Now hold on. I didn't run. I was coming back. I mean ... I'm here, right? I just needed some time. I had been attacked. My best friend had been brutally murdered. When that other man was found dead on the beach, just down from my house, it became too much. I just felt unsafe."

"What had Cynthia told you about her work," Ben asked, "about the work of her company, SMITH & CO.?"

"Like I said before, we never talked about it. I asked her several times, back when we first starting getting together. She always just passed it off. 'It's boring stuff,' she'd say, 'nothing that would interest you. I work all day long. Let's talk about other things.' She'd shrug and change the subject."

"And she never told you anything more?"

"Not while she was alive."

"What does that mean?" Clark and Ben both asked in unison.

"She left a letter at my house. I found it after she was dead. The letter explained that some man had hired her company to do illegal research, and that he had used what she had dug up to extort favors from government officials."

"Who was this guy? What officials? State? Federal?"

"I don't know, Ben. That's the entire letter, except that I should get away for a while. Let it all pass and then things might go back to normal."

Clark said, "Well, that normal part certainly hasn't come true."

"Where's the letter?" Ben asked.

"I burned it. Cynthia ended her letter saying that she had wanted me to know that much. That it would only hurt me if I knew more. That I should burn the letter, forget about it and get on with my life."

"All right," Ben said, "water under the bridge. Now tell me about the man murdered on the beach?"

"I only know what was reported in the news," Linda said. "That a middle-aged man had been found shot, lying in the surf."

"Linda. The man was shot in the head and the heart, just like Cynthia. That's quite a coincidence, wouldn't you say?"

"I'm no detective, Ben, but doesn't that mean the shooter is probably the same guy who killed Cynthia?"

"I have to ask you where you were that night."

Linda glanced at Clark. He had promised to be her alibi. But now that he was a deputy, he might feel compelled to change his mind. Her palms felt damp. Her heart picked up its pace. She would have to say something soon, something lame like being home alone that night. She could mention going for a walk. But that wouldn't have prevented her from shooting the guy.

Clark broke the silence. "She was with me, Ben. You remember, Linda. You came down around six. We had burgers and a couple of beers." Then Clark looked back to Ben, "We listened to some music and watched the ocean. The moon was bright, the surf alive. You might remember that night, Chief, it was really spectacular."

"Clark," Chief McIlhenny said, "it's getting a bit breezy. Would you go back to the car and get my cap? It's on the backseat." When Clark had gone far enough that he could no longer hear them, Ben turned to Linda. "What time did you leave Clark's house?"

Linda pointed at a spouting from a California gray whale. A pod of them lived close to the Sea Crest cliffs, feeding year round off the kelp beds. "I left around eleven," she said, "then I walked home and went to bed."

"Clark," the chief hollered, "did you find my hat?" Clark raised his arm holding the cap. Ben gave him a come-back-here wave.

"She left my place a few minutes after eleven," Clark said after walking back. "If that's what you wanted to know. Here's your hat."

"I had to do it that way."

"Sure, boss," Clark said. "I figured that's why your head got cold."

"How long you been a deputy?"

"Two days, boss. Two good days, though."

"You got yourself a future in this here police work, Deputy."

"Thanks, boss. With you as my mentor, how can I miss?" They shared a light laugh.

"Now, can I ask you a question, Ben?" Linda asked.

"Sure."

"Did anything come from all the forensics and ballistics and autopsies?"

"Nothing really. The forensics brought up a few hairs at Cynthia's but they were all female so they were likely hers or yours, or some other friend's. The national crime labs couldn't match them to anyone. Still we've got them cataloged, but right now we've got nothing to check them against. Ballistics means nothing without a gun barrel to compare markings to those on the bullet. The autopsies told us what we knew. Everyone died of gunshots at about the times we had expected."

Over the next ten minutes Linda explained that she was leaving again. That she would be back after the murders had been solved. Before they drove away, Linda hugged both men.

"Thank you for your concern for me," she said, "but please just solve this case so I can come home."

When they drove away, she knew it had been smart for her to come back to Sea Crest. If she hadn't, Chief McIlhenny would have increasingly become suspicious about her involvement. She had told them the truth, just not the whole truth and nothing but the truth. Her lies were by omission: staying silent about Cynthia's second letter. Not mentioning the money and diamonds. And of course keeping the false identities. And then there was the part about the dead guy on the beach, more specifically the part about her pulling the trigger.

She had omitted far more than she had told. But she had seen no workable alternative. Only one of her omissions bothered her, staying silent about the man on the beach and letting Clark perjure himself. Well, technically it wasn't perjury unless he said it on the stand under oath. Still, with the Chief's integrity in doubt there had been no other good choice.

Last night before going to sleep, she had written a letter telling the rest of the story, including the identity of Webster. Before leaving Sea Crest she planned to take the letter to Cynthia's attorney, and instruct him that in the event she also turned up dead he was to open it and take it to the FBI.

CHAPTER 31

*W*ebster picked up his scrambled satellite phone, dialed, and was greeted by, "Chief McIlhenny here."

"You know who this is. Anything new to report?"

"This stops now. Your dealings have caused seven deaths. I have interrogated Linda Darby at length. She knows nothing that should cause you any concern. Your obsession with Ms. Darby is over. If anything happens to her, I will blow your operation sky high. I don't care if you're government or not, and I don't think you are. Do you understand me?"

"I understand I must have dialed a wrong number."

"You heard me. Linda Darby is off limits."

"I don't know anybody named McIlhenny or a woman named Linda Darby. And I certainly had nothing to do with any deaths wherever you are. I'm hanging up now. I've dialed incorrectly and apologize for the inconvenience."

Ryan Testler had gotten up in Portland after Linda left the room and followed her to some house. Two hours later, a man came out. Testler continued to wait and when she came out he followed her to the Oregon coast. As he drove south of Lincoln City, his cell phone rang.

It was Webster. "I've got a job for you," he said, "a rush job. Chief McIlhenny is coming apart. I want him down today."

"Are we talking about the police chief in Sea Crest?"

"Who else?"

"Why?"

"I already told you. He's coming apart. The man was never committed to our work. He's threatening to blow the whistle on my operation, to ruin everything I've worked to create."

"He doesn't know your identity."

"He knows enough and as a police chief he can have the ear of the Feds. And he has undoubtedly seen you on several occasions so he knows how to describe you. Neither of us needs this problem. Make it go away."

"Cost you double."

"What?"

"He's a cop. More heat."

"Oh, all right. The usual method of payment, but get it done soon."

"Yes sir."

Testler hung up. He didn't want to kill McIlhenny. The man had killed a mobster in Jersey after that man had beaten a woman to death. Testler would have done the same thing had he been in McIlhenny's place. But then, a double fee was a double fee. What Testler was uncertain about was what to do about Linda Darby. He had her set up so he could kill her any time, and killing her would keep him in good with Webster. Conversely, to protect Darby would require that he turn on Webster. And if he was not going to kill Linda, there was no reason to kill McIlhenny. Then again, it would be nice to pick up the double fee regardless of what he decided regarding Linda Darby.

He would have to decide soon, or find a way to buy himself more time.

At eight, Testler went into O'Malley's to have something to eat. The place wasn't crowded but the dish trays in the corner were stacked high so the earlier dinner traffic had been heavy.

He had finished a beef dip sandwich and sat drinking coffee, when Chief McIlhenny slipped into the booth across from him. The vinyl seat protested against the leather of his holster.

"Hello. We haven't met, but we should."

"All right. I'm—"

"Don't bother. The name would not be real. You're the man who has been picking up the surveillance disks I've left at the dead drops."

"If I did know what you are talking about, are you sure you want to be doing this?"

"Yes. I want your boss to know I'm through."

"If what you say is true, I don't imagine he would any longer need that surveillance, given that the consulting company has burned down and the workers are all dead."

"I'm through staying silent. Tomorrow, I'm going to the state attorney general and tell what I know."

"Coffee, Chief?" O'Malley called out from behind the bar.

Ben nodded. "Black, and bring along one of your marionberry tarts." He turned to Testler. "Join me?"

"Why not," Testler said holding up two fingers. O'Malley nodded. Then Testler narrowed his eyes at McIlhenny. "Why are you telling me?"

"I figure you know who Mister X is. Without his identity, my story will lack corroboration. Go with me. Together we can bring him down and put a stop to all this."

"What if the government's behind it?"

"I don't want to believe that," the chief said, shaking his head. "But, either way, this has to come out. If it's the government, it's an abuse of power."

"Do you plan to include your killing in Jersey?"

"You know about that, do you?" The chief pursed his lips and nodded his head, before continuing, "I'm going to come clean on all of it. Still, being a practical man, I'll try to obtain immunity for Jersey in return for this new, bigger case. Come with me. It's your chance to get free of it as well."

"Have you considered that if I'm who you think I am, I may not want to be free of it?"

"I have thought about that, a great deal, and I may be wrong," McIlhenny said when O'Malley moved away after putting down their coffees, "but you've been around Sea Crest for a several weeks, off and on. I figure you're the man who saved Linda Darby in the alley. I also figure you're the man who coordinated her being grabbed off the street in the first place. That makes you conflicted. I figure you might just like to get off that horse you're riding."

"Hypothetically speaking, Chief, I know you're all stoked up about having made your decision and are eager to put it in play. Then again, your chances of bargaining for immunity for Jersey go way up if you've got me along to corroborate, and to identify the head man. Without his identity your state attorney general has nowhere to go with whatever you tell him. I'll tell you this much about the head man. He is wealthy and highly connected. You need to have him by the short hairs or all you'll accomplish is to enhance his mystique. Bottom line: you've been thinking about this for a while, but you've just dropped it in my lap. I need at least a week to decide."

"I'll leave for the capital in three days, at 9:30 in the morning. Be at my office then if you're going with me." McIlhenny stood, dropped a ten on the table and walked out, waving at O'Malley standing behind the bar holding two warm marionberry tarts.

Events were cornering Testler. He had to decide. Chief McIlhenny

had been right about one thing, Testler would love to get out of his
entanglement with Webster, but he didn't want to give up the
monies Webster would pay him over the next few years. He even
imagined shedding the name Ryan Testler and returning to his real
name. With him along to identify Webster, McIlhenny would have
a solid shot at immunity for having killed that deserving bastard in
Jersey. However, Testler knew that his own chances for immunity
were next to none, given the multiple assassinations he had carried
out. So, Webster had also been right about one thing, Chief
McIlhenny was not only a threat to Webster, but also a threat to
Testler.

CHAPTER 32

*L*inda glanced in her rearview mirror. The dark, four-door sedan was still there. Two cars back, matching her speed. It had taken the rest of the morning and a good part of the afternoon for her to drive from Sea Crest back to Portland, through it, and onto the bridge over the Columbia River that would take her into the state of Washington.

For the last half hour she had been noticing a dark, four-door sedan that had been lingering behind her. Over the next few miles she used the mirrors to keep track of the dark sedan. She eased off the gas pedal enough to drop her speed two miles per hour. Over the next mile two cars passed her, but not the dark sedan which continued to mirror her pace. Over the next several miles, except for glancing forward to maintain a safe distance from the double-semi truck in front of her, her focus remained on the dark car.

After she moved north of Vancouver, the first city on the Washington side of the Columbia River, she changed lanes. A moment later the dark sedan moved into her new lane, three cars behind. After a few miles she changed back into the middle lane, behind the double semi. After a while, the shadowing car reflected that move as well.

How could they have found me? Have they been there since I left Sea Crest? Did Chief McIlhenny tip them off? It could have been Clark. No. I would suspect the chief before Clark. The chief's body language had been suspicious and, that first night, Ahab warned me about him.

This automotive mating dance continued for another thirty miles before Linda settled on a plan.

After a few more miles, the elements of her plan appeared in front of her. She was in the center lane with the trail car the second car behind in the same lane. In the lane to her right, a double-semi, a trucking configuration not allowed in all states, moving at her speed, was a few car lengths in front. Ahead about two miles was an exit in rather open country, with an off ramp that quickly climbed high enough to allow her to look back down onto the interstate. She accelerated as if her objective was to pass the truck. The car behind her and the tail car accelerated to keep pace and also pass the truck.

Linda jockeyed her position after getting the middle of her car near the front of the long truck. She then settled down to hold her position in relation to the long truck to her right. This tactic allowed her to also control the speed of the dark sedan. At this point the dark sedan was holding alongside the rear portion of the double-semi. This meant the driver of the dark sedan would not be able to see the quarter-mile sign for the upcoming exit.

The time had come.

She tromped down on the accelerator sending the needle of her speedometer soaring past ninety, and sped in front of the truck. Then cut across the lane barely ahead of the double-semi and headed up the exit ramp, holding the wheel stiff against the high-speed pull of the pavement. The right side tires throwing gravel against the guardrail.

Half way up the ramp she began feathering the brakes and finally came to a controlled stop just before the momentum carried her into the cross street. There was no one behind her so she sat there watching the dark sedan, which had been past the off-ramp before seeing it disappear in the distance ahead, still on the interstate.

From this somewhat elevated position she looked over an expanse of flat country dotted with a few scattered trees. Then she saw something ahead, on a service road on her side of the interstate. A truck stop, at least the sign for a truck stop mounted on what was likely the tallest pole in the county. She headed there.

The truck stop was open for business and by its look had been for longer than the locals cared to remember. The building had no neighbors unless you counted a fast food place across the street whose business had slowed to the point where it had closed. Its only communal function now being windows plastered with posters announcing the nearest high school football schedule, and a flyer about free flu shots available at the drug store in town. Neither the drug store's name nor its address was shown so apparently the local folks knew whatever else they needed to know.

Inside the truck stop Linda bought a Seattle map that covered the area south far enough to include her location. At least it did according to the attendant behind the register. With the help of two truckers in the truck stop's tired diner, she identified back roads that would take her from where she was into Seattle without returning to I-5. They said it would be an hour slower than the interstate, but that was okay with her.

"Hey. Hey. Charlie, this is Bobby. The little lady outfoxed ya. The gal's got balls. Well, not balls, you know what I mean."

"Give the idiot remarks a rest," Charlie said into his cell phone.

"The boss is going to be pissed," Bobby said, "you losing her and all."

"Are you still on her?" Charlie asked.

"No sweat. I was far enough back to be able to take the same exit. She's left the interstate."

"No shit, Sherlock."

"Who's this Sherlock dude? But, yeah, I got her. She's pulled into a truck stop and gone inside. I'll let you know when she splits. Is this Sherlock guy from one of them old books you're always reading when we're holed up on a job? Oops. Hold everything. Here she comes."

"Why'd she stop?"

"I don't know. Take a piss. I guess. Women do that, too, you know."

"What else, Bobby?"

"She got a soda. No, wait a minute. There's something in her other hand. I can't make it out. Shit. She's back inside her car. Can't see her so good now. She's just sitting there."

"That's why you have binoculars."

"Fuck off. I got you covered. Wait a minute. She's looking at something. She's got whatever it is stretched out across her steering wheel... . Hey, bro, she's got herself a map. Sure, it's a frigging map. That's what she's got. She bought a map."

"Just stay with her. When she sets a pattern, let me know so I can cut over somewhere and pick you back up."

"Hey, I got her. No sweat."

"You've got your orders."

"Okay. Okay. You need to chill, Charlie."

"And remember, the boss doesn't want her taken before he gives the okay."

"What's that about?" Bobby asked. "The dude was in a hurry, now all we hear is slow down."

"Bobby, to take license with Alfred Lord Tennyson, yours is not to reason why."

"Who? You gotta stop reading all that shit, Charlie. It's already fucking up your brain."

"Forget it, Bobby, just do your job."

CHAPTER 33

*L*inda wormed her way through the small towns and side roads that eventually brought her to Seattle. The good news, she did not again see the dark sedan which had been tailing her on the interstate. Whoever had been following had either given up or gone ahead to Seattle to wait for her. But that seemed unlikely. In addition to the many exits into Seattle, they had no reason to even assume she would stop there. There were plenty of good sized cities north of Seattle, also the Canadian border. She decided to bypass downtown to the east and then circle back and enter the metropolitan area from the north.

～

"Charlie, this here's Bobby."

"Who else would it be asshole. I got caller ID you know."

"Charlie, I've had it with your attitude. If you don't get off my ass—"

"Just give me your report, Bobby. What's our little lady up to?"

"For more than an hour she's been circling around Seattle to the east. I couldn't tell where the hell she was heading until she turned back toward Seattle from the North."

"Okay. It's getting late. She'll likely settle in there for the night. Stay on her and let me know where she holes up. I'm heading your way now."

"Where are you?"

"I'm partway between Tacoma and Seattle. I just grabbed a bite waiting to hear from you. Some place that features turkey all year round. Can you believe that?"

"That's really the shits, Charlie. You lose the tail and get to chow down while I gotta stay on the job. I love turkey."

"Life can be hell, Bobby. I feel for you."

"Fuck you, asshole."

"You're still working on your vocabulary I see."

"Fuck you, asshole."

"Mr. Asshole, to you, Bobby, but I do love it when you dazzle me with those big words."

"So what are you going to do, Charlie?"

"I'm already back on I-5, heading your way. Call me when she settles in."

By ten, Linda had checked into a Best Western on the worn northern outskirts of Seattle, paying cash. After watching the news to be sure she wasn't part of it, she gave in to the restlessness that comes from sitting behind the wheel all day. She went for a walk.

The exercise felt good, but she missed a rearview mirror to observe those behind her. The pedestrians mostly held steady blank stares, people with their minds replaying their day or previewing their tomorrow while they sauntered toward the bar, ballgame, or bedroom that would fill their night.

Several blocks north from the hotel, she crossed the street and approached a brown brick building where she pushed through the padded red door of a windowless bar. The air inside was weighted with the aged odors of a career tavern. Still, its diffused light, dark woods and forest green colors conveyed a welcome. Her ears picked up clinking beer bottles, a habit started in some ancient time when men drank from pewter or pottery mugs. She traced the sound to five middle-aged guys sitting shoulder to shoulder along a bar unique in no way except for a brass lamp next the wall, adorned with small red glass dangles hanging from a green shade, the establishment's effort toward promoting the thought of making everyday Christmas.

The crash of a break shot from a coin-operated pool table called from near the back on her right. She walked deeper into the dinge, the eyes of the men pawing her front and back. Intuitively practicing the skills of a person on the run, she chose a booth shielded from the outside light that entered with each opening of the door. From there she would get a look at anyone who came in after her.

She ordered a draft beer and a shot of house whiskey. Then set her eyes on the front door. When her order came she first took a big drink of the beer, and then slid the shot glass down inside the mug to make a boilermaker. She had never drank one before, but had wanted to ever since reading in books about men drinking them, and watching them do so in movies. On more than one occasion she had walked into Millie's in Sea Crest planning to order her first, but somehow she never had. But now she didn't know how much longer she had to do anything, so it was time. Time to do a lot of the things she had never quite been able to bring herself to do. The strength of the drink dropped through her like an elevator freed by a broken cable.

Nothing noteworthy happened in the next hour except for watching a drunk leave the bar, walking out the way drunks walked, uphill on a level floor.

Two hours and two boilermakers later, she found herself staring at a neon beer sign above the bar, her stare so intense she hadn't blinked. Her eyes felt dry, and she had grown angry, bitterly angry. The bastards had torn her life apart, killed her best friend, the only sense of family she had, destroyed the tranquility of her community, and driven her from her home. This had to stop. She didn't know how, but those who were responsible should be made to pay.

After downing the last of her drink, she walked out a little unsteady herself, back to the hotel. There, she locked the door, slipped the gun under her pillow, stripped and dropped into bed. The sheets were cool, but not her temperament. She lay there listening to the tinny whirl of the window air conditioner, and the infrequent murmurs of guests passing her door until exhaustion defeated her fears.

～

"Boss, Charlie here. I'm on a secure line. The woman's in Seattle. My man's got her located in a motel. We could take her easy."

"Not tonight. Not until I tell you," Webster said. "Until then just keep me posted on her movements, but take no action. Just don't lose her."

"Why the delay?"

"Don't you worry about that. I do the thinking."

"Sure, boss. It's just that ... well, you were in such a hellfire hurry. Now, all of a sudden, we're on hold."

"I won't repeat myself. You're being paid. Do what you're told."

"You got it, boss. I'll let you know if she moves again. You call me if things change at your end. Okay?"

"One more thing. If she starts to go into an FBI office or a police station, take her out before she gets through the door. If you have to do it that way, and the press reports confirm it, I'll throw in an extra ten Gs for ya."

"You got it, boss."

Webster hung up.

～

"Testler, Webster. Can you talk?"

"Go ahead."

"Where are we on McIlhenny?"

"I've got it set up."

"I want this done."

"He's told the town he's going fishing next Tuesday. I'll take care of it while he's at sea."

"Tuesday's too long," Webster said. "It needs to be much sooner."

"Don't let impatience get in the way of a good plan. Besides, what's the hurry?"

"I got Charlie and one of his guys in position to deal with this Darby woman, she's holed up in Seattle. McIlhenny has threatened that if anything happens to her he'll go to the authorities and tell what he knows."

"McIlhenny doesn't mean it," Testler said. "If he did, he wouldn't threaten you. He'd just do it."

"You may be right. But we can't chance it. I've told Charlie to keep Darby in sight but take no action until I ok it, and that won't be until after you've finished your assignment."

"Charlie should be able to keep tabs on a woman for a few days."

"I don't like it," Webster said with a snarl. "Too much can go wrong. Tomorrow she could walk in the FBI office in Seattle."

"If she was going to do that she would've done so in Portland, Oregon, not driven through to Seattle. Isn't that where you just said she was?" Testler asked, to give Webster the impression he had no idea where Linda Darby was located. When, in fact, Testler had just parked around the corner from the Best Western where Darby had just entered a ground floor room.

"Yeah, in Seattle, she's down for the night," Webster said. "Where are you now?"

"In Sea Crest, I'm taking pictures by day and watching the

chief by night. If he goes off the edge on this, I can take him almost immediately."

"Do it then. I'll give Charlie the green light on Darby and we'll be clear on both ends in a few hours."

"Not a good idea."

"And just why the hell not?" Webster asked.

"We've killed seven people in a tiny coastal town that never before had a single murder. You've always preferred our work be kept quiet. Nothing we've done in Sea Crest has been quiet. Now you're giving me another target, and not just any target, the chief of police. If he dies in an obvious murder, the town will be left without law enforcement. That means at least the state, if not the Feds will step in."

"Why would the Feds come in?"

"Cynthia Leclair did contract work for the CIA and Defense Department. That alone will put the Feds on alert."

"You've got a point."

"Tuesday," Testler repeated, "the chief can have a simple, explainable boating tragedy. Given the options available, that's the one we should go with."

"You're right. Damn it, you're right. But we may not have the time. Darby is on the run. I've got to know what Cynthia Leclair told her, maybe even gave her."

"Where does that leave us?"

"Charlie has orders to take out Darby if she tries to enter a police department or an FBI office. You tell me you have the same kind of watch on McIlhenny. I guess that will have to do for now."

Webster hung up, praying he would get to Tuesday without any further complications.

CHAPTER 34

*T*he morning light woke Linda around nine. She got up and showered, then dressed and worked her hair into the Carol Benson look while mentally reviewing her concocted Benson family history. Then she got on the road. It was a bright and clear day, something not all that common in this area of the country during this time of the year. She loved the affection of the sun. Its warmth repeatedly kissed her face through the driver's side window.

By mid-afternoon she had driven south to Tacoma and rented a safe deposit box at Union Bank under the name Carol Benson. She left fifty-thousand in cash and approximately a third of the diamonds which she had first secured into two paper coin sleeves she had obtained from a teller before opening the deposit box. At this bank, like the others, she had given a false address.

Between the banks in Portland and Tacoma she had now deposited one-hundred thousand dollars in cash. She still had another one-hundred-twenty-five on her person, including the original twenty-five thousand Cynthia had left for her in Sea Crest. Two more banks each with fifty-thousand would leave her twenty-five thousand to carry with her.

She had felt less pressure, less fear, acting out being Carol Benson than she had felt being Nora Larick at the Portland bank.

The difference was not the name, but the poise she had developed. The confidence that she could project herself however she wished.

In total, she had six sets of false identifications. She had used Larick and Benson and planned to use two more with other banks. Her plan had been to travel as Nora Larick, keeping her other false identities in reserve. That way she could get comfortable being Nora Jean Larick, and do a bone-up study session before playing her other personas.

She spent the rest of the afternoon shopping to expand her wardrobe for the various women she could become, and having a professional rinse put on her hair to recapture Nora's color. Carol Benson's hair had been a little darker, and Carol wore hers up rather than the longer look that Nora preferred. She had also stopped in a drug store and bought a new pair of dark-rimmed glasses for Carol. She had previously bought a pair which she had worn to the bank in Tacoma, but the prescription strength was not close enough and she had difficulty seeing clearly. Fortunately, the glasses Cynthia had morphed onto her picture as Nora Larick were similar enough in style to allow Linda, as Nora, to wear her own glasses.

The entire day had gone rather smoothly. As far as she could tell, she had not been followed or watched. She decided to quietly celebrate her good fortune by going to a movie and getting a late snack.

For the length of the movie, she forgot she was a woman on the run, a woman upon whom this Webster person had issued his own kind of fatwa. But as she walked out of the darkness of the screening room, the night brought back the fear.

By eleven, she had driven south nearly to the Oregon border where she took a room on the Washington side of the Columbia River.

∾

The next morning Linda slept until eleven, had a room service breakfast and set about deciding the cities where she would choose her remaining two banks. The first two had been in the Pacific Northwest so she wanted the last two to be a good distance away. By two-thirty in the afternoon she had chosen Las Vegas, Nevada, and Sedona, Arizona, both tourist towns used to seeing strangers. By three she was in her car heading south. She had also picked a city to reach before stopping for the night, Weed, California, the first town south of the Oregon border.

"Chief McIlhenny?"

"This is McIlhenny."

"It's me," Testler said as he eased his car onto interstate five heading south. He kept back about a half mile so he could watch the pattern of movements made by the cars between him and Linda Darby.

"Me who?"

"You joined me for coffee in O'Malley's the other night."

"Oh, yeah," McIlhenny cleared his throat, "you didn't give me a name."

"You told me to skip it. Are you a place where you can talk?"

"I'm in my office. I just shut the door. If you're going with me, I leave in two days."

"Haven't decided, but I'm strongly leaning that way."

"What's holding you back?"

"I need another week."

"Too long," the chief said. "I won't wait. Where are you now?"

"Not important. Listen, Chief, you've been thinking on this for a good while. Me, I've had a day. Bottom line, by next Monday I can get my hands on some documents that will add a great deal of credibility to what you tell your state attorney general. With those documents you'll get your immunity. Your story will be supported by irrefutable evidence."

"I won't wait."

"That's your decision. But if you go alone, you've got no corroboration and you don't have the identity of the man behind it all. Not much to offer in return for immunity. If I throw in with you, it'll be a cinch. I know you're fed up and are ready to act. But don't blow the case by being impatient. Together, we'll get immunity and bring the bastard down. Alone, you'll likely not get the deal you want and the man you're really after will go on as before. And, as for Linda Darby, you'll have done nothing to remove her from danger. In fact, you'll likely increase her danger as the man will want to close off any threats."

After a long pause, Chief McIlhenny exhaled, and then said, "Monday. Not a day longer. We'll leave Tuesday morning."

"Tell O'Malley and a few others you're going fishing on Tuesday."

"Good idea, I've got a boat and the halibut are hot right now."

"Best we're not seen together on Tuesday."

"I can take out the boat and put in around Lincoln City. You can join me there."

"I'll bring the car."

"Call me Monday night. By then I'll have picked a quiet spot to put in to pick you up. I've got one in mind, just north of Lincoln. I'll check it out in the next couple of days."

"Talk to you Monday."

By mid-afternoon Ryan Testler had identified two cars he knew had to be involved in tailing Linda Darby: a black Pontiac two-door and a gray Chevy Impala. The Pontiac had settled in two or three cars behind Linda, with the Impala holding a position about five car lengths behind the Pontiac. Ryan had rented a car which got better gas mileage than either of the two cars he followed, and he had gassed up the night before. He used his binoculars to recognize the driver in the front car as Charlie Ashburn, a nail hard package of humanity with the intelligence to have been anything, mismatched with the meanness of a thug. That meant the driver in the Impala would be Bobby Vargas, a dim fellow who worked directly for Charlie. Webster preferred working with only a few men and letting those men choose helpers when they were necessary. That way, the helpers did not know Webster's identity. It would have been Charlie's idea that he and Bobby take separate cars, making it harder for them to lose the tail on Darby. For another reason, Charlie liked classical music while Bobby dug rap. In separate cars they could each indulge their respective tastes without objections from the other, all at Webster's expense. Charlie and Bobby were like John Steinbeck's *Of Mice and Men* except that these two were physically similar in size.

Testler largely ignored Linda's car, keeping his focus on Charlie and Bobby. He would not lose Linda Darby because he had put a radio-frequency transmitter on the car Cynthia Leclair had left in the storage garage for Linda. He also knew that he needed to get Charlie and Bobby off Linda's tail. Until he did that, he would not be able to have direct contact with her, which he needed in order to decide whether or not to kill Linda Darby.

Linda drove into a steady rain falling in the mountains of southern Oregon. Later, she crossed the border into California where it had recently stopped raining. But the road was wet and the air still heavy with moisture. She toggled her wiper control to make intermittent passes to cut down the glare from the headlights of oncoming cars. After a while she left the wiper on low even though the window was more dotted with mountain mist than rain.

At a few minutes before one-thirty in the early morning, she pulled off I-5 and glided down into the small mountain town of Weed, California. She had never been to Weed, but quickly found a motel with both a vacancy sign and a clean-looking coffee shop out front facing the street. At this hour, the coffee shop was closed.

Charlie and Bobby pulled up behind each other along the curb, and spoke on their cell phones while using their binoculars to watch Linda walk into, then out of the motel office. Next, she moved her car to park head in and entered a room directly in front of her parked car. Her unit was near the corner of an L-turn in the building tucked in behind the stairs next to what the sign said was a coin-operated laundry. They could easily take her here. If they did, they would not even need to get a room for themselves.

But Charlie said they could not do so without the boss's approval, and Charlie didn't want to awaken the boss who lived in the east where it was nearly five in the morning. But he also didn't want to incur Webster's wrath for having let a perfect setup pass without having taken Darby. They could knock on her door, representing themselves to be motel personnel needing to replace her pillow as the maids had run out of clean pillowcases, or whatever. They could question her, kill her, and be gone without being seen.

Charlie told Bobby to sit tight while he called the boss.

CHAPTER 35

"*Y*ou know what the hell time it is, Charles?"

When pissed, Webster always called him Charles.

"But boss, this set up's perfect."

"Listen, dunderhead. I told you to stay with her until I got back to you. Which part of that didn't you understand?"

"Well none of it, boss. But ... this'd be clean as a whistle. I just thought—"

"Don't think. Just do what you're told until I get back to you. Got it?"

Before Charlie could say yes, his phone went dead. Webster had not waited for Charlie's confirmation.

Charlie called Bobby and told him to check into the same motel. "Get a room close, but not too close, to Darby's room. Insist on the ground floor. Insist on two beds. Pay cash. I'll park on the side street and then join you in the room."

Five minutes later, Testler pulled into Weed and found the motel where Linda's car was parked. He also saw the gray Impala parked facing in about six rooms from what he was guessing was Linda's room. The motel had clustered its few guests in one tight strip of rooms, likely to make the morning maid service easier. The six cars were also crowded together, all nosed into the host building like unweaned puppies. The occupied rooms were dark except for the two directly facing Bobby's Impala and Linda's car.

The motel Linda had chosen sat on the main road through town, with a residential street on its south side. Charlie's black Pontiac was not in the motel lot. Testler turned onto the unlit small residential street and immediately saw the Pontiac parked in front of a cottage type house with a wide porch fronted by a river rock pony wall.

Testler knew Charlie liked violence, but he also knew that Charlie kept it in check, only indulging his love for giving pain when ordered to do so. Bobby joined in the cruelty only after Charlie led the way.

Because Testler had a transmitter on Linda's car he would know when she drove out of the lot, and because Charlie would not move until Linda did, and Bobby would not move until Charlie did, Testler only needed to keep track of Linda's car to know the location of all three of them. He also knew Charlie was under Webster's order not to take Linda without Webster's approval. And, further that Webster did not intend to approve her being taken until after Testler had eliminated Chief McIlhenny in Sea Crest next Tuesday.

Testler took a room at a motel across the street and down a block. Before entering the office he chose a range of room numbers on the second floor from which he could use his binoculars to watch Linda's room and her car. He requested and got one of those rooms. The desk clerk, between yawns, told him there was no place in town to get anything to eat until five-thirty in the morning when the coffee shop in the next block opened. The owner also said Testler had been fortunate he drove in when he did as the owner had just decided to turn on the no-vacancy sign and go to bed.

Testler set the alarm on his cell phone to wake him at five. He would only get a couple of hours sleep, but he had handled more demanding military assignments with less. Testler and Charlie had been in several joint meetings with Webster and worked together on three assignments. Charlie would recognize Testler in a heartbeat. But the dullard Bobby, whom Testler had met once five years before, would likely not. Ryan planned to get to the diner when it opened in the morning so he'd be fed and back to his motel room before Charlie would approach the diner, if he did at all. Charlie used Bobby as his gopher so if either of them came to the diner for coffee and danish to take back to the room, it would likely be Bobby not Charlie.

A few minutes later, the light behind the curtain over the window in Charlie and Bobby's motel room went out. Through his binoculars, Testler saw the curtain part ever so slightly. Just enough to let him know the opening was unnatural, as if held by a hand. Linda's room had been dark for at least twenty minutes. An hour later, the curtain in Charlie's room fell over the opening that had been there.

Testler eased out of his room wearing black soft-soled shoes, black jeans, and a down jacket with the collar turned up. And a black bucket hat down on his forehead. The office of his motel had been dark since a few minutes after he had checked in. The NO VACANCY sign, the only illumination other than floodlights at each end of the second floor that shone down and away from the rooms.

Testler walked quietly down the stairs, across the lot, and up the main drag. Then he turned onto the side street. When he got beside Charlie's Pontiac he stooped down as if to tie his shoe, and attached a magnetized small explosive inside the tire well of the front right tire. It was the only such device he had with him. The duffle in his trunk was in need of resupply. In the not too distant future he needed to get to one of his rental storage units to resupply. The modest blow he had placed under Charlie's car would appear to be an unfortunate malfunction. But it would be enough to disengage the steering control over the right tire and likely enough to remove that tire.

Fifteen minutes later, after having placed a small listening device next to the door to Charlie's room, Testler was back in his own room. In the chair by the window, the drapes parted, still clothed, with his binoculars in his lap, the listening receiver in his ear, asleep. He had learned long ago to sleep on assignments wherever he could, under whatever conditions existed, never knowing when the next opportunity might come.

Sometime later, he didn't immediately know how much later, except that instinctively he knew the moon had moved a distance in the sky, he heard Charlie's motel room door open. He raised the binoculars to his eyes. Charlie was a bulky man with thick thighs and a bull neck above broad shoulders. The man coming out of the room was a thin piece of fibrous tissue, Bobby Vargas.

Bobby moved quietly toward Linda's car where he used a car-jacking tool inserted along the glass window to snag and disengage the locking mechanism. When Bobby opened the door, the car stayed dark. Linda had apparently switched the dome light off. Testler smiled, Linda had good instincts.

Bobby got inside and pulled the door most of the way closed. A moment later, Testler's binoculars picked up the glow from a small handheld light. After a few more minutes, Bobby left the car, relocking the door and returned to his room. Testler now took time to look at his watch: three in the morning. He closed his drapes and got into bed, the listening device still in his ear.

~

Testler woke before his alarm went off, a backup to his internal clock which had never yet failed him. He parted the drapes and looked down to the next block and across the street. Linda's car had not moved, neither had Bobby's which meant that Charlie's Pontiac would still be on the side street. Right then the low rising sun sliced between two mountain peaks to the east to quickly fill Weed with its light and promise of later warmth. For now the outside temperature was controlled by the cold mist that visits in the early morning just after dawn.

Testler got up immediately, showered, shaved and put on clean clothes. When traveling, he tried to avoid encounters with people. Still, he dressed to present himself as a quiet, clean-cut tourist.

At five-thirty, Testler bought a USA Today out of the vending machine before walking inside the white-painted brick coffee shop. The street-front side and back walls were lined with booths. The counter fronted by swivel chairs occupied by diners rewarded with views of the inner workings of the restaurant. He took a booth at the turn from the side to the back wall from which he could watch the entire establishment. A middle-aged waitress brought a cheese omelette, toast and coffee a few minutes after he ordered it. He immediately put ten dollars on the table in case he needed to leave fast.

Twenty minutes later, through the large glass window at the side of the lobby, Testler watched Bobby Vargas coming toward the diner. Bobby, who had been in the Army but never in a war, looked more accountant than fighting man. He wore blue jeans and a gray sweatshirt in the cool morning mountain air. He scratched his head, without concern for further disrupting his sleep hairdo. His arms went up while he yawned. Then he pulled open the door and entered.

Testler held the newspaper covering most of his face, but Bobby didn't look around. Something a fighting man, particularly a Special Forces type would never fail to do. Bobby ordered something standing next to the register. Then he sat on the Naugahyde bench until the waitress motioned to him. After paying, Bobby left with a large coffee in one hand, and a big soda cup held atop a bag into which a counter person had deposited two mountain-man sized cinnamon rolls. Testler motioned for his waitress, ordered a cinnamon roll to go, and put a five on top of his ten.

Ryan watched from the lot of his motel while Linda got gas at a station across from the motel. After Linda pulled out of the station, Charlie and Bobby pulled in and gassed up. Then they rushed up the road toward the entrance back onto I-5 South. Finally Ryan filled the tank on his car and went the same way. For a while after leaving the station, Charlie and Bobby would be unable to keep visual contact with Linda. Her options were only north or south on I-5 or stay in Weed. She had come from the north, so south made sense until they got her back in sight. The electronic track Ryan had on Linda's car let him know she had in fact gone south. He also guessed that Bobby might have seen something in Linda's car the night before that told him she would be going south.

For the next half hour, Testler followed Bobby's Impala while mostly looking past the Impala to watch Charlie's Pontiac, the tail car closest to Linda's car.

Testler could no longer deny his interest in Linda Darby had become more than what it was in the beginning, an uncomplicated desire not to kill an innocent bystander. She was bright and personable. There were many women with these qualities, but Linda was somehow different. He had never lived with a woman, well, not for more than a few days, never shared a lasting, serious relationship with a woman. Yet he found himself wondering how it would be to live with this particular woman. Live as a normal couple, with her not on the run and him out of the intelligence game. Hell, the truth was he had left the intelligence game when he began taking big gobs of Webster's money in return for allowing the man to convert him into a blackmailer and assassin.

His study and surveillance of Linda told him that after her divorce and relocation to Sea Crest, she had become a bit of a recluse. But since this ordeal began she had shown some signs of coming out of her malaise, of regaining her self confidence. She was mature enough to have had the experiences that make a full woman, yet still at an age to have the perfections and flawlessness of a younger woman. Her running on the beach had kept her tush and tummy tight and her legs sculpted. He admitted to his growing interest in her, but wondered if that interest was a sufficient reason to put his own life at risk. Not to mention ending the lucrative income he received from Webster. He simply didn't know that answer, not yet anyway, and time was crowding him. He had to decide, and soon. He needed some time with Linda. And for that he needed to get Charlie and Bobby out of the picture.

As their small caravan climbed higher into the mountains of northern California the road alternated between inside curves hugging the mountain and outside curves with sharp drop offs to the right.

Other than the road itself, the area was very primitive. Large trees, mostly pines dotted the uphill side and jumped the road to pick up again on the downhill side. In some of the side canyons, small streams tumbled down to disappear under the highway to reemerge and continue their race down the canyon wall. At other places, the water was not a stream, or even a trickle, but simply rocks wetted by seepage from some ancient underground river. There were also points where the water accumulated to trail along the side of the road the way that sprinkler runoff followed the curb gutter in suburban neighborhoods.

When the road periodically wandered to the right, Testler could see beyond the next bend and the one after that. The farthest portion ahead appeared promising, perhaps just what he needed, a turn without a guardrail. He moved closer to the Impala. Then, when the center striping and traffic allowed, he held his hand to his face and scratched the stubble on his cheek while passing Bobby in the Impala. The incompetent didn't even look over. Testler didn't like being between Charlie and Bobby, but on these winding mountain roads he needed to position the radio-frequency remote closer to Charlie's Pontiac.

The four cars drove another mile or so before Testler confirmed he had seen the perfect spot, a section of road just beyond Charlie's Pontiac that eased itself to the right just before a dramatic switchback to the left. With the Pontiac about a hundred yards short of the farthest out point, Testler pressed the remote in his right hand. An instant later, a small explosion blew the right front tire free of the dark Pontiac.

The tire rolled over the edge and Charlie's Pontiac soared after it. It would not be the soaring that killed Charlie, but the sudden stop at the end.

CHAPTER 36

*I*n his rearview mirror, Testler watched Bobby jam on his brakes and skid to a stop just past the edge where Charlie's car had taken flight. Testler pulled to the shoulder beyond Bobby's Impala and walked back to where Bobby stood on the ledge looking down into the canyon. With his movements covered by the sounds of passing traffic Testler moved right up behind Bobby.

He bunched the thinner man's windbreaker in his fist. "Don't turn around, Bobby Vargas, or you'll be joining Charlie."

"Who are you? How do you know me?"

"Not important. Stay like you are." Testler brought his hand to his mouth and spoke as if talking into a cell phone, "When I walk away keep Vargas in your crosshair. If he turns to look at me, shoot. He'll drop into the canyon. If he behaves, after I've driven around the next bend, leave him be. Understood? ... Good."

Testler simulated putting the cell phone back in his pocket, then again spoke to Bobby. "Last night late, you went into Linda Darby's car. You stayed there a few minutes. What were you looking at?"

"How do you know about that?"

"Not important. Answer me. What did you find in her car?"

"A map."

"Of what?"

"The western states."

"Go on. I don't have the time for twenty questions."

"She had two places circled. Las Vegas and some place in Arizona ... Sedona. Yeah. Sedona."

"What else?"

"Nothing else. I mean, an empty coffee cup, a pair of sunglasses. Just shit. That's it."

"Did you hear me on the cell phone?"

"Yes."

"Tell me what you're going to do."

"Not move, man. Not move. But how will I know when you've rounded the next bend?"

"You can hear the cars going by. Count them. When you get to a hundred, it'll be okay to turn around."

"Yeah. Yeah. That's good. Sure. One hundred, I can do that."

"One more thing, who did Charlie work for?"

"Search me. I don't know. Really I don't. Charlie never told me shit."

"Thank Charlie. He just saved your life. Go home, Bobby. Get out of this business. You're no good at it. It'll get you killed."

Testler got back in his car, downshifted hard, stomped on the gas pedal to squeeze back into the traffic, leaving two exclamations of rubber to cool on the dry black pavement.

After reaching the highest speed he dare go without attracting attention, he tried the RF receiver, but Linda Darby's car was too far ahead on this winding road. For now, the interstate offered no viable alternatives for Linda. He would pick up what distance he could without attracting the attention of any cops. Hopefully, if he gained some miles, by the time they got out of the mountains his receiver would hear from her transmitter.

∾

Later that day, after driving through the twin cities of Marysville-Yuba City, not far north of Sacramento, Testler again turned on his receiver. He got no response, but decided to leave it on. He had no better plan so he stayed with what he had decided earlier. Continue south, keeping the speedometer at no more than five miles above the posted speed limit.

As he drove, he kept track of the passing traffic on the off chance Linda had decided to turn around and backtrack north. If she did, the RF receiver would report when she got into its range. To this point, Linda's movements had all seemed thought out so he could think of no reason she would veer off onto one of the crossing state or county roads. Not if Vegas was her destination. This meant the lack of a radio frequency reading could only be the result of too much distance for the transmitter on her car and the receiver in his to share their electronic banter. He put two pieces of spearmint gum in his mouth and turned on the radio. Eventually, she would stop to sleep at a roadside motel or in her car at a rest stop. When she did, he would hear the familiar pinging.

It was nearly eleven, California time, when Ryan decided to call Webster's secure phone in his Virginia home where it would be two in the morning.

"It's me. Hope I didn't wake you."

"No," Webster said. "What's the latest from Sea Crest?"

"Nothing. Like I told you, Chief McIlhenny has let it be known he's going fishing Tuesday, that still looks like our best plan. I'm set, just restless. Have you heard from Charlie? Is he still hanging on the woman's tail?"

"He called this morning," Webster said. "She spent last night in a motel in some Godforsaken place called Weed, California. Where in hell did these pioneers come up with the God-awful names they pinned on some of these jerkwater towns? Anyway, Charlie got into her car last night while she was sleeping and, on the front seat, he found a western states map with two cities circled: Las Vegas, Nevada, and Sedona, Arizona. When he called this morning, she

DAVID BISHOP

was on the road south. He figured Las Vegas to be her next
destination. I told him to stay on her and check in with me when
they got to Vegas or sooner if something changed."

"Why don't I fly over to Vegas," Testler suggested, "and see if
I can find her? I don't need to be here in Sea Crest now. In fact,
that would be better. I could slip back in early Tuesday before the
sun comes up, take care of McIlhenny and be out of town with the
locals unaware I had come back."

"Let me think on that," Webster said. "I'm going to catch some
sleep, then I'll call Charlie. After that, I'll call you. In retrospect, I
should have let him take her in Weed. I still don't like this hanging
back until next week."

"Relax, Mr. Webster. We're on the best course. Why don't I
head over to Vegas?"

"No. I want you there in case McIlhenny goes weird on us. In
any event, hold off until I talk to Charlie after I wake up. Either
way, I'll call you in six hours."

Ryan hung up knowing that Webster had no more information
about Linda than what Ryan had learned from Bobby Vargas,
which meant, with Charlie eliminated and Bobby scared off,
Webster was now totally dependent upon Testler for information.

It happened with Sacramento in Testler's rearview mirror and
the flatter central valley of California ahead. A solo ping, then, a
moment later, another, quickly followed by a steady rhythm. He
smiled at the thought of his receiver as the female chastising her
man with the message men so often heard from their women: you
could have at least called.

Over the next few miles the ping continued steadily. Then he
saw a sign: rest stop three miles. He pulled in and found Linda's
car headed into a parking space, unoccupied unless she was lying
over onto the seat, asleep. He looked about and saw her on foot
weaving her way through the black, metal barbeques and concrete
picnic tables randomly placed around a central building that
housed the restrooms.

Testler parked about ten spaces south of her car and took the opportunity to go to the men's room. He hadn't pissed all day, but he hadn't drank anything either. When he got back to his car, he opened a bottle of water and ate the cinnamon roll he had brought from Weed, also a Snickers bar from his glove box. A half hour later he decided Linda had gone to sleep. He reversed his car's direction so he was backed in. This position had him facing east so the rising sun would strike his face, waking him before Linda woke as her car was parked head-in, putting the morning sun at her back. He pulled his hat down and tugged his collar up, crossed his arms, and fell asleep in minutes.

The sun woke Testler at six A.M. He got out of his car at the rest stop, tugged his hat low and, with his head down, walking with a feigned limp passed close enough to Linda's car to determine she was still asleep behind the wheel. Next, he headed for the men's room to satisfy man's primal need to piss soon after waking.

Back in his car, while he waited for Linda to head out, his phone rang.

"Testler. I haven't heard from Charlie. His phone is not working. I need you to get on over to Vegas. Find them. I don't know what's happened to Charlie and his man. You might need to handle this dame yourself."

"Like always, whatever it takes. I'm on my way, sir."

Testler hung up and smiled. And you won't be hearing from Charlie, Mr. Webster. It will take the local authorities days to get to Charlie's Pontiac and when they do they won't be unable to identify him, at least not for a long while.

Twenty minutes later, he watched Linda go and come from the ladies room. After that he followed her back onto I-5. They had about ten hours of driving to reach Las Vegas.

CHAPTER 37

*A*t seven-thirty-two P.M. precisely, Testler followed Linda into the blacktopped canyon of neon signs and walls of glass known as the Las Vegas strip. No city slept, at least not like people sleep. But cities do turn their lights down and rest in their own way during the wee hours. That is, cities other than Las Vegas. Vegas is never asleep. The lights, the glitz, the winners, the losers, the live entertainers who work on their feet and those who work on their backs, all go nonstop. They say that what happens in Vegas stays in Vegas. That was certainly true for money, most of which stayed in Vegas. Money was the grease that kept all the necessary wheels turning to provide what the folks came to Vegas to do, escape from or cheat on their routine lives.

Ten minutes later, Linda pulled into the lot for the MGM Grand.

Testler liked her choice. The large crowds and greater security which came complete with cameras and guards everywhere would lessen the chances of someone trying to capture her or possibly remove her from the hotel.

Linda parked as close as she could to the entrance of the MGM Grand casino and entered. She had not slept much the night before and needed at least a short nap. After paying cash at the desk for one night she went up to a Jr. suite where she set the alarm for one hour then slipped under the soft sheets and let herself go.

Linda woke to the sounds of four lanes of traffic and the shrill cry of an ambulance. She wanted to stay right where she was, but she hadn't eaten a solid meal in more than twenty-four hours. After showering, she dressed in a pair of black slacks and a matching tank top with a silver chain belt and heels, high but not too high.

She walked through the casino, stopping to look at the posters for the lead attraction, David Copperfield, and for the Crazy Horse Paris show. Along the way, she watched waves of winners and losers darting in and out from the slots and tables like hobbled prey retreating but not escaping the relentless lure of the mechanical wolves who smelled the blood on their wallets. Then she walked into the Grand's Nob Hill Tavern where she first ordered a glass of white wine. After the wine arrived, she ordered a Maine Lobster Pot Pie that came with baby vegetables.

"Hello, Linda. It's nice to see you again."

Her head snapped up as she turned toward the voice. "Ahab."

Testler laughed softly. "Yes. Ahab. May I join you for dinner?"

"Where did you come from? ... Can't you just leave me alone?"

"Now don't be ungrateful. If I had left you alone ... well, you don't want to know what would have happened. Leave it to say that we wouldn't be here having dinner together."

"How long have you been with me?"

"Always."

"What does always mean?"

"Not important. I'm here now. You're safe. Let's just have a nice dinner?"

The waiter approached. "Will you be joining the lady for dinner?" He held a table setting for one more.

"Yes," Testler said. The waiter started placing the setting on the table then stopped when Linda said, "No. The gentleman is leaving."

"Give us a minute, please," Testler said, handing the waiter a twenty.

After the waiter left, Ryan leaned close to Linda. "If I had not been with you in Weed, the night before last, you could have been taken by the two men who followed you. They are no longer a threat. You were again vulnerable while you slept in your car at the rest stop last night, south of Sacramento. I watched over you."

"How do you know all this?"

"I'll tell you over dinner." Testler motioned for the waiter standing about twenty feet away, still holding the place setting.

The waiter came over, hesitated, and looked at Linda. She nodded. He set the placing on the table and left. Testler snapped his fingers. The waiter did an about face.

"Has the lady ordered?"

"Yes."

"I'll have the same thing, exactly the same."

The waiter left and a moment later another member of the wait staff stopped to fill his water glass.

"For starters," Linda said, "I'm tired of you smirking every time I call you Ahab. So what's your name?"

"You can call me Ryan. And what should I call you? Linda? Nora Larick? Carol Benson? Who are you tonight?"

"You think this is just one big game, don't you?"

"There are elements of a game. But a deadly, serious game, I admit."

"Is Ryan your real name?"

"Not important. It's all you need."

"Did anyone ever tell you that your habit of avoiding questions and saying 'not important' is rude and annoying?"

"Not important."

"All right then, Ryan. Tell me about all of it. You said you would over dinner."

"Dinner isn't here yet."

"Start now," she said, downing the last of her Sauvignon blanc.

"Where should I begin? Okay. There is this man. Cynthia's letters told you his name. So, Alistair Webster used your friend Cynthia to gather information he then used to leverage certain government officials into altering their normal regulatory processes according to the interests of his paying clients."

"What is your role in all this?"

When Ryan caught the waiter's eye, he moved his index finger back and forth between Linda's empty wine glass and his own. The waiter nodded.

"You still haven't told me which name you are using here at the hotel. My guess is you're registered as Nora Larick. Correct?"

"What makes you think that?"

"You're a smart lady buying your stocks and bonds, but you're in my market now. The car Cynthia left for you is registered to Larick. I figure you'd figure it would be best if your hotel registration matched the car registration. You'd also elect to get comfortable with one persona, reserving the others for the banks and other special needs."

"Damn you. You make all my planning seem infantile."

"To the contrary, you are actually doing quite well for a novice. You were particularly effective dispatching the man who came for you in Sea Crest. That took talent and a cool head. I'm proud of you."

"You know about that?"

"Until now, I wasn't certain."

The waiter brought Linda a fresh wine and Ryan a first one. When the waiter started to leave, Ryan grabbed his arm, gulped down his glass of wine and ordered a dry martini with a pearl onion. "You mean a Gibson, sir?" asked the waiter. "Yes," Ryan answered. The waiter left.

"As I was saying, you are actually doing quite well. But we only die once. You saved yourself that one time in the surf. I've saved you twice. It would certainly be easier if we worked closer together. Doing that would also increase my chances of being near you at the right time."

"I'm not going to tell you my plans."

"Oh, come on, Linda. You're here to open another bank deposit box to leave more cash and diamonds. Then you're off to Sedona, Arizona, to do the same thing."

"How do you know the towns I've chosen?"

"Your problem isn't my knowing. It's that the two men who followed you out of Seattle, who stayed a few rooms away from you in Weed, and then followed you this morning, they knew."

"I saw no one."

"That's the point. But don't worry. They're no longer of any concern."

"Did you kill them?"

Ryan smiled. "Not important. What is important is that the man Cynthia told you about in her letter, the man by whom I'm employed, knows you're here in Vegas and that your next stop is Sedona."

The food came. "That's enough for now. You're safe with me. Let's just relax and enjoy our meal. Just figure, I'm one of the men you used to meet in the cocktail lounges outside of Sea Crest."

"That's what this is about? You saved my life, so I should fuck you. Is that it?"

The couple at the next table turned toward them.

"Unless you desire to do a foursome, I see no reason to bring that man and woman into our conversation. Now, should you prefer a threesome, I suggest the woman sitting alone at the table near the wall, the lady in the red dress with the wonderful cleavage."

Linda sat clenching her napkin, staring into her plate. When she looked up, she calmly asked, "So you figure I'm some kind of whore because I went looking to get laid by strangers?"

"No. You're a woman who had talked herself into being afraid of life, but still had needs."

"I ask again. You figure you're entitled to a good roll in the hay because of having saved me?"

"If I just wanted to get laid, I could have let my two men in the alley finish you off that first night. Gotten paid, quite handsomely, I might add, and then headed here to Vegas to blow off steam with a couple of the town's best lady escorts."

"So, what is it you want?"

"For you to eat your dinner, this pot pie is delicious. You haven't started yours. Eat. You need your strength."

Linda picked up her fork and broke the pastry crust on her pot pie. "This is all so crazy. I mean, Cynthia told me nothing. Nothing! I have no idea beyond what she put in her letter and what you have told me tonight."

"I believe you, but that's of no consequence. The man wants you dead once I'm convinced you've told no one anything. If you have, I'm to handle them in the same manner."

"And that leaves me where?" Linda asked.

"Bottom line: whether you knew it before or not, you now know Webster's identity. That alone is enough to have him order you dead. You also could tell the authorities what Cynthia's company did for him, and how he used that information. So he will never rescind his order for you to be eliminated."

"Eliminated! What a polite word. You mean murdered, don't you?"

"Yes. I mean murdered."

"So what do we have here? Is this the condemned woman's last meal?"

"If I were going to kill you, I would not be here at your table. People have seen us together. I would strike without warning and without anyone being able to put us together in any manner."

"Here in Vegas?"

"The principle applies wherever it would be done."

"So I should expect to die when I get to Sedona?"

"Look. I'm not going to kill you. At least I don't think so."

"Well, isn't that reassuring? And, if I take you back to my room and fuck your brains out, then my chances go up, right?"

"Whether or not we have sex has no bearing on whether or not I kill you. One is business. The other is pleasure. But, as long as we are on the subject, your attitude is making it clear the odds of you surviving tonight are much higher than my odds of being seduced. Sad as I am to say it."

"I guess that gives me some comfort. My God, this is the strangest conversation I have ever had."

"Me, too. I think you're a real pistol, Linda Darby. I'm very impressed with your composure."

"You can't see me on the inside."

The waiter came toward them. Ryan waved him off and said, "Keep eating."

Linda took another bite, then pushed her plate toward the center of the table and lifted her wine glass. "So what do we do now?"

"No one is on your trail at the moment. Relax. Consider it a night off."

"No one except for the man who finds me everywhere. The man who might at any moment just up and decide to kill me for his own financial gain."

Ryan shrugged. "You're safe for now. I propose we sleep in. Neither of us has had a good night's sleep in a few days. Then tomorrow you go ahead and get your banking done. Then we head for Sedona. Only this time we travel together."

"What the hell difference does the banking make? If you're going to kill me, the money and diamonds become irrelevant."

"True. But then, if you're dead, it matters not whether you've put them in the bank. So, I suggest you proceed as if I'm not going to kill you."

"It appears I have your promise not to kill me while we're in Vegas. Is that right?"

"All of Nevada actually."

"Then what's stopping me from yelling for hotel security and the local police."

"You can if you wish. But you will accomplish nothing other than to damage yourself."

"And how would that hurt me?"

"You're still thinking like a law-abiding citizen, which you are no longer. You're here using an alias so your fingerprints and your ID will not check out. I could suggest they make inquiry with the authorities in Sea Crest about a dead guy found in their surf. That's without mentioning that you have a wad of cash and diamonds with you for which you cannot account. As for me, my credentials would check out just fine. I would be released, and you would be bound over as a ... person of interest in a homicide, and held for Chief Ben McIlhenny's arrival."

Linda's eyes confirmed Ryan had checkmated her threat.

"Why don't I buy you a drink in the Crazy Horse?" he said. "The show begins in ten minutes. You'll fit right in."

He took her arm as they left the Nob Hill restaurant and walked through the casino.

In the Crazy Horse they were waited on by a handsome, older woman with gray hair swept atop her head like a pewter crown. Ryan ordered two Gibsons and a white wine for Linda.

When the show was about half over, she leaned toward Ryan. "What did you mean that I'd fit right in?"

"This show is a sexy celebration of the beauty and grace of the feminine form. Your body's at least as delicious as any on the stage."

"You're a rather straightforward man."

"Do you mind?"

"No. I guess not."

"Good."

As they stepped out of the elevator an hour later, he handed her one of his room keys. "I'm three doors down from you, on the same side of the hall, if you get scared, let yourself in."

"But you said I was safe."

"You are, but the invitation is open."

"Fat chance."

CHAPTER 38

"*S*enator Abernathy, what are your plans now that you are retiring from the U.S. Senate after thirty-six years?"

"I'll be taking the little woman here back to Texas where I've bought us a nice spread outside San Antonio. I surely am ready for some quiet living for a change."

"And will your ranking member of the committee take over as chair?"

"I recommended him, endorsed him as you asked me to do. I used some of your money leftover in my campaign account to encourage the leadership to support him. It's in the bag."

Webster's bodyguard, Victor, subbing for the house staff who had been given the night off, approached Webster's guests holding a crystal cognac decanter in one hand, the stopper in the other. The senator extended his snifter. Victor poured to the normal one-third line. Mrs. Abernathy placed her hand over her glass.

"Have you got enough funds for your plans?" Webster asked. "We can't be having a former Senator living beneath his stature, now, can we?"

"Thanks to your generosity, Mr. Webster, over the years, I've salted away plenty. We'll be just fine, with more than enough left over for Theresa here to continue in luxury after I'm gone. We both thank you for this wonderful Persian tapestry you've given us tonight. It will be displayed prominently in the house on our ranch."

"That's so kind of you, Senator."

Senator Abernathy lowered his head in deference to Alistair Webster. Then quickly drank the balance of his cognac, sat his glass on the side table and rose. "Come, my dear. We've taken enough of our host's evening."

Theresa Abernathy stood, and then coaxed her dress down until it rested just above her knee. She stepped around the table, and hugged Webster while whispering in his ear. "Thank you, for bringing me the truth." Webster's hand squeezed her buttock. She didn't pull away.

"Senator, let me walk you to your car." Then Webster turned to Victor. "Will you carry out the tapestry? Use a big sheet of plastic to line the Senator's trunk. We wouldn't want anything to soil this lovely piece." Then Webster turned back to the Senator. "If you'll give Victor your keys, he'll put the tapestry in your trunk?" The Senator did so.

Victor, carrying the rolled tapestry under his arm, walked out first and opened the trunk.

When the others got outside and walked to the back of the senator's Cadillac, they saw that the plastic liner was large enough that it filled the trunk and wrapped out over the sides and front of the trunk.

The senator also noticed that the tapestry lay on the ceramic circle drive. When he turned toward Webster with a puzzled expression, Victor pushed the Senator into the trunk.

"What the hell is this all about?" demanded Senator Abernathy. Then he saw the gun in Webster's hand. "This is not funny. Not one damn bit." The senator said while struggling to raise himself from the trunk.

Webster stepped closer to the old man and touched the gun barrel to his neck. "Stay where you are, Senator Abernathy."

The senator released his grip on the trunk ledge, his behind sinking down inside, his feet sticking out into the air.

"Why?" the senator demanded, "after all I've done for you."

"And I shall be eternally grateful. No member of congress has done more."

"Then why? Why?"

"Once you've left the senate, you'll get pushed for some book deal. And the juicier the content, the bigger the advance they'll offer. You drink too much, and you talk too much when you drink, and I know better than anyone that you'll do anything for money. There is simply no return for the risk of leaving you alive."

Senator Abernathy sagged back in defeat.

Theresa Abernathy stepped up beside Webster. "Please. Let me."

Webster handed the gun to the senator's much younger and socially-graced trophy wife.

While this exchange had taken place, Victor had stepped back, drawn a gun himself, and moved into the shadow of the cover of the portico.

"What are you doing?" the senator screamed. "Why are you doing this, Theresa?"

"I'm going to shoot you, you son of a bitch."

"Why?"

"I'm not going to live in some dusty Texas town. I'm going to stay right here. This is where I belong."

"Then we'll stay here, Peaches. We can live wherever you prefer. Our house here hasn't sold yet. We'll just take it off the market."

"Not good enough. I want to watch you die. I want to do it. I want to watch your life drain from your decrepit body."

"I've given you everything you ever wanted. More than you ever imagined."

"Most of which having been made possible by our host, Mr. Alistair Webster. I will remain in D.C., the widow of the great

Senator Abernathy, giving dinner parties and hosting charity events. You're done with it. I'm not."

"We can do all that. Together."

"I suppose while you keep carrying on with your hookers. No. I'm through being humiliated."

"None of that ever touched you. I kept it under wraps. I protected you from it."

"You protected your own reputation is what you did. But everyone knew, and I carried the shame. The regular visits to the doctor to be sure I hadn't gotten infected as a result of your fucking around. When you're no longer a senator, the high caliber whores won't bother with you. After that you'll be reduced to cruising for street walkers. You're nothing but a Texas alley cat."

While the accusations and pleadings continued, Webster eased back to the porch next to Victor. When Theresa Abernathy turned and saw that Victor had a gun trained on her, Webster spoke.

"You know how I want this to play out, but it's up to you. It's time, my dear."

She turned back to face her husband who had seemingly grown smaller in the trunk, sapped of his own pomposity.

Webster pressed a remote turning on the hidden security camera that filmed outwardly from his portico.

Theresa Abernathy fired, then laughed, then fired again, then laughed again, and again, stopping only after the gun had emptied.

Webster hit the off button on the remote, turning off the camera. Then he said, "Give the gun to Victor, my dear. He'll dispose of it."

The widow Abernathy did as Webster had instructed. Victor placed the gun in a plastic bag, checked Senator Abernathy to confirm he was dead and gave the plastic bag to Webster.

The widow Abernathy, no longer laughing, sagged. Her arms dangled at her sides. Her knees began to buckle. Victor slapped her across the face.

"Get in the car, Ms. Abernathy," Victor said. "You'll drive. I want you to end up in the parking lot of the National Cathedral. I'll follow and bring you back here."

"Back here?" she said, speaking in a monotone, her face blank.

"Yes, Theresa," Webster said. "You and the late senator had joined me for dinner. His office had knowledge of the dinner engagement as well. I'm sure you recall that after dinner, your husband looked at his watch and said he had to meet someone. That he would be back. You and I and Victor had drinks and waited. He never returned. Later, we called the FBI, which we'll do after you and Victor return. Victor and I are your alibi. You were here with us."

"Put this jacket on," Victor said, holding it out for her to slip her arms into. "Now this hat and scarf. Wrap it around your neck. And, here, take these dark rimmed glasses, they're your prescription. Put on these gloves before you get in the car."

The widow looked at Victor with a puzzled expression, then slowly nodded and dressed as she had been told.

"Mrs. Abernathy," Webster said sharply. "Listen to Victor and do exactly what he tells you. Exactly. Are you listening to me?"

The widow nodded and turned to face Victor as he said, "You are to drive to the National Cathedral. You've been there many times, correct?" The widow nodded again. Victor continued. "Take Massachusetts and turn right onto Pilgrim Road. You are to park near the George Washington Equestrian Statue. Lock the car with the key and throw the key in the bushes. Cross the street and walk up the stairs to the south side of the Cathedral. I will pick you up there."

After Theresa Abernathy showed an inability to repeat the directions and instructions, Victor told her not to worry, that the glasses she now had on included a small speaker. That he would talk her through it. Theresa Abernathy got behind the wheel of her husband's black Cadillac. Victor pushed closed the driver's door with the smoke tinted glass. A moment later, she started the car and drove away without saying another word.

Victor followed, a short distance behind.

CHAPTER 39

*L*inda had slept without either setting the alarm or calling the front desk for a wake-up call. When her eyes opened, she rolled toward the clock radio: eight-fifteen. She had enjoyed the erotic show at the Crazy Horse Paris, and she had experienced dreams in which she had made love with a man. Her mind would not identify the man, but he was not her ex-husband.

By eight-forty-five she had showered, brushed and flossed, fussed with her hair just enough, and slipped into a pair of chocolate brown sweat pants and a lightweight white jersey with thin straps. No underwear. The polish on her toes was getting a bit worn, but she had no time for that now. She slipped on a pair of white sandals, the kind with a strap between the toes and picked up her purse, she wasn't about to leave all that cash in a hotel room, and the card key Ryan had given her.

Three doors he had said, on the same side of the hall. She raised her hand as if to knock, then shrugged and inserted the card key. He had said to come on in, and if she had the wrong room the door would not unlock.

Here goes.

The card worked.

Ryan sat on the corner of the bed with a cup of coffee in his hand. He was naked except for black boxers. A blonde was in his bed, propped upright against the numerous pillows the MGM Grand had left for such occasions. The sheet and comforter warmed her up to a point, just under her naked breasts.

The blonde raised her cup, smiled, and took a drink, without bothering to pull the bedcovers higher.

"You told me to come down if I was—oh, go to hell." Linda turned to leave.

Ryan's voice blunted against her back. "Linda. Don't go. Hey. Come on."

The room door closed on her second, *go to hell*.

Thirty minutes later, Linda heard a knock on her door. She squinted to look through the peephole. As she expected, it was Ryan. She pulled on a matching chocolate brown sweatshirt and opened the door.

"What do you want?" she asked, standing with her arms crossed below her breasts.

Ryan came in. "What are you so mad about?"

"If you don't know, I can't tell you."

"Come on," he said, taking a seat on the edge of her bed. "You made it clear you had no interest. And, you have to admit, the Crazy Horse show was very inspiring."

Linda sat on the opposite corner of the bed, her arms still crossed. "She was the blonde in the red dress. The one you pointed out in the restaurant."

"After you were safely in your room, I went back to the bar. She was still there. I almost called your room to see if you wanted to join us. She was willing, but after you were so uptight and disinterested in our even being a twosome—" He left his words to trail off.

"I don't do threesomes."

"Only even numbers? How about foursomes?"

"Oh, go to hell."

"Undoubtedly I will. I'm just hoping it won't be soon." Ryan broke her cold stare. "Were you coming down ... to take me up on my offer?"

"Go to hell, Ryan Testler ... or whatever your real name is."

"Lighten up. I know your vocabulary is broader than just go to hell. Talk to me. Are you angry with me for my having acted normally or yourself for not having been honest the night before?"

"I don't know. You I think. Both I guess."

"I wish I had known you were coming. I would have preferred to be with you."

"That's supposed to make me feel better?"

"I don't begin to know that answer. I can tell you that missing out being with you made her the consolation prize."

Linda started to smile, and then fought it back. "Get out of here. I need to get cleaned up. I've got some banking to do. Give me an hour."

"Come by my room," Ryan said.

"Will *she* still be there?"

No. She won't. She's already gone. I'll go with you, and wait outside the bank."

While waiting for Linda, Ryan carried a small bag down to his car and used it to pack the RF receiver along with a few weapons. Then he went to the Dollar-Rent-A-Car desk in the Grand and returned the keys to his rental car. They would continue on in Linda's car which had the RF transmitter just in case she ditched him somehow.

By noon, they drove out of Vegas south on Highway-93. "We'll be in Sedona for dinner," he said, "It's less than three hundred miles."

Linda nodded, but continued looking forward.

"Have you forgiven me for last night?" Ryan asked. "Well, this morning I guess it was. You know."

"I don't have anything to forgive you for." Linda's tone belied her words. "You got turned on. You got laid. It's none of my business."

"It was your fault, you know."

CHAPTER 40

*J*t was twilight when they rounded a bend and drove into the Oak Creek area south of Sedona. The red rock blending with the area's white sandstone made the real look lovelier and more dramatic than the pictures Linda had seen. With its creek beds, pines and the aromatic juniper, Linda imagined the area looked and smelled much as it had a thousand years ago. That is except for the commercial developments that were needed to support the local population and the heavy year around influx of tourists.

After a short drive, Ryan turned left on Highway 89-A for a distance, then got out of the car and walked into the office of the Kokopelli Inn in the part of Sedona known as new town.

"One room," he said getting back into Linda's car, "with two beds. That way, I won't need to stay awake to guard you."

"Didn't your blond bimbo satisfy you?" she asked while Ryan moved the car nearer the room he had rented.

"The room has two queen beds," he said. "You'll decide how many we use."

"I'm hungry," she said, "you?"

"Sure," he said while unlocking the door. "You like meat?"

"What, something you don't already know about me?" Linda tossed her carry bag onto the bed nearest the bathroom.

"The only time we ate together you had lobster and it made you cranky."

"I wasn't cranky."

They looked around. Linda pulled open the drapes over the window that looked back out to the parking lot.

"You certainly fooled me." Ryan said, after he tossed his bag on the other bed.

"Okay," Linda said. "Let's get this on the table. A woman goes to a man's hotel room and finds another babe in his bed, flashing her tits. What woman wouldn't get angry?"

"You know, your talk turns a bit saucy when you're mad. Still, I understand. It won't happen again on this trip. I promise."

"Did you practice safe sex?"

"I find it encouraging that you want to know."

"Oh, go to hell."

"Yes I did, practice safe sex. I take excellent care of my body. In my line of work, it's important."

"Do you have ideas on where we should eat?" she asked.

"There's a really cool place in old town, The Cowboy Club. It's been there forever. I heard John Wayne used to eat there. Also Jimmy Stewart while they were filming *Broken Arrow* just outside of town. They serve buffalo, if you like that, as well as other more standard fare."

"Give me a few minutes to freshen up."

"I'll take a walk." Ryan left the room.

He had wanted to look around anyway. To be sure they weren't being followed. He walked toward the highway looking for cars he might recognize or anyone behaving in a way that made him suspicious. He really didn't expect to. He was all but certain they were in a surveillance warp. No one working for Webster had any information except that they were likely headed for Vegas or Sedona. For anyone to find them now would only be sheer luck. Besides, Webster had no one else to send. Not unless he assigned his bodyguards which he had never done before. Webster was likely sitting tight, waiting for his call from Vegas. Testler turned and headed back toward the room where Linda was dressing for dinner. As he came around the corner of the motel, he walked into a gusting desert breeze tossing loose papers and sandy grit. He lowered his head and pinched his eyes nearly closed.

Linda had dressed in a modestly short, red-white-and blue dress with a pair of red open-toed heels. But her eyes looked the best, lightly made up on the outside, with the real magic coming from inside, open, honest, intelligent eyes.

"One of my Carol Benson outfits." she said, slowly turning in a circle. "Carol is the most sensual of my alter egos."

"And which of your aliases most closely matches Linda Darby?"

"You behave yourself, you might just find out."

CHAPTER 41

*A*t the Cowboy Club, Ryan ordered white wine for Linda and for himself a double martini.

"A Martini?" Linda asked when the waiter moved away, "you drank Gibsons in Vegas?"

"Lots of people order martinis, Gibsons are uncommon. Sedona is much smaller than Vegas. I don't want to be remembered."

Linda shook her head. "I'm learning all the time."

Ryan smiled. "If you don't wish to be noticed, don't do anything to be noticed. Every business has its ins and outs."

"That woman," Linda said, "the blonde in Vegas, wasn't she a bit young?"

"She was thirty-two, not all that much younger than you."

"I see," Linda said. "I suppose you could tell her age from her fake boobs?"

"It's a gift, what can I tell ya."

"And it's your judgment that I'm older?"

"Yes. But I like older women."

"Oh."

"I meant that as a compliment."

"And how does, you're an older woman become a compliment?"

"Older women laugh when something is funny. So many younger women have this incessant need to giggle after everything they say, funny or not, as if the giggle was some form of punctuation. Then, after the giggle, they use a head flip or a hand to move their hair."

The waiter stopped to take their order. Linda chose a steak, Ryan a buffalo burger. He then told the waiter to immediately bring another round of drinks.

"Why do you drink so much?" Linda asked.

"To better stomach my fellow man."

"And women?"

"And women."

"And yourself?"

"Particularly myself."

"So, to go back to where we were before the waiter interrupted, I'm more appealing because I don't giggle?"

"In part, I guess. But, hey, give me a break here. In Vegas I was guilty of nothing more than you've done many times when you bar hopped looking for a man."

"Okay. Okay. I forgive you."

"Thank you. But the truth is there's nothing to forgive me for."

"Hey, leave me a little something. I was shocked to find you ... your bed occupied by any woman, let alone one you had pointed out as an example of female abundance."

"She had nothing on you."

"Yeah, right. I'm ordinary, maybe plus a little. That woman was huge. Too huge."

"She was 38-DD."

"You checked?"

"Well, her bra was lying around my room all morning. I pride myself on being a very good judge, so I confirm my opinion whenever possible."

"And I'm supposed to believe that?"

"Her bra was lying around all morning."

"You know what I mean. That you were right before you looked at the tag in her bra."

"All right, I accept your challenge. I got you pegged as 34-D"

"Another gift?"

"Same gift. Different judgment."

Their meals came and Ryan spent a minute lathering his buffalo burger in Thousand Island dressing which he had ordered on the side. After he cut the burger in half, he glanced up at Linda who was looking at his face.

"You have good eyes," she said. "Easy and gentle. You never look away, yet your stare isn't intense, and you seem to miss nothing."

"What you miss can get you killed. But, thank you."

After chewing her first bite, Linda asked, "You figure I'm still being followed?"

"Not counting me?"

"Not counting you."

"No. You aren't. Not at the moment. Webster has five men in his private security force. Me, Mr. Blue, the man you left in the Sea Crest surf, and Charlie, the one I took out just after you left Weed, California."

"I went all creepy when you told me that earlier. I never saw anyone."

"Actually, Charlie and his man followed you all the way from Sea Crest after you met with Chief McIlhenny."

"How do you know this?"

"Because I was following them while they were following you."

"They didn't spot you?"

"Their focus was forward toward you, not backward toward me."

"How did you take out this Charlie after we left Weed?"

"Not important."

Linda cut another bite from her rib-eye steak. Then she said, "I'm obviously not very good at this stuff."

"Would you like me to cut your steak for you?"

"Don't be a smart ass. I meant this stuff about knowing if you're being followed."

"Don't feel bad. We're pros. You're not."

"You said Webster has five men? You've mentioned three, you, Blue and Charlie."

"Webster thinks of me and Blue and Charlie as his security team. The other two work mostly as bodyguards."

"There's no one else?"

"There are others, but they don't know Webster's identity. They work for me or Charlie or Blue, although Blue mostly works alone. So when Charlie and Blue were eliminated, any others working for them were simultaneously split off from the herd."

"The two in the alley, they worked for you?"

"Yes."

"So you sent them after me. Then saved me from them?"

"Yes."

"Why send them if you were going to stop them?"

"It gets complicated."

"Uncomplicate it."

"I hadn't made up my mind. Okay? Not definitely anyway."

"Well. That's honest. Thank you. And especially thank you for having made up your mind to save me."

"You're welcome."

"Now, tell me about this Webster guy."

"Rich. Politically connected. A fixer. He takes money from big business and others and passes it on to some members of congress to get a loophole into the law, or to a regulator to not do their job. To look the other way or sign off on something that's supposed to have been prevented through the regulatory process. Think Bernie Madoff or the BP oil spill. I don't have any direct knowledge of those two specific instances, but it's the kind of thing I'm referring

217

to. Often regulations we think are designed to protect us, are really designed to bring money to those in power, political campaigns and the like. While the conned public, particularly those who think that more government is always the answer, sits back and thinks, oh, boy, they're protecting us. Then when the shit back-flushes on one of the paid-for favors, the politicians and regulators squeal that there isn't enough regulation or the regulators don't have enough funds. The public then demands more. The political process provides more and the result is there are more rules that one can buy their way around. Not always, but often, the real problem is not lack of new regulation, but lack of enforcement of existing regulation. Sometimes that is because congress fails to provide adequate funds. Satisfy the public clamor by creating regulations, then starve the charged agency so they can't staff adequately to enforce. Everyone uses names like lobbyists or special interests. Webster runs interference for his clients, saves them gobs of money and gets paid very well. But Cynthia's letter told you about that."

"And sometimes those efforts lead to people getting killed, assassinated. Is that when you and the others you mentioned come into play?"

"Sometimes, but mostly we set up situations, ah, temptations. Sex. Drugs. Gambling. Whatever our surveillance tells us will make a given regulator or member of congress vulnerable."

"And you're okay corrupting the system like that?"

"Don't be naive. We live in a day of collapsing institutions. The church. The government. The independence of the news media. The integrity of many major corporations. Even the discipline in the public school classroom. The altruism of medical care. All of it is putrefying."

"And what has replaced it?" Linda asked.

"The twin altars upon which all of it is sacrificed: votes and money. We don't have time to raise our children, to teach them to make their beds. Mow lawns. Share a family meal. We've surrendered our children to television, video games, cell phones and text messaging."

"Is it your contention that parents no longer love their children?"

"No, no. I'm not speaking of love, and obviously not speaking of all families, just that parents are human. Two parent households are carrying too many demands, even more so for one-parent households. To a large extent, they simply don't have enough time for their children. Something has to give. They make it work by surrendering their children to TV programs that largely foster the thought that adults know nothing. That other teens, not parents, have all the answers. Am I sounding cynical here?"

"Yes," Linda said, "and old fashioned I'd say. We can't go back to the world of Norman Rockwell. If in truth we ever lived in it."

"I agree, but am I wrong about the decay of Americana?"

"Not entirely."

"Even right and wrong has been replaced by legal and illegal. We no longer say I can't do that it's wrong. We say I can do that, it's perfectly legal."

"I agree with that point," Linda admitted, "as far as it goes, but to bring us back to the here and now, when all else fails, you murder people, or entire companies like Cynthia's."

"Bribery or blackmail is so effective, that murder is rarely needed. But sometimes one of our resources turns unstable, or one of them needs someone permanently removed. When we take care of those situations, we increase our control over those whose mess we cleaned up."

"And you can live with that?"

Ryan closed his eyes, took a deep breath, and put the second half of his burger back on his plate. "Look. I'm not one of the good guys."

"Apparently not. So, why me? I mean, why haven't you just ... killed me? Or why didn't you let your two goons in the alley finish me off that first night?"

"When I find that answer, I'll tell you."

"I suspect the answer has little to do with me," Linda said, "and much to do with you. Your drinking. The uncertainty you're feeling. I think you are one of the good guys, or that you once were. I think you're getting sick of no longer living as one of them."

"I'll admit it wasn't the work I expected when I signed on."

"You don't strike me as a man who would take a job without knowing what it was."

"I got introduced to Webster by a retired Special Forces commander and a member of the congressional committee with national security oversight. It was made to sound like intelligence work outside the government."

"Black ops," Linda said. "I've read about those."

"It's been called that. Subcontracted. Off the books stuff. Private security. Lots of names. But yeah, there is a good amount of intelligence and paramilitary work done by experts no longer directly employed by the CIA or the official military. It gives the government a measure of plausible deniability."

"But you eventually learned Webster wasn't part of even that."

"Affirmative, I mean, correct."

"Why did you stay in his employ?"

"Cynthia told you in her letter, money. Webster pays enough to buy your soul. Well, your convictions anyway. So, like Cynthia, I started thinking about how much longer I needed to do the work to fund a rest-of-my-life plan. Isn't that the American dream?"

"And you're not there yet?"

Right then the waiter came into view. "Did you two save some room for dessert?"

"No," they said as a duet. Then, before the waiter could leave, Ryan ordered another double Martini. Linda shook her head and said, "Not for me." The waiter left.

"And you've not yet funded this rest-of-your-life plan?" Linda repeated.

"Not all the way. No."

"And then I came along?"

"And then you came along."

"Why me? How did I tip over your greedy gravy train?"

"I don't know exactly. Maybe you were just one too many. Maybe any *next one* would have been one too many. But I don't think so. I think it's you in particular."

"I don't mean to push this, but, pleased as I am by it, I wonder why I'm the target you can't execute?"

"You're everything that represents America to me. I hope this doesn't sound ... well, too corny. I joined the military. I became a sniper and then worked counterintelligence, all of it as a wide-eyed adventure-seeking young man. Defend my country. Protect its people. All that patriotic mumbo jumbo. Over the years, it soured. I became more familiar with the inner workings, and my allegiance gradually swung from country to cash. When I personally had you under surveillance for a couple weeks, you became all the reasons we had started our military careers. If I kill you, I've killed who I'd like to be again. I've killed what I ever believed in."

CHAPTER 42

*L*inda lay beneath him, but not in surrender. She had welcomed him into her, taking her pleasure and, hopefully, giving as much in return. She had closed her eyes as she climaxed. Something she had always done since her divorce. But this time, unlike all the others, she had not seen her ex-husband's face. This time she had seen Clark Ryerson's face.

What am I doing? I've carefully avoided relationships. Now I'm experiencing one with Ryan and imagining a second with Clark. God protect me from me.

～

Ryan woke immediately when Linda did, her head on the bicep of his left arm. He put his nose into her hair. Despite the passing of the night and having made love, the fragrances of shampoo and soap remained, a clean smell. He longed that one day he could again think of himself as clean.

"Good morning, Linda," he said, "let me apologize for last night."

"What for?" Linda said, turning her face toward Ryan.

"I was out of line. You might have thought you had to make love with me because you needed my protection."

"You want us to forget it? It's forgotten."

"I didn't mean to take advantage of you."

"What is it with you men?" Linda grabbed one of the extra pillows she had dropped beside the bed, propping it under her head along with the one she had used to sleep. "Why do men always think they took advantage of the woman? Like we're weak and can't control our own legs."

"I don't want it to confuse things."

"Oh, please. I'm a big girl. But it's forgotten, so I don't know what you're talking about."

"Let me start over. Good morning, Linda, last night was another reason I like older women."

"That's starting over? I suppose you're going to say it's the way we older gals look in the morning?"

"You look wonderful in the morning, all day for that matter. But, no, it's because older women know how to make love."

"The same thing can be said of men," Linda said. "The younger man is concerned with his own satisfaction. The mature man turns his attention to pleasing the woman." She smiled. "Thank you," she said, "I needed last night."

"It was great for me, too."

"Don't you think it's time for you to tell me your real name?"

"Ryan Testler is just fine. Consider it my real name, I do."

"May I ask you something else?"

"No guarantee I'll answer, but ask."

"Last night, when you were telling me of your metamorphosis from a young man joining the military to a strong-arm man for Alistair Webster, you said, 'all the reasons *we* started our military careers.' Who's the *we*?"

"You don't miss much, do you?"

"I try not to, particularly when my life's on the line."

"I was including my best friend growing up. We went to the same elementary school and remained best friends through prep school, college, and into the Marines."

223

"What was his name?"

"Gene."

"Where did you and Gene live?"

"Not important. An American small town, Norman Rockwell you'd call it. I would, too. It was a fabulous place in a fabulous time. Our parents bought summer houses on the opposite sides of a small lake. For our first Christmas there, our parents bought us walkie talkies that worked between our two houses. We usually fell asleep talking. Imagining Special Forces work behind enemy lines. Snipers. Whatever. We grew up wanting to be heroes. We pledged that our lives would not be ordinary. No way. We grew up sharing books like the *Corsican Brothers*, and *The Three Musketeers*, and Louis L'Amour's stories about the Sackett brothers."

Linda rose up to sit on the edge of the bed. "Two boys who grew up dragging their youthful imaginations."

"Something like that," Ryan said.

"What happened to Gene?"

"He died."

"How?"

"On a covert action in the Middle East, under my command. After that, I left the military. The records were fixed to show Gene and I died together."

"How could you get the records to show that?"

"Not important."

"And you figured you were at fault?"

"I was."

"And that's part of why you quit? Why you chose money over patriotism? Why you soured on yourself?"

"I caused Gene's death."

"I'll bet Gene wouldn't agree."

"Well, enough about all that. It doesn't change anything. Besides, we need to get started. As I recall, you've got to get into one of your other identities and do some banking. While you get ready, I'll go find us some good coffee and a newspaper. I hate this hotel room stuff. Black?"

"Artificial sweetener," Linda said, "and a little cream, please."

"Lock up behind me." Ryan said before leaving the room.

"This is Testler, thought I'd check in."

"Where are you?" Webster asked.

"In Vegas, where you sent me." Testler said, while standing outside the Kokopelli Inn in Sedona, Arizona.

"Have you found what you went there to find?"

"I found her. But I don't have her yet. There were too many people around. I'm waiting for her hotel room number, then I'll take care of it."

"Here's your coffee," Ryan said as he came back into their room in Sedona.

"Thanks," Linda said coming out of the bathroom, a towel cinched under her armpits. "Despite our big dinner last night, I'm famished." She smiled. "I wondered how we worked up such an appetite."

He smiled. "Working up an appetite is good, not to mention fun."

Linda hugged Ryan.

Through her towel, he felt her squish against his chest. "There's an interesting place just up the road," he said. "The Coffee Pot Restaurant, the place serves over one-hundred different omelettes. I also got this touristy book about the red rock formations around here. There's a rock shaped like Batman, another like a bell, even a Snoopy rock. Up the road from the omelette place there's a tall rock shaped like a coffee pot. Why don't we hang around an extra day and see the sights? I got a brochure on jeep trips up into the red rocks."

"Sounds like fun. I can finish getting ready out here if you want in there."

He grabbed his dopp kit and headed for the bathroom while talking. "I'll be ready when you get back from the bank. Come pick me up and we'll go eat. Sound okay?"

"Do they serve omelettes after breakfast hours?"

"They do. I checked with the front desk."

Linda leaned on the bathroom door jamb to say she was leaving.

"Now you're coming back for me, aren't you?" Ryan asked.

"I might as well. You'd only find me again, and I don't think I want you for an enemy."

"No, you don't."

CHAPTER 43

"*E*verything go okay at the bank?" Ryan asked while getting into the car after Linda pulled into the lot at the Kokopelli Inn.

"Yeah. Easy. I may have discovered a new career, impersonations."

"They're easy" Ryan said. "Mostly people accept who and what you say you are. When they request an ID, they see it as a necessary formality. They're pre-conditioned to take a cursory glance, and if it checks you become who you say you are. The hardest part is learning to relax and play the role. There it is on your left, next block. See it, The Coffee Pot Restaurant."

They had ordered and were sipping coffee when Linda turned the conversation serious.

"Tell me more about this Alistair Webster?"

"You got it last night. He subverts the American government by arranging for people to be compromised, blackmailed. He orders assassinations when he determines them necessary."

"Tell me about him in a more personal context. Health? Family? Like that."

"Why is it women like to know that stuff? He's in his early sixties and, as far as I know, his health is fine. His wife died some years ago. No children. He likes young girls."

"Young girls? Children?"

"Not kids," Ryan said, "but very young."

"The guy's a real upstanding citizen."

"I wouldn't piss on 'im," Ryan said, "if he were on fire."

"That's certainly graphic."

"It's how I feel."

"How can you work for a man like that?"

"For the first few years I found working for Webster peaceful. That's not the right word, but sort of. No causes. No sides. No defeating the wicked or saving the world. I could just focus on the *how* and *where*. Let Webster decide the *who*. Do the deed. Take the money. Move on."

Their omelettes came. Ryan added ketchup to his guacamole and green chilies omelette. Linda did nothing to enhance her turkey, avocado, bell pepper and cheese concoction.

Then she said, "What you just said will likely never make sense to me. Our worlds are so different. Still, we should be able to do something to stop this parasite."

"You can't end evil. It exists. All you can do is stop evil people, one at a time."

"Isn't this Webster answerable to the law?"

"In theory, sure, but America is currently taking its two major overlapping principles way too seriously: law and individual rights. Guys like Webster, crooked and wealthy and politically connected, live in the seams of that overlap. Webster keeps himself insulated. He uses men like me, men who would never go to the authorities because of, if for no other reason, their training and self interest. The Webster types of the world use us, our special talents. The targets of men like Webster are others vulnerable because of their own weaknesses. Their forte is crime against individuals. Men like Webster stay away from societal crimes such as bank robbery and embezzlement. Bottom line: the self interests of their employees and their victims prevent both groups from going to the authorities. And these men have the wealth and high-priced lawyers to provide an additional layer of protection."

"That can't always work," Linda said. "I mean, some victims must experience a pang of conscience."

"Rarely. But sometimes and when that happens men like me arrange accidents. And no one ever knows for certain. Look at the death of President Kennedy. Then there's that recent death of the former defense department big shot whose body was found in a landfill. Also that congressman a few decades back, the one killed in the explosion of an airplane near Russian airspace. Were these accidents or assassinations? Who knows? One side claims conspiracy while the other side laughs it off and accuses them of being nut cases. There are always opinions both ways. The point is, no definite answers are found and no one of sufficient power is ever held accountable."

"You mean, if they were not accidents to begin with?"

"That's how it works, yes."

Ryan picked up the carafe on the table. "Can I warm up your coffee?" Linda nodded and he refilled both cups.

"How does it feel to plan and carry out a killing?"

"You should know. You put Blue down in the surf."

"That's not the same. He came after me. I was defending myself. I didn't plan it."

"Yes you did. You planned on the run. You improvised."

"I mean to coldly plan a killing over a period of time, without an imminent threat."

"It's really the same whether the threat is immediate or not. If someone wants to kill you, you defend yourself. The major difference is where you have time you can plan. With a good plan you gain the upper hand. In table tennis they call it, 'your add.' "

"This isn't a game!"

"That's exactly what it is. The stakes are life and death. The better your plan and tactics, the more likely you'll win. This isn't some two-out-of-three wager. This is the quintessential sudden death playoff. The prize is staying alive."

"If you're sick of all of it, why don't you just kill Webster?" Linda's face showed the shock she felt. "Oh, my God, I said it."

"It's been under consideration. You want in?"

"What?" Linda asked.

"You heard me. He's trying to kill you, after first torturing you to find out what else you might have learned and to whom you might have repeated it. As you said, you have a right to defend yourself. He sees you as a threat to his grand scheme. He won't stop coming. You have only one decision to make: will you pick the time and place, or will you leave it for him to pick? If you let him, it's his 'add.' "

"But he won't come himself. Will he?"

"That's no real difference. Whether he comes or orders someone else who comes. You're still dead. He still caused it."

"Why can't we just go to the authorities? With what you know, he'd be arrested."

"You think so? It would be his word against the word of a former mercenary, and a woman who has never seen him or spoken to him. You learned of him only through Cynthia Leclair's letters and me."

"You know many of his victims. They'll corroborate what you say."

"We already covered that. They're not going to step forward and admit they've been blackmailed or circumvented government regulations. Why would they confess to having done that? To having taken bribes or had a mistress compliments of Alistair Webster. Why would they do that?"

"Like you said before, they wouldn't, their self interest."

"In the end," Ryan said, "Webster's victims would stand with him, not us. His high-priced lawyers would dismiss our accusations with little effort. Forget the fairy tales. On this level, justice is rarely found in a courtroom."

"But to kill someone, to just ... " Linda's words drifted away, unfinished.

"Some people deserve to die. It's that simple."

"Okay. Okay. I accept that. The world would have been better off without Adolph Hitler. Charles Manson. Sure. But who gets to decide?"

"The folks who pay."

"That doesn't make it right," Linda said.

"But that's how it is."

"Buying someone's death? No. You can't justify that."

"What about the people who will continue to die if Webster doesn't? Last week it was your friend, Cynthia Leclair and her coworkers. This week, he wants it to be you, missy. Tomorrow, someone else, after that other people in other matters of which we are unaware."

Linda nodded slowly. "I'm convinced. How do we do it?"

CHAPTER 44

*R*yan and Linda drove out of Sedona under a cold blue sky swept clean by the wind. The sun was still low and the red rock crags to the east, still draped in shadows, looked like shading in a pencil drawing.

Ryan had put together a rough plan, subject to improvisation, and with it came a strong sense of urgency to put it into play.

After driving north a relatively short distance on I-17, they picked up I-40 out of Flagstaff, Arizona, and headed east.

"So," Linda said, after a few miles, "you told me Webster had five Special Forces types in his small private army. We've accounted for you, Charles and Blue. What about the other two he uses as bodyguards?"

"To understand the other two requires a bit of backstory: Their names are Victor and Mark. They have a third brother, Fabian. Their mother named the three of them after ancient Catholic popes. She—"

"Pope Mark?"

"Well, Marcus is his actual given name. Fabian made it and is at one of the catholic churches in Baltimore. Victor and Marcus, Mark, rejected the church, turned from their mother and became soldiers. I met Mark after we all came to work for Webster. Victor I knew. He started in Special Forces under my command. He's personable, but mean, likes violence. Years later, their mother got cancer and suffered long and hard. During her suffering, Victor and Mark were racked with guilt for having ignored their mother's wishes. Mr. Webster stepped up and got her the best of care. In return, the two sons remain loyal to Webster."

"She reminds me of my own mother."

"Was your mother also intensely Catholic?"

"My mother was the poster woman for intensely Catholic. Every morning, she started her day by going to the church to pray, her little girl in tow. The first words I heard every morning were get up, brush your teeth, and get dressed. I don't want to be late for church. I never understood that, often there would be no mass. We would be there alone, so how could we be late?"

"Tell me some other things you remember about your mother, random thoughts."

"A hair grew out of a large mole on her neck. She always smelled of baking something. She wore super thick glasses. Back then, they hadn't invented plastic lenses so people's glasses just got thicker and thicker as their vision worsened."

"Forgive me for saying so, but your mother doesn't sound like an attractive woman."

"Not after about age forty. Before that she was a real looker. That's what my daddy always used to say after she had let herself go. 'Your mother used to be a real looker,' he'd say."

"Tell me the event that involved your parents that you most clearly remember from when you were young."

"Oh. That's easy. I was twelve. My parents thought I had gone to bed. I had, but I often snuck down the hall upstairs to lie on the carpeted landing and watch the adults downstairs."

"And?"

"That particular night, my father put on a record he had bought that day at the record shop downtown, a Cole Porter song, Love for Sale. Well, my mother started moving around the room in front of my father, stripping as she went."

"Whoa! I like your mother. What did you think about that?"

"I'd never heard that song before, and I'd never seen anything like that before. I didn't think it happened outside of the books I snuck to read under the covers with my flashlight. But here was my mother ... my mother! I could feel myself blushing, just watching. She was glorious."

"I take it your father liked it."

"Liked it? My father was throwing money at my mother. That made her laugh and shimmy all the harder. It was really something. After all these years, I can still see the whole thing in my mind, every detail. Like it's happening again right now, right in front of me."

"Have you ever done that for a man?"

"No."

"Is that regret I hear in your voice?"

"I've always thought that one day, I would, but no, not yet anyway."

"Tell me about your father?"

"Ah. There was a man for the ages. He died two days before my twenty-first birthday. We were going to go down to his favorite tavern and he was going to buy me my first legal drink."

"What's your fondest memory of him?"

"His taking me with him sometimes when he went to the park where he played chess. Some men play golf every Saturday. My dad and his buds played chess in the park or, with bad weather, in the tavern. The other men were all like uncles. I loved them all."

"You know, you won't find your father in one of the men you pick up in taverns."

"What are you now, assassin slash psychiatrist?"

"It's a gift."

"That's enough about my family. Tell me more about that town where you and Gene grew up."

"There's not much to tell. Just a little town, there's a million of 'em, a small school, Daughters of the American Revolution chapter, firemen's pancake breakfast fund raisers, lots of fishing and hunting. Those Norman Rockwell paintings could have been done in my hometown."

"Your parents?"

"Both dead."

"Ex-wives? Kids?"

"None. None."

"So you're really the Lone Ranger? Gene was your Tonto, but now he's gone, too."

"Something like that."

"Does that concern you?"

"Sometimes, I suppose. Look, we need to get on to the business at hand."

"Okay. How is the mother of the three popes doing?"

"She's dead. I thought I said that. Despite the doctors Webster brought in, the disease was unstoppable. In the end, Webster had bought himself two loyal soldiers."

"And you said, those two rarely go out on ... what do you call them, assignments or missions?"

"Military types often say missions. Webster speaks of assignments. But, no, Victor and Mark are mostly at Webster's side. When one travels with him, the other stays at home. They've gotten softer from lack of action. However, make no mistake both are stone cold killers with their hands, a variety of weapons, and have the ability to improvise that is inbred during Special Forces training."

Ryan, who had taken over the driving about an hour before, had driven into New Mexico before either of them spoke again.

"So, you've never been married," Linda asked.

"Never. Marriage is less relevant than it once was."

"Why do you think that?"

"The social and sexual emancipation of women. They've become more honest about their physical desires and are less needy, less clingy. On the man's side, he can buy whatever he wants, pretty much whenever he wants, wherever he is, without involvement or the discomfort about how to walk away the next morning, with none of the difficulties of ending a relationship that isn't working."

"That may be true," Linda said, "but what about the desire for true intimacy beyond sex?"

"Women still equate sex with love. For most women, it's part of the cultural imperative that lets them feel they remain good after sex."

"And men?"

"Men equate sex with lust. They equate fidelity with love. At least those who make good husbands do."

"You are quite the philosopher, aren't you?"

"In my business there's lots of free time. Helps rationalize what I do."

"How does love and sex help rationalize what you do?"

"No. Not love and sex, the philosophical thinking."

"Is that what led you to have reservations about what you do? Look out. There's a cop up ahead on the left just beyond the overpass."

"I see 'im. My speed's within the limit. The last thing we need is to be pulled over."

"You were saying?"

"I don't have reservations about what I do. Like I said, some people deserve to die. Many people know such a person. They might even wish that person were dead, but they lack the resolve to turn their desire into action. The famous attorney Clarence Darrow once said, 'I have never killed a man, but I have read many obituaries with pleasure.' From there it isn't all that far to just taking the matter in hand and doing the killing."

Linda looked over at Ryan. "Webster certainly appears to be deserving."

"That he is. Still, I find it difficult."

"Why?"

"As they said in the old west, 'If you take a man's money, you ride for his brand.'"

"What's that, some kind of Louie L'Amour philosophy of the plains?"

"Don't laugh. We all do it. Everyday people follow the orders of their employers and do things they know are wrong, maybe even illegal. You don't think Bernie Madoff had employees that suspected something wasn't on the up and up. Then there are the employees of the banks who played games with foreclosure documents. That kind of shit goes on all day, every day. Salespeople who lie about the product they're trying to sell."

"I'm sorry, but that doesn't climb high enough to equate to killing people."

"Like I said, some deserve to die. And you, Miss Darby, have agreed that Webster is one of them."

"Okay. But for me, it's self-defense. You've made a business out of it."

"I told you, I'm not one of the good guys."

"But you are. At least you are to me."

"Life is never quite what it seems, is it? Everything must be viewed from a given perspective, considered in one context or another. It changes things, doesn't it? I like to think there's a difference. I rarely kill women, never children, and only men who qualify."

"And there's the crux again," Linda said. "Who decides?"

"Like I've said, it's up to the person paying."

"And that's how it should be?"

"How it should be matters little. That's how it is," Ryan said, as he angled the car into the right lane that would take them into a rest stop that had bathrooms. "That's how it always will be. It's the golden rule: he who has the gold, rules."

After getting back on the road, Ryan asked Linda to tell him about her ex-husband.

"We've got Webster to deal with. Let's focus on one vermin at a time, please."

"Aha. The lady is still carrying a torch."

"That's ridiculous. I hate 'im."

"You sure about that?"

"Yeah. I hate him like—another cop on your left beyond the overpass."

"We're fine," Ryan said. "Go on, you were saying you hate your ex."

"That's the emotion that lingers. But even when you hate a man, you're not sure ... really sure there's not still some love mixed up in it. Love and hate are two rooms divided by a very thin wall."

"Would you go back to him if he asked? Right now, well, as soon as our current unpleasantness is finished."

"No. I might want to, but no."

"Do you want to get married again?"

"Before all this started happening, I'd have said no and meant it. Or at least believed I meant it."

"Now?"

"Funny how all this has gotten me thinking. My life the last seven years has been isolated, lonely, bordering on reclusive."

"You know who would be a good man for you?"

"First you were a philosopher, then a psychiatrist, now a matchmaker, and through it all, a soldier of fortune."

"What can I say, it's another gift."

"All right, I'll bite. Who?"

"Clark, the waiter in O'Malley's Bistro. Well, I guess I should say Chief McIlhenny's new deputy."

"Clark? What made you say him?"

"He's a good man. I've watched him. He's solid and dependable."

"Yeah. I think so too."

"And he cares about you."

"He likes me. I know that."

"His feelings are deeper than that. I'm not just talking about the blood you donated for him. That gets you gratitude, but that's not what he's feeling. Trust me. I know."

"Okay. I'll look into it, let him audition." Linda laughed and moved her seat all the way back, putting her bare feet on the dashboard. "That is, I will if I ever get back to Sea Crest."

"So, what changed your outlook about getting married again?"

"The prospect of dying I guess. Knowing there is no one who will much care. That you've left no one behind. It's like, I don't know how to say it, giving up my place in the universe."

"Now who's the philosopher?"

"I guess all of us to some degree."

"Maybe," Ryan said, "after this, you and I should get married?"

"Ask me again in a couple of days, if we're still alive."

"If we don't survive, who will raise our children?" Ryan asked. "Your mother?"

"My mother's dead. But we don't have any kids."

"Then we better not get killed."

Hours later, as they drew nearer Albuquerque, Ryan said, "We'll catch a plane here and fly into Pittsburgh. From there we'll drive."

"Why not just fly into D.C. or Baltimore? They're both closer to where you told me we're going."

"This is what I do. Trust me. Drive. Fly. Drive. Fly. First go to a point south of your destination, then one to the north of your destination. Change names. I assume you have a couple of false IDs left?"

"I do. Should I use one for the flight?" He nodded. Then she asked, "What about you?"

"I generally don't need them. Ryan Testler is a dead-end identity. No records, just a false trail of papers. However, I will use another identity for the flight to Pittsburgh to avoid the possibility of Webster's data center spotting someone traveling under the name Ryan Testler."

"Then Ryan Testler is not your real name?"

"No."

"What is?"

"Not important."

"Is that your answer to everything you choose not to answer?"

"Pretty much."

CHAPTER 45

$\mathcal{F}$our hours later they were on a direct flight to Pittsburgh. Ryan spoke little on the plane, choosing to snooze. Linda's mind, on the other hand, was a battlefield raging between hopes and fears.

Before leaving the Pittsburgh airport, Ryan rented a gray two-door car using one of his sets of false identification. In the future, without Webster, he would need to buy these on his own. After driving outside the city proper, he abandoned the car two blocks from an Enterprise in-town car rental center. He walked there alone, rented a black four-door and drove back to pick up Linda. Less than an hour later he stopped and rented a room, again paying cash.

Once inside, he said, "I need to go out for a while. Don't leave the room. If you want ice or anything to eat, use room service."

"Where are you going?"

"Not important."

When Ryan got back and entered their hotel room, Linda was watching television.

"Where have you been?"

"We ditched our guns before our flight, remember, so I did a little shopping for things we'll need. Now, let's get some sleep. I'll set the alarm for five-thirty. We'll go over the plan then, have some breakfast and get on the road. Destination: the area near Falls Church, Virginia."

⁓

By seven the next morning, Ryan had reviewed the high points of his plan with Linda. He had also answered or deflected her questions. Through it all she paced the room, periodically running her hands through her hair. She also drank the hotel room coffee he had made before waking her.

He finished with, "One hard and fast rule: If you want to survive, you'll do what I tell you, and do it immediately. Get your questions over with before we get there. I'll go over the weapons a little later."

"I can't believe this. I'm on my way to kill someone."

"I can handle it alone. Then meet you back here."

"Cynthia was my friend. Besides, it's me Webster is after. That makes this my fight. I'm in."

"Okay. I know Webster's estate, so we'll need very little reconnoitering. Until tonight's activities are finished, do nothing to draw attention to us. Keep this hat on unless I tell you to take it off. While I was out last night I also filled up the gas tank and stopped at a supermarket. We have bananas, apples, rolls, candy and water. If you need to use a restroom give me lots of advance notice. I'll find a fast food restaurant with a side entrance that comes in near their bathrooms."

"Why not a gas station with a convenience market?" Linda asked.

"More than likely they'll have a video recorder for security."

"I would have never thought of that."

"This is your last chance to stay here. I can come back for you."

"I can't condone what we're going to do, but it somehow feels right. No. It feels wrong. Necessary's the word, not right. It's my fight so I can't walk away and let you carry it off alone."

"In some ways, it would be easier alone. Last chance."

"No. I'm in. That's final. What do we do next?"

"Okay. Check out time is twelve. I've arranged for an extra hour. The alarm is reset for noon. We need five hours to get there, and we've got about twelve before we need to arrive. We don't want to be loitering anywhere along the way, so we'll sleep until noon. Then we'll leave. There'll be a place where we can stop to review things and rest for a while on the way."

"My God, I can't sleep now."

"You're going to burn huge quantities of nervous energy. Depending on how it goes we might be able to sleep tomorrow night, then again, we may not. So get to sleep. That's an order, soldier."

"I don't know how much sleep I'll get," she said.

He put the do-not-disturb sign on the outside knob, and pulled shut the blackout drapes while Linda got under the covers.

"Focus on relaxing your feet."

"What?" she asked. "What good is that?"

"When your feet are relaxed, focus on relaxing your legs. Then your butt, on up until you get your head to relax."

"Then what?"

"Then you'll be asleep."

"It's that simple, huh?"

"If you let it be."

~

Linda liked the idea of sleep, but didn't believe it would come. She thought about how her entirely placid life since moving to Sea Crest had turned tumultuous. Perhaps the changes she now faced were exactly what she needed to rebalance the rhythms of her life. Then she felt Ryan stroking her hair. "Remember," he said, "your feet. Concentrate. Then move up little by little."

Ryan opened his eyes a few minutes before noon. He woke Linda, telling her to lie quietly while he called Webster. She wrinkled her brow, but said nothing, just nodded.

"Boss. Testler. I've located the target. She's having breakfast in the hotel coffee shop. I'll follow her up after she eats."

"Which casino are you at?"

"No time. I need to get in position to follow her. I expect to have this wrapped up in time to give you a final report by late tonight, or early tomorrow morning depending on how long I question her."

"Call me when it's done. I'll be home tonight. Alone."

"You won't be going out? No visitors?"

"No. Call no matter the time. I want to know this is done. After that get back to Sea Crest and take care of Chief McIlhenny."

"Okay, boss. Oops. She's getting up from her table. I gotta get in position. The next time you hear from me it should be wrapped up."

Ryan hung up and turned to Linda who had gotten up and was standing in the doorway to the bathroom, her arms crossed. "Webster will be home," he said. "He won't be expecting us. Now you go on and get ready. We need to be out of here in one hour."

"Get ready?" Linda said, incredulous. "What does one do to get ready? Should I brush my teeth? Does a lady wear lipstick to a murder?" She felt her lips trembling—oh no.

Ryan went over to her and put his arms around her. She cried and held him. When she stopped, she stood back and looked embarrassed.

"Now," Ryan repeated softly. "Go get ready. Wear the clothes I gave you. No jewelry. None. We leave in fifty minutes."

"I thought you said an hour?"

"I did. Ten minutes ago."

While Linda showered, Ryan called Chief Ben McIlhenny on his cell phone. "Chief, this is me. We need to make it Thursday, rather than Tuesday."

"No way. You've delayed me long enough! ... Why?"

"I'm in the east. I'll need to mix and match some driving and flying to get back there. I'll be able to leave tomorrow."

"You knew our plans for Tuesday. Why did you go?"

"Back here I can get my hands on some documents that will corroborate our story. Nail it down air tight. I wanted to be sure I could get them before I called you. I'll meet you as planned in the cove north of Lincoln City, on Thursday."

"I don't like this," McIlhenny said.

"You will when you see what I'll be bringing. It'll assure you'll get your immunity for the Jersey killing," Ryan said, confident this would entice Chief McIlhenny to cooperate.

"All right," McIlhenny said after a long sigh. "Thursday, but everything else remains the same as we had planned for Tuesday. Agreed?"

"Agreed."

CHAPTER 46

*R*yan turned off his lights a mile from the entrance to the Webster estate. Then he drove by at a low speed. Had he turned into the driveway it would have taken him through a small grove of trees along a casual curve that led to the guard gate about seventy-five yards inside the property line.

From the street, he and Linda could see only two portentous peaks pocked with gabled windows peering down like dark eyes trimmed out from the wall ivy. Faint shards of light escaping from somewhere on the estate silently punctured the matte sky.

Five minutes later, at two minutes after eight to be exact, Ryan pulled their rental car off the road, through the dark rain into the swallow of a densely treed area south of Webster's property. For the next minute or so he drove slowly through low wet weeds. Then he swung hard left and pulled the rented Taurus to a stop under the tar-papered roof of a lean-to supported on one side by a decaying adobe block wall. The corners of the other side were supported by two round wooden posts resembling old telephone poles. That shelter, such as it was, ended the plink of the rain against the roof and hood of the car. He turned off the windshield wipers. Next, he opened the windows halfway to begin their adjustment to the outside conditions and to prevent the windows from fogging.

The old shelter appeared to have been built long ago to protect burlap bags of feed and fertilizer. The nearby fields had surrendered their tillable dignity, forgotten farmland locked in an endless time warp between harvest and spring plowing. Whoever had forsaken the fields no longer cared about the decaying shed. The corner post to the right front gimped enough to tilt the entire structure, the roof rain pouring down from that corner.

They were about a half mile from the outer wall of Webster's estate, a half mile from their mission.

"Are we going to get through this alive?" Linda asked, her eyes staring into the wet darkness.

"Piece of cake. Webster hates dogs, so that's one less thing to worry about. And the housekeeper/cook should be gone by now. That leaves Webster, Victor and Mark."

"So we're outnumbered."

"Surprise makes us an army."

"Will all three of them be in the house?"

"Mark is likely in the guard gate up at the entrance. Webster and Victor should be inside."

"Why Mark? Couldn't Victor be in the guard shack?"

"Not likely. Mark is smart like his brother, but less likeable. Victor is more personable, more conversant. Webster likes Victor better. So do I. But one of them will be up front, the other inside."

"Damn this rain," Linda said. "I can't see anything."

"Oh, no. This is great. People go outside less when it rains. Noise dies in the rain. It's even likely that Mark will stay in the guard shack and skip his rounds. Security at Webster's estate is a cushy job. It's made the brothers sloppy about procedures."

"Is there a chance," Linda said, "that we could reason with Webster? Convince him I know nothing?"

"None whatsoever."

"I'm afraid."

"There's good fear and bad fear."

"It can't be good to be afraid."

"Bad fear clogs your mind, slows your reactions. Good fear makes you cautious, keeps you alert. Don't fight fear. Let it work for you." He reached over and squeezed her thigh. "You got balls, little lady, to come this far. You can wait here. For me, this is a go, with or without you."

Linda got out of the car. They were both dressed in black rain gear from hat to sneakers, with more black under the rain gear, all military style clothing Ryan had selected to remain quiet when they moved. Ryan had gotten the clothes somewhere in Pittsburgh the night before, the night he had gone out to purchase the guns they carried as well as regular and night vision binoculars.

The wet, cold air created the kind of atmospheric pressure that caresses a bullet and keeps it on course.

Linda looked up at the sky.

Ryan said, "These rain clouds will help us get to the house without being detected."

"Absolutely?" she asked.

"Nothing's absolute."

"And if not?"

"We improvise."

Ryan slipped a 9-mm Beretta into a shoulder holster inside his rain jacket, then put a second Beretta into some kind of apparatus behind his neck, inside his jacket collar. Linda's Rossi .38 snub nose he put into her jacket pocket.

"Do not draw this gun outside the house. Not unless I've fired first and the target is close." He put his face close to hers and raised his eyebrows. She nodded. Then he continued. "When we're inside with Webster, keep your hands mostly in the pockets of your jacket, but take your hands out and put them back in a few times. I want him to see your hands in your pockets as nonthreatening."

Again, she nodded.

"The Rossi is most accurate and effective from in close. But don't worry, inside you'll be pretty close. If necessary you can fire without taking it out of your pocket. The hammer on the Rossi will not foul in the fabric. If time is critical, fire right through your jacket."

Again, she nodded.

Ryan flipped the strap on his regular binoculars over his head with the glasses resting on his back; then did the same with the night-vision binoculars only putting them so they would hang to his front.

He took her arm and they walked out from the protection of the lean-to roof.

Webster buzzed Victor to come into his home office.

"What do you think about Ryan Testler?"

"Strong. Capable. Ice under stress. He's reliable to work with. You know we were together in Delta."

"I meant more with respect to our work."

"He's a good man, sir. Hasn't he always gotten done whatever missions you've given him?"

"What if I told you I'm starting to doubt him?"

"I find that hard to believe, sir. But then, your judgment has never steered me wrong."

"I'm not certain, mind you, just suspicious. His delays in his current assignment seem plausible, yet untypical. He normally gets things done clean and quick. In and out, you know. Not this time."

"Well, if you decide he needs to be taken out, I'm your man."

"You realize I've always considered Ryan number one, ahead of you."

"As I said, sir, should you decide, I'm your man."

"Thank you, Victor. That'll be all for now."

To Linda, her heartbeat alone seemed loud enough to announce their approach. With each step the wet underbrush grabbed at her ankles, impeding her stride, twisting her feet. She strode forcefully, pulling her legs through the dense wet growth. The overhead trees, a palette of greens and browns, hung heavily with water. In the daylight, she imagined, the area might be pretty in a rugged sort of way. Tonight it seemed a graveyard.

As they moved closer to the outside wall around Webster's estate, Linda, startled by sounds nearby, pulled her gun and pointed it toward nothing more precise than the darkness.

Ryan put his hand on her arm, turning her until their faces were no more than three inches apart. "Now we went over this. That gun is useless unless the target is close. When we're inside, keep it in your pocket. Your hands now and again coming out, then going back in. You remember what we talked about?"

"I know how to handle a gun."

"This is not about how to handle a gun, but about when to use it. If you can't follow orders, go back to the car and wait. I can't have you putting us both in jeopardy."

"I'm sorry."

"Can you follow orders?"

"I'll do whatever you say."

"There will be some improvisation, but I will always take the lead. Don't hesitate in anything I tell you. Don't question. Don't think about it. Just do it."

"I'm okay. Really. Really I am."

The wind forcing its way through the underbrush whipped Linda's black pants against her legs. She kept her head down, the rain dripping off the lowest point in the front of her hat.

Ryan touched the front side of her left shoulder. They were at the wall of the estate, beneath an old large oak. Linda could see meager light dancing about in the higher branches of the tree. Light that had to be coming from somewhere on the estate, but standing this close to the wall, they were in its shadow.

Ryan had told her the horrible weather was perfect for what

they were about to do. Linda wanted to believe that, but had trouble balancing horrible and perfect in the same description.

"This wall," he said, "has sensors built into the top of it. If anything bigger than a bird or a squirrel touches it, a security alarm will go off inside the house. We won't hear it, but they will. If that happens the advantage swings from us to them. Do not touch the wall, not even down low, not even if you are falling. Do you understand?" Linda nodded. "Not even a light hand to steady yourself. No contact whatsoever." She nodded again.

"Stay here. I'm going over."

"Don't leave me."

He opened his hand and showed her a rock. "See this?" She nodded. He put it in his pocket. "In ten minutes, I'll arch this rock back over the wall. When it falls, you climb into the tree just as you'll see me do in a moment. I'll be on the other side to catch you when you drop feet first. Remember, don't touch the wall."

"What if you're not back in ten minutes?"

"Then run back to the car and drive like Lucifer himself is on your tail. Forget about me. It'll be too late."

"That's a comforting thought."

"The hell with comfort, its good advice. If it comes to that, do it. Ten minutes. Not eleven. Do you understand me?"

Linda grabbed his arm, started to open her mouth, then shut it and just nodded.

CHAPTER 47

*L*inda watched Ryan easily gain height in the tree and move out onto a main branch that had to be more than a foot thick.

She moved a few steps to her left where she could make out his silhouette against a cloud backlit by the moon. He didn't move. He just sat there. Motionless. Large. Powerful. She believed he had the physical strength to do whatever they had come to do, and from what he had told her about his life, he also had the mental strength. She remembered when he took out the two thugs in the alley in what was no more than ten seconds. He was capable all right, but was he capable enough for both of them?

Then Ryan dropped out of sight, down on the other side of the wall. It might as well have been off the edge of the planet. Except for glancing at her illuminated watch, she didn't move, her eyes remaining on the spot in the tree from which he had disappeared.

The next time she looked two minutes had already passed.

Did he mean ten minutes after he climbed into the tree or ten minutes from when he dropped down?

The guard shack sat near the entrance to the estate, about fifty yards from Ryan's current position. A person leaving Webster's home would drive roughly the same course as Ryan now took on foot, parallel to the driveway with one side of the estate wall to the right. The area between him and the guard shack was planted in grass studded with an irregular pattern of large shrubs. Ryan moved from one shrub to the next, angling to always keep the next shrub between himself and the guard shack.

He stopped behind the closest shrub, five yards short of the shack, ten yards from the point where the block sidewall joined the rod-iron fencing that fronted the estate, that iron fencing included the gated entrance itself.

Mark was wearing a down jacket and sitting with his arms crossed. A soda can on the side table, a clipboard hanging on a hook. Had those in the house detected anything, they would have warned Mark and he would be standing, at least sitting alert. But Mark was slouching down in a tilt-swivel chair. So far their presence had gone undetected.

Ryan had walked down from the house several times to visit Mark in this shack. He knew that on cold and damp nights Mark used a plug-in space heater. The noise from the heater was not loud, but enough that with the rain, Ryan would be able to get right up to the shack without being heard.

In a silent move, Ryan stepped into the doorway of the shack, the noise suppressor attached to his Beretta. Mark was asleep. Ryan made his rest eternal.

Five minutes. Ryan had now been gone five minutes.

Six minutes.

Seven.

At eight minutes, a tuft of leaves above Linda's head moved enough to release a load of water that struck Linda's hat and her shoulders. She stepped back. Her heart quickened. Her hand tightened on the gun in her pocket. She looked up.

Ryan had come back.

Thank God.

"I thought you were going to throw the rock over the wall?" she asked as soon as he dropped down beside her.

"The tree's a bit slick so I thought you might like me with you while you climbed."

"Yes. Thank you. What happened over the wall?"

"I took out the guard."

"Mark? Was it Mark?"

"Yes."

"Did you have to kill him?"

"The dead can't hurt you."

She grimaced and then nodded. She was glad she had never met Mark.

Ryan led her back deeper under the canopy of the tree. "Give me your watch," he said.

"What?"

"Your watch, woman. Now."

Linda handed him the watch.

He put it in a zipper pocket inside her jacket and zipped it shut.

"Why did you take my watch?"

"The dial illuminates, I could see the faint glow rising into the tree."

"No way."

"Then how did I know you had it? Now get your mind off your watch. Are you straight with your responsibilities?"

"Yes. Sure. Will we also need to kill Victor?"

"Not important."

"Now wait a minute. I need more than your trite 'not important.' This is a man's life."

"No one in this business expects to retire with a pension."

"But is it necessary?"

"I told you Victor and Mark are brothers. Mark had to be eliminated. We could not go in with an unprotected flank. If we killed only Mark, Victor would hunt us. For this to end, tonight, we need to remove both brothers and Webster."

"Is that it? No one else?"

"It looks that way."

"When will we know?"

"We'll know when we know. Now unclutter your mind. Your job hasn't changed."

"I know. Just do what you tell me."

"When?"

"Immediately. Without question. Okay?"

"And your gun?"

"In my pocket. And the bit about my hands, I got it. I got it."

"But will you do it?"

"If I want to stay alive, I guess I'll have to."

"Now you've got it. No more do-gooder platitudes. We've cut it to the bone. Do it or die."

CHAPTER 48

*R*yan again shimmed out on the large branch, only this time Linda was moving in front of him, with his hands steadying her. When they were both beyond the estate wall, he spoke into the back of her head. "Grip the tree and stay here until I motion for you. When you drop, keep your arms about a foot from your sides. I'll help break your fall."

On the ground, Ryan moved forward until he was behind a large shrub about ten feet from the wall. He held that position to study the house and grounds. The only lights were two floods on the brick facing above the upstairs windows, the light diffused considerably by the vines of kudzu which robbed much of the brightness before it reached the ground. More floods were on the corners of the house, dual units positioned to illuminate each side. Another lit the concrete area where Victor's and Mark's cars were parked just north of Webster's three-car garage. Ryan went back to the wall, looked up at Linda and raised his arms.

Linda felt confident that her legs, strong from beach running, would allow her to drop the ten feet to the ground, but from sitting on the branch, her head was more like thirteen feet from the ground so the drop seemed more frightening than it would be, or so she told herself.

She looked down again. Ryan motioned again. She dropped. Her arms angled outwardly from her sides.

Ryan eased her descent, then put his arm around her shoulders and moved her about ten feet until they were both behind the large shrub he had a few minutes earlier paused behind to study the house and grounds.

"Are you all right?" he asked, his lips near her ear. She nodded and gave him a thumbs-up.

From in close, the brick two-story house appeared a fortress conjured from some gothic story, the unyielding gaze of the upstairs windows like empty eye sockets. The ambient light reflecting oddly as the wind buffeted the panes.

"You see the front door?" Linda nodded. "The big double French doors to the right, you can see room light diffused by drapes?" She nodded again. "That's Webster's office. He's in there now."

"How do you know it's Webster?"

"I don't absolutely know. But it wouldn't be Victor in the boss's office. There are no extra cars at the house, and I've never known Webster to invite a guest into his office. The only other thing I know is we don't have time to discuss everything. If you want to walk away from tonight, take what I tell you as gospel. We are on a schedule based on when the outside security lights come on. Understood?" She nodded.

"When you see those drapes open, that's your signal to come. The door will be unlocked. Come fast and walk right in."

"You're not going in alone?"

"Remember rule one: follow orders."

"But what if the drapes don't open?"

"If I'm in there more than fifteen minutes without opening the drapes, get out of here."

"I know. Back over the wall and run like hell."

"No. You can't get over the wall without setting off the alarm. The guard has been eliminated. Run to the front of the property. Out the gate. To the car and beat it."

"And just leave you?" she asked, with rain spit spraying from her lips with each word.

"If those drapes don't open within fifteen minutes, you won't be able to do anything for me. Just get out."

"You took my watch. How will I know when it's been fifteen minutes?"

"I'm sure you've counted one-one-thousand, two-one-thousand, like that, everyone has. Do like that and use your fingers to keep track of the minutes. That'll occupy your mind. Help you focus."

Linda reached up and placed her wet palm against his wet cheek and then touched his lips.

"Okay," Ryan said, his mouth next to her ear, "the rain's our friend, and the sky's dark. I don't want to talk when we get near the house so let me go over a few more things now. There's a series of can lights in the roof over the long portico. If he had guests, those lights would be on now. They're off, so like he told me on the phone, he should be alone. However, those lights, along with landscape lighting around the grounds, come on at ten to act as further security. That gives us an hour, that's plenty of time. Webster won't come out in this weather. But Victor could come out to take food to his brother in the guard shack or to go to his car. Stay alert. I'll keep my hand on you in case we need to move quickly or drop down."

"Why didn't you tell me this stuff before we got here?"

"It would make more sense if you could see the house and grounds while I told you. Out this far, with the noise from the rain, we're okay talking long enough to set this up."

"What do we do first?" Linda asked.

"First I get in. You stay here. Under no conditions are you to go onto the porch. There are lights they will turn on if they hear

258

something. And you'd leave wet tracks on the slate flooring. We're going to move about twenty yards to that group of large bushes to our right." He pointed. "That's where you'll wait. They will shield you if Victor comes out to his car or to see his brother at the guard gate. Just don't move, not at all, and he won't see you."

"But he'll find his brother dead?"

"If he goes up that way, I'll know it and deal with it. You just stay where you are until you see the drapes open over those double French doors. Then come quickly and get inside."

"So, you're definitely going in without me?"

"Yes. My point of entry could be upstairs. That means climbing. Alone I can adapt to the conditions and any resistance I encounter. Then again, I may just open the front door for you from the inside."

"Isn't all this a bit iffy?"

"Sometimes split-second planning is needed. The current situation calls for a looser, flexible plan."

"What if you don't find a way in?"

"Then we'll ring the bell."

"Are you insane?"

"Not important."

CHAPTER 49

*L*inda felt Ryan's hand tighten on her arm. Then he said, "Let's get moving." The next thing she knew they were running. She looked back to see her footprints disappearing in the wet grass.

My God. I'm actually doing this.

She wanted to stop and pray for their success, but there was no time. Besides, she doubted a prayer for a successful murder would be answered.

They reached their first goal, the group of bushes about twenty yards from the house from which she would have a good view of the double French doors through which Ryan would signal for her to enter.

"You'll be safe here. Don't move if Victor comes out." He reached up and wiped a raindrop from her nose. Then he kissed her. Then he left her.

When Ryan passed the double French doors, he could see a pale shadow through the drawn drapes. Webster was in his office, at his desk. Locked French doors were not that hard to bust through, but he didn't know Victor's location and he didn't want to turn the night into a firefight with Victor.

He was guessing his quiet point of entry would be a single French door into Webster's master suite. An eight-foot wall surrounded a twelve-by-fifteen private garden/spa area immediately outside that French door. The private garden included an in-ground hot tub that Webster sometimes used to ease his arthritis before retiring for the night. Ryan had helped Webster design and test the security system on the outer estate wall several years ago so he knew this smaller private-area wall had the same security sensors. There were also motion detectors positioned about three feet out from the wall. However, Webster generally kept the motion detectors off because small critters often tripped the system. He also knew that Webster had spoken of having that system upgraded. Bottom line: Ryan would need to proceed under the assumption the motion detectors had been enhanced and were fully operational.

Despite these restrictions, this private garden and the door into the master suite would be his first choice entry point. Victor would not be in Webster's private wing so if he got inside as he hoped, he should be able to get deep into the house without being detected.

Ryan circled the private patio wall, staying ten feet out to avoid any chance of somehow tripping the motion detectors. When he was ten feet past where the wall abutted the house, he found what he had remembered, a control box for the automated watering system. The box was on the outside wall of the master bedroom near where it jutted out to accommodate the larger media room adjoining the master suite. The control box stuck out less than a foot from the wall and would not likely hold his weight for any length of time.

Ryan placed his right foot on top of the box and heard the stress brought on by the pressure. He made his move quickly, hoisting himself up from the box while literally falling away from the wall to which it was attached. As he gained height, he grabbed the edge of the adjoining roof with his left hand. Then he grabbed the cornering wall with his right and pulled himself up onto the roof.

He silently moved toward the back of the house directly above the private garden and the door into Webster's master bedroom. From there he lowered himself, hung from the edge, and dropped onto the outside slate tile flooring.

The French door was on the alarm system, but the alarm would not be engaged until ten o'clock when it came on along with the automated lights and alarms system. The alarm for this door also had a manual turn-on in the event Webster went to bed before ten, something he rarely did and apparently had not done tonight. The door had a normal knob and a deadbolt. Both had been engaged.

Ryan unzipped his outer rain jacket and his inside jacket. Then he glanced at his watch: nine-fifteen. He had forty-five minutes before the alarm and lights would go on. From inside his jacket he took out a diamond glass cutter and began center cutting one of the glass panels in the French door. If Webster had gone to bed early, Ryan would need to quickly immobilize Webster and then find and eliminate Victor. He finished the cut and, using the suction cup he had first attached to the glass, removed the cut circle and placed it in the garden under the leaves of one of the nearby plants. After putting the glass cutter and small suction cup back into one of the pockets inside his jacket, he reached through the hole, released the deadbolt and turned the knob.

The door opened.

He drew his Beretta and stepped through the door. Once inside, he took a plastic bag from inside his rain jacket. Then he removed his outer rain pants and jacket, his hat and overshoes so he would not leave a water trail to reveal his presence or his location should he get into it with Victor. He placed the wet clothing in the plastic bag, and began moving toward the light spilling into the hallway.

~

The heavy rain continued to shoot out of the dark sky that roofed everything as far as Linda could see. She was wet and cold, but not shivering thanks to the thermal underwear Ryan had given her to wear. The water heavy shrubs she stood behind provided some cover, but as the winds swirled, the rain came at her from differing angles. She wanted to turn her back away from the rain that was now slamming into her face, but she couldn't. She had to keep her eyes riveted on the slightly illuminated drapes over the double French doors, and pray for Ryan to open them in the next minute, if not the next second. When he did, the light inside would tumble out across the driveway toward her and she would dash for those doors, trusting Ryan had things under control and she would be safe inside. The idea of finally facing this monster, Webster, made her both eager and frightened. The short-term attraction of running away continued to claw her mind, but she stood her ground.

Fifty-nine-one-thousand. She looked down at her hands as the cold thumb on her right hand curled inward, joining her fingers to form a fist on that hand. The other hand, already a fist, told her that ten minutes had passed. Ten minutes that had passed like ten hours. With the passing of the eleventh minute she would need to start uncurling her fingers. Still, she waited for Ryan Testler, trusted the killer, gambling her life.

One-one-thousand.

Two-one-thousand.

Ryan continued down the hallway, his Beretta in one hand, the bag of his wet clothes in the other. The honey-colored light oozing out from Webster's office silently blunted against the picture of Webster's deceased wife that hung on the wall at the turn of the hall. The light cast a strange shadow across the face of Meredith Webster, a hard looking woman, slender, dressed all in black, with black hair cut in bangs a little long for the elevation of her eyes.

The woman had not been attractive, yet she had possessed certain warmth. She had also been wealthy, extremely so, and had left it all to Alistair Webster. Since her death, to Ryan's knowledge, Webster had engaged in no serious relationships.

From the last time he had looked at his watch, Ryan estimated that the fifteen minute point where Linda was to cut and run was drawing near. He couldn't divert his attention long enough to again access his watch. He guessed he had two minutes, three tops.

He stepped into the office doorway.

Webster looked up.

CHAPTER 50

"*W*hat the hell are you doing here?"

Webster's voice had not sounded like him. Not tired exactly, more like he hadn't spoken in a while.

"Good evening, Mr. Webster."

"You're supposed to be in Vegas. What is this about?"

Ryan dropped his bag of wet clothes near the wall. While keeping his eyes on Webster, he reached behind himself and closed the door back into the hallway. Then he lowered his Beretta, holding it along the side of his thigh.

"Linda Darby was never a threat," Ryan said. "She's an ordinary woman, actually quite an extraordinary woman, but she never posed a risk to you. She is not the kind of person we set out to deal with. You've gone kill crazy."

"How dare you talk to me like that."

"I'll talk to you any damn way I want. The person holding the gun always gets to do that."

Webster pushed his chair back, the wheels crunching as they dropped into the grout lines in the tile flooring.

Ryan raised his gun.

"I'm just getting comfortable. Don't get excited, Ryan."

"Oh, now I'm Ryan. I've worked for you for years. Killed six people for you and I've always been Testler. Now I'm Ryan."

Webster turned his tilt-swivel chair, angling it so he was looking right at Ryan.

Ryan moved past Webster until he was near the double doors about ten feet behind the desk. He reached up and hand-pushed the drapes open farther, then slid open the door. A moment later, Linda came inside, and he closed the door behind her.

"I'm guessing," Webster said, still looking at Ryan, "that you had something to do with my not hearing from Charlie and the death of Blue on the Oregon beach."

Ryan saw Linda's lips begin to move. His mind moved quicker. If she said anything about shooting Blue, Webster would see her as a threat. "Be quiet, woman," Ryan said angrily. Then he spoke to Webster. "Good guess."

"What is this about, Testler?"

"Mr. Webster, say hello to Linda Darby."

The muscles in Webster's face said he had decided to clam up. Then the tension eased. He had changed his mind. "Why in the hell did you bring her here? This is gross insubordination."

"We passed insubordination when I pulled a gun on you. Now, be polite. I've seen you do it before. Welcome to my home, Miss Darby. Like that. Now you try it."

So this is the guy. The man who had Cynthia and so many others tortured and murdered. The man who has destroyed my life. The asshole who wants me dead.

Linda just stood there, the rain attacking the glass door behind her, her heart attacking itself. Again she momentarily considered turning and running back out through the door, beyond the Webster estate, back to the car and driving as far as it would take her. Ryan, the most self-contained man she had ever known, could kill Webster. But she didn't. She just looked at Webster, the personification of evil.

266

His soft blue eyes appeared enormous behind his reading glasses. He was clearly shaken by this unexpected invasion of his home. He took off his exaggerating glasses and put on a pair that downsized his eyes. His old face looked boyish in some manner she couldn't exactly identify, and for that matter didn't care. Webster ran his hands over his paunch, then down his thighs and crossed his legs. His pants rode up to reveal short socks, his calves white and hairless. Then he pushed his wire framed glasses up against the bridge of his thin nose and looked directly at Linda.

"Good evening, Miss Darby. Welcome to my home."

She moved her eyes from his face long enough to notice a modest sized crucifix mounted above his head on the side wall. The room was framed in dark mullioned panels. A small gooseneck desk lamp brightened part of his desk.

Webster turned slowly to face Ryan. "The Bible dictates that we should honor our mother and our father. I gave birth to you as Ryan Testler. I am your mother and father. How dare you betray me?"

"I've seen dogs that wouldn't claim you as kin."

"So you think you can make it without my protection? Without the generous sums I pay you?"

"When one rejects the consequences of any course, one accepts the consequences of another."

"You were always quite the philosopher, Ryan."

"That's not my main goal."

"What is your main goal?"

"I wanna be rich, or a hero. I'd rather be rich, but Ms. Darby here would prefer me as a hero, so it works for me either way."

"I can take care of the rich part," Webster said. "I'll give you one-hundred-thousand dollars to kill her right now. Right here. And dispose of the body."

"For that amount, I'll take hero."

"Two-hundred-fifty thousand dollars. That's one quarter of a million dollars."

"You aren't convincing me."

"That's a lot of money. You've done a lot of assignments for a lot less."

"True. But Ms. Darby has had days to work on my sympathy. Just look at her body. She's very convincing. As for money, it comes and it goes, but her desire to please continues."

"Okay. Let's quit screwing around. One million dollars."

"Show me the money and it's done. And I'll dispose of her body."

CHAPTER 51

*L*inda felt panic. Shock. Had Ryan conned her? Had he brought her here only to bid up the price for killing her? Had this been about his achieving his retirement goal with one last killing? If Ryan had decided he would kill her now, she had no chance. She'd never get out of this room.

The Rossi fires through the jacket. The hammer won't snarl on the fabric. I could shoot Ryan. Then take the gun out and kill Webster. But that would alert Victor who would have the advantages of knowing the house and greater firepower.

Linda gripped the Rossi, her index finger gentle inside the trigger housing.

Ryan moved a few feet to the side away from Linda's deadly pocket. He did so slowly, but she recognized he had moved just enough to make a shot from inside her jacket more difficult. He grinned, but kept his eyes on Webster.

Linda angled her body enough to recapture a straight line of fire.

Ryan grinned again, his focus still on his employer.

"I'll need some time to raise that much cash."

"Mr. Webster. Mr. Webster. You once told me you could put your hands on a couple million without leaving your house. You are not a man to idly boast, so cough it up. Or I go back to choice B: hero." Then he turned to Linda, "Are you okay?"

"I'm cold, freezing is more like it." She took her hands out of her pockets, formed them into a circle and blew into the circle.

"Sit down, Linda. Over there." Ryan's tone made it an order. "You can keep your hands in your pockets if that's warmer. But sit down."

Linda sat.

"Well, Mr. Webster, which will you make me? Rich or hero?"

"Wait here," Webster said.

"No way. You'd keep in it in this room. I figure a safe."

"Yes, of course, only please put that gun down. Certainly, you don't need it to protect yourself from me."

Ryan shrugged and slipped his Beretta behind his belt at the front of his pants. He grinned again at Linda.

Webster got up, moved to his left, and took a picture off the wall to reveal a safe, then began moving the dial for the combination.

"I figure you've got a gun in that safe," Ryan said. "If you turn back fast, you'll be dead before you come full around."

"You don't trust me?"

When the safe door swung open, Ryan stepped close to Webster's back, his gun against the back of his neck, and looked over his shoulder.

"As you can see, Ryan, there is no gun."

"Make it two million."

"We agreed to one."

"And I shall only take one. The second million is for Ms. Darby."

"But the payment to you is for killing her."

"Things change. Instead, you're paying us to walk away, keep quiet, and leave you alone."

"Ryan, I know I can trust you. But I can't trust her. Kill her and take the entire two million for yourself."

At that moment, the door leading back to the hallway flew open and Victor filled the void as if he were the door itself. He stood six-two with robust shoulders, and gray shark-like eyes above a joyless grin. His gun centered on Ryan broad midsection.

"Doesn't seem right me holding a gun on you," Victor said. "You having been my mentor and all."

"Doesn't have to be this way, Vic. Put the gun away and join us. Get free of this maggot."

"But Mr. Webster pays me well. And once you're gone, I move up in the pecking order. That'll make the pay even better. Right, Mr. Webster?"

"Right, Victor, at least double what I have paid Testler."

"So," Ryan said to Webster, "that's why you encouraged me to put away my gun?"

"Along with my getting to the safe where I could press the hidden remote to summon Victor. Forgive me, Ryan."

"God forgives, Mr. Webster. I don't."

Then Ryan returned his attention to Victor. "So, how have you been?"

Victor ignored Ryan and spoke to Webster. "You can sit down boss, be comfortable. I'll take this garbage out."

"There's at least a third million in that safe," Ryan said. "That's enough to set you up for life."

"No dice. Mark and I owe Mr. Webster for taking care of our mother."

"Okay," Ryan said. "I wanted to offer you a piece of tonight's haul. Still, it doesn't seem fair, you holding the only gun. Why don't you let me take mine out?"

"Not on your life."

"I thought not, but how 'bout just my finger gun?" Not waiting for an answer, Ryan slowly raised his arm and pointed his hand toward Victor. His index out and thumb back, like a child does to simulate a handgun.

"Now be careful," Victor said after he and Ryan shared an uneasy laugh. "You won't shoot me with that thing, will you?"

"I think I will," Ryan said as he slowly pressed his thumb down to fire the child gun.

Linda had watched the two men bantering over joyless smiles. Then it ended. Nearly simultaneous to Ryan firing his finger gun, she heard the sound of breaking glass from behind her. Then saw Victor's head snap forward suddenly, and then just as suddenly snap back. His knees gave way and he went down heavily.

Linda looked at Webster who sat stunned with a questioning look on his face, one that probably matched her own. The shot had come from outside.

Someone outside is supporting Ryan. But we came alone. But Ryan had not been surprised. He had used his finger gun to call in that shot from outside.

"You got something we can put the two million in?" Ryan asked.

Webster nodded, and then opened a cabinet in the credenza on the side wall below the crucifix. He took out a black satchel and stacked the two million inside.

Then Ryan said, "Give us the rest. Empty the safe."

"But we agreed. Two million and you kill this woman."

"You bargained in bad faith. You had no intent of giving us the two million. That releases me from my agreement. So, new deal, we take it all."

"That's three million," Webster said, "maybe a little more."

"Good. Do it."

"You bastard."

"Yes, sir," Ryan said, "in my case, an accident of birth. Now you, you're a self-made man."

Linda watched Webster hand the satchel to Ryan, then collapse into his chair. He was defeated and he knew it. He crossed his legs, his left hand sliding off his lap, down along the edge of the cushion. Then his hand came back. Fast. His fist filled with a Glock. He fired at Ryan, hitting him in the chest.

Ryan went down.

Linda fired her snub-nosed Rossi three times through the front of her jacket. All three bullets hit Webster so close together in time that the convulsions of his body seemed as one.

The anger that had fed her rage drained from her. She felt empty. Her whole body began to shake. She ignored it and rushed to Ryan. He was not moving.

Ryan looked up. "Good shooting, missy."

"But you've been shot."

"I dealt myself a hand in your game. None of this is your fault. It was my plan, and my failure to allow for that old fox keeping a gun in that chair."

"What'll I do?"

"Get on with your life. Go home. Be yourself. The real you. You're a hell of a woman, Linda Darby. I'm proud to know you."

"But I killed Webster," Linda said.

"Damn straight you did. He definitely deserved to die. He would have shot you next."

"I need to call an ambulance."

"I'd be dead before they got here. And your identity would be blown. I'm still in charge of this operation. Get out of here. Leave one million in the safe so it won't look like a robbery. Take the other two million and go. The authorities will never know you've been here. Split the money with Clark."

"Clark?" Linda said, having forgotten all about the shot from outside. When she looked up, she saw the former waiter from O'Malley's, now Sea Crest deputy, standing just inside the door. He came over and kneeled.

"Sorry, Captain. He fired before I knew what was happening."

"No regrets, Sarge. You did your job. Thanks for your help. Now get Linda out of here."

"I will," Clark said, his hand on Ryan's shoulder. "She can go back to Sea Crest now." Clark then turned to Linda. "You've got your life back. It can be just like before."

"No," Linda said. "My life will never again be like before. I want to go back to Sea Crest, but this time not to hide."

"You need to go, Sarge," Ryan said.

"But we can't leave you," Linda said.

"You can and will. I'm done. If you don't leave now, you'll have wasted what I did."

Clark put his hand under Linda's arm and lifted her to her feet. "The captain's right."

Clark walked out behind Linda, closing the drapes behind them.

EPILOGUE

*C*lark and Linda alternated driving his car the several days it took them to get back to Sea Crest. Along the way, they followed the news reports about the murder of Alistair Webster. The stories told about two other men also found dead at the Webster estate. At this point, the two other men had not been identified beyond reference to them as bodyguards in Alistair Webster's employ. There was no mention of any third man or of the police finding an abandoned, burned out Taurus under a rickety lean-to not far from the Webster estate. The papers were talking about it as a robbery because Webster's safe had been left open and empty. Linda and Clark had left a million in the safe. That million had to have been taken by someone if the safe was found empty, or perhaps the police first at the scene had divided it up.

There were unconfirmed rumors about files being found in Webster's office that implicated many Washington, D.C. insiders, members of Congress and several agency regulators. One article also mentioned a gun found in a plastic bag, the FBI was checking for fingerprints. The local police had been quoted as saying the FBI had taken the contents of a two-drawer lateral file that might not have been found had the hidden wall panel not been left standing open.

"We never found any hidden file cabinet," Linda said.

"I figure the captain wanted the files found," Clark said, "so he opened the hidden cabinet after we left."

"But Ryan was dead?"

"The papers said three dead," Clark reminded Linda, "Webster and two bodyguards."

"But Ryan was dead. I saw him. So did you."

"He wasn't dead when we left."

"Oh, my God," Linda said. Do you think he survived? That he took the other million?"

Clark smiled. "The captain needed to finish funding his own retirement plan while also helping us fund ours."

"Why did he let us think he was dying?"

Clark put his hand on Linda's forearm. "He felt it best you thought he was dead."

"Why?"

"I stopped asking the captain why a long time ago."

"Why do you call him Captain?"

"That was his last rank in Delta."

"Why did he leave the military?"

"Rules of engagement are politically motivated, and he had seen too many good men die because of those restrictions. Politicians rule through authority not through competence. The captain's rule one: if someone is trying to kill you, kill them. The rule applies for individuals or countries. Rule two: see rule one."

"Tell me more about him."

"There is so much to tell, yet so little that can be. I will tell you he greatly admires you, feels you're a real winner."

"Why does he think I'm a winner?"

"Because you're gentle and compassionate, yet tough enough to do what needs to be done. He admires that. So do I."

"Will we ever see him again?"

"Perhaps, some day."

After entering Oregon late that Friday, Clark and Linda stopped for the night. Over breakfast the next morning, they read about the death of Sea Crest Police Chief, Benjamin McIlhenny. He had died in a boating accident on Thursday, in the deepwater channel off the coast of Oregon.

Clark leaned toward Linda. "Ben was in many ways a good man. But he was on Webster's payroll. If he had not helped Webster, your friend Cynthia would not have been killed. And no one would have ever come after you."

"Why would Ben help Webster?"

"Ben had killed a man in New Jersey, a man who needed killing. Webster could prove Ben did it and end Ben's law enforcement career. So he chose to do Webster's bidding, and now Ben has paid the price for that choice."

"And that made killing Ben okay?"

"Maybe not okay, but necessary. Efficient."

"Why?"

"Ben was having an attack of conscience. He had decided to go to the authorities. That would have brought all of us into the light, Webster, Cynthia, you, the captain, maybe me. Cynthia is dead, no reason to sully her memory. Webster has already been exposed. So why let Ben create problems for you and the captain. It's more efficient to just let the guilty suffer and that included Ben."

"It would have exposed the corrupt public officials who sold out to Webster."

"Now you know why the captain left Webster's hidden file cabinet open to be found. Get them exposed without involving you, me, or himself."

They had finished breakfast, returned to the car, and driven for a half hour before either of them spoke again.

"So," Linda asked, "what are your plans? Are you and Ryan off on another adventure?"

"Not me. I told the captain I planned to call it quits. Actually, I had before this but, well, when he told me it was for you, I relented."

"Will you be sticking around Sea Crest for a while?"

"Actually, I thought I might apply to fill Ben's job. I am his only deputy, and at the moment Sea Crest is without a police department. The county sheriff is likely providing temporary coverage. There's a military file on me as Clark Ryerson, so that name'll hold up when they do the background check. Beyond that, there's a lady in town I haven't quit trying to date."

"Then Clark isn't your real name?"

"No."

"What is your real name?"

"Gene."

"And you and Ryan have been friends since you were boys, right?"

"Yes."

"Ryan told me you were dead," Linda said, looking at the man she had just learned was really named Gene.

"The captain, well, both of us really, feel that in his line of work, it is best he be seen as an island. No family. No long friends. Alone. He's less vulnerable that way. His family, more safe. So, yes, Gene is dead, sort of. But Clark is alive and well, and I like the name."

As they turned onto the coast road that approached Sea Crest from the south, Linda asked, "What is your last name?"

"Ryerson. Clark Ryerson. That's my name now and forever."

"What's Ryan's real name?"

"Not important."

The end

An excerpt from **HOMETOWN SECRETS, the next story in the
Linda Darby, Ryan Testler series** begins on the next page.

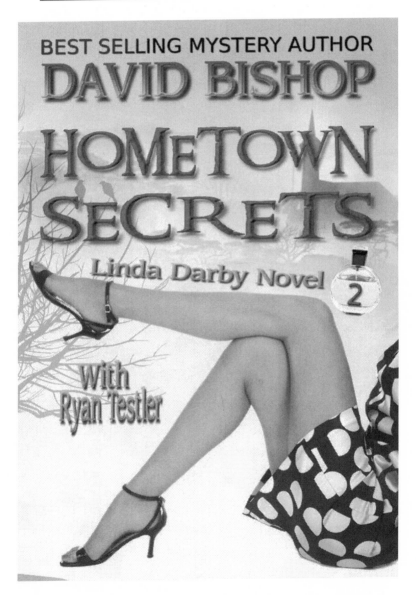

PROLOGUE

*M*artha Cranston sat inside the ranch house in a hard rocking chair and watched her husband's eyelids flutter, his nostrils flare. Her hand tightened around the short glass of whiskey she brought it to her mouth. The soft light from the moon oozed around the back of her shoulders to build shadows of the bedposts against the far wall. This was their nightly vigil: flutter, flare, swallow. Repeating endlessly with nothing, absent her prayers, to suggest Billy's breathing would not go on at least as long as her own.

Unknown to Martha, things were about to change. Outside, when clouds gauzed over the moon, a man moved through a group of parked pickup trucks to the back of the old barn used to house the family's pleasure horses. He had carefully chosen this against-the-wind path to break up any minor sounds arising from his steps.

Three minutes after arriving at the back of the old barn, he retreated across the open field to a cluster of trees and thick brush sixty yards beyond the far side of the corral. He made no effort to hide his tracks as he went. He wanted them discovered. He wanted the tracks seen as the likely escape path taken by the person who did what he came to do.

From there, he circled back to the road bordering the front of the Cranston property. When intervening clouds dampened the moonlight, he scurried to the back of the new, modern barn. With the next shrouding cover, he darted over heavily-trod ground to a nearby toolshed, then a pump room. He repeated this pattern until he recaptured the position he had left at the rear of the old barn.

Over time, the Cranston family's unchallenged control of the town had bred a general laxness, arrogance, and overconfidence that made the man's invasion rather easy.

Carefully shielding himself behind a small collection of empty 55-gallon drums scattered behind the barn, the trespasser lit a cigarette puffing it adequately to be certain it would stay lit. He slipped the cigarette into the top of a book of matches so that it trailed above and slightly behind the heads of the paper matches. He carefully nested this simple ignition device into a gathered stack of loose dry hay at the back of the old barn, cresting it to a peak partway up the grayed boards. He then tossed an opened metal cigarette lighter into the hay, leaving it to char in the fire and possibly be identified as the fire-starting tool.

After working his way back around to the corral and along the fence line, he returned to the street. From there he walked to his vehicle parked behind some scrub brush off the side of the road about fifty yards away. Sitting behind the wheel, he saw a brief spit flash in the distance. The row of matches had burst into a sudden, silent fire. The dry hay a willing partner, the flames hungrily licked their way up the back of the dry barn, his arson device consumed in the process.

He drove away with his headlights off, the fire busily feasting on the barn and a split rail fence. The commotion he could see in his rearview mirror disclosed the fire had been discovered. That was fine. Whatever the extent of the damage, he was satisfied with the first round in his plan to assault all things Cranston.

Let the game begin.

CHAPTER 1

In the quiet turnings of her own emotions, does a woman ever fully let go of her first lover?

SUNDAY

Linda Darby knew she should have returned home long ago. Now, her mother was dead and she was going back. Since leaving twenty years before, she had always found convenient reasons not to visit. Mother wasn't a bad person, simply joyless. Had they lived near the storied seven dwarfs, her mother would have hung around with Grumpy, not Happy. As Linda grew into adolescence and beyond, the primary issue wedged between her and her mother was men. Her mother's hard-crust toasted view of them versus Linda's desire to be a warm, buttered muffin.

For many of us there is some measure of unfinished business lying in wait in our hometowns. A school we failed to realize represented the best of times. Friendships sacrificed to the getting-on-with-it of our careers and lives. Emotional issues involving unjust parents, real or perceived, and, for some, unsettled issues

283

with siblings. Then there's the young loves we just didn't quite know what to do about, and, through that uncertainty, left fallow without closure.

Linda had taken the normal steps before departing for her hometown, as well as steps far from normal. For this visit, she would not use her real name, Linda Darby. Maybe she would eventually, but not right off.

She alerted her mercurial friend, Ryan Testler, a man with whom she had kept up since their first meeting. They had been torrid lovers, but somewhere along the way, her relationship with Ryan mellowed into something more akin to hot pudding, covered and cooling. She believed Ryan remained interested in more than just friendship, but that he felt it inappropriate to bring Linda into his world, a world of which she couldn't be critical. His skills saved her life two years ago. His feelings for her had prevented his taking her life. Last year Ryan had hired her to do a small, quick job in Phoenix, Arizona, a job which paid her most handsomely.

When Linda told Ryan her mother had died and she would be going back to her hometown, he offered to go with her. She refused. Her trip was a family and personal matter. Over time she had told Ryan a great deal about her upbringing in Cranston, Kansas, and her involvement, to use the polite word, with Billy Cranston. Before hanging up she told Ryan she would travel to Cranston by train. At his suggestion, she purchased a ticket that ended not in Cranston, but continued on to Kansas City, a good distance farther. That way, since she was traveling under a false identity, if it became necessary, she could describe Cranston as an impulsive stop in a longer trip, one she needed to continue, and leave.

No nearby airport served Cranston. Only a private airstrip on property owned by Billy Cranston and used by those he favored. Long ago, that would have included Linda, but not today. Billy Cranston was her primary reason for using an alias.

All morning her eyes, ears, and nose reported the train's tireless work as it chugged and jerked its way through cattle country. That had monotonously continued until about two hours ago when the tracks found a crease and entered what seemed the world's largest wheat field.

In late May the wheat in this part of Kansas was nearing maturity. The color was still golden and the heads were still standing tall. It would not be long before harvest. Linda expected to be gone before the heads of the winter wheat nodded sufficiently to signal the crop was ready to be disconnected from the soil. After that, the in-ground stubble would be churned under to begin the process for the next crop.

Linda stood on the train platform, mesmerized by the rush of the close wheat, backed up by the windswept wave of the never ending distant golden crop. The sky seemed bluer than she remembered and the clouds whiter. Then suddenly, as if by magic, the wheat field parted and her hometown of Cranston, Kansas, appeared before her. Not more than a couple miles up the tracks, a modern Midwest version of Moses parting the Red Sea.

The train stifled its high-speed click-clack and settled into a hushed strain as it eased forward toward the platform. The scene ahead looked much as it had when Linda used to ride her bike down to deposit a portion of her allowance into the boxy red soda machine that boldly stood against the outside of the stationhouse. That box now a tiny red dot against the weathered wooden wall.

CHAPTER 2

The breeze would billow our skirts, tickling the soft whites of our thighs

The first sound to reach Linda's ears as she stepped off the train was the bell atop Saint Christopher Catholic Church. Her first sight was a small dust devil at the top of the modest rise in the ground west of town, a veritable mountain in this flat part of America. The wind usually blew this time of year, all times of the year for that matter, at something less than ten miles per hour, but often at a more aggressive pace. All in all, her hometown of Cranston looked the same, felt the same. As if she had not arrived by train, but by time machine preset for minus twenty years.

No other passenger got off in Cranston, Kansas.

The first smell reached her nostrils before the train pulled to a complete top. The odor of the Cranston feedlot was always there, everywhere, swamping anything rising from the kitchens of the town's few downtown eateries. Like towns with paper mills or certain other industries, the aroma of feedlot hung on the town like a wet, putrid shroud no longer noticed by the locals.

The first person Linda saw was a small woman of around fifty. She didn't recognize her. The woman walked beside a man fingering his toupee, a large man who shaded her the way a double-parked delivery van dwarfed a curbed car. Just before passing the couple stepped to their right and crossed the street. The woman looked over at Linda and smiled. The man glanced and then looked down, his fingers exploring his hairpiece the way ants duck about in a bowl of sugared cereal. Linda was a stranger to them and, she hoped, would be a stranger to the entire town.

The Cranston family had been devoutly Catholic since the founding of the town and outwardly remained so today. The town hinted at religious tolerance by having a second church—a poorly attended Methodist. That congregation included no one who worked for Cranston directly as an employee or indirectly. There was no overt pressure or demands, just subtle leverages applied beneath the surface. A word here, a denial of something wanted there. Over time, most locals who had chosen to remain had fallen into step. If you relied on the Cranstons, as did many of those who called Cranston, Kansas, home, you attended the Catholic Church and supported the Cranston family's businesses, in particular the latter. For the most part, the ambitious and confident had migrated out of the town, and a go-along-to-get-along attitude settled in.

Helpful to the Cranston's maintaining their fiefdom was that, in the big picture, those who didn't reside in town or nearby didn't give a rip what happened as long as the mess didn't drift far enough to touch them. Political contributions by Billy Cranston further muffled any infrequent concerns percolating among state officials.

Linda walked from the train station toward the town square which looked as it did in the header for the town's small website, the same as it existed in her mind from before she left. Every sixty minutes, a high clock struck the number of bongs necessary to signal the new hour. Concrete walkways ran in grid-like fashion around and through the town square with a center circular area covered in brick. There was a large gazebo for the use of local musicians and politicians. The rest of the town square was comprised of two grass areas for picnicking during the spring and summer months, and some roses planted and lovingly tended by the Daughters of the American Revolution. Most days, the square was inhabited by the urchins of the town. The firemen used it annually for their pancake breakfast, the Kiwanis for their chili cook-off, and several other groups for numerous bake sales put on as fundraisers for local activities.

Everything Linda learned about Cranston for the last twenty plus years had been filtered through cyberspace, further seasoned by her mother's infrequent and exceedingly brief letters. She never called. Mother had no phone in her home. She avoided the mail because she believed Billy Cranston read her letters before they were transported out of town. Linda imagined her mother being paranoid, but then one of Billy Cranston's cohorts was the postmaster and another managed the local phone exchange. To cater to her mother's concerns, Linda had provided the address of a rental box in Portland, Oregon, which Linda visited whenever she traveled from her home in Sea Crest, Oregon, to the state's major city.

Every year Linda received a few letters from her high school classmate and best friend, Vera Cunningham. Upon entering high school, Vera began making herself available to boys. Nearly every high school class has at least one female who shares herself as easily as did Vera. Of course, the boys needed to take her to the movies or wherever. Without ever having to buy her own ticket, Vera got to see every movie that came to town. When there was no picture Vera wanted to see, or hadn't already seen, she was plied with dinner or a drive to the local swimming hole. Vera was a solid student and never a troublemaker. She just loved sex and was refreshingly candid about it. Linda suspected there wasn't a girl in Cranston who, to one degree or another, at one time or another hadn't envied Vera.

Vera had remained in Cranston, stayed single, learned dressmaking from her mother, and eventually inherited her family home and took over the business, Vera's Threads. The store had always been favored by the Cranston women. The favor of the Cranston women meant that, despite Vera not attending Saint Christopher Catholic Church, Vera escaped the subtle punishments meted out to others who didn't fully fall in step with Cranston's unwritten rules. Vera's letters, also sent to Linda's Portland postal box, were always postmarked from Wichita. Linda planned to ask Vera why.

The identification Linda carried reported her name to be Carol Benson. That name was one of the sets of false IDs given to her by Cynthia LeClair, an elderly lady of somewhat mysterious skills, in Sea Crest, Oregon, with whom Linda had been great friends. The color of Linda's hair as well as the clothing and accessories she brought oozed the style and image she had carved out for Carol Benson, a persona quite different from vintage Linda Darby.

Today was Sunday, so the ringing of the church bell was not unexpected. Only the timing of that first bong felt odd. The bell had pealed just as her foot reached down from the train to touch the possessed ground of Cranston.

Did Billy arrange this? Had he somehow learned I was coming home? Is my paranoia showing?

Billy Cranston would be close to fifty now. He had always turned her on, actually just the thought, as she remembered him, turned the spigot on her juices. Would he still have that effect? King Billy had married. This she knew from the Internet. Billy, undoubtedly, had set up his marriage with a prenuptial that limited his wife to a modest sum, modest for the Cranston brood anyway. The family motto held that whatsoever belonged to Cranston blood would always belong to Cranston blood, which substantially meant Cranston male blood. During the early years, while Billy and Linda were still all tangled up with each other, he told her that should he ever marry, he would insist on a prenuptial agreement just as had existed between his father and mother, and between his older brother and his wife.

The land and businesses controlled by Billy Cranston were legally held in one of three Cranston corporations. The voting shares in these corporations were owned only by Billy Cranston—the younger, but only surviving Cranston son. Billy's older brother had died while serving in the U.S. Marine Corp. Wives were never allowed to work in any of the family businesses. There were two Cranston sisters who held minority interests of nonvoting shares.

A small squad of CPAs and attorneys were employed to maintain a clear paper trail with the hope this would evidence that no wife's money or joint marital funds were ever invested in Cranston businesses. And that no events could inadvertently create sweat equity claims if any of the wives decided to end their marriages.

One question for which Linda intuitively knew the answer: Does Billy have a mistress? Sure Billy Cranston had mistresses, attractive women of negotiable virtue, buying them for less than the folding money he likely held at any time in the warm depths of his pockets. Billy Cranston still looked to temporarily hide his dick under skirts which did not hang in his wife's closet.

If Billy hits on me, perhaps I should say when he hits on me, will I succumb? If he doesn't, will I feel offended? Is my vanity showing?

Linda slung the strap of her purse cross-shoulder to keep it secure, picked up her two suitcases, and started her three-block walk to the Cranston-owned two-story Frontier Hotel on the corner of First and Main.

She chose a route that required her to walk a couple extra blocks, taking her up Second Street along the side of the home of Vera Cunningham who lived on the second floor above Vera's Threads. There was no reason for doing this other than wanting to make some personal connection, even if only to pass the

Cunningham home, a house where she spent a great deal of time while growing up.

Suddenly, there was Vera, the back of her anyway. She sat a few steps down from the landing at the top of the wooden staircase that descended from her upstairs residence to Second Street.

When they were teens, Linda and Vera often sat on those very steps. Afternoons, the staircase rested in the shade, gentled by a breeze that regularly funneled down Second Street. Vera's mother used to holler at them to not sit there saying it was immodest to do so in their dresses, but it was the coolest place in town. The air gusts would billow their skirts, tickling the soft whites of their thighs. Linda smiled at recalling they had another reason for sitting there, the attention of the boys with whom Vera was always in demand. During those years, Linda enjoyed basking in the banter that took place between Vera and the bolder boys.

The clerk behind the Frontier Hotel counter was a stranger. She signed in, paid what was required, and schlepped her own bags up to her room. She paid five dollars more per night for a second-floor room with a window that looked across the street toward the Cranston Bank & Trust, the local drugstore, and The Drop Inn.

Over the years, Linda and Vera never exchanged pictures. It just didn't seem necessary. The image of Vera that Linda carried was of her friend decked out in the sexy red dress she wore to her twentieth birthday party. Linda stayed for that party and left town the next morning.

CHAPTER 3

ot being recognized is as much about not allowing your behavior to be familiar, as it is about not allowing your appearance to be familiar

After unpacking, Linda decided to go to The Do Drop Inn to listen, observe, and to get something to eat. She put on some heels and a black and white dress which cut a clean line just above her knees. The Drop, as it was known locally, had always served burgers and fries. She figured they still did.

The Cranston-owned Do Drop Inn was roughly across the street from her hotel. As she stepped off the curb, she felt herself rushing as if returning to a memory. The warmth of the sun touched her head and shoulders. The sky was light blue with a few distant rain clouds, but she didn't expect rain today. Neither did she expect what would soon follow.

As soon as she cleared the doorway she knew the answer to her first question: The Drop still served burgers and fries. The place had been painted a new shade of brown slightly lighter than the rough-cut stained boards used as a chair rail. A new juke box adorned the far wall, but the same wallboxes accompanied each booth, allowing patrons to select songs from where they sat. A large picture she didn't remember hung on the sidewall, something undecipherable with lots of bold colors that didn't seem to be getting along with each other.

She stepped up to the bar and ordered the All-American which included a soda with free refills. She was engulfed in the shadow cast by the bartender. He was no more than six-foot-two, but he seemed nearly as wide. He had massive shoulders and arms developed by lifting more than beer kegs. There was no paunch resting on his western style belt buckle, not even a small one. A swarthy looking man, she guessed of Greek descent. He did not look familiar.

She sat in one of their wooden, unpadded booths and opened a fascinating mystery novel she had started reading while on the train. After several pages, the bartender, who appeared to be the only working employee, brought her food. The plate cuddled in his broad hand like an eaglet in a nest.

"Hi, miss, you new in town?"

"That's right."

"Going to be here long?"

"At least long enough to have lunch."

He smiled, left her food, and returned to a position behind the bar.

She put the book aside, slathered the burger bun with the thousand-island dressing she had requested on the side, picked up the burger, and took a first bite. As she chewed, the tavern filled with light as the west-facing front door swung in. A young man, who had likely been in elementary school when Linda left town, stood in the center of that light, his hand atop the open swinging door.

At that moment, routine behavior in Cranston abruptly ceased.

Dead silence drowned the jukebox as the man went down. Easily at first, as if they watched was a film in slow motion, then hard and sudden. Two guys at the bar, the dark-complected bartender, and a couple sitting two booths over, and Linda watched until a heavy thud shattered the silent limbo. His head pounded the concrete floor, then repeated, slightly muted, when his forehead bounced before settling against the hard gray flooring.

As if by reaction, the bartender flattened his hands on the bar and catapulted over the counter and the barstools, to the customer side. When he got to the fallen man, he knelt, rolled him onto his back, and immediately checked his pulse at the side of his neck.

"Carlos has been shot," he said looking toward the men at the bar.

"Will he be okay, Mud?" asked one of the men.

"I'm afraid he's dead," the bartender said, his nickname apparently Mud.

For a bartender, Mud had been not only nimble, but easily able to recognize death.

"You should call the sheriff," said one of the men sitting on a barstool. "Or maybe Billy, Yeah, Billy, whatdaya think?"

"I'll take care of it," Mud said.

"Oh, my God," said the woman sitting in the booth with the man. "His mother works for the Cranstons. She's a maid in their home. She'll wanna know what's happened. Honey, go get her."

"What's her name?"

"Maria. You know. Maria. Maria! Go on."

"You know her much better than me. You go, Terry. I'll stay."

The woman got up and hurried toward the door. She stopped suddenly as she neared Carlos's body, turned and went around behind the bar and through a door. The aroma from a deep fryer rushing out through that door revealed it to be the kitchen, likely with an exit to the back alley.

By this time, Mud had moved around the end of the bar, raised the hinged section and returned to his position on the working side of the counter. He immediately picked up a phone on the back counter and dialed.

As he did, an older man with an obvious hunchback and a scruffy beard, the collar on his rumpled shirt partially turned up, walked up to the bartender, said something and pointed at both his eyes using both his index fingers. The bartender opened a drawer in the counter and handed the old man a pair of glasses. The old man slid the glasses up under the bill of his soiled ball cap which carried the name of the grain cooperative near the interstate highway. The old geezer smiled and nodded before squeezing past the bartender. He picked up a tray of dirty glasses and dishes and went back into the kitchen, limping slightly.

After a moment, the bartender turned, faced the wall, and spoke. When he hung up, he dialed again, keeping his back toward the patrons. Linda figured he called the sheriff first and then his boss, Billy Cranston, or one of his underlings.

As far as the others knew, Linda was a stranger in town. As such, she stayed put and watched while finishing her burger and nibbling on the heaping pile of fries which had been scattered on her plate the way tossed kindling bunches in a fire pit. Eventually, the bartender brought her a fresh cola, a refill. Mud had seemed completely in his element when he checked Carlos and calmly declared he was dead—almost too calm.

Not counting numerous lynchings Linda had read about, carried out in the old days by the town's vigilantes, she couldn't recall ever reading of a homicide in the Cranston Gazette. She had religiously read the Gazette online, once a week in the library near her home in Sea Crest Oregon. The library had subscribed at her request, showing it, not Linda, as the subscriber. She donated an amount sufficient to cover the costs associated with their doing so.

While eating, Linda watched a pale, thin man at the bar draw hard on a cigar the width of his nose, both showing red on the ends. His cheeks collapsed inward in response to his harsh inhale. Then she heard someone at the bar say the victim's name, adding a last name: Carlos Molina. That same man said Carlos worked, *had* worked Linda thought would now be correct, as a laborer of some sort at the Cranston feedlot. However, Carlos, his shoulders in his own blood, now wore slacks and a blood-soiled button-down collar long-sleeved shirt. Not the dress of a farm laborer. From what she could tell, given the distance and the less than ideal light, his fingernails looked clean and the skin on his hands was not embedded with soil or heavily calloused. One of the men at the bar said Carlos had no family other than his mother.

The light from the open door again dashed past Linda to crash against the back wall. This time, a sheriff's deputy walked in and told everyone to stay put that Sheriff Blackstone was on his way.

A few minutes later, a man Linda immediately recognized as Billy Cranston walked in followed by another man. As they came in, she heard enough trailing words to know they had been talking about a fire and not the town's first murder in God knows how long. Judging by his uniform, the second man, the one who held open the door for Billy, was Sheriff Blackstone.

The clock in the town square screamed once, followed by a second bong to announce it was two in the afternoon, a little early for a feedlot worker to be dressed business casual and entering a bar. Perhaps today had been Carlos's day off.

"Mud," Billy said in a stern voice, while making a couple of jerky moves with his hand, his thumb out like an impatient hitchhiker. The bartender picked up some papers and slid them under the bar. The racing forms Linda had seen on the bar when she walked in. Right after ordering, she had heard the men discussing wagers on horses. Someone was making book in Cranston, and doing it rather openly. At this point a good guess would be the bartender, Mud.

Had this all been going on before I left Cranston? Maybe it had always been here, but I was too young, self-absorbed, and naïve to see some things plainly there to be seen.

Billy Cranston and Sheriff Blackstone looked around. As he panned the room, Billy's eyes met Linda's. Her first face-to-face immediately wet her palms, but nowhere else. She froze, but didn't panic.

Billy removed the remainder of a fat cigar from his face. He looked at the stub, the way a man does when taking a pipe or cigar from his mouth. He sputtered his tongue against his lips a couple times before using his fingers to remove a morsel of tobacco that had somehow gained freedom from the stalk in his mouth. He looked at it before flicking it from his fingers. Then Billy looked at Linda again, holding his gaze for more than a moment.

Billy's hair had thinned some, his body widened some. More softened, than widened, likely from an excess of everything but exercise. She forced herself to hold still, not smile or look away.

I'm a stranger who has just seen a man shot dead. Look disturbed, she told herself, *curious, even somewhat frightened, nothing more. Recognize nothing and no one.*

The entire establishment had been stone still since the authorities walked in. That quiet was broken by the gimpy-legged dishwasher who again came out from the backroom carrying a stack of beer mugs which he proceeded to put in the cooler beside the row of draft beer pulls. Other than that action, no one moved. No one spoke. The few customers watched Billy. Not the sheriff. Billy.

The bartender stood center on his own side of the bar, his arms slid outward, stiff, his hands cupping the edge of the bar, his elbows slightly hyper-extended. Without fanfare or anyone speaking, he reached for a clean shot glass, then a second one and filled both with whiskey. By the red wax around the neck of the bottle, Linda recognized the brand to be Maker's Mark. Mud set both shot glasses, now dark in color, on the end of the bar.

Billy's stare moved to the man sitting in the booth alone, the one whose female companion had left to get Carlos's mother. Billy also looked at the men at the bar. They each looked at him, smiling or nodding in submission, or fear, or simply deference.

So far, Billy hasn't recognized me. Then again, the light in The Drop is dim and Carlos, not I, holds center stage.

The sheriff, or whom Linda assumed to be the sheriff, moved across the carpet to stand in the middle of the small parquet dance floor. He hunched his shoulders before stuffing his thumbs behind his wide black belt, his shiny boots reflecting the low lighting sent out from the jukebox.

"Most of you know me. I'm Sheriff Reginald Blackstone."

His identity surprised Linda. The Reginald Blackstone she had known in high school would be the last young man she would ever imagine growing up to become sheriff. Reggie had always been big on the outside, but Jell-O like on the inside, using his bulk to bully those he could, which were most of her classmates.

The man's clearly still a bully. Funny how things change, but stay the same.

"All of you stay right where you are," he said, "for the time being. Don't talk amongst yourselves about what you observed here. Speak only to me." He punctuated his order by banging his left thumb against his chest.

How silly, Linda said to herself. *What the hell does he think we all have been talking about ever since the shooting?*

The sheriff walked to the jukebox, grabbed the cord and jerked, pulling the plug. The music died and the jukebox's light reflection immediately retreated from what appeared to be his hand-tooled snakeskin boots.

While the sheriff commanded the floor, Billy took a seat at the bar. The bartender brought him a draft beer and a salt shaker. They didn't speak, but slowly and down low along the bar top, Billy extended his closed fist toward the barkeep for a macho fist bump. Billy salted his beer and took a drink. He wanted to come across as unconcerned, but he had come as quickly as Sheriff Blackstone. King Billy was concerned all right. From what Linda knew, this was the first murder in his private fiefdom, at least since the beginning of his personal reign.

The sheriff went to the end of the bar and used the house phone for a moment. While on the phone he picked up one of the shot glasses and threw down its contents in one gulp.

"Who are you?" the sheriff asked two minutes later as he slipped into the booth across from Linda. "I don't know you. Just get into town?"

"That's right, Sheriff Blackstone. I came to town a couple of hours ago on the mid-day flyer."

Named after the comic strip character, Reggie had been a junior the year Linda graduated from high school. Even at that age Reggie was known for his consumption of beer. Apparently he graduated to the hard stuff. She was glad he came to talk with her. This interview would be a good test run before her inevitable up close and personal meeting with King Billy.

"I could tell it stopped," the sheriff said. "The mid-day sounds different when it does. Not that it stops all that often." In a juvenile and naked display of authority, he reached over and took one of her three remaining fries. "What's your business in Cranston?"

Before answering, she ran the pad of her index finger along the lines of a name which had been gouged into the wood table top. Then she looked up. "Respectfully, Sheriff, everyone in this place can verify I was sitting right here when that poor man was shot, so clearly I'm not a suspect."

"Then perhaps you can help me with another ongoing investigation, an arson that burned down the horse barn and part of the corral fencing out on the Cranston ranch. That there's Billy Cranston at the bar—the man who came in with me."

"I haven't heard a thing, Sheriff, but then I just got here. When did this happen?"

"Coupla days ago. I was just wondering if someone you know hereabouts told you about it. You know, idle talk that don't get repeated all that much in front of the sheriff."

Reggie Blackstone still doesn't speak properly, Linda thought before saying, "I don't know anyone in town, Sheriff. Like I said, I just got here. It was a random stop on my part. I was ready for a break from train travel."

During this exchange, his eyes never left hers. Without looking away, he placed the pilfered fry on his outstretched tongue and suggestively drew it slowly back into his mouth. After using his versatile tongue to move the yet-unbitten fry to one side, he said, "I ask again, what's your reason for being in our town?"

The best way to deal with the sheriff is the way I dealt with Reggie Blackstone the bully when we were children. Not allow him to intimidate me.

"All right, Sheriff, let me put it this way, I'm an American citizen exercising my right to go where I please without having to account to anyone for my reasons. ... No disrespect, Sheriff Blackstone, but my travel plans are my own business. However, in the spirit of cooperation, I will tell you I was just passing through. I love train travel but after a few days of it I need some time on terra firma. I love small towns so I got off here for a respite."

"Then you plan to move on immediately? Tomorrow, Monday's midday flyer, perhaps?"

"I had planned to do just that. Now, being part of, in a manner of speaking, a murder, I may hang around for a while. I love to read murder mysteries." As she said that, Linda held up her print copy of Who Murdered Garson Talmadge, a Matt Kile Mystery that she had been reading when Carlos hit the floor. "This is my first opportunity to experience a murder up close and personal. I hope that doesn't sound morbid. I've always been an unapologetically curious person."

"No other reason for being here?"

"Asked and answered, Sheriff."

When she said that, his eyebrows went up. This phrase was most often heard from attorneys.

"What do you do for a living, Miss?"

"Because I was a witness to this unfortunate crime, you have a right to ask me some things. My name is Carol Benson and I am staying at the Frontier Hotel. I saw only what I overheard the men at the bar tell you: Carlos, at least that's the name I've heard, opened the door and fell. The bartender checked him and said he had been shot and was dead ... . I think we're through here, Sheriff."

His eyebrows went up again. She expected he would check her out, try to find out if she was an attorney, which she was not. Linda supported herself mostly through day-trading publicly held stocks and the interest off some certificates of deposit. Her manner had clearly left the sheriff unsure how to proceed with her. He would likely handle her carefully until he learned enough to ascertain whether or not she had the wherewithal to bite back.

She wanted the sheriff and Billy to have these uncertainties on their minds, rather than reaching back and trying to find her in a mental sea bottomed with rusted memories.

Not being recognized is as much about not allowing your behavior to be familiar as it is about your appearance being familiar. That was the image she wanted them to have of her: poised, articulate, and confident, far different than the shy and insecure Linda Darby, schoolgirl, who lingered somewhere in the dusty corners of their past. She had Sheriff Blackstone curious, and would have Billy Cranston curious once the sheriff reviewed his encounter with her after the two men left The Drop.

Just as the sheriff started toward the booth where the lone man waited, that man's female companion came back in with a Mexican woman Linda assumed to be Carlos's mother. The mother froze upon seeing Carlos on the floor. She stared at an irregular puddle of her son's blood jagged as a muffler partially unwound from around his neck. She dropped to her knees next to her son. Her hand over her mouth, she remained silent, her obvious pain loud.

The sheriff went to her, placed his hands under her elbows and picked her up as if she were a sack of grain wedged by a door during a prairie rainstorm. He led her back to the booth where the man had waited. The man got up and motioned for his woman and

Carlos's mother to sit together on his side of the booth. The woman who had escorted the mother to The Drop sat close and took Maria Molina's hand.

The sheriff shook hands with the man. "Hello, Harry. Thanks for going and getting Ms. Molina."

"My wife, Theresa, went to get her."

"Sure. I saw them come in together." The sheriff turned to the woman. "Thanks, Terry. I appreciate your doing that." She nodded slightly.

The sheriff slid into the booth across from the two women. Harry snatched a chair from a nearby table and sat at the end of the booth.

The sheriff leaned against the wall at the end of the booth, his shoulders, angled away from Linda, slouched down about level with the top of the booth. With the music off, the room was quiet enough that Linda could hear the answers pretty well as they came toward her, but only bits and pieces of the sheriff's questions, which moved away.

In the background, the bartender filled another glass with soda from his bar dispenser.

."He's a good boy, Sheriff," the mother said, "never in any real trouble. Mr. Whipple at the feedlot tells me my Carlos is a good worker. No trouble, Sheriff. Why would anyone want to kill him?"

While the mother spoke, Linda quickly glanced toward the bar. One of the two men sitting there shook his head slightly while the other did the same with his eyebrows raised. Mud looked down. Clearly, these men did not agree with the mother's characterization of her son.

The dishwasher came back out from the kitchen. The bartender pointed his index finger at the fresh glass of soda he had just filled and, rolling over his palm, used his thumb to point at Linda.

The sheriff asked something Linda couldn't make out, but she did hear him enunciate one word, "enemies" somewhere around the middle of his question.

While the dishwasher limped over to her table, Linda heard the mother say, "No. Everyone likes my boy. He has no enemies. My Carlos is a good man. No trouble."

Linda again distinctly heard one word in the sheriff's next question, "Girlfriend."

"Carlos has no one special, Sheriff. My boy is, how you say, gorgeous. No, no, handsome. The girls like Carlos. He likes them. He is good to them, but he spends too much of his money on them. No bad blood. No trouble. Who killed him, Sheriff?"

The old man left Linda's cola, spilling a slight bit when he put his hand on the table to steady himself. He nodded without speaking or smiling, picked up her empty plate and turned to take it to the dirty dish tray at the end of the bar. Her attention drifted back to the sheriff who had moved to sat tall in the booth.

"My investigation is only beginning," he said. "At the moment, I have no idea who killed your boy. Carlos was shot in the back of the head as he entered."

The mother's hand covered her lower face, squeezing her lips, pinching them in from the sides as her hand fisted over her mouth. Her eyebrows, thick and dark, furrowed in. Her forehead wrinkled as she fought to hold herself together while wrestling with the sheriff's words.

After giving the mother a moment, the sheriff continued. "We just don't know. I hope to find out. No one saw anything other than your son coming in the door and falling to the floor. No shots were heard and, far as I know right now, it appears only one was fired. I am sorry."

Maria Molina turned her face into Theresa's shoulder. The movements of her body revealed she was sobbing, hard, but not wailing. She let go of her mouth and turned back to face the sheriff. "Will you find out who did this, Sheriff?" She swiped at her tears without concern for smearing her modest eye makeup. "Promise me you will find the man who killed my boy, my Carlos."

"I promise I will do what I can to find the man ... or woman. I'll make my inquiries, but I can't be promising anything. As things develop I may need to talk with you some more. If I do, I'll come by your place or stop in at your job."

Maria closed her eyes and sat still, grappling with her misery. When she opened her smeared eyes, she nodded her head, hesitatingly. "Of course, Sheriff. Thank you."

From the corner of her eye Linda saw Billy and Mud talking again, leaning close, the barkeep doing most of the talking. Mud using his head as a pointer, motioned toward her.

Billy moved down the bar, about the width of his body, far enough to block her direct view of his employee. Sheriff Blackstone moved to the end of the bar and downed the contents of the second shot glass.

Over the next half hour, Linda watched the local doctor, who from what was said, also acted as the county coroner, take Carlos's body from The Drop. Fifteen minutes later, Sheriff Blackstone held the door open for Billy Cranston who, walking behind the sheriff, pushed the dishwasher out of his way. The old man staggered a bit but didn't fall. Linda started to get up to help him. He looked at her and gently motioned with his hand for her to sit back down.

After the sheriff and Billy left, Linda closed her book, drank the last of her soda and got up. On the way out she paid her bill at the bar. The bartender followed her toward the door walking on his side of the bar.

"Goodbye, Miss. Thanks for coming in. Bad scene here today, sorry you had to be part of it."

She stepped as near as she could, the bar between them at the end in the direction of the door. Away from the two men who remained on stools at the other end.

"Good burger. Thank you."

"Call me Mud. Everybody does."

"Sure, Mud. Was Carlos Molina a regular?"

"He stopped by most days, before or after work, to get a burger, have a brew, talk with the boys, normal stuff."

"I thought I heard his mother say he worked at the feedlot," Linda said. "He wasn't dressed like a ranch worker."

"No he wasn't," Mud said, confirming the obvious. "I don't know anything about his work. Maybe it was his day off."

"Yeah, maybe," Linda said, while thinking: *Carlos stopped in most days before or after work. This is a small town. It's hard to believe the bartender didn't know what kind of work Carlos did.*

END OF EXCERPT.

An excerpt from David Bishop's novel, **Who Murdered Garson Talmadge, a Matt Kile Mystery** begins after the next page. This is the first in the Matt Kile mystery series which currently includes four stories, a fifth Matt Kile mystery will be released in the coming months.

#1 Amazon Bestselling Author

DAVID
BISHOP

Author of 'The Woman'

A MATT KILE MYSTERY – BOOK ONE

Who
Murdered
Garson
Talmadge

PROLOGUE

*I*t's funny the way a kiss stays with you. Lingers. How you can feel it long after it ends. I understood what amputees meant when they spoke of mystery limbs. It's there, but it isn't. You know it isn't. But you feel it is. While I was in prison, my wife divorced me. She said I destroyed our marriage in a moment of rage in a search for some kind of perverted justice. I didn't think it was perverted, but I didn't blame her for the divorce.

But that's enough sad stuff. Yesterday I left the smells and perversions of men and, wearing the same clothes I had worn the last day of my trial, reentered the world of three-dimensional women, and meals you choose for yourself. My old suit fit a bit looser and had a musty smell, but nothing could be bad on a con's first day of freedom. I tilted my head back and inhaled. Free air smelled different, felt different tossing my hair and billowing my shirt.

I had no excuses. I had been guilty. I knew that. The jury knew that. The city knew that. The whole damn country knew. I had shot the guy in front of the TV cameras, emptied my gun into him. He had raped and killed a woman, then killed her three children for having walked in during his deed. The homicide team of Kile and Fidgery had found the evidence that linked the man I killed to the crime. Sergeant Matthew Kile, that was me, still is me, only now there's no *Sergeant* in front of my name, and Detective Terrence Fidgery. We arrested the scum and he readily confessed.

The judge ruled our search illegal and all that followed bad fruit, including the thug's confession. Cute words for giving a killer a get-out-of-jail-free card. In chambers the judge had wrung his hands while saying, "I have to let him walk." Judges talk about their rules of evidence as though they had replaced the rules about right and wrong. Justice isn't about guilt and innocence, not anymore. Over time, criminal trials had become a game for wins and losses between district attorneys and the mouthpieces for the accused. Heavy wins get defense attorneys bigger fees. For district attorneys, wins mean advancement into higher office and possibly a political career.

They should take the robes away from the judges and make them wear striped shirts like referees in other sports.

On the courthouse steps, the news hounds had surrounded the rapist-killer like he was a movie star. Fame or infamy can make you a celebrity, and people treat celebrity like virtue.

I still see the woman's husband, the father of the dead children, stepping out from the crowd, standing there looking at the man who had murdered his family, palpable fury filling his eyes, his body pulsing from the strain of controlled rage. The justice system had failed him, and, because we all rely on it, failed us all. Because I had been the arresting officer, I had also failed him.

The thug spit on the father and punched him, knocking him down onto the dirty-white marble stairs; he rolled all the way to the bottom, stopping on the sidewalk. The police arrested the man we all knew to be a murderer, charging him with assault and battery.

The thug laughed. "I'll plead to assault," he said. "Is this a great country or what?"

At that moment, without a conscious decision to do so, I drew my service revolver and fired until my gun emptied. The lowlife went down. The sentence he deserved, delivered.

The district attorney tried me for murder-two. The same judge who had let the thug walk gave me seven years. Three months after my incarceration, the surviving husband and father, a wealthy business owner, funded a public opinion poll that showed more than eighty percent of the people felt the judge was wrong, with an excess of two-thirds thinking I did right. All I knew was the world was better off without that piece of shit, and people who would have been damaged in the future by this guy, would now be safe. That was enough; it had to be.

A big reward offered by the husband/father eventually found a witness who had bought a woman's Rolex from the man I killed. The Rolex had belonged to the murdered woman. The husband/father convinced the governor to grant me what is technically known in California as a Certificate of Rehabilitation and Pardon. My time served, four years.

While in prison I had started writing mysteries, something I had always wanted to do, and finally had the time to do. When I got out, I had a literary agent and a publisher. I guessed, they figured that stories written by a former homicide cop and convicted murderer would sell.

My literary agent had wanted to meet me at the gate, but I said no. After walking far enough to put the prison out of sight, I paid a cabbie part of the modest advance on my first novel to drive me to Long Beach, California, telling the hack not to talk to me during the drive. He probably thought that a bit odd, but that was his concern, not mine. If I had wanted to gab, I would have let my literary agent meet me. This trip was about looking out a window without bars, about being able to close my eyes without first checking to see who was nearby. In short, I wanted to quietly absorb the subtleties of freedom regained.

CHAPTER 1

SIX YEARS LATER:

$\mathcal{I}$ had been about to walk out my door to have breakfast with the tempting Clarice Talmadge and her septuagenarian husband, Garson Talmadge, without knowing Garson would be skipping breakfasts forever, not to mention lunches and dinners. The Talmadges lived on my floor, at the end of the hall on the corner with a balcony overlooking the white sand shoreline of Long Beach, California. Then my phone rang. It was Clarice, but she hadn't called to ask how I liked my eggs. The cops were with her and they hadn't been invited for breakfast.

A uniformed officer halted me at the door to the Talmadge condo. "My name's Matt Kile," I said, "I was asked to come—"

The saxophone voice of Detective Sergeant Terrence Fidgery interrupted, "Let 'im in."

For seven years before my incarceration Fidge and I had worked homicides together for the Long Beach police department. Fidge was a solid detective, content with his work, a man who appeared to need nothing else. Well, perhaps a diet-and-exercise program, but Fidge was a man who would do anything to stay in shape except eat right, exercise, and drink less beer. I left the force ten years ago but stayed in touch with Fidge and his wife, Brenda, whose pot always held enough to fill one more plate. I often sought out Fidge for his up-to-date cop's angle for my mystery novels.

The master bedroom, where Garson Talmadge slept alone, was immediately inside to the right; his door loitered partially open. Clarice stood in the middle of the living room, clutching her Chihuahua, her wet eyes pleading for help. I put my open palm straight out toward her so she would not come to me, then my finger to my lips signaling her to stay quiet.

"I'll be with you in a minute Matthew," Fidge hollered from somewhere deeper into the condo.

I waited in the foyer while the police photographer finished shooting Garson's bedroom. A liquid had been spilled or thrown against the bedroom door. I touched the wet carpet and smelled my fingers. Coffee, with cream, I thought. A moment later, the photographer came out of Garson's bedroom. I couldn't place his name, but I'd seen him around. We exchanged nods as we passed in the doorway.

Sometimes you strain so hard listening for the quietest of sounds that you don't hear the loudest. The shot that had hit my neighbor Garson Talmadge just above the bridge of his nose had come so fast that before he consciously heard it, he had stopped hearing everything.

The edge of Garson's bedcovers was pulled back exposing a foot too white to be a living foot. A modest amount of dried blood soaked Garson's pillowcase, and stippling surrounded the entry wound. My elderly neighbor had taken it from up close.

I started toward the bed and heard a crunching sound. I stopped. The gold carpeting between the door and the bed had been sprinkled with what looked to be cornflakes. I stood still and looked around. A man's billfold sat on the dresser in front of the mirror, the corners of a wad of cash edging out where the wallet folded over. Five boxes of cornflakes stood at attention along the wall at the end of the dresser, the flaps on the end box rigid in mock salute.

A hissing sound led my gaze to the sliding door to their ocean-facing balcony. The slider was open two inches with the air fighting to get inside. The room was cold enough that I would have closed the door, but not in a crime scene. I pulled the sleeve of my sweater down over my fingertips, reached as high as my six-three frame allowed and opened the slider far enough to stick my head outside. Halfway between the door and the railing, a zigzag print from the sole of a large deck shoe smudged the dewy balcony. The sole print testified that the step had been toward the condo. I pushed the slider back to its original two inches. Moving to avoid the cornflakes, I went into the walk-in closet. There were no shoes with that sole pattern, and no shoes of any kind under or beside the bed. Whatever clothing Garson had worn, had not been left over the high-back leather chair or the bed's foot rail. Garson had always struck me as an everything-in-its-place kind of guy; his room proved it. He would not have wanted to see the jagged out-of-place blood stain on his pillow.

Sergeant Fidgery came through the doorway, his posture slouched, his stride short. "Hey, Matthew, just finished your latest, *Murder on Overtime*. Your best yet."

"Thanks, Fidge. As always, your technical tips helped. Where's your new partner?"

"What's this new stuff? You know George has been with me since, well, since that stupid stunt you pulled on the courthouse steps ten years ago."

"Anybody since me will always seem new. So, then, where's George?"

"Sick," Fidge said. "I'm soloing. That's why I approved your coming down here."

"By the way," I said, "happy birthday old man. Sorry I didn't make the party last weekend. Forty-seven, right?"

"Yeah, sure," Fidge said sarcastically. "We go through this every year. I'm forty-seven, you're forty-six, but only for a couple of months, then you'll be forty-seven like me. Brenda said to tell you she hasn't forgiven you for missing the party."

"Hey, man, you know I would've been there if I could. My agent scheduled an out-of-town book signing without checking the date with me; she won't do that again."

"No sweat, Matthew. I'm just yanking your chain. Brenda understands."

"Thanks. Look, I stepped on the cornflakes before I saw them. They blended with the carpeting. It looks like the flakes had been walked on before I got here. You?"

"Who the hell expects cornflakes on gold carpet?" Fidge asked. "Christ almighty, on any color carpet." Fidge put a steadying hand on my shoulder, crossed one knee with his opposite ankle and looked at his sole, then did the same with the other foot. Neither of us saw anything on the soles of his shoes.

"Did Clarice walk on 'em?" I asked.

"Says so. Says she got up, threw a load of clothes in the washer, put the coffee on, showered and slipped into what she called 'a little thing,' then came in here to wake her old man."

"What about the uniform at the door," I asked, "did he come in, too?"

"I cursed when I stepped on the flakes," Fidge said, shaking his head. "A bit too loudly, I guess. Officer Cardiff came running. Now stop poking around, Matthew. I let the wife call you because she said she had been with you last night and that you might have a key to this place, not so's you could play detective. Tell me about her, and keep your voice down."

"What can I say? She's got her own teeth, great hair, and this and that."

"Yeah. Right off I noticed her this and that. Also the 'little thing' she said she put on this morning is hanging behind her bathroom door. You ought to take a look, or maybe you've already seen it, with her in it." He looked at me from the corner of his eye, and then added, "I haven't heard you deny she was with you so tell me about her visit."

"Clarice came down during the night. Said she thought someone would try to kill her husband. Looks like she had that right."

"What time did she get there?"

"It had been dark for a while. She woke me and I had been zonked. I went to bed around ten. So, midnight would be a good guess."

"What did she say? I want all of it and I want it exactly."

"Page one, colon: The doorbell woke me a few minutes after midnight. I found Mrs. Talmadge leaning on my door jamb wearing a man's white button-down shirt, a strategic gap formed by the mismatching of a southern buttonhole with a northern button. Her blond hair teased her shoulders. She was wearing a pair of shiny gold sandals, her toenails painted red to match the bloody mary she held, a celery stalk standing tall in the short glass."

"Knock it off, Matthew; this isn't one of your novels. You know what I want. Give."

I nodded. "Her opening line was 'something bad's gonna happen.' She brushed past me, her sandals slipping as she stepped down into my sunken living room, her shirttail failing to fully cover her backside. Oops. I forgot. You said no descriptions. I asked her what she was talking about. She said, 'Somebody's going to kill Tally.' That's her pet name for her dead husband."

"Then what did she do?" Fidge asked.

"She took a big drink, chomped the end off the celery stick that had poked her in the cheek, and oozed her bottom over the arm of my leather chair, creating two small miracles. She didn't spill a drop, and her face showed no reaction when her bare bottom settled onto the cool leather."

Fidge screwed up his face.

"Okay. Okay, just the facts, Sergeant. I asked why she thought that. She said, 'Three days ago, I answered the phone. Some guy with a raspy voice asked for Gar. Only he made it sound like jar. I told him there's no jar here and hung up.'"

"Was her dead husband there?"

"No. But her live husband was." Fidge gave me the finger. I ignored it and continued. "She said her husband just sat at the table drinking coffee but that he turned white when she mentioned *Gar*. To illustrate the color she held up her short white shirttail, her unblemished skin the color of light milk chocolate. She had no tan line. I know you said to can the descriptions, but I figured you'd like that one."

"What did her husband say?"

"He told her that some former business acquaintances in Europe used to call him Gar. Then he told her to hang up when they called back."

Fidge put one hand in the air like he had been busted back to directing traffic. "When? Not if?"

"I asked her that, too. She definitely said, 'when they called back.' And, before you ask, she said there were no more such calls, at least not while she was home. She got in Garson's face about that call again the next morning, and they fought."

"How well did you know this guy?"

"Not all that well," I said. "I went out to dinner two or three times with the Talmadges. Garson was a bon vivant. He and I played poker with a few men in the building, maybe four times."

"Did the Talmadges go to dinner with you or you with them?"

"What's the difference?"

"Who invited whom?"

"I don't recall."

"Who drove? That's usually the person who extended the invitation."

"That I remember. Clarice. She gets motion sickness in a car. She found it didn't come when she drove. Garson said it had something to do with her vision and hearing senses getting the same stimulus."

"When I was a kid," Fidge said, "my uncle always drove for the same reason. You mentioned you played poker with the deceased and a few other men in the building. The wife's about thirty-five and a real looker. The dead guy's around eighty. Was she also playing with some of the other men in the building?"

I ran my hand through my hair, wrinkled my lips, and then said, "Yeah."

"You?"

"I expect it'll come out, so here it is. One afternoon, two days before they moved in last summer, Clarice knocked on my door. I had seen her and Garson in the building earlier, but hadn't been introduced. She said ... no, she didn't say, I assumed she and Garson were father and daughter."

"But she didn't say otherwise, right?"

"She didn't say otherwise. Before she left, we, well, you know. Then I found out they were married. It's rumored several other fellows in the building have also taken turns. I don't know any names, but I suspect you'll find wives eager to spill their suspicions."

"Someday," Fidge said, "I need to give you my sex-without-deep-feelings-is-worthless speech. I just don't have time right now."

"Oh, too bad, I've been so looking forward to that one. But it's a load of bull. Sex for pure lust is not worthless. Not all of us are fortunate enough to have someone we love deeply in our lives every time we get a case of the hornies."

"You've obviously given this a lot of thought, Matthew. But may I bring you back to why we're together this morning?"

"You brought it up." I sighed. "Go ahead."

"What do you know about Garson Talmadge's background?"

"Less than I know about his eating habits. During one of the dinners, Garson said he came from Europe, but shied from anything beyond generalities. I can tell you he spoke some words with the softer consonants common to the French. Once when the poker talk came around to Iraq, Garson pronounced 'Allah' with the back of his tongue raised to touch his soft palate as is done with Arabic."

The sun broke through the clouds to reflect off the ocean and brighten Garson's bedroom. We moved a bit to avoid the glare.

"What else happened while she was at your place?"

"She took another bite from the celery stalk. A drip of bloody mary fell onto her skin to slalom down her abundant cleavage until blossoming into a pink splotch on her white shirt."

"Knock off the colorful bullshit, Matthew."

"You know, you're the only person since my mother who regularly calls me Matthew. Brings back memories. I like it."

"I told you to knock it off."

"Sorry. It's the novelist in me; I think that way now. Clarice said the next morning when Garson went into the bathroom she saw a bunch of passports in an attaché case he'd left open on his bed. They all had his picture, but different names. She didn't remember any of the names, but from the way she told it he had enough to start his own phonebook."

"They fight a lot?"

"According to her," I said, "at least since that call asking for Gar. She also heard him on the phone speaking some language she didn't understand. Said it wasn't French. That she didn't speak French anymore, but had taken French in high school so she'd recognize it. After the 'Gar' call, she said her husband never again left their condo except a couple of times to go to the workout room and spa area in the building."

"What else?" Fidge widened his stance, taking care not to step on more of the cornflakes.

"Did I mention her fingernails were painted to match her toenails?"

Fidge flipped me off again, then asked, "What time did she leave?"

"I didn't look."

"Guess."

"I'd put it at a little after three in the morning. And, yes, the skin on her fanny made a popping sound when she pulled free of the leather chair."

"She stayed more than three hours? Just what were you two up too?"

"We talked. Her life, well, her life some. Mostly mine, I guess."

"And you spilled your guts, right?"

"Some stuff. Yeah. The woman knows how to get a man talking."

"I'll bet. Her naked under a man's white shirt, mismatched buttonholes and all. I suppose you told her your wife got a divorce after you went to prison?"

"Yeah."

"And that she had been ready to file even before that, because you shot her father's prize hunting dog? You told her that, too?"

"That damn dog was hunting me, Fidge, charged me in the study, saliva hanging from its teeth. For heaven's sake, you had to be there. That animal took down game with that mouth. What would you have done?"

Fidge laughed. "I'd've brought along Milk Bone when I visited the in-laws."

"Ha. Ha. Hell, my marriage was kaput by then anyway, only a matter of time."

"So you shortened the time."

"It was self-defense. Hey, you got a murder here. Shouldn't you be doing something more important than critiquing my messed-up life?"

"You're right. I'm here about the murdered man, not the

murdered dog. You were telling me about you and Clarice and your three hours in paradise."

"I can't really tell you what we talked about. It was late. You know, you get sort of groggy, the mindless talk comes and the time goes."

Again his silent finger preceded his question. "What about the key?"

"I don't know why she said that."

"That don't answer my question, Matthew. Says you were her old man's only friend in the building. She figured her husband might have given you a key for emergencies or whatever. That woulda been convenient for you when you wanted to visit with his wife."

"Okay. Here it is direct. I do not and never did have a key to the condo of Garson and Clarice Talmadge. Is that plain enough, Sergeant Fidgery?"

"Don't get hot, Matthew. You know how this works."

"I wasn't dodging your question. How do you size this up?"

The sergeant stepped closer. "The wife's a pastry on legs, but her deck is missing a few cards. She plugs her old man, and then leaves the front door dead bolted from the inside." Fidge gestured toward a .22 revolver on the bed. "Says that there's her husband's gun. It's loaded with longs. Only one shot's been fired. I expect ballistics will find the missing long is in the old guy's brain. Says the red scarf draped over the gun handle is hers, so's that pretty little pink pillow with the ugly little black hole. Her dog sleeps on it, or used to."

"Why the pillow?" I asked, "a .22's pretty quiet. An expert would know that."

"She ain't no expert."

"Oh, come on, Fidge." I shook my head. "Clarice isn't the kind to kill a man unless it's with loving."

"And just what kind is she, Mr. Writer?"

"The divorcing kind. She'd move on and find a new rich guy.

Think of it as legal prostitution with fewer customers and better working conditions, with a topnotch severance package thrown in."

Fidge grinned. "Maybe you should write one of them columns for the lovelorn."

I imitated his finger, using my own. "What's the story on the cornflakes?" I asked.

"Says her husband was a very light sleeper. That he sprinkled the flakes on the floor so no one could sneak into his room. How's that for nutso?"

Clarice's voice shrilled from the living room. "I didn't do it, Matt. Honest to God, I didn't do it." Her Chihuahua whimpered, perhaps in agreement.

I had never before heard the dog make a sound. Garson had refused to buy the condo unless his wife could keep her dog. She proved to the condo association that Asta had been trained to always stay quiet indoors and, after Garson paid a large nonrefundable deposit, Asta became the only pet in a building posted: no pets.

I looked at my old partner. "Just what points this at her?"

Fidge started with a facial expression that screamed I've already told you, then he summarized: "The deadbolt. No forced entry. Nothing's missing. The neighbors have heard lots of screaming. The gun was in the house. The scarf and pillow are hers."

"That won't get you a conviction."

"That's just the part I'm telling ya. We got more and we're still in the first inning."

"What else do you have that ties her in?"

"I'm not paid to report to you, Matthew. But I'll tell you this, when the wife used her scarf and her dog's pillow she moved it up to premeditated."

"Maybe Garson did himself in?" I said.

"Usually they leave a note, and suicides don't worry about

fingerprints and keeping their work quiet, not to mention the awkwardness of plugging themselves in the front of the skull."

Fidge shrugged after discrediting suicide. I agreed with him; this wasn't suicide. Still, I hadn't seen Fidge shrug that way in years, but habits become habits by lasting over time. This Fidgery shrug meant, *open and shut.*

"I'm not going to tell you again, Matthew, get outta here. The medical examiner could be here any minute."

"I'm going." I used the back of my hand to pat the sergeant on the breast pocket of his dark-blue suit coat. "She can phone her attorney after you get her downtown, right?"

"Sure."

"Who called this in?"

"Her."

"What about the coffee?" I asked.

Fidge coughed into his fist then answered. "Says she dropped the cup when she saw the hole in her sugar daddy's noggin."

I left my ex partner in Garson's bedroom and went to Clarice in the living room. "I'll come see you once you're permitted to have visitors."

She shifted Asta from one arm to the other while blotting her eyes with the soft pads of her straightened fingers, the way women do to avoid smudging their eye makeup.

"Please take Asta," she pleaded. "There's no one else I can ask. I got her a continental clip three days ago. She won't need another grooming for weeks. I'll be home before that."

I had once thought about getting a dog, but figured on one I could name Wolf or King. Then, after the incident with my father-in-law's mad creature, I repressed the whole idea of a dog.

"Matthew, I need another minute in the victim's room," Fidge said, leaning out of the doorway of Garson's bedroom. "When I come out, I want a decision on that dog. It's you or the catcher."

"What'll I do with a little chihuahua?" I asked looking at Clarice.

"She won't be any trouble." Clarice's eyes went all funny. "Please, Matt."

I had always envied the way Sam Spade could stand up to the femme fatales who tried to play him. I had also given that skill to my fictional detective, but no one had given it to me.

"All right," I said, hoping I sounded less defeated than I felt. "Asta can stay with me."

"Are you sure?" she asked.

"I'm sure of almost nothing. But, yes, Asta can stay with me." I put my fingers against her lips and headed for her bedroom where I found no deck shoes with zigzag soles. I quickly looked in the bathroom, the kitchen, and the laundry room and found no zigzags there either. Fidge had likely already done this. He was a solid detective so he would have seen the shoe print on the deck and the partially open glass door in Garson's bedroom.

Back in the living room, I asked, "When did Garson start with the cornflakes?"

"Tally went all crazy after that call. He started carrying his gun around in his waistband, sleeping with it on the night stand. He kept insisting I go get six boxes of cornflakes. We fought about that. We fought about everything, about nothing. Yesterday, I stopped at the post office to mail a few house bills and something Tally wanted mailed; on the way back I bought the damn cornflakes. Guess what? We still fought." She leaned closer and whispered. "He scared me real bad. I wish I hadn't—"

I grabbed her shoulders. "Save it for your attorney, you have no privilege with me." But she kept talking anyway.

"Damn it, I didn't shoot him. I was trying to say I wish I hadn't gotten mad at him so much those last few days." She stood clutching the dog, breathing slowly. Her eyes shut. Then she put down Asta and said, "Go with Uncle Matt."

The hair ball leaped into my arms.

"She'll sleep on the foot of your bed. You'll need to get her a new pillow. Her pink one has a ... hole in it. Take a few of her toys. She'll be fine."

Fidge again filled the bedroom doorway, "Just the mutt."

"But Asta needs her toys. She—"

"Lady. Just the mutt or we call the pound. None of this is up for negotiation."

I put my fingers under Clarice's chin, raising her head. "Get your mind off that damn dog. You're in a real mess. Do what Sergeant Fidgery tells you but don't talk about this to anyone until you get an attorney, a criminal attorney, a good one."

Fidge came out of the bedroom wearing a grin wider than his flat nose. "I hope you and Asta will live happily ever after." His eyes sort of twinkled, which is hard to imagine on the hangdog face genetics had passed down to Fidge.

"Now," he said, "for the last time, Matthew, get lost."

I lowered the dog to stop it from licking me on the mouth and walked out with Asta scrambling up my front, watching Clarice over my shoulder.

CHAPTER 2

$\mathcal{L}$ ike yesterday, today started way too early. After a shower, three cups of coffee, a scan of the sports section, and four words in the crossword puzzle, I pulled my Chrysler 300 out of my building's underground parking and pointed it toward town. The veil of salty wetness that had sneaked in while the city slept still coated everything that had spent the night outdoors. I turned on the windshield wipers, hit the defroster button, and headed for the city jail. Clarice had been temporarily held at the smaller Long Beach jail inside the police department. After her arraignment, she had been moved to the larger main jail on Pacific Avenue near Twentieth Street.

Last spring, my ex-wife and I started sharing dinners, movies, and what was now her bed a few nights a week. We still cared, but she couldn't get past the anger and betrayal she felt over my having gunned down the thug outside the courthouse. After nearly a month of our running in place, I put a stop to the experiment. The ending of most relationships digs an emotional hole that refills with emptiness; ours was no exception.

Hemingway had said something like the best way to get over a woman is to get a new one. I hadn't decided whether to take

Hemingway's advice or to write a novel, use her name, and have her killed—heinously. For a few weeks after I pulled the plug on our mutual effort, I considered both, a sort of double exorcism.

Then I met Clarice, who was bright and funny as well as passionate. The only problem, Clarice was married. I hadn't known that, and I hadn't bothered asking. My libido was screaming, "Any port in a storm," and Clarice was a dock slip built to hold a good sized yacht so I powered on in.

The Long Beach jail, one of California's largest, booked about eighteen thousand inmates annually. That seems like a huge number of bookings, but then Long Beach was California's sixth largest city, and America's thirty-eighth biggest with a population around half a million. To most people Long Beach doesn't seem that big, probably because it butts up to Los Angeles without an obvious border crossing.

The lobby chairs of the Long Beach jailhouse were all occupied with people jabbering in multiple languages. I figured all of them were talking about seeing a loved one and cursing someone else for the poor choices made by the loser they had come to visit. The air felt tight from the fear which grips everyone in a jail, even those working hard at showing tough. The mothers who had brought babies were trying to keep them from crying. But the babies had it right. Jail was a place that could make anyone cry.

For now, Clarice's world was the place writers had given names like stir, the slammer, the joint, the pokie, and a thousand others. But not the big house, that name referred to prison not a jail. Whatever the name, except in the movies, escapes were rare. Once you went in, you stayed in until they let you walk out or they carried you out.

Eventually I was called through a heavy door and left to walk behind a row of uncomfortable looking chairs. Visitation was limited to fifteen minutes. I chose the first place to sit where the chairs to each side of me were not occupied by other visitors. A moment later, Clarice entered through a door like the one I had come through, only her door was on the inmate side of the glass partition. This was a big difference, huge, I could leave at will, while she would be forcibly detained. Her entrance started the clock on our fifteen minutes. She walked toward me behind a row of chairs on her side, forced a smile, not much of one, and sat down.

We were separated by a pane of glass as thick as old coke bottles. I picked up the dirty phone on my side. She picked up the dirty phone on her side. She put the flat of her other hand on the unbreakable glass, the pads of her fingers turning white from the pressure. I covered her hand with my own, the insulation of the cold glass denying the heat from her fingers.

She ignored the tide of tears spilling through her black lashes. "The prosecutor convinced the judge I was a flight risk. He denied bail. They photographed and fingerprinted me, then some dyke with a mustache felt me up during a strip search. After that I got shoved in the shower."

By the time Clarice finished, her voice had raised several decibels. The visiting room guard walked over and leaned down next to her. I couldn't see his face, but a good guess went something like: behave yourself or this visit's over and that gorgeous fanny of yours goes back in lockup.

She lowered her head and nodded. The guard stepped back. I gave her a minute to compose herself.

I had called ahead to get the official words. Clarice Talmadge had been charged with capital murder, also known as first degree murder with special circumstances, under California Penal Code 187 (a). The fancy title meant that if she was found guilty of having murdered her husband for financial gain, one of more than twenty different situations which constitute capital murder in

California, she would face either the death penalty or life imprisonment without a possibility of parole.

Clarice jerked her hand up to swipe at a running tear. Then let her hand freefall onto her lap. Her face looked whiter than I had ever seen it, probably due to the shower and no makeup. Still, the woman was lovely. The jailhouse orange jumpsuit brought the emerald out of her bluish-green eyes. Her naturally creamy skin made me wonder why she ever bothered with makeup. Even her lips had a natural hot-pink hue, her tongue having the enviable task of keeping them moist.

She brought the phone back up to her ear.

"Asta's a strange name for a dog." I said, hoping to pull her out of her funk.

Her unpainted lips thinned and trembled. "How is my baby? Is she okay?"

"She's fine. Slept on the foot of my bed just like you said she would. We're getting along swell. I got the food and snacks you told me about. No problem. Where'd you come up with the name Asta?"

Clarice's head and shoulders swiveled to her left as a heavyset Hispanic inmate moved toward her, then quickly spun to the right to confirm the big woman had continued on by. Caught up in her jailhouse vigilance, I also watched the large woman until she sat in a chair two cubicles beyond Clarice.

"Tally bought Asta for me," Clarice said, returning from the distraction. "He named her after a dog owned by some guy named Nick Charles. I told him this Charles must be one of his friends I never met. Tally just smiled. He likes his jokes—liked his private jokes. Then he said something about my being too young to understand."

"I don't think the police are going to be looking too hard for anyone else to pin this on." It was a hard message, but one she needed to hear. She took it without reaction.

"After we met," she said, as if she had not heard my harsh

message, "I researched you in the online archives. You don't know it, but I'm hot stuff searching on that Internet." She moved the phone to her other hand, the aluminum wrapped cord draping across her mouth like surreal braces. "I read all I could find about your career as a cop."

"Then you know I went to prison and why."

"I know, and I agree with the majority of the people in the poll. I'm glad you shot the bastard. He deserved it."

"I appreciate that. In any event, I doubt I would have lasted much longer as a cop."

"Why?"

"The easy answer is the department thought I had too much Mike Hammer in me, while I thought the department had too much Casper Milquetoast. In my novels, I define and dole out justice the way it feels right to me. My readers must agree that justice isn't always best found in a courtroom. They keep buying my books."

"So your departmental papers show, terminated: too much Mike Hammer?"

"Well, they glossed it over as insubordination. I never have been any good at letting someone play smart when they're talking stupid, just because they're the boss."

Clarice moved in her chair, my gaze moved with her. She said, "One of the articles mentioned you're also a private detective."

"True. After my pardon they couldn't deny me a PI's license. Investigative work was my profession, but the law wouldn't allow me a permit to carry a weapon. I'm not sure why I got the private license. Maybe I thought it would add to my mystique as a crime novelist."

"Maybe because it lets you feel in some way you're still a detective." She grinned for the first time since I arrived, and then said, "The job that made you happier than being a novelist."

When they were being nice, the biddies in our building referred to Clarice as the airhead on the fourth floor, but my instincts told me Clarice was Phi Beta Kappa in street savvy.

"Methinks the lady has brains as well as beauty."

"My mother was a lady. I think of myself as a woman. There is a difference you know?"

"No. I didn't know. As a writer, I'm naturally curious."

She explained. "When a lady sees a man who attracts her she thinks of herself as a flirt. When a woman does, she thinks of herself as a prick teaser."

"I like it. May I use it?"

"Of course, but it requires you recognize one from the other."

"I'll do my best. Now, our time is limited so let's get back to your situation."

"You said the cops won't look much beyond me, so I need you to find out who killed Tally."

"Except in the pages of my books, I haven't worked a case in a lot a years. You don't want me. At best, I'm a rusty ex-detective."

"I've known a few smart men, Matt, even a couple of honest ones. But you're both. That's rare and it's just what I need."

"Don't make me out to be holy, you know my record."

"You plugging that guy shows you cared about the victim and about justice. That you're passionate about what you believe in. I need you to believe in me."

"I don't know." I kept shaking my head long after I finished saying it. "I just don't think I'm the man for this job."

"You are exactly the man for the job. You were with me. And you know I couldn't kill Tally … You know that, don't you Matt?"

Sam Spade would easily know whether or not Clarice was working me, but I couldn't tell. In the end it mattered little. I had always had difficulty re-corking an opened curiosity.

"No promises," I said. "I'll think on it. But, as long as I'm here, I do have a question about last night."

The always perfect polish on her fingernails was chipped when she turned the back of her hand toward me and wiggled her fingers. "Bring it on."

"When you got home from my place, did you look in on Garson?"

"No. His door was shut. He usually went to bed before me. He'd close his door when he turned off his TV. Unless he called out, I would never go in after he shut his door ... Why do you ask?"

"It would have told us whether or not he had been killed while you were with me." Her expression told me she understood.

"I expect," she said, "the autopsy will show Tally died while I was with you."

"That will show a range of time that will likely cover part of the time you were with me and some time you weren't. But we don't have the autopsy yet."

She didn't say anything, just looked down and pursed her lips.

"You handling this place okay?"

She shrugged. "It's nasty and that's just the surface. Look at these outfits. How's a girl gonna look good in this ugly thing?" She tugged hard enough to billow the loose-fitting orange material over her bust, then glanced toward the door and the guard.

"You'd look good in anything," I said, meaning it, "but this is not a place for looking sensuous. Let your hair go. Don't bathe unless they insist, but cooperate when they do."

"No sweat, Matt. I hold a brown belt in karate. If any of the lesbos in this place put a hand on me, they'll wish they hadn't."

"Also, this is not a place to get in a fight. Walk and talk with confidence, not cockiness. Stay to yourself, but don't act like a victim or like you're too good for the rest of 'em."

She smiled for the second time. "Seeing we're talking outfits here, I see you wore your trench coat. That ought to help you get into your detective persona."

The trench coat may have been a little over the top into my novelist side, but I wasn't about to confess that to Clarice. "Morning fog," I said. "Wet. Now, did you get an attorney?"

"I called Sidney Blackton." She stroked her fingers on the glass the way she might to tickle the open palm of my hand. "He was Tally's lawyer for all his U.S. business deals."

"You need a criminal mouthpiece, not a corporate attorney."

"That's what Blackton told me. He sent over Brad Fisher who went with me to the arraignment. I gave Fisher your name and told him you'd help. Was that okay? Do you know Fisher?"

"Only by reputation, which says he's a topnotch criminal lawyer. No promises, but I'll talk with him."

End of Excerpt

Who Murdered Garson Talmadge, a Matt Kile Mystery, the first in the Matt Kile Mystery series is available now in either eBook or print. Signed, print editions for collectors and to be used as gifts are available on my website, www.davidbishopbooks.com. My email is david@davidbishopbooks.com.

ABOUT THE AUTHOR

David Bishop enjoyed a varied career as an entrepreneur during which he wrote many technical articles for financial and legal journals, as well as a nonfiction business book published in three languages. Eventually, he began using his abilities as an analyst to craft the twists and turns and salting of clues so essential to fine mystery writing. David has several mystery and thriller stories available for your pleasure reading. For more information on David and his other novels please visit his web site. He would appreciate hearing your thoughts on this or any of his novels.

http://www.davidbishopbooks.com
mailto:david@davidbishopbooks.com
facebook.com/davidbishopbooks
twitter.com/davidbishop7

Manufactured by Amazon.ca
Bolton, ON